Leslie Kelly

she Drives me crazy

HQN™

ISBN 0-373-77031-6

SHE DRIVES ME CRAZY

www.HQNBooks.com

Printed in U.S.A.

With sincere thanks to my agent, Ethan Ellenberg.
Ethan, without your encouragement and support,
this would never have been possible.

And to Bruce. You make it all worthwhile.
Thanks for making me truly believe in what I write.

PROLOGUE

"JOHNNY, YOU GOTTA SEE THIS. There's a giant set of hooties hangin' over exit 23."

County prosecutor Johnny Walker, named for his father's favorite brand of fire in a bottle, barely looked up as he continued to pump gas into the tank of his SUV. It was too early in the morning to try to decipher Lester's sexobabble.

Coming from anyone else, the pronouncement might have raised Johnny's curiosity. But this was Lester, owner of one of the only two gas stations in Joyful, Georgia. Lester might not remember his nickname from high school, but Johnny—and most of the female population—still mentally referred to him as Lester the Lecher.

"Here you go, Les." Johnny tugged a twenty out of his pocket and extended it toward the other man.

Lester paid no attention. He continued to stare skyward. A tinge of curiosity finally made Johnny turn around. Following Lester's stare, he beheld what had so captivated the man.

The letch was right. A big giant set of hooties…er, woman's breasts…was clearly visible on a billboard by the highway exit. "I'll be damned," Johnny muttered, not believing his eyes. He couldn't help adding, "Nice rack."

Now, wouldn't that give the residents of this nasty town

something to gossip about when they woke up this morning? Yessir, the townsfolk of this warm, syrupy burg—as falsely sweet as a sugarcoated lemon drop—would glance out the window while munching their corn flakes and behold a pair of snow-capped mountains standing over the interstate. Because from here, the white tassels barely covering the five-foot-in-diameter nipples did indeed resemble snow.

Lester continued to pay silent, drooling homage to the fleshy hills glistening in the morning sun. Finally, he whispered, "Whaddaya suppose it's for?"

Johnny shrugged. "Haven't you heard? Sex sells. It could be advertising anything from toothpaste to Viagra."

"Nah, it wouldn't work," Les said with a snicker. "One look at that and a man'd realize he don't *need* Viagra."

Personally, Johnny hadn't needed to be titillated by pinups, magazine centerfolds or Victoria's Secret catalogues in oh, about forever. Nope, it had been the real thing or nothing since he was fourteen and a girl named Cherry Hilliard had lived up to every one of those "on top of Cherry Hill" jokes he'd heard whispered about her in the locker room.

Darn shame Cherry had found religion and married Reverend Smith. Cherry Smith just didn't have quite the same ring to it.

"One way to find out." Lester reached for the passenger side door handle of Johnny's SUV. "Let's go check 'er out."

"I can't. I've got to drive down to Bradenton for a meeting. Besides, you have another customer," Johnny said as he watched Fred Willis, a local deputy who Johnny had gone to high school with, turn his squad car into the station.

Fred had apparently noticed the breasts, too. He was

paying no attention to his driving, and almost clipped Johnny's back fender as he pulled up a few inches from the pump. His ancient, dingy tan squad car gave a rusty belch as it shook, rattled and rolled to a stop. "You see that?" he yelled from the window.

"You bet…let's go!" Lester dashed around to Fred's passenger door and hopped in. The two drove off, not sparing Johnny a second glance.

That wasn't too surprising, since Johnny couldn't fairly call himself one of Fred Willis's favorite people. Particularly because Johnny got such satisfaction in setting free the poor bumbling criminals Fred and his boss, Sheriff Brady, managed to round up in this relatively crime-free area.

Give him a real crime or criminal, and he might give a damn about doing his job. But, hell, here in Joyful? The jail cell doors might just as well stand open for all the effort Johnny took to keep their occasional occupants inside them. Course, that was probably more effort than Sheriff Brady made to ensure the innocent folks who had the misfortune of being from the wrong side of town were kept *out*.

In Joyful, the justice system was equally balanced. If you were rich and arrogant and committed a crime, the police took care of you. If you were poor and trashy…Johnny Walker did.

Still holding the twenty, Johnny walked into Lester's grimy office and left it on the counter near the register. He gingerly picked up a half-squashed plastic water bottle and set it on top of the bill, so it wouldn't blow away in the warm summer breeze already wafting through the open door.

Looking around, he grimaced in distaste. Hopefully no one else would come to the station and enter the office looking for Lester. The magazine photos plastered across the back of the door would probably make Virginia Davenport, president of the Daughters of the Confederacy, drop dead of sheer outrage.

And with his luck, the sheriff would call it murder and want Johnny to prosecute.

"Hooties over Joyful," he mused aloud as he again glanced at the billboard and got into his car. "Now there's something you don't see every day."

As he drove out of town, Johnny was struck by the strong feeling that something interesting was about to happen.

He couldn't wait to find out what it was.

CHAPTER ONE

"EMMA JEAN FRASIER'S coming back to Joyful."

Cora Dillon wondered if the years of sleeping beside her husband Bob, who sawed logs louder than any lumberjack, had finally taken their toll. Her hearing, without doubt, had just failed her. She stared at fancy-pants Jimbo Boyd, whose round face was filled with self-importance. She didn't know why, considering what a rotter he'd been as a boy. And leopards didn't change their spots. Not in Joyful, Georgia, anyway.

"Emmajean Frasier," Cora said, drawing out the name.

Jimbo nodded, then reached into his desk. He pulled out a bunch of keys stuck on a ring shaped like the hood ornament on the namby-pamby car he was so proud of. "I need you to get the house aired and cleaned today. And I want it done right."

Cora straightened and narrowed her eyes. Imagine, snot-nosed, dirty-pants Jimbo Boyd telling her how to clean a house! Hadn't she worked as a cleaning woman for him and half the town for the past ten years? Something was definitely wrong with him. Maybe the glue he used on his shoeshine-black toupee, which looked about as real as the one worn by that Captain Kirk on the TV, had seeped through his skin and affected his brain.

"Emmajean Frasier's coming back to Joyful. Now

there's a trick I'd like to see," Cora replied with stoic calm, "considering she's been dead more'n a year."

"Dead?" Jimbo began to sputter. "No, no, Cora. I don't mean Emmajean…I mean *Emma Jean*…the granddaughter."

"Granddaughter?"

Jimbo shook his head and huffed. "Yes. Her mama's folks have money and raised the girl overseas. She spent a year here, though, her last year of high school. 'Bout ten years ago."

Cora thought on it. "Possible, if it was *exactly* ten years ago. That's the year my youngest girl lost her husband and me'n Bob went out to be with her. Always told her the rotten sum-a-gun she married was a brainless fool."

Jimbo pasted a look of false sympathy on his face, managing to look more concerned than annoyed, though Cora knew better. "I hadn't realized your girl had been widowed."

Cora snorted. "Widowed? He didn't *die*. I just toldja he got *lost*. Got drunk in the woods and wandered around for days rantin' about giant beavers. Ended up in the nuthouse in Terre Haute. We stayed a while to take care of Cora Jr. and the kids."

Jimbo made a rude sound and Cora's fingers itched to give his ears a good boxing. She didn't, though. Jimbo Boyd *did* own the only real estate office in Joyful, and sent a lot of work her way. Not to mention he was the blasted mayor.

"She'll be here late today, so I need this done now."

She scowled. "I didn't see a granddaughter at the funeral."

"She wasn't there. She was sick or busy or something."

That made Cora pause. Too busy to come to her grandma's funeral? Disgraceful. She harrumphed as she took the keys from Jimbo. Then she paused, remembering a wicked old scandal. "Wait, the Frasier girl...is she the one..."

Jimbo nodded, his own eyes glowing with speculation.

Cora smirked, no longer surprised Emmajean's grand-child hadn't had the nerve to show up in Joyful again. Not given the way she'd *left* it. "I suppose I can have the house cleaned to Miss High-and-Mighty's satisfaction."

THOUGH IT GALLED HER, Cora spent the morning getting Emmajean Frasier's two-story Victorian-style house spar-kling. She was determined no spoiled long-lost grandchild would come to Joyful and turn up her nose at the life her grandma had lived.

Cora talked to herself while she worked. She talked to Emmajean, too, though they hadn't been very friendly in life, what with Emmajean holding the title of "Champion Pie Maker" five years running, and Cora feeling more en-titled to it.

Though Cora didn't really believe in haunts, she figured she'd best be sure Emmajean didn't take offense to Cora being in her house. Particularly when she started looking through her recipe box.

"Drat," she muttered, realizing the other woman must have hidden her best recipes, or memorized then burned them.

Cora had tried that once, when she was having chest pains and thought she was dying. When the doctor'd said it was just gas, and she realized she'd forgotten to memo-rize her red slaw recipe before she'd burned it, Cora had fumed. She'd tried for days to re-create it until Bob swore the next time she put a helping of red slaw in front of him, she'd be wearing it atop her head.

Wanting to take one more peek around for Emmajean's

recipes, Cora opened a drawer in the old-style rolltop desk in Emmajean's bedroom. Funny, everything in there was all jumbled up, not neat like the rest of the house. Like someone had looked through it.

Cora shrugged off the thought and began to dig through the drawer, which was full of memories. Photos. Letters. Pictures of a little girl, probably the scandalous brat who hadn't bothered coming to her grandma's funeral. There were postcards, newspaper clippings and flyers with Emma Jean Frasier's name on them. And, near the very bottom, a glossy color brochure.

Cora Dillon sucked in a shocked breath and stared at the brochure in her hand. "Dirty pictures," she muttered.

Emmajean Frasier's granddaughter had peddled nasty pictures of naked people, and statues of even more naked people, at some New York gallery that pretended the pornography was art.

"Well, wait until the town of Joyful learns Emmajean Frasier's granddaughter went off to sell dirty pictures." Considering the scandal, the details of which she'd finally remembered, they'd likely not be too surprised.

She wasted no time in spreading the word, and the game of "whisper down the lane" was well underway by lunchtime.

By 1:00 p.m., the women at Sylvie Stottlemyer's bridge club were tittering over it. They gleefully repeated the scandal of May 1995 involving Emmajean Frasier's granddaughter as they trumped and made their rubbers.

By two, the guys working on the line at the machine parts factory north of town were speculating on precisely what kind of pictures had been involved. Whether they were X-rated or triple-X. And whether they might still be available on the Internet.

By three, the two different rumors about Emma Jean and the billboard had caught up with one another and been mixed together in the great seething cauldron of gossip. Now things began to make sense…because the club advertised on the billboard was being built on old Emmajean's land.

By four, the term "gone off to *sell* dirty pictures" had been replaced by the term "gone off to *make* dirty pictures."

And by 5:00 p.m., the whole town of Joyful knew with titillated certainty that the person building the new club was Emma Jean Frasier—aka the porn star.

EMMA JEAN FRASIER hit Joyful late Friday afternoon, not sure whether to be glad her long trip had ended, or sorry she couldn't just keep on driving.

Florida sounded good. West Palm. The Keys.

"Not happening," she muttered. Joyful had been her destination, and Joyful was where she'd arrived.

At least no one pointed. Nobody ducked their heads together to whisper. She felt pretty sure she didn't see any tar being boiled, feathers being plucked or big scarlet letters being cut out for prominent display on her chest. Not that they did that kind of thing anymore.

She hoped.

Glancing at herself in the rearview mirror, she smothered a groan. Sixteen solid hours of driving with the top down under the blazing sun, or the humid, cloud-filled night sky, played absolute hell on a three hundred dollar color job. Even if the color job *had* been done by Floyds on Fifth in New York.

"No more three hundred dollar color jobs for you, babe," she told her sun-pinkened reflection. No more lunches at trendy New York restaurants. No expensive cooking classes she could try, but inevitably fail due to her notorious inability in the kitchen. No more trips upstate in the autumn, or wine-tasting clubs or sponsoring shows for promising young artists. No parties in her pretty Manhattan apartment, either.

Gone. Done. Finito. Over and out, with a single hour-long meeting with her attorney.

"Flat broke," she whispered, unable to hear her own voice.

The summer air rushing over the windshield stung her eyes, bringing a harsh tear to them. *It's only the wind,* she told herself. She certainly wasn't crying over stolen money. Nor over lost jobs, SEC investigations or worthless stock.

Emma had received the invitation to return to Joyful two weeks ago, on the very day she'd found out. An interesting twist, being invited to come to Joyful for her high school reunion the same day she'd learned her only remaining asset was her grandmother's house in that same town.

She didn't know if she'd have ever returned if she'd had any other choice. Not for the silly teenage reasons that had driven her away—and *kept* her away for several years—but simply because there was no one to come home to anymore.

Grandma Emmajean was gone. Just the house remained, not the *home*.

Her grandmother's death was a blow from which Emma was still recovering. She'd been unable to face the memories in the warm, sunny-yellow house the old woman had left to her. Her parents had handled all the legal paperwork surrounding Emmajean's will, and had arranged for her property to be managed by a Realtor in town. Emma had tried not to think about it since.

"Better think about it now," she mused as she saw more and more that looked familiar to her.

Her foot lifted slightly off the gas pedal as she spotted the old lumber mill on the outskirts of town. Just west of here, near the highway leading down to Atlanta, would be the old pecan orchard her grandmother had owned, the orchard that was now Emma's. Her heart clenched. She wasn't quite up to visiting the orchard yet.

She'd soon come to the Chat-n-Chew. The combination gas station and restaurant—where Emma and her high school friends used to try to buy beer—sat right on the main road. She decided to stop, needing to fuel up and grab a cold drink. She also needed to deal with the memories hitting her from every direction, some eliciting a gentle smile but most bringing a hint of sadness for their association with Emmajean.

The blaze of sunlight sent a shimmer of heat reflecting above the blacktop road, and Emma's eyes grew a little hazy. The tears lurking behind her lids began to spill onto her cheeks.

She was home. In Joyful. But the one person who epitomized the meaning of the word "home" wasn't here to welcome her.

She blinked rapidly. Fatigue from being behind the wheel for so long was making her overly emotional. Shrugging her shoulders, she ran a quick hand through the tangled mass of short curls surrounding her face and took a deep breath. The air was warm and thick, redolent with the smells she'd always acquaint with the South—earth, pine and a faint wisp of fruit from some nearby orchard. Her tears dried almost immediately.

Before reaching the Chat-n-Chew, Emma suddenly remembered the little park, down a gravel road that cut back to the local grange building. Almost holding her breath, she slowed as she drove by, peeking down the road, unable to see much, other than a tangle of woods and the roof of the grange rising above it.

But she knew what was hidden behind those woods. The park. The gazebo. Emma's breath came faster as a different memory overcame her, and a new face intruded on the images of the past.

"Johnny," she said, his name tasting unfamiliar on her tongue.

She hadn't thought of him in ages. Well, at least not in weeks. His wide, heartbreaking grin and the spark of devilment in his eyes had never been *too* far from her thoughts, even though the rest of Joyful had been.

Johnny Walker had been her savior and her downfall, all in the very same night. He'd given Emma her first lesson in raw, hot passion. A lesson she'd never forgotten— and had never come close to repeating.

Then he'd given her a lesson in betrayal.

"The bastard."

Could he still be here?

No. He'd hated this town. He'd wanted nothing more than to shake its dust off his boots and get out even then. Johnny would be long gone from Joyful. No question about it.

And Emma Jean Frasier wouldn't have it any other way.

"THE PORN STAR'S pulling up outside!"

Johnny paused, his fingers resting lightly on the can of spaghetti sauce he'd picked up off the grocery store shelf. *Porn star?* Now, there was something you didn't hear mentioned often in Joyful, Georgia. Livestock auctions, yes. Dances at the VFW hall, storm warnings, gossip about whose husband was spotted with a female impersonator down in Atlanta…yes.

But porn stars in Joyful? Nossir, he didn't think he'd heard that one before. Though, given the controversy of a proposed new twenty-four-hour strip club on the outskirts of town, he couldn't claim too much shock.

Wouldn't that give the biddies something to chew on? As if they all weren't already in the middle of a frenzy over the billboard advertising Joyful Interludes, the new club, which had shown up this morning. Now they were likely planning pickets, boycotts, religious protests. Soon they'd be talking legal action. Then they'd be knocking on his door.

Add a porn star to the mix and Joyful might just erupt of sheer titillation.

"Didja hear me?" the voice continued. "Joe Crocker down at the Chat-n-Chew says the porn star who's opening up that new strip club is heading into town, right here to this very store!"

The words hung in the sunny, late-afternoon air of the Joyful Grocery Store. Johnny thought even the dust motes stopped swirling at the announcement made by the teen who'd burst in off the street, his face red, eyes wide with excitement. The kids buying penny—now dime—candy, dropped their loot and froze. The cashiers at the two front checkout lanes, who'd been exchanging man-tales and smacking bubblegum as they rang up the purchases of the handful of customers in the store, also paused.

Then, as if they were all puppets on the same string, they turned and gawked out the huge front window of the store. Eighty-year-old Tom Terry, who used to own the town's only barbershop, hitched his pants up and tucked his shirttail in.

The expectant silence, as charged as the air in the bingo

parlor before each ball was drawn, was suddenly interrupted by a demanding voice. As demanding as only the voice of a three- or four-year-old little girl could be. "I spilled my juice, Mama!"

Johnny cast a quick glance at the child, whose lower lip was stuck out in a belligerent pout. She tugged on her mother's dress. The mother—Claire Deveaux, former newspaper reporter turned chubby housewife—ignored the kid. Claire was just as focused on the front door as everyone else in the place.

"Mama…"

"Not now, Eve," Claire whispered with a shushing motion. "Somebody important's coming, baby."

Somebody important. Miss Fanny Tail? Miss Venus Triple-D'Milo? He almost snickered. Why in God's name would a porn star be opening up a club here in Nowhereville, Georgia? And why was he the only one who seemed surprised by this news?

Johnny shook his head. Apparently he'd once again been completely oblivious to some juicy bit of fodder on the town from Joyful's infamous grapevine. That's the way he preferred it. Growing up in a family that was usually the target of such gossip had left a sour taste in his mouth, and he generally shut down his ears when people were whispering nearby.

This time he'd apparently missed some *very* serious gossip, which had probably started thirty seconds after the billboard had gone up this morning. He almost wished he'd detoured past it to read it for himself.

Porn stars and strip clubs. Joyful was becoming downright wicked.

Not that he believed Joe Crocker knew a porn star from an opera singer—the man thought any female blessed with an abundance of northern curves liked to be leered at and drooled over. So did ninety percent of the rest of Joyful's male population. Almost made him feel sorry for the mystery woman. She could be anybody from a college professor to a congresswoman. And sure as hell, some man here in this very store would likely ask her to autograph his butt with a red felt-tip marker as soon as she arrived.

He grinned, picturing her response if she was simply a wayward traveler or a harried housewife doing some shopping. It was almost worth sticking around to see if anybody got slapped in the face. Or kicked in the...

"I had me a porn star once," Tom Terry muttered to no one in particular.

Johnny couldn't resist glancing at the old-timer, who stared into the air wearing a look of reminiscence.

"Kep' her in a box under my bed. 'Bout broke my heart when Buddy, my best hunting dog, found her and bit right into her. Great big holes, right in her leg."

Johnny could only shake his head. It wouldn't do any good to try to change the subject. Old Tom was as predictable about his dirty stories as he was about spitting on the sidewalk whenever his archenemy Joe-Bob Melton was approaching.

"Tried to use some packing tape t'fix her up," the old man continued, not even looking around to see if anyone was listening to his tale of woe. "But it didn't work. Dern near took m'head clean off when she popped and started flyin' around the room." And then, as if he hadn't painted a good enough picture, he added, "Just imagine one'a them Thanksgiving parade balloons hittin' a light pole and flyin' all over the city folk, flashin' her glory-be-ta-Jesus parts in front a' the kiddies waitin' fer Sandy Claus. That's what she looked like all right."

Johnny closed his eyes and thought about work, his car. Anything except the image Mr. Terry had put into his head.

"She scared poor Buddy right outta the house and under the porch," old Tom continued, apparently not noticing that everyone within earshot had edged away. "Whizzed 'round the livin' room like a balloon pricked with a pin." He gave a wheezy, dirty-old-man snicker. "Pricked." Then he puffed his scrawny chest out. "Now, I'm not *pin*-sized, mindya."

"Mr. Terry, *please,*" a nearby woman hissed as she tried, unsuccessfully, to cover the ears of her wide-eyed little boy.

Yeah. This was how rumors got started in Joyful. Pretty soon, the story of Tom's relations with a plastic sex doll would turn into one of the greatest love stories in the state of Georgia. Tom Terry and Plastic Polly would rank right up there with Jimmy and Rosalyn Carter. Or Newt Gingrich and himself.

As much as he disliked admitting it, Joyful's gossips might not always have the whole story, but there was often at least a kernel of truth in the rumors, way down there amidst the dirt. So, it wasn't entirely impossible that he was about to see some buxom goddess of stag films and late-night cable movies.

"Which porn star?"

No one answered Johnny's question. Now that Tom had shut up, they'd resumed their wait. They stared, slack-jawed, wide-eyed, as a sporty red convertible whipped too fast around old Tom's pickup and zipped into a spot directly out front.

"Mama, my *top,*" the little girl voice of sugarcoated iron wailed. This time, the pitch was high enough to irritate the ears. All except the child's mother's ears—Claire didn't even seem to hear. She was too busy watching the action unfolding on the movie screen created by the flat surface of the front windows.

Even Johnny watched, interested in spite of himself, more by the reaction of the townspeople in the store than anything else. At least, until he spotted the blonde at the wheel.

Then he heard a low wolf whistle. It took a moment before he realized it had come out of his own mouth.

He couldn't see her features yet, just the bright blond mass of curls, short, framing her face which was shadowed by an outrageous pair of tortoiseshell, cat's-eye sunglasses. While he—well, everyone—watched, she reached to the passenger side of her car, bending out of sight. She came back up with a filmy, pink scarf, which she wound tight. Running one hand through her hair, she tied the scarf around her curls like a headband.

The anticipation rose in the store as the blonde leaned close to her rearview mirror to apply some lipstick. Johnny could tell even from here that it was pink—to match the scarf. Her car was parked so close that he could see her purse her lips to check her makeup.

The rush of heat descending from his brain to his gut astounded him. Johnny knew plenty of attractive women— there were a dozen he could call right now if he was in need of female companionship that merely seeing a woman put on lipstick did such interesting things to his lower half. This one, though…well, he couldn't take his eyes off her.

Somewhere in the near distance he heard, "Gotta clean my top, Mama. It's my fave-o-rite!" He recognized the increasingly desperate sounding Deveaux kid. But he couldn't truly focus on anything except the stranger.

She wore a flouncy-looking white blouse that hung just

at the edge of her shoulders. Noting the expanse of bare skin on her neck and chest, he swallowed another wolf whistle. She *had* to be a northerner. Women from around here wouldn't dream of exposing so much pale flesh to the hot afternoon sun, particularly while riding around in a convertible.

Plus, of course, not one woman in Joyful had that outrageous platinum-blond hairdo or those cat's-eye sunglasses.

When she stepped out of the car, he nearly echoed old Tom's groan of appreciation. "She's got *some* legs," the old man said.

A favorite old ZZ Top song started playing in his mind. Because he'd bet the blonde knew how to use them.

She paused beside the car, and somehow managed to avoid tipping over in the strappy high-heeled sandals that barely covered her feet. A sudden flash of gold told him she was wearing a flirty ankle bracelet. Johnny took a deep breath. He'd had a thing for ankle bracelets ever since he'd first seen one on his brother's teenage girlfriend, years ago.

The woman's legs went from the ground clear up to heaven, and were shown off not only by the heels but also by the short, flimsy pink miniskirt she wore. It wisped around her thighs. With a strong gust of wind, it might well have flown even higher.

"Wind's died down. Too bad," old Tom muttered with a wheezy, heartfelt sigh, audible from several feet away. Johnny, who'd been thinking much the same thing, couldn't say a word.

When she turned and bent over the closed door, reaching through the open convertible roof for her purse, Johnny held his breath, along with everyone else in the place. She apparently wasn't a complete exhibitionist, though. She kept the flat of her hand against the skirt, just below the curve of her backside, to keep from showing the world whether or not her favorite color extended to her underclothes.

Having retrieved her bag, she turned and walked toward the sidewalk. Johnny noticed her wobbling a bit on her heels and wondered if she was going to trip on the curb. No one else appeared to notice the moment of unsteadiness. But he knew he was right when he saw her cast a quick guilty look side to side, as if to see if anyone had observed her narrowly avoided fall. For some reason a smile crossed his lips at that one tiny chink in her filmy pink armor.

"Don't stand here gawkin," one of the cashiers said as the blonde reached the store entrance.

With a flurry of motion, a dozen pair of hands found something meaningless to do. Shaken out of his daze by the moment of uncertainty displayed by the bombshell…er, porn star…or whatever she was, Johnny walked toward the checkout counter, still carrying his spaghetti sauce. He swallowed a laugh as he watched Tom nervously grab for something, and then blanch when he realized he held a box of tampons. The man dropped the box to the floor, kicking it under the nearest shelf where it would probably remain until next Christmas when the aisles were rearranged for the holiday goods. Some lucky lady would find a dusty box of feminine products in the half-off basket come New Year's.

He'd just stepped past Claire, who didn't even notice him to nod hello, when he heard the young mother shriek. "Oh, no, Evie, what did you do? I have to wash it in the washing machine!" The woman swooped the child up and carried her toward the back of the store, beelining for the bathroom.

Johnny didn't even have time to wonder what had happened before the stranger from the convertible entered the Joyful Grocery Store. She almost barreled right into him.

"Oh, I'm sorry," she said, and her voice startled him. He'd expected breathy, sultry or honey-sweet tones. Hers sounded controlled, clipped, evenly modulated, with maybe even a hint of a British accent.

"No harm no foul," Johnny replied with a shrug.

For some reason, the woman sucked in a sudden gasp of air and jerked away from him. Though she still hadn't removed her ridiculous glasses, Johnny peered at her, trying to see why she seemed so startled. He couldn't see her eyes, but did notice that the nose on which her glasses rested was lightly dusted with freckles. Aside from the bright pink lipstick, her face was bare of makeup, and a few more freckles dotted the high cheekbones. Not exactly how he'd picture a porn star. Then again, he'd never met one up close. So maybe freckles weren't so unusual, even if they were damn near adorable.

"You…you…" she said.

Johnny had to wonder about that. A freckled porn star who stuttered?

She wobbled again on her heels, and Johnny instinctively reached out to steady her. He grabbed for her arm but connected with her shoulder instead. The loose cottony fabric of her blouse slid beneath his hand until his palm touched her bare skin. She was soft, pale against his dark fingers.

This time he was the one who pulled back, or, rather, he thought he did. His brain reacted, sent the message, but he had to wonder if his hand had become disconnected somehow, because his fingers were still there. On her. Sliding across the soft flesh of her nape to brush across her collarbone.

Hearing a bark of laughter, Johnny realized every set of eyes in the store was fixed on them. His hand finally remembered who was boss and obeyed his brain's command to let her go. He took a step back, seeing the faint pink outline his touch had left on her skin, then let his gaze travel down the rest of her.

The first thing he noticed was that she was *not* built like a brick...well, she wasn't stacked. He hadn't seen many porn flicks in his life—never needed to, if truth be told—but one thing he remembered: the females starring in them appeared to be a plastic surgeon's best friend. Not this one.

While average height, her ridiculously high heels put her at just a few inches shorter than he was. Not hippy. She was nicely curved—had some particularly fine *northern* curves—but was certainly nowhere near as well-endowed as he'd expect from an X-rated movie queen. So she definitely wasn't the downright bovine creature pictured on the billboard.

But the legs. Oh, boy, the legs and that thin little strip of gold dangling above her left ankle nearly had him gasping for breath. This woman could probably have any man she wanted at her high-heel clad feet.

"Have a foot fetish?"

A rueful grin spread across his lips as he raised his eyes to meet hers, which were still hidden behind the glasses. Her enigmatic, close-lipped smile told him he'd been caught staring.

"Something like that." When she made no move to remove her sunglasses, he leaned closer. "What about you? Doing the Jack Nicholson thing?"

She looked confused.

"Traveling incognito?" he asked, gesturing toward her sunglasses.

She shrugged. "Is it working? Am I blending right in?"

He choked out a laugh. "Yeah. Like an ant in a sugar bowl."

"Are you saying I'm sweet, or are you comparing me to an insect?"

"Oh, I'm certain you're sweet, darlin'. I doubt this town has seen so much cotton-candy sweetness in one package in a very long time." He waited for her response, wondering why he enjoyed baiting a complete stranger.

"Do you like cotton candy?"

"Love it," he replied, narrowing his eyes and shooting her a dangerous look he hadn't used on too many women recently. "Melts on the tongue and tastes *so* good."

She swallowed. Once. Then leveled her gaze on him from behind the dark lenses. "Liar."

"Am I?"

"Cotton candy makes you throw up and you know it."

Her voice held a note of certainty and Johnny suddenly realized she wasn't flirting. She was speaking fact. This time, when his eyes narrowed, it wasn't flirtatiously, but in concentration. "How do you know that?"

"Same way I know about your appreciation for nice legs."

He didn't say a word.

"Not to mention your thing for ankle bracelets."

This time it was Johnny who nearly gasped. *Who the hell is she?* He felt like he should know. There was something familiar, something that was nagging at him about her voice. He couldn't really know her, could he?

"Lucky guesses," he said, testing her.

She shook her head. "Nope."

She lifted her hand and raised one index finger, straight up, then crooked it at him, beckoning him closer. Johnny couldn't resist. Sliding one foot forward, he leaned as near to her as he could get without actually touching her. He nearly felt everyone else in the store shifting forward, too, but ignored them.

"How do you know?" he asked when he was close enough that the tip of his shoes came within a hairsbreadth of her bare toes. Her deep, even breaths reached his cheek.

She leaned up, almost on tiptoes, and Johnny bent closer. Her perfume, light and flowery, wafted from her warm, creamy skin. It called out to him, something in his brain recognizing the scent and making his whole body grow tense and aware, before his brain could analyze why.

His lips were mere inches from her temple, and he focused hard, trying to figure out the strange feeling of anticipation gripping him.

Then she whispered, "Because you told me. Right before you stole my favorite gold butterfly ankle bracelet right off my ankle."

And suddenly he knew. Even before she stepped back and pushed her silly sunglasses onto the top of her head with the tip of her index finger, revealing her golden-brown eyes, he knew.

"Emma Jean."

CHAPTER TWO

THE WORLD certainly kept spinning, and the clock probably kept ticking and the sun likely kept shining and the town of Joyful definitely kept whispering. But right here, right now, for Johnny Walker, time stopped. A decade disappeared. Ten years fell away. And he looked into a set of eyes he'd never thought to see again, though he'd seen them in his brain nearly every day since.

"Son of a bitch."

"Hello to you, too, Johnny," she said with a tight smile.

He didn't return the greeting. "So," he murmured, knowing she'd be able to hear the edge in his voice. "Emma Jean Frasier has done what she swore she'd never do—return to the pits of hell disguised as the hills of Georgia."

"And what do I find, but the devil waiting here to greet me," she said, her expression not nearly as jaunty as her tone.

He tsked. "Still sassy."

She cast a disparaging glance at the spaghetti sauce can in his hand. "And you're still a big spender. Don't tell me—you have a hot date tonight? My, you always did entertain with style."

He instantly remembered their one date. As her eyes shifted away from him, he knew she was kicking herself for bringing up such a loaded subject.

"Guess I should hurry right out to that field over by the Nelson place to pick a bouquet of wildflowers."

Her quickly indrawn breath told him his jab had hit home. And suddenly, seeing a flash of hurt in her eyes, he regretted the comment. Coming back to Joyful couldn't have been easy for Emma Jean. Not with the way she'd left. Correction…the way she'd *run away*.

The thought helped him thrust off the moment of remorse.

"I have to go," she insisted, trying to push past him. The brush of her arm against his sent a jolt of hot awareness rushing through him again. As they froze, face-to-face, breath to breath, he mentally tripped again into the world of Emma Jean Frasier's sweet, caramel-eyed stare. Without warning, his senses went on overload, filled with a sudden, quick stream of memories.

Hot summer days when it almost hurt to draw the thick air into his lungs—particularly as he watched her walk down the road in her tight shorts and tighter tops. The way the sunshine caught the sparkle of gold in her long, honey-colored hair every time she walked by.

And that one incredible night. The cicadas taking up a nighttime chorus as they sat and talked for hours. The moisture of her tears against his neck as he'd held her in his lap while she'd cried over his no-good idiot of a brother. Then the return of her good mood, the way he'd teased her into giving him one of those joyous, dimpled smiles that had stopped his teenage heart.

He almost heard the soft strains of Garth Brooks from his truck radio as they danced in the moonlight. Almost smelled the scent of her hair—lemons and tangerines, sweet and tangy, just like Emma Jean had always been. Almost tasted the sugary, slick taste of her strawberry lip gloss.

His brain tripped one step farther, into truly dangerous territory. Right here and now, in the brightly lit store surrounded by people, he heard the echo of the forbidden, sultry whoosh her satiny dress had made as it fell to the ground. And the way she'd whispered his name over and over again when he'd been buried deep inside her body, certain he'd died and landed straight in the arms of an angel.

"Johnny?"

He flinched as she spoke, losing his grip on the can of sauce in the process. They both looked toward the floor at the sound of the loud clunk. Watching the spaghetti sauce roll away, Emma stepped to the side to avoid getting her toes crunched. Johnny took the moment to get a major grip on himself.

By the time Emma looked up again, he felt much more in control. He'd thrust the mirage of memories back to the depths of his subconscious where they belonged, along with all those other stupid, dangerous teenage memories— like hot-wiring cars, putting firecrackers in mailboxes and making out with girls underneath the bleachers after cutting class. Kid stuff. Just like his feelings for Emma Jean Frasier.

If he told himself that often enough, he might actually start to believe it was true.

"Seeya, Emma Jean," he managed to mutter, pretty damn sure he sounded almost normal. Almost sane. Almost not crazy with wanting to reach out and either pull her into his arms and kiss the hell out of her, or shake her for leaving. And for coming back. At this moment, he couldn't say which angered him more.

She nodded and stepped away, gingerly avoiding the sauce he'd dropped. Unfortunately, however, stepping over one can didn't help Emma save her own. Because two seconds after she moved, she slipped on something, causing her feet to fly out from under her.

Then she hit the floor, falling on her butt like a big old sack of rocks.

IF SOMEONE had told her that within her first several minutes in Joyful she'd be lying flat on the floor, with her legs askew and Johnny Walker crouched between them, Emma would have laughed in that person's face. Particularly if also told that half the slack-jawed, gaping town would be looking on.

What'd they call this? Déjà vu all over again? Because this was, pretty much, the same position she'd been in on her *last* night in this town, ten years ago.

Fate, she decided, was a mean-spirited bitch with a really long memory and a twisted sense of humor.

"Em, are you all right?" Johnny asked from where he'd hunkered down between her ankles to see if she was okay.

"No, I'm not all right," she managed to bite out.

She'd slipped in some unseen puddle on the floor, paying such close attention to avoiding the can—and the man who'd dropped it—that she hadn't even seen the other danger. Now her ankle and foot felt like they'd been twisted into a pretzel shape. For that matter, so did her stomach.

Not to mention her heart.

She scrunched her eyes shut, waiting for the initial rush of pain to subside. Maybe then she could deal with the fact that the first familiar person she'd seen in Joyful was the one she'd hoped to avoid altogether. And that he looked so damned good.

Johnny as a teenager had been heartthrob material. Pure

wicked, honey-tongued, hunk-a-licious male. The baddest of the bad boys. The motorcycle-riding, cigarette-smoking, heartbreaking guy who'd been featured in every teen movie ever made and in every good girl's most secret fantasies.

Time hadn't been kind enough to tug frown lines on his lean, handsome face, put circles beneath his stunning blue eyes or gray streaks in his thick, walnut-brown hair. Gravity hadn't sucked down that flat, muscle-striped chest and stomach. He definitely didn't have the poochy belly and man boobs she'd occasionally—when in a vengeful mood—wished on him. He wasn't saggy, pasty and pale. Devil take the man.

No, Johnny Walker was nothing like she'd sometimes hoped he'd be. Of course, the other times, she'd been vacillating between wanting him maimed, dead or imprisoned.

Liar. What she'd really wanted was him pining.

But, huh-uh, just her luck, he looked better than he had ten years ago. Bigger. Harder. Fully masculine in his adult body, with little remaining of the whipcord-lean youth she'd known. Definitely he had not wasted away having spent the past decade mourning the loss of the best thing he'd ever had. *Her.*

Nope, he was all hunky, smiling, flirty man. The jeans and leather jacket might be gone, as were the chains and silver stud earring he used to wear. But the "Yeah, I really can deliver what my eyes are promising" look was all, one hundred percent Johnny.

"Let me help you," he insisted. "Hell, Emma Jean, I didn't imagine you'd drop away in shock at the sight of me."

She narrowed her eyes.

"Because I have to admit, seeing you was a definite surprise, but I don't think I'd go swooning over it."

His surprise certainly couldn't match hers. She'd been so sure Johnny would be long gone. Instead, here he was, crouched between her calves, trying to ease her foot out of her sandal, as if they'd seen each other in the flesh every day for the past decade…instead of only in each other's nightmares.

"I didn't swoon," she muttered. "I slipped in something."

He just shrugged, continuing to try to unbuckle her shoe.

Emma took a moment to remember the look on his face when he'd first recognized her. She had to admit it—that expression had almost made the subsequent pain of twisting her ankle worthwhile. Surprise didn't cut it. He'd been shocked. Stunned. And for one quick, nearly unseen instant, he'd been very, very glad.

Emma didn't care so much about the shock. The glad, however, had almost been worth the sixteen-hour car ride which had ended with her falling on her fanny with her legs askew and the hottest guy she'd ever known in her life crouched between them. In front of the gawking shoppers in the Joyful Grocery Store, no less.

Who were all *still* gawking.

She sighed. Quite an entrance after ten years away. She supposed it was a vain hope to think no one here would remember her being caught in pretty much this same position on prom night.

Oh, well, at least she wasn't stark naked this time.

As she ruthlessly shoved the hint of pleasure that Johnny was glad to see her out of her brain, she acknowledged the other parts of her body that were also sparking in reaction. My, oh my, those hard, lean hips of his were between her legs and she was looking at his thick, dark head of hair, remembering tangling her fingers in it. Suddenly she was feeling damp—down low—and it had nothing to do with whatever spilled liquid she'd fallen in.

Closing her eyes, Emma took a deep breath, trying to work up the courage to deal with her current predicament. Hmm…she was flat on her butt in public, lusting for a guy she should hate, wishing her panties weren't so tight and her skirt wasn't so short and her sex life hadn't been so miserable lately that her own body would betray her in spite of the pain in her ankle. And in her heart.

Today was going onto her top ten list of bad days.

"I'm sorry, Emma Jean, your foot's already swelling."

Sorry for causing her to slip on some unseen wet spot? Or for breaking her heart? Not that she'd give him the satisfaction of voicing that question. No, Johnny Walker had no idea he'd broken her heart…because he'd never known it was his to break.

"Nobody calls me Emma Jean anymore," she said, wincing as he gingerly touched her heel with the tip of his finger.

He visibly stiffened and met her stare, his deep blue eyes still incredibly dramatic against the dark brown hair. "Do you go by another name? A screen name?"

Not sure why on earth he'd care about her Internet name, she frowned and leaned over to gingerly unbuckle her sandal. "I mean, I go by just Emma now."

"As in just Cher? Or Madonna?" he asked, his voice thick with something she couldn't identify. She put it down to embarrassment—he couldn't be feeling any better about the situation in which they'd suddenly found themselves than she did, particularly with the wide-eyed onlookers all around them.

"No," she explained her patience growing thinner as her embarrassment increased. "As in just Emma Frasier. No Jean. Now, if we've straightened out my name to your satisfaction, would you mind leaving me alone so I can stagger to the nearest emergency room for X-rays and a cast?"

He muttered under his breath and she'd swear she caught the word "sassy" again. "I'll take you over to the clinic," he finally said when he saw her staring at him.

"Forget it," she muttered. "I can get up." She glanced around the floor. "What did I slip in?"

They both spotted a big, smeary blue puddle of sticky goo at the same instant. "Did two Smurfs battle to the death in here or something?" she said with a disbelieving groan.

Johnny tsked. "Laundry detergent. Or fabric softener. I think a little girl was trying to get some spilled juice out of her clothes."

"Great. Welcome home, Emma, enjoy your fall," she said.

He shrugged. "You always did know how to make an entrance." Then his eyes narrowed. "And an exit."

She shot him a glare, not appreciating his humor—nor his reminder of the last time they'd been together—one teeny bit.

"You're sure it was a little girl? Maybe it was you who had to suddenly clean up his clothes…though I never figured you for a man who'd wet his pants at having to look me in the eye again."

The insult skimmed right off his gorgeous hide. "Aww, honey, I hate to disappoint you, but you didn't have me shaking in my shoes." He lowered his voice. "Or needing to get out of my pants in a hurry." His grin was positively evil. "For a change."

Zing. Another dangerous recollection. Johnny sure hadn't needed much urging to get out of his pants the last time they'd been together. The dog.

Before she could give into her first impulse, which was to laugh in spite of herself, or her second, which was to smack him, he continued. "It was the Deveaux kid. I don't think she's quite mastered the whole sippie cup thing yet."

"So then what?" Emma asked, raising her voice and looking around the store. "Was there a run on mops or something today? Blue light special on paper towels?"

The two young cashiers, as blatantly nosy and fascinated as their customers, exchanged a look. She read it easily. Both silently ordered the other to take care of the mess. Then they each refused. She could almost predict how this one was going to end—with a game of rock, paper, scissors, loser gets the floor duty. In Joyful, some things never changed.

"Doggone, I sure wish I had a camera to get a picture for the paper," the old man said with a snort. "I can see the headline. Star slips…"

"Enough, Tom," Johnny muttered, giving him a warning look.

Star? Before she could even ask what on earth the old-as-dirt guy was talking about, one of the cashiers reached around her register and grabbed a disposable camera.

That was enough for Emma. Without another word, she yanked two fistfuls of Johnny's shirt between her fingers. Using his shoulders for leverage, she pushed herself up into a half-standing, half-leaning position. She ignored the sudden rush of heat in her belly. It was almost certainly caused by embarrassment and *not* the warmth of his exhaled breaths against her stomach as she leaned over him.

Not his breaths. Not his lips. Not his mouth.

Definitely not.

Another giggle from the crowd made her straighten her back. Her ankle screamed in protest, but she turned and hobbled toward the door, anyway. She just couldn't do this right now. Not after the night she'd had. Not after the *month* she'd had!

Emma had no problem laughing at herself when she deserved it. But this was too much. She was stressed, jobless, exhausted from driving. Oh, yeah, and penniless. Then, she'd come face-to-face with the guy who'd stolen her virginity and broken her heart.

And finally, the cherry on this particular hot-fudge sundae of her life, she ended up flat on her butt next to a big puddle of sticky blue goo in front of half the town.

Dammit, some days it didn't pay to get out of bed. Then she remembered: she hadn't been able to afford springing for a cheap hotel room along I-95 last night. So she'd actually been out of bed for more than twenty-four hours.

No wonder she was on the verge of tears. Not because of pain or humiliation. Not even because of the ache in her heart, and the other one between her legs at seeing Johnny Walker again. It was merely fatigue making her eyes sting and her lids flutter to keep any suspicious moisture from flowing down her cheeks.

This didn't go into the top ten worst days, it was in the top five.

She was almost to the door when she realized Johnny had followed. He stepped around her, blocking her exit. "Where do you think you're going? You can barely walk."

"Away. From. Here." She punctuated each word with a harshly snarled breath.

"Running away. Your M.O, isn't it? You get embarrassed and hit the road." He shook his head in disgust. "Typical Emma Jean Frasier."

She clenched her back teeth so hard her jaw hurt. But she'd already given the town gossips quite enough to chew over tonight on the gossip lines, thank-you-very-much. She was not about to get into a screaming tizzy of an argument with Johnny over who'd run out on whom. "Please leave me alone."

She tried to walk around him, finally giving up on the stupid shoe, which made the ache in her ankle even worse. She bent over and yanked it off, letting it dangle by the strap from the tip of her finger. Then she marched toward the door, with her head held high. Or, at least as high as it could be, considering she descended a good three inches each time she went from her good foot—still in the high-heeled sandal—to the bad one, which was completely bare. The bad one also made her cringe with pain every time she put her weight on it.

Johnny, however, wasn't going to let her make her grand exit. Emma could barely suck in a shocked breath when she felt him scoop her up from behind. "Stubborn woman."

He held her easily, bracing her behind the shoulders and beneath the knees. She might have been a stuffed doll for all the effort it took him. Emma had just enough time to clutch at her dangling shoe before it fell out of her fingers as the grocery store door opened before them with a swish, letting in a thick blast of stale summer air.

Before they could exit, however, a titter and a few whispers reached her ears. Emma groaned. It wasn't bad enough that she'd fallen, but now she was being swept out of here like some romance heroine…by the guy who'd given her her first adult taste of heartbreak as a teenager.

She leaned close to his ear to avoid being overheard.

Forcing her nose to stop working so she wouldn't smell the familiar earthy scent of his skin, and her eyes to stop noticing the cute way his hair still curled behind his ear, she whispered, "Put me down right now or I swear I'll kick you."

He raised an amused brow. "With a broken foot?"

"My other foot's not broken."

"It will be if you kick me. Those shoes of yours are pretty useless, aren't they?"

"Johnny, please don't do this."

"I already did. Now shut up, Emma Jean, and let's get you X-rayed."

Over his shoulder, she saw a cluster of shoppers inching closer. They made no bones about trying to hear every word she and Johnny exchanged. Surely nothing this exciting had happened in Joyful since, oh, say, ten years ago. That would have been the night this bastard had seduced her in public, then roared away, leaving her to explain to a bunch of gawking onlookers while trying to fasten two-dozen tiny, silk-covered buttons up the back of her pink prom dress.

Before they could escape the store altogether, however, a female voice said, "Hey, Johnny, what about your sauce?"

Emma glanced at the cashier who'd spoken, a young woman with teased up bright red hair and a serious case of acne. The woman watched them with eyes as big as dinner plates, and a definite pout on her heavily glossed lips.

"I'll be back for it," Johnny informed her.

"You have to buy it. You bent it all up when you dropped it," the belligerent cashier exclaimed.

"Yeah, and your date's gonna be real disappointed if you don't make her a gourmet meal," Emma muttered.

The woman's voice rose in pitch. "My boss'll make me pay for it if you don't."

Right. As if her boss wouldn't have heard the whole sordid story within six-point-five minutes on the infamous Joyful grapevine. Every person in the store was practically shifting on their feet, itching for Johnny and Emma to get gone so they could spread the news to the four corners of the Joyful kingdom.

Emma tried to wriggle out of Johnny's arms. "Go pay for your sauce and I'll go out and get back in my car. I can drive myself to the clinic." Then, giving him a slightly malicious smile, she whispered, "You damaged the can. I wouldn't want you to get falsely accused of vandalism... *again.*"

Direct hit. His eyes widened at the insult, and his lips thinned. He obviously remembered when he'd told her about being accused of vandalizing the town fountain as a kid. Another memory from prom night—during their hours of talking, he'd told her what it was like growing up a member of the trashiest family in town.

Not too unlike what it had meant growing up a rich kid in boarding school.

Lonely.

"Damn, you got bitchy while you were away, didn't you?"

The camera-hungry old man, whose pants were hitched up almost to his nipples, snorted with laughter. Yes, he probably approved of the caveman tactics. Emma shot him a glare and he quickly turned away, pretending to carefully examine a sign advertising a weekly special on toilet paper.

Over near a breakfast display, a harried-looking mother shoved a box of marshmallows and sugar masquerading as breakfast cereal into her toddler's hands to get him to stop crying. Heaven forbid she miss a word of Emma and Johnny's confrontation.

"And you got hard of hearing," Emma finally retorted, making no effort to keep her voice down. She didn't much care if everyone in the store heard and took notes. "I said put me down."

"Uh, okay, that'd be a big *no*."

Without another word to anyone, he strode out the automatic door, still holding her securely in his arms. Emma watched over his shoulder as the cashier, her co-worker and every shopper in the place rushed to the front window. They might as well have pressed their noses against the glass for a better look.

He didn't even pause as he passed by her convertible. When he reached a black SUV, he lowered her to the ground, effectively trapping her against the car with his long, firm body. Another flood of memories invaded her brain. She remembered what it had been like to dance with him, both vertically at the prom, and later, horizontally under the misty, moonlit sky.

"Don't you understand the meaning of the word 'no'?" she asked, wondering why she sounded so darned weak all of a sudden. "Or has it been so long since a woman said it to you that you've simply forgotten what it sounds like?"

He raised a brow. "Jealous?"

"Oh, puh-lease."

"Emma, answer me one question. That little car you squealed in here on. Manual or automatic?"

Flustered by the change of subject, not to mention his, umh…closeness…she admitted, "Manual."

He nodded, unsurprised. "Of course. You would never buy a car you couldn't drive like a screaming bat out of hell. Your poor gears are probably already ground down to nothing."

She couldn't deny it. An automatic transmission had

seemed almost sacrilege in an eight-cylinder car meant to go from zero to ninety in the length of time it took to touch up her lipstick in the rearview mirror.

"Which ankle did you twist?"

She followed his pointed stare toward her left foot, already looking swollen and tender. Then she knew where he was heading. The clutch would be a killer. "Oh."

"Right."

He opened the door, and lifted her, putting her in the passenger seat.

"My car…"

"Will be fine here," he insisted.

His tone allowed for no more arguing. It was time to admit the truth. To her eternal mortification, she really did have to accept the help of the one man on earth she'd hoped never to see again.

Correction. This day was going to her top *three* list of bad days. Maybe even top two.

"All right," she finally conceded, hearing the dismay she couldn't keep from her voice. "Let's go."

DANEEN BRADY WALKER buttoned her blouse and smoothed her skirt in the tiny bathroom off the reception area of Boyd Realty, wishing yet again that they had a shower on hand. Paper towel cleanups just didn't cut it after quickies on the boss's desk.

"You swore there'd be no more quickies," she told her reflection, angry at her lack of willpower when it came to Jimbo Boyd, her full-time boss and her often-times lover.

He'd had her in the palm of his hand for years. Whenever she tried to back away, knowing he'd never give her what she wanted—a real commitment—he always managed to seduce her back into their long-standing affair.

This latest time, she'd managed to resist for a month. Long enough to start looking beyond him, beyond the fruitless dreams of him leaving his wife for her. She'd begun thinking she could live without him, though he'd been a major presence in her life since she'd been young and dumb, wowed by the attention of a handsome, much-older man.

He was still handsome and she was still dumb, as evidenced by today's naked wrestling session on his desk.

He'd sounded so unhappy last night, that's what had done her in. He'd called her at home, telling her how terrible his life was without her. *That* she believed. Jimbo was the most put-upon man she'd ever known, controlled by his rich wife. The mayor would never admit it, but Joyful knew exactly who was in charge, at work, at home and at city hall. First Lady Hannah Boyd.

Jimbo might cheat on her, but he wouldn't leave Hannah. Daneen had thought the realization would give her the strength to stand firm when he started begging her to come back to him.

Uhh…wrong.

"Idiot," she called herself, then left the powder room.

She'd known this morning that Jimbo would lay on the charm today, wanting an after-hours *dick*—yuck, yuck, hardy-har-har, emphasis on the *dick*—tation session. Nope, no surprise there. Not after last night's teary phone call, and the loud argument Jimbo'd had with Hannah this morning. Fighting with Hannah always made Jimbo want to have sex…with someone else. Not that Hannah suspected that Daneen was the someone else these days.

Since it was after five-thirty, she began to gather her things to leave. Maybe she'd beat Johnny to the house and he'd never hear her phone message. She'd told him she was working late and he should heat up some leftovers in the microwave for supper.

Grabbing her purse and keys, Daneen knocked lightly on the closed door of Jimbo's office. When she didn't receive an answer, she pushed it open and saw him at his desk, talking on the phone.

"I told you it wouldn't matter," he said. "The paperwork is perfect. There's nothing she can do."

She waited, wondering who he'd called, knowing the phone hadn't rung. Five minutes ago, they'd been panting and naked on his desk. He must've reached for the handset before he'd zipped up his fly. Well, didn't *that* make her feel special.

"The tracks are covered. Nobody can do a thing. Do you think I don't know this town? Stop worrying."

"Jimbo?" she whispered.

He looked up and saw her standing there, then impatiently waved her out with his hand, not saying a word. Daneen stiffened, hot moisture rising in her eyes, to her absolute mortification.

God, it killed her that she loved the son of a bitch. At least, she usually loved him…on the days she didn't hate his faithless guts.

Backing out of the office, she blinked rapidly, righteous anger drying her tears. She turned on her heel and walked to the exit, prepared to give the door a good slam as she left. But as she reached it, she saw someone standing outside.

"Came to get paid," Cora Dillon said as soon as Daneen unlocked the front door, which Jimbo had locked shortly before their five-minute interlude in his office. The woman tried to push inside. "I did some cleaning for Mr. Boyd today."

Cora, one of Daneen's late mother's friends, was known far and wide as the nosiest busybody north of Atlanta. She'd just love to come inside and catch a hint of scandal, perhaps something as damning as Daneen's lipstick on Jimbo's chin. Not to mention the unmistakable aroma of illicit sex.

"Sorry, we're closed." Daneen stepped out and tried to pull the door shut behind her. "You'll have to come back tomorrow."

The steely-eyed old bat had the gall to stick her foot in the door and shoulder it back open. "Mister Boyd said I could get my money today. I know he's here, so I'll wait inside for him."

Daneen gritted her teeth, wishing she'd left earlier, or at least sprayed down Jimbo's office with some air freshener. Busybodies had the noses of bloodhounds. Since their eyes were almost as deadly keen, she didn't even dare to glance down at her blouse to make sure she hadn't missed a button.

That'd be the last thing she needed—for her father—or worse, *Johnny,* to hear rumors about her and Jimbo. He'd be devastated. Humiliated. And Daneen would die before hurting him.

"You're wasting your time," she said to Cora, trying to sound unconcerned. "It'll be a very long wait. He's been in on that phone all afternoon, I barely got a minute with him today."

God, it was hard to stay steady and meet the other woman's eyes. She did it, though, because Cora Dillon collected gossip the way some old ladies collected ceramic pigs or antique dolls: with single-minded precision.

Daneen didn't want anyone to know about her secret affair with Jimbo. Not Hannah Boyd. Not Cora Dillon.

And especially not Johnny.

CHAPTER THREE

TRYING TO ESCAPE the view of the onlookers still pressed against the front window of the Joyful Grocery Store, Emma sank into the passenger seat of Johnny's SUV. Through half-lowered lashes, she watched him go around to get into the driver's side.

Of all people in the world she hated to be indebted to, it was Johnny Walker. Well, him, and the bank that held her car loan. She'd have to figure out how to pay them *after* she figured out how she was going to buy her next meal.

But right up there in a close tie was Johnny Walker, the man she'd never been able to forget. Or forgive.

Getting in on the other side, he jerked the door closed, his every movement taut and tense. He obviously disliked the situation as much as she did. His jaw remained stiff as he yanked his seat belt across his lap and fastened it.

She watched, her eyes going where they had no business going before she managed to scrunch them shut. Johnny's lap was no man's land. No woman's land, at least. *Not this woman, anyway.*

Probably plenty of others, though. She imagined with his looks and smile and those wicked blue eyes he'd probably had a *lot* of women in his lap over the years. "Bastard."

He turned his head and quirked a brow. "Excuse me?"

"Hurts like a bastard," she mumbled.

He stared, practically daring her not to blink at the lie. She wouldn't. She couldn't. And she didn't. Not even when her eyes began to feel like they were full of sawdust.

When he finally looked away to start up the car, she almost cried with relief. She did not want him to know she had any feelings for him one way or the other. Sadness would tell him how much he'd once hurt her. Anger implied he meant something to her.

Complete indifference was definitely the best way to go.

"'Cause, you know, I felt pretty sure you couldn't be talking to me," he said as he backed out of the parking space. "The guy who just carried your ass out of not only a painful situation but a damned embarrassing one."

"Which wasn't entirely my fault."

"Wasn't mine, either," he countered. "In case, you know, you were, uh, cursing more than the pain in your ankle."

Darn. She hadn't fooled him at all with the brief staring contest. He was still too intuitive for her own good.

But he was also correct. "You're right," she admitted, the words dragged out of her throat almost against her own will. "Thank you. That wasn't quite the way I'd expected to renew my acquaintance with the residents of Joyful."

"How'd you expect to do that?" he asked with a frown. "On a stage wearing nothing but a big smile?"

She sucked in a shocked breath, then barked out a laugh. "Good grief, hasn't this town seen me naked enough?"

This time, she surprised a laugh right back out of him. He glanced over at her, good humor making those irresistible dimples of his deepen in his lean cheeks. "Is that a trick question?"

She raised a brow.

"*Is* there such a thing as seeing enough of a naked woman?"

Deadpan, she replied, "I suppose it depends on the woman. Are we talking Lady Godiva naked here? Or the old lady from the Shoebox greeting cards naked?"

"How about porn star naked?" he asked, his eyes narrowing.

Then she snorted. Porn star, indeed. "Is that how you're getting your kicks these days? Was the can of spaghetti sauce you dropped really supposed to be a dinner for two—you—and a two-dimensional date on your big-screen TV?"

He chuckled again, shaking his head. Johnny always could get her to say the most outrageous things, when other people generally thought of her as the sweetest spoken, most ladylike girl around. Once upon a time she'd liked him for that.

With Johnny, she hadn't had to be an angel. And lordy had he tempted her to be a devil. On one night in particular.

"You haven't changed much," he finally said.

"You have."

"You're still a smart-ass."

"You're still a bossy, arrogant so-and-so."

He snorted. "You obviously still know how to be the center of attention."

"*You* obviously still have a hero complex," she responded.

They fell silent for a moment, then, she heard him say one more thing. "I've thought about you."

The absurd fluttering his softly spoken words caused in her stomach made her retort airily, "I haven't spared you one minute."

That shut him up. And officially upped her time in purgatory for lying. Big huge fat liar, that was Emma Jean's new title.

But it served its purpose and was worth a few more years of penance. Because it got him to quit being cute and teasing and playful and sexier than any man had a right to be.

Johnny angry she could handle. Johnny flirtatious and cute she definitely could not. No sane, reasonable, breathing woman could. It was bad enough that she was half-crippled and helpless, she hated to be emotionally helpless on top of it. As emotionally helpless as only Johnny Walker had ever been able to make her.

Helplessness had never agreed with her, emotionally *or* physically. Nor, she realized as she thought about him taking her to a clinic with pricey X-rays, had poverty. An Ace bandage from the clinic would probably cost more than a bag of groceries. And right now, a little pain seemed preferable to starvation.

Having sprained her ankle enough as a kid, she recognized the symptoms. All she needed was a good soak, a strong bandage—which her grandmother had always kept on hand—and some aspirin. Or a belt of something strong to numb the pain in her ankle and the confusion in her brain.

She doubted her grandmother had ever stocked *anything* strong enough to numb the abject humiliation of the scene in the store.

"I don't need to go to the clinic," she said.

He just shook his head. "Don't start that again."

Knowing he probably figured she was arguing for argument's sake, Emma turned in her seat. She placed her hand on his arm, just below the rolled up sleeve of his dress shirt, to try to convince him she was serious. Bad move. Waaaaay bad. It was impossible to ignore the sudden blast of heat shooting through her fingertips at the feel of his smooth skin against hers. General Electric could have learned something about stoves from this guy's skin.

Hot. Fevered. Powerful.

She gulped away the momentary insanity. "I mean it," she finally said when she felt capable of speech. "I've sprained and twisted my ankle enough times to know what it feels like. This one's not bad." Even to her own ears, her voice sounded thin and unconvincing. Not surprising. She could barely focus on anything but the knowledge that she was really here, breathing the same air, actually *touching* him after all these years.

Though behind the wheel, he seemed unable to tear his gaze away from her hand, starkly pale against his own deeply tanned skin. She finally pulled it away, wondering why her fingertips still tingled even after she'd clenched her fists in her lap.

Then, noting where her fists had landed, she jerked her hands lower toward the knee part of her lap. Away from the, umh…upper *thigh* part. That territory was too alert already. It had been ever since she'd seen him in the grocery store.

Emma, you are one pathetic, sex-starved woman.

Yeah. She definitely was. Which was why she needed to get away from the six-foot tall walking pile of solid sin.

"My grandmother had a well-stocked medicine cabinet at the house," she mumbled, knowing the house wasn't too far away. "I can bandage it myself. I've had lots of experience. Can you just give me a ride to her place?"

He cleared his throat, gave one nod and turned at the next corner. They rode in silence for a few moments, but finally, as they pulled out onto Main Street, Johnny glanced at her again. "I'm sorry about your grandma. She's sorely missed. Most of the town turned up at her funeral."

She heard an unspoken question in his voice. "I was in the hospital after a car accident."

He cast her a quick look that might have been concern but was more likely curiosity.

"I'm fine now," she quickly explained. "But I was laid up for a few weeks." She glanced out the window, unable to hide the regret in her voice. "My parents didn't even tell me she'd died until two days after the funeral. They knew I'd have tried to get here."

"I'm sorry, Em."

"Me too," she whispered, then she cleared her throat. "But at least I got to see her right before she died. She came to visit me in New York while I was in the hospital."

"What happened? Were you in traction? Broken legs?" he asked, glancing at her thighs, exposed to an almost indecently high level due to her short skirt. Then he quickly glanced away and a funny tick started in his temple.

Johnny always had been a leg man.

She thrust the thought—and the flash of unmistakable heat it caused—out of her head. Swallowing hard, she forced a note of nonchalance in her voice. "Nope, not legs. Broken head."

He gaped. "Are you kidding?"

"Minor swelling on the brain knocked me out but good for a few days. I woke up after surgery bald as a cue ball, a little confused about who I was and wondering whether Brad Pitt really had been painting my toenails while I slept."

This time, he hit his brakes, coming to a stop in the middle of the street. Darn good thing they weren't being tailgated, or he would have been rear-ended for sure. "You're serious?"

"Yeah," she said with a rueful sigh. "Unfortunately, Brad hadn't been visiting me during my unconscious state. That part was just a dream. Did you know they take off your nail polish when you have surgery? I didn't know until I woke up and peeked at my toes. They were dreadfully bare, so that's how I knew Brad hadn't come around."

He shot her a glare. "Would you shut up about your nail polish and get back to the bald part? Jesus, Emma Jean, did you have brain surgery?"

"The swelling had to be relieved." She fingered a short curl beside her cheek, twisting it around her finger. "Ah, well, I'd always wanted to do something drastic with my hair."

"Baldness is pretty drastic."

"So are scars on your head. Believe me, this hairdo is positively lush in comparison."

He stared at her hair, at the curl wound around her index finger. At her face.

Emma's heart skipped a beat in her chest as she took stock of the moment. God, of all the things she'd envisioned about her homecoming, there'd never been anything close to this.

Alone with Johnny. And him looking at her with the same old combination of interest, frustration and aloofness that had always driven her crazy. She wondered what he could be thinking to make his eyes sparkle such a brilliant blue, a vivid color she'd only ever before seen in the waters of the Caribbean.

Behind them, someone laid on a horn, and Johnny jerked his attention back to the road. Emma took the moment to order her heart to get back to doing its job, regular and even. And she reminded herself to breathe.

In. Out. Slower. Deeper. Calm. Relax.

Hitting the gas, Johnny took off down the street, shaking his head and muttering something beneath his breath.

"Ahem, if you're going to speak to me, could you do it louder? I didn't quite hear you."

He mumbled again, then glanced at her out of the corner of his eye. She grinned.

"A lush hairdo? You always were one to see the silver lining, weren't you?" he finally said.

Not always. Not on prom night, anyway. Not until he'd *shown* her the silver lining. And a lot more.

"So you don't like my hair?" Emma wasn't particularly vain, but she'd thought the Marilyn Monroe look suited her. And at least, it got people to stop seeing her only as the sweet, long-haired golden girl.

The hairdo had inspired other changes, including a wardrobe renovation. Not to mention her cute sporty car. Within weeks, Emma Jean had transformed into a slightly bad girl. That was one positive thing to come out of her accident, anyway.

"I like your hair Emma Jean," he admitted. "But I meant the other silver lining. I guess you bless your accident a bit, since you got to see your grandmother one last time."

Definitely. "Yes. I'm very thankful I got to see her again."

It hurt to think of their last visit, fourteen months before, and not just because it had been the last time they'd been together. A very concerned Grandma Emmajean had said she was thinking of making some changes. She'd talked about leaving Georgia. Someone was interested in buying her land, and she'd thought to sell the house, too, and buy a small place in New York to be near her family. Namely her.

Those words had shocked Emma. Joyful was her grand-mother's life. The house and the grove had been in her family for decades. It had been heartbreakingly clear how lonely Grandma Emmajean had become, and how selfish Emma had been to stay away just because of some embarrassment she'd suffered as a teenager.

She'd asked Grandma Emmajean not to do it, and had promised to come for a long visit once she was well enough. Nothing would have stopped Emma from keeping her promise. Nothing…except the twist of fate that caused her much-loved grandmother's tired heart to stop beating in her sleep the following week.

"You must have been pretty upset with your parents for not telling you," he said. "They're still trying to keep their princess safe, huh? Bet that one was hard to forgive."

He understood. Instantly. Unlike anyone else, Johnny could sympathize with her anger at her parents. They'd been so worried, they'd denied her the chance to grieve the most important person in her life. Like always, they'd protected her. "Yes. It was."

"They ever find out why you left Joyful before graduation?"

She listened for an edge in his voice, but didn't hear it. "No. Grandma Emmajean kept them from hearing everything."

He gave a dry chuckle. "Good thing. I remember how much they fought against you staying with her and going to Joyful High for a year."

She vividly remembered the conversation when she'd told Johnny about her life. It had been eleven summers ago. Spotting him tinkering under the hood of his truck on the side of a country road near her grandmother's pecan orchard, she'd stopped to give him a lift. Her heart had pounded wildly, sweat making her hands slick on the steering wheel.

It had been dangerous. Exciting. Thrilling to finally be alone with the baddest of the bad-boy Walkers.

During their brief ride, when he'd teased her about picking up strange guys, she'd told him how happy she was to live like a normal teenager. With her parents busy getting on with their jet-setting lives on the other side of the globe, they couldn't constantly protect their "little girl" from danger.

At seventeen, being alone in a small car with the object of her most torrid virgin fantasies had ranked pretty high on Emma's danger meter. Considering the tense, aware atmosphere between them now, she suspected things hadn't changed much.

Not even thinking about it, Emma moved her hand to her face as she stared out the window. Another memory filled her mind…of the teasing kiss Johnny had given her that day to thank her for the ride. It had been on her cheek, but not high up, not chaste and friendly. Not at all. He'd kissed her close to her mouth, as if wanting to taste the tiny dimple in her cheek. Then he'd shifted to brush his lips against the corner of hers. Even more amazing, he'd stolen a wicked taste of her lip gloss with a heart-stopping flick of his tongue.

Right before he'd gotten out of the car, that sexy hunk who'd already had her shaking in her seat had moved his mouth to her ear, nibbling on the lobe as he whispered, "I have *such* a thing for ankle bracelets." Reaching down, he'd caressed her calf, then stolen her anklet right off her leg. She hadn't even had the strength to protest as he'd put it in his pocket.

His wicked expression had told her he'd taken it as a souvenir.

The pounding in her heart had said, *let him*.

That had been the last time she'd been alone with Johnny for a while. Because the next time she saw him—when he was home from college for Thanksgiving weekend—she'd been wearing another guy's jacket. So she could never tell him that from the first time she'd laid eyes on him, she'd fallen headfirst into the most intense infatuation of her life. She couldn't have owned up to her many erotic dreams after their one, much-too-brief kiss.

No. Those were not exactly the kinds of things a girl could tell her *boyfriend's* older brother. Especially not one as rebellious—and hot—as Johnny Walker. Because she would never have been able to tell what he might do with such information.

Or how she might react to it.

He interrupted her musings. "Tell me more about this car accident you had."

"I'm fine," she assured him, "it wasn't that serious."

"You never could lie worth a damn."

Smiling, she elaborated. "I got T-boned by an uninsured, unlicensed driver. It took a while, but I'm fully recovered. Though I don't know if my insurance company is."

"I figured it had to have been bad, Emma Jean, because I know even a bald head wouldn't have stopped you from being here if you could."

"Just Emma," she murmured, surprised by the concern lacing his tone. Not to mention his certainty that she would have been in Joyful if she'd been able. She'd figured other people would notice her absence at the funeral and make some negative assumptions. Not Johnny.

His unexpected confidence in her was a strong reminder of one thing she'd tried to forget in her years away from this place. Though he hadn't known her long, Johnny Walker had known her better than anyone else. She'd spilled her most secret heart to him in the few short hours they'd shared together.

The acknowledgement almost hurt, making her flinch.

He glanced over. "You okay? In pain? Emma?"

"I'll be fine."

"We're almost to the house. If you want to give me your keys, I'll get somebody to bring your car over later."

Keys. The keys! She looked at him sheepishly. "I'm so sorry, Johnny, I forgot. I don't have keys to the house. I have to go by and pick them up from the Realtor."

He stiffened.

"I really hate to be such a bother."

"It's not a bother," he insisted. "But, knowing there's only one realty office in town, can I assume you mean Jimbo Boyd's place?"

At her nod, she heard him give an audible sigh. Then he looked at his watch. "It's twenty till six." He lowered his voice, almost as if speaking to himself. "The office should be closed by now. I'm sure she's…the secretary's… left."

She shrugged. "Probably. But I told Mr. Boyd I'd be getting in around dinnertime. He said he'd be working late on some paperwork and that I should just knock if the front door was locked."

The tenseness in his shoulders appeared to ease a bit. "Okay, no problem," he said with a nod as he pulled over to turn the SUV around. "Let's go to Mr. Boyd's office."

THOUGH SHE'D RAISED her voice and refused to budge out of the way, Daneen Walker had finally realized that nothing short of the miraculous landing of a spaceship in the middle of the street—or possibly a blue-light special on support hose—was going to prevent Cora Dillon from barreling into the Boyd Realty office. The woman was as relentless about her money as she was about her gossiping, and she wanted to get paid *now*.

She didn't see a spaceship, and the closest K-Mart was miles away, but Daneen got a miracle, anyway. The rumble of an engine pulling up along the front curb made Cora take a step back and turn around so Daneen could come all the way outside.

"Isn't that Johnny?" Cora asked. She moved one work-worn hand up to shield her eyes from the late-afternoon sun shining directly onto the front of the building.

Daneen nodded, recognizing the SUV. Her heart sank and her stomach tightened. As if Cora wasn't bad enough, now she had to try to act naturally in front of Johnny? This was bad. Johnny Walker knew her better than just about anyone. He usually saw through her lies whenever she tried to tell one. He had that prosecutor thing down pat, as Daneen had learned more than once in the years since she'd been related to the man.

She should've hung up on Jimbo as soon as she'd heard his voice last night. Or never answered the phone to begin with, since she had caller ID. Then she might not have been such a pushover this afternoon and wouldn't have been caught unaware by the biggest busybody in town…and by Johnny.

Since Cora was no more able to turn her eyes away from the hunkiest, most talked-about man in Joyful than any other female, Daneen took advantage of her distraction and risked a quick button-check of her blouse and skirt. *All clear.*

"Who's that with him?" Cora continued.

Daneen hadn't even noticed the other occupant of the car. Like Cora, she shielded her eyes, tightening her jaw as she spied a woman's blond head inside the vehicle. "I have no idea."

Then Johnny was out of the car, walking around to the passenger's side. He looked up and saw them, but instead of returning Daneen's friendly wave, he froze, as if surprised to see her. Why he'd be surprised to see her standing outside her own place of employment, she couldn't say.

Nor could Daneen say much of anything else when the other door of his SUV opened and a long, slim female leg slid out. The day suddenly seemed to get a little cloudier, and the mouthful of air she'd just inhaled turned stale in her lungs.

Daneen tensed, watching Johnny square up those big, broad shoulders of his, then help the woman out. They exchanged a few words as he easily lifted her down.

The blonde leaned into him, hobbling a bit as they approached the front of the building. Daneen rolled her eyes...typical woman's trick, she'd used it herself. A twisted ankle was a good way to get chest to chest with any hunky male with a hero complex. Straight Vixen-101 stuff.

The question remained—who was the blond-haired bimbo trying women's tricks on Johnny Walker, the man Daneen had grown used to thinking of as her personal property?

IF JOHNNY hadn't already gotten out of the truck by the time he spotted Daneen standing outside Jimbo's office, he would have come up with some lame excuse and driven away. The last thing he wanted was to bring the two women face-to-face within the first hour of Emma Jean's arrival back in town.

Too late now. Emma wanted her key, and Daneen would be even more angry if she realized they'd tried to avoid her. Nor would Emma consider staying in the truck. She wanted to speak to Mr. Boyd and no twisted ankle was going to stop her. Besides, she insisted she was already feeling better—an outright lie if he'd ever heard one, given the way her lips trembled and her eyes teared up when she tried to stand up unaided.

"'Evening," Johnny said with a nod as they approached the front door. Emma was leaning into his side, his arm supporting her around her waist as comfortable and easy as could be. Only a cardiologist would have been able to tell his heart was beating hard enough to bust out of his chest. He told himself it was merely the thought of having to deal with Emma and Daneen together. But somewhere, deep inside his gut, he knew it was more likely because of the way Emma felt pressed against his side.

Just about perfect.

"Mrs. Dillon," he said, easily recognizing the dour-faced woman standing beside Daneen.

Cora Dillon had once worked as a lunch lady at the Joyful Primary School and now did cleaning work wherever she could get it. He half expected her to rap his knuckles with a wooden spoon, the way she would way back in second grade when he'd try to sneak an extra piece of fruit from the lunch line. "Reduced price lunch for poor folks means *one* apple, Mr. Walker," she'd say, loud enough for every kid in the cafeteria to hear. "And no cookie!"

That pretty much summed up his childhood. One apple and no cookie. Some steely-eyed adult like Mrs. Dillon always seemed to be around to make sure no trashy Walker kid tried to snitch anything more than his charitable due.

He half wished the old woman would get charged with

jaywalking, or lifting a piece of candy out of the Brach's sampler display at the grocery store without paying for it.

There was one case he'd sure as hell prosecute.

Mrs. Dillon gave what for her probably passed as a friendly smile. "Mr. Walker," she said in greeting.

Johnny kept his hands well out of spoon range, just in case, even though he knew she couldn't very well rap the knuckles of the county prosecutor. Particularly not when one of her own rowdy grandsons was a recent beneficiary of Johnny's goodwill toward the high-spirited youth of Joyful.

"Nice to see you, ma'am," he replied, every bit as evenly.

Then the woman turned her attention on Emma Jean, studying her like someone might study a particularly difficult crossword puzzle or riddle.

"This is Emma Jean Frasier. I'm sure you knew her grandmother," he explained.

"It's just Emma," his companion murmured under her breath.

Her words were lost under Daneen's surprised gasp, which Cora Dillon echoed. Daneen's reaction he could have predicted. Mrs. Dillon, though, was probably annoyed at being caught not knowing the name, marital status and credit history of a new arrival to Joyful. Maybe Cora was losing her touch—she wasn't often caught unaware when it came to gossip-worthy newcomers.

"Hello, Daneen," Emma said when neither of the other women made any effort to speak. Johnny had to wonder how she hid her tension beneath that smooth, cultured voice. Her whole body was tight enough to snap in half.

Little wonder. Daneen had, after all, stolen Emma's man away once upon a time.

"Emma Jean," Daneen whispered, sounding the tiniest bit unsure of herself. Very unusual for this particular woman, who hardly ever let anyone see her weaknesses.

A variety of expressions crossed Daneen's face, ranging from dismay, to dislike, and perhaps even a bit of embarrassment. With reason, of course, as they all well knew.

But Daneen quickly did her thing, tossing her head and ignoring whatever guilt she might still be feeling about what had happened back in high school. "Well, I had no idea you were coming back to Joyful." Daneen's tone sounded forced as she straightened her shoulders in a failed attempt at indifference.

"Never can tell where one of us bad pennies is going to turn up," Emma said with a too-bright laugh. "How…*nice*…it is to see you, too."

That sounded about as sincere as a televangelist asking for forgiveness for screwing over his flock, but Johnny figured Emma Jean had a right to be spiteful. Daneen had done her dirty, all right. In front of the whole town, to boot.

"Johnny, wherever did you find her?" Daneen asked. "I didn't even know you two were…acquainted."

He frowned slightly at the blatant lie. There was no way Daneen hadn't heard about prom night, even though she hadn't been there to witness it firsthand. She'd run off, leaving Joyful in a tizzy that same day. Still, she'd come back soon enough afterward to hear the story. It had been whispered over and over, just like all the other scandalous tidbits of local folklore.

The prom night interlude between rebel Johnny Walker and golden girl Emma Jean Frasier was probably repeated almost as often as the tale of how Joyful had gotten its name. Frankly, Johnny had always found the name story a lot more interesting. Reportedly two hundred or so years ago, one of the town's founders had stopped at the tiny two-road crossing and pronounced, "This place is about as joyful as a fi'ty cent whore with a toothache." And Joyful had been christened.

How could a couple of teenagers caught bare-ass naked at the gazebo by most of the members of the senior class of Joyful High compare with that?

Unfortunately, he appeared to be the only person in Joyful who believed it couldn't.

"Emma and I ran into each other at the grocery store," he finally said. "She needed some help. I'm going to drop her off at her grandmother's place, but we need the key."

Cora, who they'd nearly forgotten about, reached into her pocket and dug out a small key ring. "Here you go," she murmured, still staring with avid interest at Emma. "I cleaned it up for you this morning. I was dropping the key back off to Mr. Boyd."

"Thank you very much, Mrs. Dillon," Emma said, sounding as refined and genteel as her late grandmother, who'd been every inch a lady. Had Emma sounded as dignified when asking him to make love to her? He couldn't really remember.

Liar. He remembered everything about that night. And no, she hadn't sounded proper and refined at all. She'd sounded sweet and hungry. Enticing, alluring and innocent. A lot more innocent than he'd ever expected, to his utter shock.

Which made it difficult, if not downright impossible, to believe the rumors that she'd been off making dirty movies since she'd left here ten years ago. He hadn't had time to wrap his mind around the whole gossipy rumor, but his first instinct was to suspect the Joyful grapevine had this particular story totally screwed up, particularly given the way she'd joked about porn movies during their drive.

"I haven't been inside the house in a very long time and I do appreciate your efforts," Emma continued.

Mrs. Dillon looked as if she didn't know whether to take Emma's words as a compliment or not, so she just grunted and turned toward the door. "I'll wait for Mr. Boyd inside," she told Daneen, who still appeared too shocked to protest. Then Cora entered the building, leaving the three of them alone.

"So, why are you back, Emma Jean?" Daneen asked. "I thought we'd seen the last of you."

Emma, apparently not as easily cowed, or, at least, as polite, as she'd been in high school, raised a brow. "Funny. Seems to me you were the one who skipped out of town first, Daneen. Speaking of which, how *is* Nick?"

Nick. Nick Walker. His younger brother, and once upon a time the object of affection of a number of teenage girls in the township of Joyful, Georgia. He'd have to include Emma Jean Frasier and Daneen Brady in that list.

Daneen Brady—now Walker. His former sister-in-law.

"Emma, maybe we should leave now," Johnny said, trying to turn her back toward the car. The last thing he wanted was to get Daneen started on the subject of his brother.

Too late.

"Probably burning in hell, for all I care," Daneen said, her voice hard, as it always was when Nick's name came up. "Wherever he is, he's certainly not here, so if Nick's the reason you came back to Joyful, you might just as well turn around and go back up north." Her tone turned sugary sweet, though her green eyes remained cool and assessing. "Gracious, it's been ten years, Emma Jean. Haven't you gotten over Nick yet?"

Yep. Daneen was sharpening up her claws. When she got around to remembering the rumors of what had happened between him and Emma Jean on prom night, they'd become even more cutting. Though there had never been any romantic involvement between him and his ex-sister-in-law—and never would be—she did seem to think her family status gave her the right to tell him how to run his life. The only reason he gave her a tiny bit of leeway on that was because she was, truly, family. Once a Walker, always a Walker, no matter how much Daneen hated to claim the name.

"Let's go, Emma."

Emma wouldn't be moved. Instead, smiling as she tapped the tips of her perfectly manicured pink nails on her collarbone, she stared at Daneen. "Oh, you sweet thing, to be worried about me," she said, lacing her voice with a sugary hint of Southern cordiality. "But, no, Nick was only a boy. A sweet, innocent teenage crush. Obviously our relationship wasn't anything like yours—since you were the one he *had* to run away with and marry so your daddy wouldn't kill him and all."

Johnny lowered his head so his ex-sister-in-law wouldn't see his grin. Not too many women could pull off that perfect blend of sweetness and cutting sarcasm. Emma's grandmother had had it down to an art form. Emma had apparently learned one or two things during her time in the South.

He had no idea where she could have learned anything about the adult film business.

As steam almost began rolling out of Daneen's ears, Emma gave a little smile and leaned heavier against Johnny's side. "I am really hurting now. You will help me back to the car, won't you? I'll speak to Mr. Boyd tomorrow." She gave him a wide-eyed, limpid look which, he supposed, probably appeared helpless and intimate to Daneen, as Emma had likely intended.

For an instant, he was tempted to let her fall on her ass again, leaving her lying on the ground outside Boyd Realty. She deserved it. Damned if he was going to let Emma Jean Frasier use him to salve her ego or bolster her pride one more time. Been there, done that. Pick another sucker, lady. Once in a lifetime was enough for anyone.

But there was something else in those golden-brown eyes of hers, something beyond flirtation or teasing. Her lashes flickered as she blinked rapidly, appearing on the verge of tears.

She seemed tired and hurting. In pain, both emotionally and physically. His heart twisted in his chest at the sleepless circles under her eyes and the paleness of her skin accentuated by a light dusting of freckles.

"Please, Johnny?" she whispered, this time not sounding cajoling but instead nearly desperate.

He sighed. Just like old times. The town had always known him as a rebel, but those closest to him had always realized he was a soft touch, always stupid and sappy enough to step in and take care of people who needed help. Which she did.

Besides which, to his eternal consternation, he never could resist Emma Jean Frasier when she said please.

EMMA DIDN'T MEAN to use Johnny out of spite by asking him to help her to the truck. In fact, when she saw his hesitation, she regretted having to rely on him at all. But she did. She needed to get away and he was the only one who could help her do it.

"What's the matter with her?" Daneen asked, sounding

falsely solicitous. "Shouldn't she come inside and sit for a while?"

Before Emma could nix that idea, Johnny hurried to thank Daneen and refuse her offer. He went on to briefly tell the other woman what had happened at the store.

Emma barely listened, wondering why she'd let Daneen get to her. Heavens, she was no longer the new kid in school being baited by the most popular girl, like she'd been during her senior year at Joyful High.

God, it seemed another lifetime. Who cared what had happened back then? Teenage dramas had nothing on Emma's adult life. High school certainly hadn't prepared her for men like her former boss, Wes Sharpton. Or for women like her former best friend in accounting, Lydia Bailey.

She idly wondered if Wes and Lydia were enjoying their South American honeymoon. And if the last remnants of the money they'd embezzled from the firm—which had put dozens of people out of work and landed them in the middle of an SEC investigation—was all spent yet.

Their money couldn't have disappeared any faster than Emma's life savings. Since her last few paychecks had bounced, and her mutual fund investments with the firm had become worthless, her balances had hit zero dollars and zero cents before she and the rest of the staff even knew what had happened.

Her checking account had gone even lower. The resounding *boing* of the checks she'd bounced all over Manhattan still rang in her ears at night. It was almost as loud as she imagined the metallic clang of the cell doors would have been if she hadn't immediately covered those checks through the sale of her furniture and jewelry back in the city.

She'd never imagined when she finally settled into brokering and finance—thinking she'd finally found her niche after she'd sampled so many other interesting creative outlets—that she'd end up losing all her money because of her job!

She'd have been better off sticking to archeology. Or art—the show she'd helped fund for an erotic artist a few years ago sure had been fun, though it'd shocked Grandma Emmajean when she'd sent her one of the brochures.

Grandma Emmajean. *Her savior.* Because coming to Joyful hadn't been a mere pleasure trip to lick her wounds and wait out the controversy. It'd been a downright necessity, if she wanted a roof over her head...*without* having to go to her parents for help. It still might come to that. But it hadn't yet, thank heaven.

"Well?" Johnny asked, interrupting her thoughts. "Are you ready to go, Emma?"

"Absolutely. It was so nice to see you," she told Daneen over her shoulder as Johnny helped her down the sidewalk. She leaned against him, almost not even noticing the steadiness of his hand on her arm, the steely strength of his chest against her side and the warm, musky scent of his cologne.

Well, that was a bald-faced lie. She could no more fail to notice those things than a person could pretend not to notice the color of the sky or the metallic way the air tasted right before a wicked thunderstorm. Some things were so elemental they simply couldn't be ignored. Like him.

Emma suddenly wondered if she'd made a big mistake. Maybe bickering with Daneen would have been a better way to spend her evening. Because after only an hour back in his company, she began to wonder if she would have the strength of will to resist those crazy old feelings she'd always had for Johnny Walker.

Somehow, she feared she wouldn't.

CHAPTER FOUR

CORA HADN'T HESITATED a moment once she'd gotten inside the waiting room of Boyd Realty. She'd turned right around, made herself a nice peeky-hole between two slats of the miniblinds—which were shamefully dusty, no surprise there—and watched what was going on outside.

The trio continued their chit-chatty conversation for a few minutes. It didn't take an expert in body language, however, to know there was no friendliness between the two younger women. They were like two cats in a box, trying to stay away from one another until it was safe to swipe, drawing first blood.

She smirked. Daneen Walker was way too uppity, to Cora's mind, and always had been. It hadn't helped that her daddy, Sheriff Brady, had spoiled the girl to bits when her mother had passed on fifteen years ago. Lately, she'd been darn near impossible with her claims. She'd been hinting that since Johnny was single, and she was kin, she was gonna serve as his first lady when he got elected mayor after Jimbo Boyd retired.

"Maybe cows'll fly down Market Street one of these days, too," she whispered sourly. Because that'd be just about the day any of those white trash Walkers got elected mayor of Joyful.

Prosecuting attorney was bad enough. But since there

weren't lawyers lining up for the low-paying job, she supposed he was the best they could do. She knew it darn near killed Sheriff Brady to have to work with the brother of his ex-son-in-law. Especially with Johnny's reputation for going easy on the criminal element.

Cora gulped down a bit of guilt. As much as she hated to admit it, Johnny had done a good turn by her grandson, Matthew. The sheriff probably would have seen the boy sent up to juvie hall for tipping over one of the Port-o-lets at the county fair last fall. It might not have been such a fuss and bother if Deputy Willis hadn't been inside the doggone thing at the time. Johnny Walker had worked things out with the public defender, so the boy had done some community service, but no time in jail.

Anyway, it wasn't like the portable piss-pot had been damaged. Much. And the township should have paid little Matty and his buddies for the spectacle. Deputy Fred had put on quite an entertaining—if a bit smelly—screaming performance once he'd been rescued. It had been a darn sight more exciting than the sideshows, like the two-headed chicken—obviously a rubber toy with an extra beak super-glued to its butt. Or the hootchie-cootchie girls wagging their saggy fannies all over the midway.

"Mealy-mouthed Fred Willis probably liked getting the attention, anyway," she muttered, remembering how quiet and whiny he'd been as a child.

Outside, she saw Daneen's body was stiff with indignation. The snooty Frasier girl with the tattered reputation had a confident look on her face as she and Johnny turned away. Looked like the blond chippie had won this round. Cora had no love for city girls who sold dirty pictures, but it did a body good to see Daneen Walker set back on her round heels once in a while.

Sensing the scene out front was almost over, Cora let go of the blinds. She took a moment to examine the office, even peeking into the small bathroom. When she saw a tell-tale red wrapper floating in the toilet, she smirked.

Just as she'd suspected...Jimbo Boyd was sticking more than For Sale signs into some of the cheap real estate in Joyful. She sure didn't suppose Daneen had been filling up rubbers and using them for water balloons.

Filing the information away into the back of her brain for future use, she stepped over to the closed door of Jimbo's office. She heard his voice, but no one else's, and assumed he was on the phone, arguing with someone.

Cora smiled. Lucky for her, when Mayor Jimbo argued he did so the same way he did everything else. Loudly. If she'd showed up a half hour earlier, she might of heard the mayor calling out for the lord while his fake-pearls-wearing secretary told him to be a good boy or else mama'd have to spank his bottom.

She snickered, then leaned closer to the door, listening. Catching a few words, she wondered who the mayor was talking to. And why he seemed so interested in that new strip club being advertised on the highway billboard...Joyful Interludes.

EMMA SHOULD have known better than to think Daneen would let her get away without one more shot at ruining her day.

"Wait," the other woman called before they could step off the curb onto the street.

She gritted her teeth as Johnny paused.

Daneen sauntered down the sidewalk, like a woman who knew she looked good in her silky blouse and tight skirt, and grabbed Johnny's arm. Tilting her head back, she gave him a welcoming smile. "Are you coming over to dinner tonight?"

Johnny appeared confused. "Was I supposed to?"

"Well, it's Friday."

Johnny raised a brow. "So?"

"You know. Little Johnny's pizza and movie night."

Little Johnny? Emma tensed. There was a little Johnny somewhere? Good grief, had she been so bloody distracted seeing her first lover in the flesh—and such fine flesh it was—that she'd never even cast a quick, surreptitious glance toward his left-hand ring finger? Emma Jean Frasier, usually a connoisseur of eligible bachelors, had slipped up big time.

She looked now. No ring. The rush of relief surprised her. She shouldn't have been glad. After all, she hated the bastard, she really did. But something that felt suspiciously like happiness did ooze through her before she could stop it.

"Why do you call him that?" Johnny asked, shaking his head in obvious annoyance. "You know he hates it. The kid's been called Jack for nine years. Why all of a sudden you've started calling him Johnny is beyond me."

Daneen cast a glance at Emma. "What boy wouldn't want to be called the same thing as the man he considers his daddy?"

Growing visibly tense, Johnny didn't answer right away. He stared directly at Daneen. The woman finally stopped giving Emma sly looks, and focused on Johnny's unsmiling face.

"Jack is my nephew and I love him," Johnny said, his tone tight. "But I'm not his father, I'm his uncle. He knows it. You know it. Everyone in town knows it. Changing his name isn't going to do anything but make him resent *you*, Daneen."

Emma at last understood. Little Johnny…Jack…had to be the baby Daneen had been pregnant with back in high school. The baby she'd conceived with Emma's boyfriend, Nick Walker. The baby the whole town had been whispering about on the day of the senior prom, when word got out that the king—Nick—had deserted his queen—Emma—because he'd knocked up the daughter of the sheriff.

And that the sheriff was cleaning his gun.

Daneen didn't say another word as Johnny helped Emma to the SUV and held her arm while she got in. Once he joined her, taking his place in the driver's seat, she couldn't help rolling down her window to face Daneen. Somehow, her face didn't even crack as she forced a pleasant expression. "Nice seeing you, Daneen. I never got a chance to say goodbye all those years ago." She managed a completely unconcerned laugh, still having enough of that old dumped-high-school-girl pride to act as if she didn't care what had happened. "You sure missed one *wild* prom night."

Daneen began to frown, then her mouth dropped open, as if she'd just remembered something. She looked ready to grab the door handle when Johnny revved the engine to life.

"Now you did it," Johnny muttered as he pulled away from the curb, leaving a slack-jawed Daneen behind them.

"What'd I do?"

He shot her a frankly disbelieving look out the corner of his eye. "*Wild* prom night? Did you really have to remind her about what happened between you and me?"

It took her a second to process the accusation. He thought she'd intentionally set out to bait Daneen by making her jealous of her and Johnny? "Back up, big guy," she said with a frown. "For your information, I was trying to blow off what happened between your jerk of a brother and that—*person*—back in high school. Why would she care…" Then she remembered the whole Daddy nonsense and groaned. "Oh, God, don't tell me you're following in Nick's footsteps. You're involved with Daneen?" She shuddered, not feigning her complete dismay. "Ewww. Two brothers. I didn't think bad taste ran in families."

He glanced over and raised a brow. "As opposed to what…good taste?"

She had to think for a moment before she caught his meaning. Then she got it. He and Nick had both gotten involved with *her,* hadn't they? She almost punched his arm for putting her in the same category with Daneen, who'd been about as big a bitch as Emma had ever encountered during their high school days. But she didn't want to cause an accident.

"Anyway," he continued, "no, we're not involved. Never have been, never will be."

Emma blew out an impatient breath. Men. Such simple creatures. "Have you told her that?"

He gave her a pointed look as they stopped at a red light. "Yeah, I have. Nine years ago, right after she came back to Joyful, she made a play. I shot her down."

The thought of Daneen trying anything with Johnny made Emma feel a sudden stab of annoyance she had no business feeling. She swallowed it away, asking, "Is she in love with you?"

Johnny shook his head. "Hell, no. She knows me too well."

That was an interesting comment, considering how loveable he was. Correction. Had *once* been. "Oh?"

"She knows it'd be a waste of time since I don't want

anything to do with love, marriage or any of that garbage. Walker men just aren't cut out for it. At least not the ones from my branch of the family tree." He shrugged, probably realizing how heavy that had sounded. "Daneen and I are friends, that's all."

Emma remained silent for a moment, hearing a hint of resignation—though not bitterness—in Johnny's voice. He obviously believed what he said about commitment. Little wonder, considering his background…his father. And apparently Nick. The only surprising thing was how his words had affected her—with a sudden flare of something almost painful in her belly.

"If you say so. But Daneen sure looked territorial."

"There's nothing else between us, and there never will be," he added. "Daneen knows it as well as I do."

He apparently believed that. Gullible as well as simple. "So what's with the Daddy stuff?"

Turning the car onto Peach Grove Lane, he headed toward her grandmother's neighborhood. "Jack doesn't really have one. Nick bailed on her and joined the Marines before Jack was even born." Johnny frowned, looking disgusted.

"Why?"

"I don't know. I've only seen him once since."

That surprised her, knowing how close Johnny and Nick had been. But the tightness in his jaw warned her not to push.

He continued. "Daneen moved back here when Jack was a month old. My mom and I do what we can to help." Rolling his eyes, he added, "Daneen has realized I'm never going to get married and have kids, so she pictures Jack as my heir or something—as if I've got a ton of money. Which I *don't*."

Never marry. Never have kids. Again that stab of something hit her in the stomach. *Hunger. It's just hunger from a long day of driving with no food.* But deep in her heart, she knew she was lying to herself.

"She seems to think her status as my 'sister' gives her the right to interfere in my personal life," he said. "Look, can we talk about something else?"

"Like?"

"How about we discuss how wild prom night was?"

The louse. She really couldn't believe he wanted to have this conversation while she was trapped, practically crippled, and at his mercy. "Let's not. Ever."

"Still feeling sorry for yourself?"

"Still mad at the world?" she snapped right back.

"Nope." He shot her a look out of the corner of his eye. "Just you."

She sagged back into the seat. *He* was mad at *her?* What a laugh, considering he was the one who'd gotten into his truck and taken off after they'd been caught at the gazebo.

The mention of their prom night brought up lots of emotions. Humiliation, of course. Embarrassment. Sadness at the white-hot anger that had made them both say some pretty ugly things.

Enough.

"Let's not talk at all," she said, fighting for emotional distance from Johnny, in spite of their close proximity.

"Suits me fine," he muttered as he fell silent.

Closing her eyes, she battled to think of something else. But the thought of their final confrontation reminded her of everything else that happened that night.

Prom. Ten years ago. It should have been a disaster. The town had spent the day whispering about Nick and Daneen's elopement. Emma had spent the day crying about having no date for the most important event in high school.

Then Johnny had been there. He'd knocked on her grandma's door, wearing the tux Nick had rented. It was a little tight across the shoulders and the sleeves were a bit short, but he'd still been heart-stoppingly handsome. Smiling that wicked Walker smile of his, he'd handed her a bouquet of freshly picked wildflowers. Ordering her to dry her tears and put on her dress, he'd informed her he was taking her to the dance. Whether she liked it or not.

She'd liked it. As a matter of fact, considering she was already crazy for him—and had been since the day the previous summer when he'd kissed her in her car—she'd loved it.

And for a few hours, she'd truly loved *him.*

"You're thinking of that night," he said softly.

His whisper didn't startle her out of her reverie, and she could only nod, her wisp of a smile probably telling him she was recalling the early part of the evening. The nice part. "Remember the look on their faces when we walked in?"

He chuckled, obviously picturing—as she was—the gaping upperclassmen gathered beneath the twinkling lights and clumps of fresh magnolias decorating the VFW hall. "They expected you to stay home crying and instead you came in on the arm of the wickedest of the Walker boys."

The scent of magnolia always took her back to that place. Always made her feel the heady thrill she'd felt when she'd walked in with him. Not because of how her classmates had reacted, but because of the way his hand had felt on the small of her back. His fingers had dipped low on her spine, touching her with a kind of intimate possession his brother had known better than to even try.

For all his talk and swagger, Nick Walker had been a boy, contained by the boundaries she set.

Not Johnny. He'd already been a man. A man who'd completely intoxicated her, physically, and emotionally. A man to whom boundaries meant absolutely nothing.

"You said something sweet to make me smile for the picture," she murmured.

"I told you I had your ankle bracelet hanging on my bedpost in my dorm room."

Yes, that was it. She idly wondered what had ever happened to the anklet but didn't have the nerve to ask.

"We danced every dance," she added, still looking out the window, not at him. She didn't *want* to look at him, didn't want to know if this unexpected stroll down memory lane was as confusing for Johnny as it was for her. She'd been angry about how the night had ended for so long, she'd almost allowed herself to forget how magical most of it had really been.

They'd stayed in each other's arms, swaying to the music—even the rock songs—for ages. He'd flirted with her shamelessly. He'd acted as if he had eyes for no one else. Then he'd whisked her out the door. But not before giving her a bone-meltingly romantic kiss under the slowly spinning mirror ball, right in the middle of Whitney Houston's "I Will Always Love You."

Then they'd gone to the gazebo. And the night had become truly amazing.

Did he remember the way she'd cried as she tried to thank him for showing up at her door? Did he ever realize she hadn't been crying over his stupid brother, but over his own kindness?

Probably not. He'd probably never again thought of how they'd slow-danced in a darkness lit only by the stars and some watery moonlight. Dry leaves had snapped beneath their feet and the breeze had made a faint whistle as it swept through the gazebo, but she'd never felt cold.

A ghost of a smile crossed her lips as she thought of how they'd talked and laughed. Laughter had been followed by long, deep kisses that had gone on forever. Sweet touches giving way to more intimate ones. Tenderness turning to passion. The first real arousal of her life. And the amazing feel of his body on top of hers…inside hers….

"Stop," she whispered, wondering how on earth she'd allowed her thoughts to completely overwhelm her. She wriggled in her seat as a memory-induced tide of heat slid through her blood, settling with insistence between her legs.

"What? Are you okay? Hurting?"

"I'm fine," she insisted, taking a few deep breaths.

If he'd realized what she'd been thinking about—and the way her body had reacted—she'd just have to die. Right here and now. Dammit, what kind of woman got turned-on remembering her first sexual experience which, considering many females first had sex with teenage boys, usually sucked?

Hers hadn't. She had to admit it, if only to herself…it had been the best of her whole entire life. Not necessarily the intercourse part, which had been slightly uncomfortable at first. But the emotion. The tenderness. And, oh, yeah, the orgasms.

Nineteen years old or not, Johnny had known *exactly* what he was doing. With his hands. With his mouth. With every bit of his big, firm body.

"You're sure you don't need the doctor?" he said, obviously not believing her and taking her silence for discomfort.

Well, she was uncomfortable, but not in the ankle area.

No, the throbbing sensation was now much higher. As in, right between her thighs. And no doctor could make her feel better.

"Quite sure," she mumbled, drawing in a few deep breaths to try to focus. "My, it's already awfully hot for early June."

He shrugged, either not impressed with her conversational skills, or realizing she wanted to leave the subject of prom night behind. She was saved from having to make any further effort by his nod. "Here we are."

She hadn't even noticed how quickly the ride had flown by, since she'd been a little…er…distracted. Now, however, she froze as she stared out the windshield of his SUV at the gently familiar tree-lined street onto which they'd turned.

"Miss Ellen's house," she murmured, spying the huge elm tree in front of what had once been a white bungalow. "Her piano students used to wake me up every Saturday with their scales."

The house was green now. A tricycle and a scooter in the driveway, plus a bat and ball lying in the grass, gave evidence that old Miss Ellen had moved on, in one way or another.

Next came the white picket fence surrounding the immaculate lawn maintained by Mr. and Mrs. Willoughby, her grandmother's next-door neighbors. And then…

"There it is," she whispered. The lemon-yellow, two-story house that she pictured whenever she closed her eyes and thought of home. Of happy times and warmth. Of sweet hugs and the papery smoothness of her grandmother's strong hands. Of endless summer days being allowed to climb trees and get dirty.

She'd expected tears to fill her eyes when she saw it again. But somehow, after everything she'd been through, she didn't feel sad at all. As a matter of fact, staring at the house—so warm and bright, and best of all, entirely hers—she began to smile.

This was Emmajean's house, Emmajean's world, Emmajean's town. Her grandmother wouldn't be here to welcome her, but all the warmth and hospitality she'd epitomized lived on right here in Joyful. She could lose herself in that warmth and hospitality, let it salve her wounds and heal her spirit while she figured out what she was going to do with the rest of her life.

In spite of the dull pain in her foot, the fatigue in her shoulders and her pitifully empty wallet, she truly felt good. For the first time in a long time, Emma Frasier began to believe everything really would be okay.

Because she was home.

JOHNNY DIDN'T stick around once they got to Emma's grandmother's house. He helped her inside, then made sure the electricity was on and the place secure. Though he wanted nothing more than to get out, to put a mile of physical distance between them—immediately if not sooner—he also made sure to find her an Ace bandage in her grandmother's medicine kit.

By the time he left, she was soaking her foot in an old washtub in the kitchen. She was also nibbling on a piece of fruit from a Welcome Home basket Jimbo Boyd had left on the counter. Good old Jimbo. Never one to pass up an opportunity to kiss the ass of a voter—or a campaign contributor.

She'd thanked Johnny sincerely, accepted his offer to have someone bring her car over to the house and agreed he should let himself out. She might as well have been a fare he'd picked up in a taxi for all the intimacy between them.

It wasn't too surprising that Emma had tried to put up walls. Just the faint beginnings of a discussion about what had happened between them had made her go silent and distracted.

"The little coward."

If Deputy Fred Willis had been around, Johnny would have earned himself a hundred dollar fine as he blasted out of her driveway. Even if he'd seen the dusty old patrol car, he didn't know if he could have lifted his foot off the gas pedal.

He needed space. Distance. Needed to get away from those golden-brown eyes of hers and her soft voice. The longer he spent in Emma's company, the more likely he'd have been to shake the hell out of her and ask her why she'd done what she did.

First, why she'd used him as a physical substitute for his brother when it came to something as important as sex. Then, why she'd run away the very next day…when that sex had been so damn good! And finally, how in the name of God she could have gone on to have sex for money in the name of movie-making.

Sex, sex and sex again. That's what it all came down to. If he'd stayed in that house another minute, the subject would have come up. And sex was one thing he could not talk about with Emma Jean Frasier. At least not without being sorely tempted to find the nearest flat surface and fully explore the meaning of the word with her in every position known to man. Plus a dozen yet to be invented.

He shook his head in disgust. He obviously needed to get laid. Preferably by someone who didn't list her proficiency with various coital positions on her résumé.

Then he snorted. "It's bullshit. If she's a porn star, I'll prance up Market Street in those spike-heeled shoes of hers."

No, there had to be another explanation for the stories flying around town. *Had* to be. And once he got a firm grip on his libido again, he'd find out what it was.

In the meantime, there was her car to deal with. Grabbing his cell phone, he hit one of the speed dial buttons. "Virg, can you meet me down in the parking lot of the grocery store?" he asked when a familiar voice answered.

"Sure," his cousin said. "Can I finish my hot dog first?"

"Hot dog. Minnie working tonight?"

"Uh-huh. Third weekend in a row." Virg tsked in disgust. "That skunk boss of hers tells her if she wants to be head cook on Sundays, when the regular guy's off, she has to bounce at the door every Friday and Saturday night."

Minnie had recently moved up from bouncer to cook's assistant at the Junctionville Tavern. After she and Virg got married, she'd put her foot down saying it wasn't seemly for a bride to be physically tossin' drunks out of bars. Her boss had apparently found a way to finagle her back where he wanted her.

"If she didn't have her heart set on getting a job as head cook somewhere, I'd make her quit," Virgil continued.

He'd make her quit. Yeah. Right. Virgil Walker would be able to *make* his two hundred and fifty-pound wife, Minnie, do something on the same day Johnny made snow fall in July. Still, he might be able to sweet-talk her into it. They were disgustingly cooey with each other.

"Okay, meet me by the red convertible parked right in front of the store in about a half hour," Johnny said.

Virg audibly chewed a mouthful of his dinner. Johnny knew without asking that the hot dog was smothered with onions and mayonnaise. A disgusting combination if ever there was one, but that'd been Virgil's favorite meal since childhood.

"Red convertible," Virg finally said. "You mean the porn star's car?"

Johnny winced. "She's not…just meet me there, Virg."

He cut the connection before his cousin could answer, then headed back downtown. When he arrived at the store, he pulled into the parking lot next to Emma's car. Before cutting the engine, he opened the window. Johnny sat back, watching the last of the evening shoppers pushing their carts inside. It'd be closing soon, right around the time the town of Joyful rolled up its sidewalks for the night.

"Hey, Johnny," he heard from outside. Glancing up, he saw Claire Deveaux, the harried woman whose little girl's spill had caused such a fuss earlier. Claire was walking toward the store, a frown on her pretty brow.

"Hiya, Claire. Didn't finish your shopping earlier, huh?"

She grimaced. "I tried to clean Eve up in the bathroom, but she was a mess. I had to leave an entire cart full of groceries behind and take her home. I bet those twits didn't even have the sense to put the ice cream back in the freezer case."

He snorted. "Better hope they did. Otherwise they'll want you to pay for it. Where's the baby?"

"Home with her daddy. Probably telling him for the tenth time about how mama wasn't paying close enough attention so she spilled her juice on her fave-o-rite top." She sighed, sounding amused, yet weary. "Daddies and their little girls."

He wasn't much of an expert on either one, not being a daddy, and ever having had one to speak of. At least not one he wanted to acknowledge.

"So, I hear you scooped up the porn star and carried her out after she fell." Claire nibbled the corner of her lip. Johnny couldn't tell whether she was embarrassed, amused or disappointed because she'd missed the spectacle.

"She's not a…look, Claire, it was Emma Jean who fell."

Claire's mouth fell open far enough for him to count the fillings in her teeth. "Emma Jean Frasier? Good lord, why didn't she call me and tell me she was coming?" She peeked into the car as if expecting to find Emma inside. "Where is she?"

Johnny now remembered that Claire and Emma had been close friends in high school. "I dropped her off at her grandmother's house. She twisted her ankle, but she'll be okay."

"Emma Jean," Claire murmured again, and a soft smile crossed her lips. "I haven't seen her in…oh…ten years."

Johnny nodded and murmured, "Prom night."

A soft flush rose in Claire's cheeks, and her eyes widened. She stared at Johnny, obviously remembering. "Oh, my goodness, that's right." Then she began to smile. "And just think, you were here to save her this afternoon. Again. You do always seem to be in the right place at the right time to take care of Emma Jean, don't you, Johnny?"

Yeah, but, she'd better not get used to it. He was done taking care of Emma Jean. He had enough people to take care of in his life. The last thing he wanted was to be needed by a woman he'd once wanted with every ounce of his body.

From now on, she was on her own.

"Well, I'd better run," Claire said as she glanced toward her watch. "Store closes soon, and I've got to get home and feed my family. I don't guess you or Emma Jean got to finish your shopping either?" She looked down, sheepishly. "I still feel awful about that. If you see Em, tell her I'll come by soon to apologize and catch up on old times, okay?"

He wouldn't be seeing her. No doubt about it. But he merely shrugged, then bid Claire goodbye.

True to his word, Virgil came strolling up Market Street right on time. Virgil, two years younger than Johnny, was one of the Bransom-Walkers. Meaning, his mother, a rather well-liked member of the Bransom family, had married a no-account Walker thirty-odd years ago. Their offspring were marginally more respectable than the plain old Smith-Walkers, such as Johnny and Nick. Their own mother hadn't been much higher on the socioeconomic scale than their father, though Johnny was the first to admit she was pretty much a saint in their eyes.

Virgil didn't mind the Walker prejudice. He'd never aspired to do much more than tinker with his junkyard-bound hot rod, work as a handyman doing odd jobs and have a happy marriage with his wife, Minnie. Since he came from another side of the Walker family—one that seemed to have escaped the bad-marriage curse that had affected Johnny's—he might actually have a shot at achieving his dreams.

Virg didn't much look like a Walker, except for his dark blue eyes. He stood a good six inches shorter than Johnny and weighed forty pounds more. Still, Johnny had always considered Virgil as much of a brother as Nick.

"This the porn star's car?" Virgil asked.

Getting out of his car, Johnny shot Virg the kind of quelling look that had been known to make even Sheriff Brady watch his mouth. "She's not a porn star. The car belongs to Emma Frasier. I told her I'd get somebody to bring it over to her grandma's house because she hurt herself and couldn't drive."

Virgil whistled. "So, Emma Jean Frasier's the porn star? The woman in the thong underwear who slipped in All-Tempa-Cheer and fell in the store today is Miss Emma-jean's granddaughter?"

"Thong underwear?" Johnny bit out.

Virg nodded. "Black and tan. Jungle pattern. Leopard spots."

Johnny rolled his eyes even as he gulped at the sudden visual of Emma Jean's underclothes. "Nobody saw her underwear, Virg. Spots, jungle or anything else."

"Tom Terry said…"

"Tom Terry is a nasty old reprobate who plays pocket hockey looking at the mannequins in the window of the dress shop. You gonna believe him? Or me, your flesh-and-blood relative, who was standin' closer to her than anyone when she fell?"

Virgil looked disappointed.

"And she's not a porn star."

Virgil's disappointed expression grew more sad. "You sure?"

He nodded. "You remember her, Virg. Do you seriously think she could have left Joyful and gone off to make adult movies?"

Virgil glanced into the distance, smiling like a man reminiscing over a particularly fine meal or a good cigar. "Oh, yeah, she coulda."

Virgil was saved Johnny's fist in his gut by virtue of their blood kinship. "I don't mean physically," Johnny snapped. "Do you think the hoity-toity daughter of some rich people who live overseas would star in stag films?"

"They're not all stag films," Virgil argued. "Some are really art. *Sleepless With A Paddle* shoulda won an Oscar."

Johnny didn't even ask.

"Virg, will you just drive the damn car over to the Frasier house? I'll follow you and give you a ride home."

Virgil looked like he wanted to argue about it, but shrugged and got into the convertible instead. "She's got long legs," he said as he bent down to adjust the driver's seat forward. "Porn stars always have long legs."

"And the village idiot always gets the crap beat out of him for not shutting up when he's talking too much."

Emma Jean was not a porn star. Period.

His cousin gave him a sly grin. "Touchy, touchy."

Johnny didn't say another word as he tossed Virg the keys, then got into his SUV. He followed the sporty red car over to Emma's house, tapped the horn briefly to let her know they'd arrived and waited while Virgil sauntered down the driveway.

"You left the keys in the sun visor?" he asked as Virg opened the passenger side door.

His cousin nodded. "I can always mosey on up to the front door and hand them over to her. Maybe even step in for a visit."

"Get in the car, Virg." Johnny frowned, recognizing his cousin's amused expression. Virgil was ragging on him. Which meant Johnny hadn't been very discreet about his interest in Emma. Something he'd have to remedy immediately.

Virgil shrugged, then hoisted himself into the SUV. "She still as pretty as she was back in high school?"

"Prettier," Johnny admitted.

Emma Jean as a teenager had been just about the sweetest thing he'd ever seen. She'd been a sunshiny angel, in looks and personality. But now, she was a woman. She was an all-grown, all-seductive, all-knowing female. Her eyes held knowledge now. Knowledge, and challenge. Her body was riper, more inviting. Her face smoother and less vulnerable, yet still perfectly angled with that creamy complexion and dimpled smile.

Pretty was insipid, like violets and rainbows and sappy

crap like that. Pretty didn't come close to describing the woman Emma had become. Now she was stunning.

Virg continued. "And you rescued her again, huh? Picked her up and carried her on outta there like the Prince Charming you played on prom night?"

His cousin had been a junior at Joyful High School and had attended the infamous prom. No way could Johnny feign ignorance. "Can we not talk about this?"

"Sure," Virgil said with a chuckle. "Wish I'da seen her, though. I bet I could place her."

Almost afraid to ask, Johnny said, "What do you mean?"

"Well," Virgil said, with a raised brow that warned he was intentionally going to say something provoking. "Minnie did get me that 'special' movie subscription for our anniversary. If I see Emma Jean, maybe I'll recognize her from *Banging Private Ryan,* or *Lord of the Cock Rings.*"

Johnny's hands tightened on the steering wheel until they went white. When he finally trusted himself to speak, he said, "Virg, another word and you're never gonna give Minnie those kids she wants. You hear me? You say one more thing about Emma Jean Frasier and I swear to God you'll be eating your balls for breakfast."

CHAPTER FIVE

THERE WAS NOTHING to eat for breakfast. The fruit from the basket Mayor Boyd had left had served as late lunch, dinner and midnight snack last night. This morning, though, rejuvenated after a good night's sleep in her old bed, Emma was starving.

She'd had enough money to buy coffee and necessities at the store yesterday, which was why she'd stopped. Her shopping had obviously been interrupted. So today she was desperate. She wasn't picky—lord knew she wouldn't be getting her standard double mocha cappuccino from her favorite trendy little coffee shop on Fifth Avenue anytime soon. Right now, though, she'd give her right arm for a cup of Maxwell House. Instant.

A quick glance through her grandmother's pantry revealed a few dusty old cans of vegetables, but nothing that could pass for caffeine. She needed something strong to wash down the aspirin she intended to take for her still slightly sore ankle.

Then she spied the big coffee can on the top shelf of the pantry, nearly hidden behind a spice rack. Saying a quick prayer that it was sealed, she stood up on tiptoe. Emma shifted to keep her weight off her sore foot as she reached for it, balancing herself on her grandmother's old cane, which she'd found in the hall closet. She hadn't let herself focus on the smoothness of the cane against her palm. It hurt too much to think about Emmajean's strong but tired hand wrapped around it.

"Oh, please, please be unopened," she whispered. "Or at least not moldy." If the can had even a few coffee grounds left in the bottom, she was desperate enough to brew it up.

Her fingers brushed the metal surface of the container, and she cajoled it within reach by poking at it through the shelf grating. When she finally lifted the can and tested its weight, she didn't know whether to laugh or cry. Something was inside, judging by a slight jingle, but it definitely did not contain coffee. Then she pulled off the plastic lid, and began to do a little laughing *and* a little crying.

Grandma Emmajean's pin money. She'd forgotten all about it. But like pennies from heaven, here it was. The can held lots of bills, mostly ones and fives. Enough cash to get her through until she could find a job.

Two jobs, really. She'd need one here in town to get her through the next couple of months until the scandal died down. Right now, she and all her former co-workers were persona non grata in the financial world. She had a better chance of becoming Miss Universe than of getting in with another large New York brokerage.

So she'd stay here in Joyful for a while, finding some easy little job to pay her bills, which wouldn't be bad since the house was hers, free and clear. She could spend the summer regrouping, sending out résumés back in the real world—*her* world—and planning a new course for her future. Without ever, hopefully, having to ask her parents—particularly her mother—for a thing.

They'd be furious when they found out. *If* they found out. But it was worth the risk. She couldn't stand the thought of them stepping in to try to "help" her. Translation: trying to retake control of her life, as they'd tried to do last year after her accident.

She loved them. But a pushier, more smothering couple she'd never met. As their only child, she'd been the one smothered for years. At least until Grandma Emmajean had stepped in to support Emma when she'd taken a stand at the age of seventeen and demanded the freedom to decide where she'd go to school.

"Thank you, Grandma, for being there for me again," she whispered with a smile, staring at the cash. "Now, if only Joyful had restaurants that delivered Cheerios, we'd be in good shape."

Unfortunately, she suspected there weren't any cereal deliverymen in Joyful. If she wanted breakfast, she was going to have to drive for it.

Before she could go back to her room to dress, she heard a knock at the front door. Since it was only 8:00 a.m. on a Saturday, she couldn't imagine who'd be stopping by. Then she remembered what it had been like living here, where neighbors knew one another's first names. On many a Saturday, one of her grandmother's friends would pop in with a basket of muffins and a cheerful "good morning." She smiled, touched that someone had heard she was back and had come to welcome her home.

It wasn't one of her grandmother's neighbors or friends.

"Oh, no," she said when she opened the door and saw Johnny on the porch.

"That's a nice way to greet a person bearing food."

Eyeing the paper grocery sack he held in the crook of one arm, she raised a brow.

"And coffee," he added.

Almost cooing in relief, she reached for the smaller bag in his other hand. He glanced at her cane. "I've got it."

Stepping back to let him in, she inhaled, catching a whiff of the coffee. It was almost good enough to make her forget she was still wearing the raggedy shorts and T-shirt she'd put on for bed. They went well with the mass of tangled hair she hadn't yet gotten around to brushing.

"Hmm, I take it you're not a morning person?" He didn't even try to hide his amusement.

Bleary-eyed, she couldn't even take offense as she slowly led him into the bright and sunny kitchen. "For coffee, I'll forget that I'm not exactly at my best." She sat at the butcher block table and watched him remove two large foam cups of coffee, as well as creamer and sugar, from the bag. "What are you doing here, anyway?"

Grabbing a handful of napkins, he reached into the larger bag and pulled out a few more items. Finally he smiled and showed her a box of powdered sugar doughnuts. "I figured you were stopping at the store last night to get supplies before you were…interrupted. So I picked up some things to tide you over."

She supposed she shouldn't have been surprised he'd shown up at her door, bringing her exactly what she needed. He had a track record of doing just that: flowers on prom night, coffee and toilet paper today. Touched by his thoughtfulness, she murmured, "This was very nice of you. I'd almost decided to try to drive down to the store."

"Now you can put it off another day or so, until your foot's okay." He cast a quick look at her ankle.

"It's not bad at all," she insisted. Stirring some cream into her coffee she sipped it, almost sighing with pleasure. "Diner coffee. Is there anything better?"

"Diner pie. My cousin Virgil's wife makes the best peach pie in the state of Georgia."

She pursed her lips and shook her head. "No way could

it beat my grandmother's pecan. We used to go out to her daddy's old farm outside of town every year when we'd visit for Thanksgiving. My dad would tie ropes to the branches and we'd shake the nuts onto tarps on the ground. Then Grandma would take them home and dry them to last her the year."

She thought for a moment of the lovely afternoons in the orchard. Her grandmother would talk about the old days, and the last little piece of her family's farm—the orchard—which she'd held onto and promised to leave to Emma. She inhaled deeply, almost smelling the fragrance of Emmajean's baking. "She'd always have a fresh pecan pie waiting when we came for our summer visit. I'm going to dig through her recipes as soon as I can figure out where she hid them and make one of those pies."

"I'd like to taste a piece of pie *you* baked."

He obviously remembered her lack of ability in the kitchen. She didn't tell him about her Manhattan cooking school experiment…so she wouldn't have to tell him she'd, uh, failed.

"I might not have Grandma Emmajean's creative flare, but I've learned to follow a recipe to the last pinch. I do okay."

"Maybe I'll risk my life someday by letting you bake for me." The twinkle in his eye took any sting from his words.

"If somebody had told me a month ago that I'd be serving up pie to *you* in my grandmother's kitchen this summer, I'd have thought they'd been hitting the kind of moonshine the old-timers used to brew up in the hills," she muttered.

"They still do."

She raised a curious brow.

"My uncle Rafe and his brood live up there."

More Walkers. Why was she not surprised.

Johnny drank his own coffee, then got up to put away the groceries. She watched him silently for a moment, seeing glimpses in his strong profile of the teenager she'd known.

Yesterday, wearing a dress shirt and trousers, he'd been conservative, powerful and mature. Not to mention gorgeous.

Today, dressed in faded, worn jeans and a tight white T-shirt that did sinful things to the strong muscles in his arms and shoulders, he was downright devastating. Unshaven, rugged, completely masculine. Yet he looked perfectly comfortable in the kitchen, putting milk, juice and eggs in the fridge, taking care of her like he would any old friend who'd been laid up.

Only they weren't quite old friends, were they? And being with Johnny didn't exactly make her think of being laid up. Just laid, maybe.

Don't even go there.

No, friendship couldn't describe what was between Emma and Johnny. There was something else, something instinctive and deep. It had been present from the very beginning, even while she'd been dating his brother and he'd been playing the role of town rebel to the hilt.

It hadn't been mere attraction. Looking back with adult perspective, she knew that now. Heck, even then, when she'd been practically a kid, she'd suspected the charge she and Johnny sparked off each other went a lot deeper than teenage hormones.

When Johnny got around to finishing with the groceries, and they actually looked at one another, the awareness that had always existed between them would return. They'd begin dancing around the tension and intimate knowledge they'd shared from the first time they'd met. And then he'd leave.

For some reason, she didn't want their truce to end too soon. After she'd eaten her fill of the doughnuts and swallowed another gulp of coffee, Emma leaned back in her chair. "You know, I meant to ask you last night, why are you back here? I always figured the way you hated this town, you would have gone far, far away."

"Oh, so you thought about me a lot, hmm?" he asked, a note of teasing in his voice. Not returning to his seat at the table, he leaned a hip against the kitchen counter. He crossed his arms in front of his chest, until his muscles flexed against the white cotton of his shirt. "I thought you hadn't spared me even a moment's thought."

Sipping her coffee, Emma ordered her heart to return to its normal rhythm. "No, I never did." *Lie*. "It was so long ago, I hardly even remember what happened when I lived here in Joyful." *Lie number two.*

A knowing smile crossed his lips. "Right."

She knew better than to protest too much. "What's the story? I haven't seen your picture on the cover of any sports magazines, so you obviously didn't turn pro after playing football in college."

"Nope. With the help of a three hundred pound offensive lineman from North Carolina State, I blew out my knee in junior year."

She swallowed hard. "Your scholarship?"

"Can you believe by then I qualified for an academic one?"

"Yes, I can believe it," she murmured, knowing Johnny had always been much smarter than anyone in this town had ever given him credit for. "So you did finish college?"

"Even worse," he said. "My professors liked the poor white-trash Georgia boy so much, they helped me get into law school."

Her draw dropped. Johnny, the most-suspended teen in the history of Joyful High School, a lawyer? It boggled the mind.

He must have seen her shock because he chuckled softly, a gentle, delighted sound that reminded her of the way his laughter had always made her feel. Like she'd just sipped something luscious and sweet and her whole body had gone soft with the pleasure of it. She closed her eyes briefly, then opened them to find him watching her intently.

"Tough to imagine, huh?" he continued. "It gets better." His eyes glowed until he finally delivered the punch line. "I came back to Joyful to take the job as county prosecutor."

If she'd had a drink in her mouth, she would have spewed it all over the kitchen table. Because there was no way she believed that one. Johnny had liked the legal authorities as much as Emma liked going to the gynecologist.

"You're *such* a liar." She shook her head and rolled her eyes. "I can't believe I actually fell for any of it. Don't tell me, let me guess. You're really in business with your Uncle Rafe making moonshine up in the hills."

"It's true, Emma Jean, I swear." He made a crossing motion over his heart. "Every word."

Emma didn't have much faith in anyone's "I swear." The last time she'd heard one, Lydia, her former best friend from accounting, had been swearing Emma didn't have a thing to worry about by leaving every penny of her money invested in her company-backed portfolio.

Look how that had turned out. With Lydia partying with the rich and corrupt in Buenos Aires, and Emma flat broke but for Grandma Emmajean's pin money in teeny-town Georgia.

Johnny's expression, however, made her pause. "You're serious? You're not kidding?"

"Not kidding. I've been the big bad prosecutor of Joyless for eighteen months now."

"You're a prosecutor. Good grief, Johnny, I know how much you hated the sheriff's office. Heck, any authority figure! So please, using small, nonlegalese words, try to explain something I find completely incomprehensible."

He crossed the room, taking his seat at the table as he reached for another of the doughnuts. After he bit into it, he deftly licked at a spot of powdered sugar on the corner of his much too kissable lips.

Emma's world rocked a little bit as she watched. Hit hard with a sudden flash of sense memory, parts of her body tingled, reliving the way that tongue of his had felt. How he'd adored her, exploring every inch of her, introducing her to parts of her body she'd barely had a passing acquaintance with.

He'd been better than anyone after. There hadn't been any befores, *or* many afters, probably for that very reason. Once she'd had something so good, she'd wanted nothing less than perfection. Unfortunately, no other man had ever been able to give it to her.

She forced herself to focus by jerking her injured ankle. Hard. Pain dissipated the momentary haze of horny dementia.

"I worked in the public defender's office in Atlanta for the first year after I passed the bar," he explained. "Then I heard this job had opened up. My mother was still here…."

Emma didn't ask about his father. She knew full well how Johnny and his brother had felt about him.

"She's not getting any younger. Besides which, like I

said, Daneen had moved back to town with Jack, and he was getting older. I thought the kid could use more people looking out for him." His tone grew tight. "Obviously my brother wasn't bothering."

She skipped that subject, too.

"What happened to Mr. Early? He was the prosecutor forever."

"He got tired of it and decided he wanted to be public defender for a while." A look of amusement crossed his face. "Between the two of us, we manage to keep Sheriff Brady from doing too much damage. At least, whenever I can pry Cyrus Early's fishing pole out of his hands long enough to get him to show up in court."

Ahh, there was the key. Johnny was still finding ways to do what he always did—help people in need, while also thwarting the local authority. Leave it to him to find a rather unique position from which to do it.

"I'll bet your mom loves having a county official for a son," she said. She hadn't met Nick and Johnny's mother too often, but she'd been impressed by the woman's innate kindness and obvious love for her two boys.

He nodded. "That makes it worthwhile. She retired, you know, a couple of years back. When I was in my senior year at Georgia State my father was killed."

"I'm so sorry," she murmured.

She hadn't ever met Johnny and Nick's father. Neither one of them talked about him much, and Nick had always insisted she never come out to their small farm on the outskirts of town while they were dating. But anyone who lived in Joyful had heard the rumors about the man, as renowned for his drinking as he was for his mean temper.

"Feel sorry for the woman whose car he crashed into

when he was driving home drunk that night," Johnny said matter-of-factly. "She miscarried her baby."

She shook her head, not sure how to respond. Johnny didn't sound bitter, merely aloof. She wondered again what it must have been like growing up as the son of a man the whole town considered the most useless—and mean—of all the trashy Walker clan.

"Now, Em," he said, settling back in his chair and staring her full in the face. "Why don't you tell me exactly what you've been doing for the past ten years?" He reached for his coffee. "And why you've come back to Joyful."

DANEEN DIDN'T LIKE working on Saturdays. It was hard enough getting someone to stay with little Johnny...all right, *Jack!*...during the week. Weekends were nearly impossible. "Come on, bud. Time to go," she hollered, glancing at her watch.

Jimbo understood her limitations as a single mom and was usually flexible. Today, however, he was insistent. He'd called last night asking her to come in. Her dismay at having to work on a Saturday had been equaled by her annoyance at the interruption of the phone conversation she'd been having. She'd been getting an earful about the high-and-mighty Ms. Emma Jean Frasier.

She couldn't believe the stories. The town thought Emma was the owner of the new club, Joyful Interludes. Therefore, they figured, she must be the mysterious "porn star" advertised on the billboard. Something about her going to the city and making dirty pictures had made perfect sense to the gossipers. They'd connected point A to point B and come up with a big whopping *X*.

Daneen didn't know much about any porn star rumors, but she honestly didn't think Emma owned the club. Jimbo had handled the sale of the property, she knew that because he'd made a boatload of money off it. He was still representing the new owners here in town. The checks that came across her desk from the holding company building the club were nice and regular.

Surely she would have seen Emma Jean's name *somewhere* by this point if she was involved in the project.

Or maybe not. Jimbo was playing this one awfully close to his chest, so she supposed anything was possible. Still, remembering Emma Jean's prim and proper teen years, and her town matriarch grandmother, she doubted the story was true.

But that didn't mean she didn't enjoy gossiping about it.

She swallowed a bit of guilt in her throat because of the way she'd stolen Nick away from Emma Jean in high school. Then she shrugged. Emma Jean could have had any guy she wanted. She didn't have to go after Nick Walker—the one Daneen had been after forever—the minute she hit town!

It was just too bad Daneen had eventually gotten him. Nick had been one hell of a lover, but not quite as gullible as most teenage guys. She'd learned that the hard way when he'd started reading up on pregnancy during her second trimester. That'd been the beginning of the end. Because even if he was a big goofy teenager and a bad student, he sure hadn't had any trouble with basic math. He could easily count to nine—nine *months*. Then he'd figured out the truth.

"Mom, why can't I go to the park for the morning? I know some of the guys'll be there." Jack emerged from his room and met her at the front door of their little house, the one Daddy had helped her buy when she came back to town.

She glanced at her son as they walked out. "I've told

you, you're not going to hang around in the park like a ju-
venile delinquent. Your last name might be Walker, but you
don't have to act like one." At the frown on his face, she
cursed her quick tongue. "I'm sorry, babe. Listen, I don't
mind you being alone for an hour after school, but not a
whole weekend morning."

"What happens when school lets out in a couple
weeks?" he asked with a knowing grin. "You don't need
to waste money on a baby-sitter all summer. How about
we decide together, like two mature people, that I'm old
enough to take care of myself?"

She laughed as they got into her car. Jack…what a
wheeler-dealer. Just like Jimbo. "How about we don't and
say we did?"

He rolled his eyes and nagged her all the way to the office. When they got there, Daneen was both surprised and
relieved to see her father's cruiser parked outside, next to
Jimbo's Lincoln. "Look, Pa-paw's here. Maybe he'll take
you back to the station to hang out or something while I
work."

Jack's eyes lit up. "Last time he let me radio Deputy Fred
and tell him a spaceship landed in the Wal-Mart parking lot."

"That's not very nice," she murmured.

Fred was a decent man. Nicer than most men in this
town. He always treated her like a lady and was very protective of her, even though she'd made it clear she was not
going to follow her father's advice and go out with him
again like she had a few times in high school.

Her father. Whew. If he ever found out about her and
Jimbo, there'd be pure hell to pay. He seemed determined
that Daneen was still his "innocent" little girl who'd been
done wrong by a rotten Walker.

One of these days, he'd probably find out the truth. *All*

of it. Daneen looked forward to judgment day more than that one.

Inside the office, Daneen pointed to a chair and whispered for Jack to sit in it. Walking toward Jimbo's door, she heard her father's voice. "Damn, you swore she'd never come back."

"I didn't think she would," Jimbo replied easily. "But it doesn't matter. Everything's filed, legal and tidy. And what's she going to do about it? Huff and puff and blow the place down?" Jimbo gave one of his big, hearty politician laughs. "Dan, my friend, you need to relax. I've got things under control."

Wondering who they were talking about, Daneen knocked lightly on the office door. "Hello, there," she said as she walked in and smiled in greeting.

"There's my baby girl," her father said, giving her a bear hug. Then he glanced out into the reception area and spied Jack. "Come on in here, boy. Mayor Boyd was telling me your mama had to work today. I was hoping you might be able to spend some time with me."

Jack ambled into the room, as if he wasn't busting with excitement about getting to spend time with his blustery grandpa. "You gonna let me turn on the siren in the squad car?"

"You betcha," Dan said with a big laugh. "You believe this kid, Jimbo? My grandson knows how to work all the angles."

"Quite a boy Daneen's got there all right," Jimbo replied.

Daneen nudged her son in the shoulder. "Say hello. Then say goodbye. We got work to do."

"Yes, son, we surely do," Jimbo said, hunkering down eye to eye with Jack and giving him one of those big, genuine smiles. Then he looked up at Daneen and gave her an intimate look. "I don't know what I'd do without your mama."

Daneen clenched her jaw, ordering herself to be strong. Unfortunately, her whole body was reacting to that warmth in his eyes. She cursed her own weakness, knowing it was inevitable.

Well, at the very least, she would make him beg for forgiveness for his inattentiveness the previous afternoon. Because she suspected this morning she'd be helping Jimbo file away more than just legal deeds.

JOHNNY DIDN'T EXPECT Emma to open up and be honest about what she'd been doing for the past ten years. At least not if she'd really been off making dirty movies… which he doubted. But there was no question in his mind she was hiding something when she breezily informed him about how great life had treated her.

She was blissfully happy. She was successful. She was thrilled to pieces.

She was lying through her teeth.

Emma looked stressed, tired and worried about more than a twisted ankle. She definitely wasn't the happy-go-lucky Em he remembered. Besides, whenever Emma Jean Frasier lied, her cheeks turned bright red. He knew it was true, he'd seen it firsthand in the old days. Right now she looked like a circus clown, complete with two bright spots of face paint on her pale skin.

Even with that, she still looked better than any woman ever had to him. And he'd admit that to her about the same time he'd admit he'd once owned a Michael Bolton CD.

"So, life's a picnic and you're thrilled as can be. And you came back to Joyful for what?" He tilted one corner of his mouth up into a humorless grin. "To go to a reunion with a bunch of people you told to go straight to hell the day you left?"

She narrowed her eyes. "What would *you* know about the day I left? You were long gone by then, weren't you? Probably still driving like a maniac back to college."

He nearly laughed. No, the day she left he'd been circling Joyful in his old, beat-up pickup. He'd spent the morning after prom contemplating slamming into a tree. It was either that or drive back to her house and kick in the door. Then he'd have demanded to know why she'd felt the need to rip his guts out the night before. Because, by making it perfectly clear that she'd settled for him when she'd really wanted his brother between her pretty white thighs, that's essentially what she'd done.

"Yeah," he finally retorted. "While you were busy packing."

She didn't deny it, but went quiet, as if thinking about that night. He couldn't help remembering, either.

He hadn't shown up in Nick's stupid, too-tight tux and taken her to the prom with the intention of nailing her. He'd planned to take her arm, let her hold her head up, then walk away, having righted the wrong Nick had done her.

But, no, she'd made him believe she needed more. Hell, any guy would have gone for it when a girl as beautiful as Emma Jean had made it clear she wanted him. Since Johnny had been half-gone on Emma since the first time he'd seen her, he hadn't thought twice. No question, he'd been a Walker through and through in those days. Hot blood combined with no frigging common sense.

Emma hadn't, however, been playing by the rules. Because, dammit all, she'd been a virgin. And virgins did *not* decide to give it up to a guy on the spur of the moment.

Which meant she'd planned all along to lose her virginity on prom night.

To his kid brother.

Christ, it still rubbed him raw to think about it. What made it worse was that he and Nick had been close at the time. Two boys who'd raised each other when their workhorse mother wasn't around and their drunk father didn't give a shit.

He couldn't let himself think about Nick too often, now, other than to curse his refusal to be involved in his son's life. It wasn't Jack's fault Daneen had trapped Nick into marriage. Johnny figured Nick must never have forgiven Daneen for costing him Emma. Because, as Johnny had learned, his brother and Emma Jean Frasier had been a lot more serious than anyone ever knew.

A part of him had died that night when Emma had looked up at him with guilt-filled eyes and started crying over her stupid necklace. She'd gone all to pieces over a hunk of dime store, gold-plated jewelry, which had broken when they'd made love.

Nick had given it to her.

Her tears had rushed out while they lay there, still naked, in the gazebo. The look in her eyes when she'd told him Nick had asked her to wear the necklace on their honeymoon—had sent Johnny over the edge.

From mild discomfort to major guilt trip. Combined with a heaping helping of that hot-blooded Walker temper.

He'd already been tearing himself up with regret. Bad enough to have stabbed his kid brother in the back by relieving his girlfriend of her virginity. To find out Nick had planned to marry Emma was worse. The real shocker, though, judging by the way she was crying, was that Emma wanted to marry his brother. Which left Johnny feeling completely sucker-punched.

He'd reacted like any hormonal nineteen-year-old who'd found out the girl of his dreams was in love with a jerk who'd cheated on her. Badly. Meanly. Saying things he wasn't proud of. .

Then he'd left her there, naked and crying, illuminated in the spotlights of a bunch of cars when the rest of the senior class showed up for a late-night, after-prom party.

"Jeez, Johnny, did you even change out of your tux before you headed back to campus?" she asked, interrupting his waltz down the not-so-pleasant lane called Memory.

"You sure you want to go there?" he asked, knowing she heard the challenge in his voice. "You ready to talk about prom night?"

The color rose higher in her cheeks. "No. I want to forget it ever happened. It was one more lousy teenage moment to go into the record book of lousy teenage moments."

Lousy? Huh-uh. Not on her life. It might have ended badly, but the sex itself had been phenomenal. The best he'd ever had up until that night. Though he could admit it only in the confines of his brain…the best he'd had *ever*.

That was probably the one and only time he'd made love to someone, rather than just having sex. With Emma Jean, he'd allowed himself to fall into her fantasy and imagine he was the hero she'd thought him to be. He'd wanted to be the stupid, sappy Prince Charming. For a while, there in the gazebo, he had been.

Then they'd both turned into warty green frogs. Him with his temper. Her with her unspoken admission that she'd given it up to the wrong brother.

"You sure have a selective memory, Emma Jean," he said, leaning toward her across the kitchen table. "Because I somehow doubt 'lousy' would have prompted your… shall we say, appreciative and *vocal*…reaction that night?"

Though she shot him a contemptuous glare, she couldn't disguise the deepening pinkness in her cheeks. No, Miss Emma didn't like to be reminded she'd been a screamer.

"I'm all grown-up now, Johnny. And I've learned orgasms aren't gifts that have to be bestowed by small-town studs who like to *take* off five minutes after they *get* off."

He pushed his chair back and stood, stepping closer until he practically towered over her. "Yeah, and I guess you have a lot of experience now to know."

Professional experience.

Emma tilted her head back and stared up at him, refusing to back away though he knew he was crowding her. Not a bit cowed, she also rose to her feet, until they were practically eye to eye. "That's none of your damn business."

Her face was so close, her warm breaths touched his chin. Her tousled, bed-messed hair begged to be tangled between his fingers, brushing his cheeks…or spread across his groin. The image and the sweet, morning smell of her skin proceeded to suck every thought out of his head.

Take a big, giant step back.

He leaned closer. "I have a vested interest when you're standing here lying like a politician caught with an intern."

She obviously chose to misunderstand him. "I'm not lying about it being none of your business."

He gave her a taunting smile. "No. But you're lying about it being lousy. Admit it, that moment was one for the record books."

Stubborn to the last, she set her lips in a straight line. "You're delusional. It wasn't that great, Johnny." She gave an exaggerated look of pity. "I don't blame you, it wasn't your fault. You were a teenager. Heck, I don't imagine any teenager could be classified as *good*."

Shaking his head, he tsked, letting her see his amusement. Not to mention his determination. "You're the one deluding yourself," he told her. "Which I can prove anytime, anywhere."

Her eyes flashed at his mildly voiced threat, and her lips parted on a quickly sucked-in breath. God, those lips. That mouth. That tiny hitch of a sigh she couldn't hide.

His threat hadn't scared her. It had excited her. And with that realization, his last tiny bit of resistance evaporated.

Hot blood. No friggin' common sense. *Just like old times.*

Before he even realized he was going to do it, he crowded close to her, and growled, "Like right here, right now."

CHAPTER SIX

JOHNNY KNEW he'd regret what he was about to do, but he was determined to do it anyway. He didn't give her time to figure out what he meant. Instead, he showed her. Before she could protest, he slid his fingers into her short tangle of hair, cupping her head and tugging her mouth to his. She gasped a little, deep in her throat, just before their lips touched. Then the same old spark ignited. He fell into that hot, burning place where thought didn't exist, only sensation.

Only *her.*

When she parted her lips, he took full advantage, inhaling her, sweeping his tongue against hers to savor the taste of warm, sweet coffee and hot, sweeter Emma.

In his memories, she'd always tasted like strawberries. Now there was no slick lip gloss. Nor had any tears fallen down her cheeks to make her skin taste salty like it had on prom night. There was only Emma, who had driven him crazy with lust from the first time he'd seen that flash of gold on her ankle when they'd both been practically kids.

She tilted her head, inviting him deeper. He accepted the invitation, his entire body seeming to spark and burn. Hers felt equally hot beneath his hands. He cupped her hip, dropped his other hand down her spine until his fingers brushed the small of her back. She whimpered against his lips, pressing herself hard against him as she slipped her arms around his neck.

"Tell me again how I'm deluding myself," he muttered as he drew his mouth away from hers to suck in a shaky breath. He didn't wait for her answer as he bent lower, to taste the hot pulse point on her throat, then the vulnerable spot where her neck met her shoulder.

"You're deluding yourself," she mumbled, twisting against him even harder, bringing the vee of her legs in contact with his. Her moan of pleasure drowned out his own.

"So it wasn't memorable?" he asked, nibbling her collarbone, even as he cupped her waist with his hands, then began to tug her T-shirt free of her shorts.

"No. Completely forgettable," she replied, as she just as greedily stroked his sides.

"Truly awful, huh?"

"Uh-huh." She sounded nearly incoherent. "Hate to tell you this, but it really sucked."

Yeah. Sucked. Now didn't that bring up a few interesting visuals? He wanted to suck on the tender place at the back of her knee. On the soft skin where her thigh met her ass. On those sweet, pouty nipples pressing hard against the cotton of her shirt. For a start, anyway.

"As bad as it is right now?" he continued. Though almost out of his mind with want for her, he still silently dared her to admit the truth—she'd *loved* it then. Following her admission, they could proceed to how bad she *wanted* it now.

"Every bit as bad."

Picking her up by the waist, he turned around and sat her on the sturdy, butcher block table. He pushed her knees apart and stepped between them. "You make me crazy," he mumbled. "And you make me want to kiss those lies right out of your mouth."

"Don't you dare kiss me again," she growled back.

Then she made a mockery of her own words by wrapping her fingers in his hair and pulling him down for another kiss. A slow, deep, welcoming one that reminded him of the slow, deep, welcoming way they'd made love in the gazebo.

His hands moved of their own accord, under the loose T-shirt, sliding up her sides. No impediment whatsoever. Her smooth skin tingled under his hands as he edged up and around, tracing patterns on her bare back and her rib cage. Coming closer and closer to the front, until she started to shake and moan.

He really didn't know how far they might have gone. One second they were on the verge of clothes hitting the floor and him showing her the meaning of the words multiple orgasm all over again, like he had ten years ago. The next there was a ringing sound and Emma Jean was sliding away from him, shimmying back on the table.

"Oh, my God," she said, looking mortified.

Her eyes were glazed, her mouth full, pouty and swollen. Her shirt was twisted, almost hanging off her shoulder and he could see a faint red mark on her neck where he'd been nibbling on her a few moments before. Her heaved-in breaths made her chest rise and fall until his hands clenched with the need to touch her, cup her, *have* her.

"What was that?" she finally whispered.

"I think it was the doorbell. And I think I'm going to have to do bodily injury to whoever rang it."

She glared. "I didn't mean the doorbell. I mean *that*." She pointed to his body, then to hers. "This. Us!"

Her anger and embarrassment finally sunk through the hazy red cloud of lust and satisfaction permeating his brain. Emma still wasn't ready to admit a thing. Not about their past. Not about what had just happened. Stubborn as ever.

"I think that was called a lousy moment."

Her face reddened. "You kissed me."

"You kissed me back."

She opened her mouth to deny it, then jerked it closed, unable to do so.

"If prom night was a *moment,* then I guess that kiss happened at the speed of light." He tsked. "Or maybe not at all."

"Not at all would have been better."

"When'd you get to be such a damn liar?"

"When'd you get to be such a damn caveman?"

They were both panting, staring at each other across the width of the table. Emma's choppy breaths drew his attention back to her loose cotton T-shirt, which had slipped down off one shoulder. The skin there was reddened… from his touch. From her excitement. From the heat sparking around them both. He wanted to kiss the spot, both to soothe away the redness…and to nip at her again because she made him insane, and hot, and ready to lose his mind.

He'd never wanted like this before. Never been stupid with it before—at least not since prom night. Christ, of all times to start acting like a Walker again, it had to be here. Now. With *her.*

"You think I'm a caveman?" he finally asked, wanting her to admit that, though he'd started it, she'd ended up every bit as much a participant in their embrace as he'd been. "You're saying I forced you? That you had no active part in this at all?"

Her mouth opened. Closed. Then she nibbled on her

bottom lip. Finally she admitted, "Maybe I did. But you were still lousy to do it. You kissed me to try to prove something, and all you proved was that we both have overactive libidos and long-term memory problems."

He raised an inquisitive brow.

She continued. "Because if there are any two people in the world who have no business kissing on my grandmother's kitchen table, it's you and me."

Her words rushed out, choppy, thick with frustration and anger and maybe even a hint of vulnerability.

It was the vulnerability, combined with the redness on her shoulder and the brightness in her eyes, that made him try to make light of what had been the most explosive moment of his year. "It was just a kiss, Emma Jean. Your grandma's kitchen table is a hundred years old and I'm sure it's withstood a lot more."

She didn't relax. Instead, she just continued to glare at him until they both flinched at the insistent ringing of the doorbell. Johnny had almost forgotten what had driven them apart to begin with.

Whoever was ringing had apparently grown impatient because the ding-dongs were incessant. "I'll get it."

Not waiting for her reply, he turned and went to answer the door. He didn't want to stand there for one more moment, knowing the spark of righteous indignation in her eye would have him ready to prove something to her all over again.

Like the fact that she was a screamer.

Hearing her clumping along after him within a second or two, he felt a sharp stab of regret for forgetting her injured ankle. "I said I'd get it, Emma Jean," he said as she followed him out of the kitchen. "Stay there."

She passed him in the hall, ignoring his command.

When Emma opened the door, Johnny somehow wasn't surprised to see Claire Deveaux standing outside. Next to her, on the porch, stood her daughter, who was reaching out to jab at the doorbell again with the tip of her index finger.

"Enough, Eve, the door's open," Claire said with a sigh.

Eve, a tough little cookie whose daddy doted on her before the whole town, was wearing a pink ballerina outfit. She looked like she'd rather be wearing a tool belt. Her ferocious frown dared him to make one crack about how pretty she was. He had a feeling if he did, she'd head-butt him in the gut or kick his ankles.

"Oh, my God, Claire!" Emma shrieked. She dropped the cane and threw herself into Claire's arms, the two of them hugging and jabbering a mile a minute.

The longer they ignored the kid, the more she frowned and pouted. Johnny crouched down until he was face-to-face with her. "My mother used to tell me when I stuck my lip out that far that a bird was going to land on it and peck at my nose."

She sucked the lip in, catching it between her teeth. Giving him a closemouthed grin, she raised a cocky eyebrow.

He grinned back. "Better."

"Oh, Claire, is this your baby?" Emma said, staring down at Eve in amazement.

Claire nodded, then put her hand on her daughter's shoulder. "Yes, this is Eve. And she has something to say to you."

Eve scuffed her little ballet shoe clad foot on the wooden porch and scowled up at her mother.

"Go on," Claire prompted.

"I'm sorry you fell in the blue stuff I spilled at the

store," she mumbled. The girl sounded as pained at having to apologize as she would have at having to eat a plateful of brussels sprouts.

Johnny chuckled as a look of understanding slowly spread across Emma's face. She bent down to face the child. "It's okay, I'm sure you didn't spill it on purpose. Everybody has accidents."

Eve's eyes widened into twin saucers. Then she glared up at her mother. "You said big girls don't have accidents."

Claire sighed and shook her head. "We try not to, sugar. And she didn't mean *that* kind of accident!"

"She's adorable," Emma said as she straightened up to face Claire. "I still can't believe it. You, a mother." Then she grinned. "And married. You swore you'd never get married."

Claire gave her a cheeky grin. "Ahh, ahh, I didn't say never. Remember the article we read in *Cosmopolitan* magazine in senior year? I said the only way I'd get married was if I ever found a man who could do *that*." She cast a glance at Johnny and her face pinkened.

As Emma laughed, Johnny rubbed a hand over his brow. He did *not* want to know what they were talking about, particularly because Claire's husband, Tim, was a friend of his. He wondered how he'd ever be able to face him again without being tempted to ask the guy if he could lick his eyebrows.

"Can you come in and visit?"

"I'm sorry, no," Claire replied after casting a curious glance between him and Emma. "I have to get her to ballet class. Another round of 'terrorize the ballerinas' is on the schedule for this morning. But I wanted to stop by and say welcome home, and see if you need anything."

"Johnny brought me a few things this morning."

Johnny instantly saw the look of knowing amusement on the other woman's face and mentally cringed. He could almost hear her now—*still looking out for Emma Jean?*

Nope. Uh-uh. Not this guy. No matter what had almost happened back in the kitchen, he was definitely not sticking around to get kicked in the teeth again by Miss Emma Jean Frasier. It was time for this ol' boy to get outta here.

"Gotta go," he muttered. "Take care of yourself, Emma." With a friendly nod to Claire, a wink at Eve and barely a glance at Emma Jean, he walked down the front steps, got into his SUV and drove away.

"TELL ME EVERYTHING."

Emma raised a brow as Claire grabbed her daughter's hand and walked into the house. "I thought you had to get to ballet class."

Claire shrugged and plopped onto the stuffed sofa in the front room, which Grandma Emmajean had always called her sunroom. "That was when I thought Johnny was staying." She turned to her daughter. "Baby, you don't mind if we're late to dance class today, do you?"

Eve shook her head, hard, sending a riot of light brown curls dancing on her forehead. "I don't never wanna go back there." She stuck out her bottom lip and scowled as she explained. "Courtney Foster kicked me with her tap shoe and broke my leg."

Claire let out a loud sigh. "Eve, that was almost a year ago, your very first lesson and you don't even take tap anymore."

The child's frown didn't ease one bit. Emma had seen New York City cops who didn't look as fierce.

"Besides, you did not have a broken leg," Claire continued. "And it was an *accident*." She met Emma's stare and rolled her eyes. "Unlike when you retaliated by punching Courtney in the nose."

Emma bit her lip to hold back a laugh. Remembering Claire's propensity for slugging anyone she thought needed it, she figured this was proof positive of the old "what goes around comes around" caveat.

Not that Emma could complain. After all, Claire had decked Daneen Brady on her behalf the first week of senior year. She'd told Emma that if she was too ladylike to blacken the eye of the girl who'd called her a man-stealing tramp, Claire was not. All three of them: the man-stealing tramp—Emma; the brawler—Claire; and the all-around bitch of the high school universe—Daneen, had gotten detention. What a start to her only year in public school.

Man, she'd missed Claire.

"Hey, Eve, there's doughnuts on the table." Emma pointed toward the kitchen. "Right through there. If your mama doesn't mind, you can help yourself to one."

Somehow, she got the feeling Eve didn't much care whether Mama minded or not, because she was edging toward the hall before Claire even managed a slight nod of approval. "But don't get sugar all over your leotard!"

The minute they were alone, Claire patted the sofa seat next to her. "Sit. Tell all. What was Johnny doing here? Your lips are red, and oh, my God, is that a hickey? Did something happen between you two? Please tell me you at least brushed your teeth this morning. Why haven't you written for so long? Did you really let Johnny in with your hair looking like that? And when did you cut it? I *love* the color! But start with Johnny."

Emma burst into laughter. Same old Claire…not one

moment of hesitation, no shyness, no reserve. Had she ever had another girlfriend who could let ten years drop away with a smile and a hug, and fall right back into a pattern of easy companionship? No, honestly, she didn't think she had.

Claire seemed more than ready to welcome her back to Joyful with open arms. Unlike Johnny...who'd probably only welcome her back with an open zipper, judging by the crazy passion that had erupted between them minutes before. Then he'd push her away again. Same old story.

"It's like I said," she finally replied. "Johnny knew I was stranded without any supplies, so he dropped off a few things."

Claire crossed her arms. "Condoms, handcuffs and silk sheets?"

"Oh, please."

Her friend gave an evil laugh. "Oh, please nothing. Remember who you're talking to. I'm the one you poured your heart out to in your letters after you left town ten years ago."

"My heart was never involved," she said, trying to convince herself as well as Claire. *Just my libido.*

"Bull. Come on, Emma Jean, do you think I don't remember the way you talked about him whenever he'd come home from college that year? Even when you were dating Nick, it was *so* obvious he wasn't the Walker you wanted."

"Ancient history."

"Unexplored opportunity."

Emma gave an unladylike snort. "Oh, it was explored all right. On prom night."

Claire answered with a Cheshire cat grin. "And that's all?"

Feeling heat stain her cheeks, Emma declined to answer.

Claire, of course, saw the truth anyway. "Whoa, girl, you've been back eighteen hours and you're already going at it with the most sought-after bachelor in Joyful."

"We didn't go at it!" Then she thought about Claire's other comment. "Johnny's…sought after?"

"You'd think the single women in this town had never laid eyes on a man before," Claire said with a disgusted snort. "So he's gorgeous, single, a lawyer, good to the poor folk and can get it up five times a night."

"What?"

Claire pointed an index finger. "Gotcha."

"Ha ha." Then she glanced at her own hands, trying to sound completely nonchalant. "Does Johnny…is he involved with someone?"

Claire was courteous enough not to look triumphant at Emma's definite interest in Johnny's romantic status. "There are some women in this town who like to brag. But truthfully, Johnny stays to himself. I think he intentionally stays away from the local man-eaters. Despite what some people might hope, he's good at avoiding the snare nets and bear traps the women around here set for him." She rolled her eyes. "He sure is talked about, though."

Emma had to ask. "And I'm sure the prom night story is still hanging around out there?"

Nodding, Claire patted her hand in commiseration.

"Am I still referred to as the 'loose-buttoned Frasier girl?'"

Claire stood with a shrug. "Nope. You're the girl who turned Johnny Walker into a bachelor for life." Winking, she called for Eve and walked toward the door. "Everyone thinks you broke his heart as retaliation for what Nick did to you. Then you skipped town."

Shocked, Emma thought about Claire's words. Everyone thought she'd intentionally hurt Johnny to get even with his brother? Even for a gossipy little burg like Joyful, that was pretty darn cruel. "I didn't…"

"I know, honey. I drove you home that night, remember?"

Of course she remembered. Claire had helped Emma back into her pretty pink dress, shielding her protectively from the leers and stares. After telling the gawking seniors to go screw themselves, she'd ordered her date to hand over his car keys. Then she'd driven Emma home and they'd proceeded to get drunk on a bottle of Grandma Emmajean's blackberry brandy.

Emma still couldn't stand the smell of brandy. Or of blackberries. And she'd never stopped loving Claire.

"Don't worry about it," Claire continued, obviously not noticing Emma's distraction. "Your timing's perfect. Joyful's got a whole entire new scandal to whisper about. Strip clubs, porn stars, this little slice of Georgia heaven is feelin' downright corrupted these days."

The wicked sparkle in Claire's eye said she didn't much mind that development. Then what she'd said sunk in. "Porn star? Strip club?"

After calling for Eve again, Claire nodded. "Yep. And I've thought about you every time someone's mentioned the club."

Emma raised a brow. "Do I want to know why you think of me in connection with a strip club?"

"Don't worry, honey," Claire said with a low chuckle. "You're awful cute, but I haven't switched sides. I still prefer to play with the men's team."

Grinning as she understood what Claire meant, Emma joined her at the front door. "*Men's?* As in plural?"

"All right, I admit it. One man's. Singular. My husband, Tim." A quick frown crossed Claire's forehead and she muttered, under her breath, "Or I used to, anyway."

"Used to what?"

To Emma's shock, Claire's face pinkened. She couldn't remember her boisterous friend ever blushing before.

"Never mind. I was thinking of something else."

Though curious, Emma sensed that Claire didn't want to continue the conversation. For the first time, she paused to wonder whether Claire's marriage was entirely wonderful, in spite of having a husband able to live up to a *Cosmo* standard of sexual prowess.

"I'm looking forward to meeting your husband," she said. When Claire's mouth pinched a little tighter, Emma knew she was on to something. She also knew Claire would talk about it when she was good and ready, and Emma wasn't about to push her.

"Now," Emma said, "get back to this whole club thing."

Claire visibly relaxed. "Oh, right, sorry, the club. I think of you because of the site where the place is being built. The billboard just went up yesterday. Before that, we all thought it was a diner or something." She chuckled. "Some diner…I don't see Mayor Boyd or Mrs. Davenport sidling up to the counter at dinnertime ordering Jell-O shooters or Slippery Nipples, and getting them served by a sex kitten in a thong and pasties."

As usual, a conversation with Claire left her slightly unbalanced. Emma sighed, remembering Claire's tendency to ramble. Getting the scoop from her without taking a bunch of detours into some funny and completely irrelevant stories was like trying to get from Manhattan to JFK during rush hour. Nearly impossible, often darn frustrating, but full of some interesting sights along the way.

Emma went back to the important part. "I still don't get why you associate me with a strip club."

Claire called for her daughter again. "Eve, I said now!"

A loud thumping signaled the little girl's return down the wooden floor of the hall. Eve was either stealing the kitchen table, or dragging her feet big time in protest at the thought of the dreaded ballet lesson.

"Sorry," Claire continued. "I think of you because of where the club's being built. At your grandmother's old place. Remember how we'd go out there at night after football games, and light up bonfires? Lordy, that one time the fire sparked and spread too close to one of the pecan trees, I thought you were gonna bash Nick in the head with a burning log."

Not sure she'd heard her friend correctly, Emma touched her arm. "What are you saying, Claire? What about my grandmother's old place? Are you talking about the orchard?"

Claire groaned when she spied Eve, who looked like a piece of chicken ready for the fryer, all covered with white powder and grease. "Baby, now we're gonna have to go home and change."

"Claire," Emma insisted, "tell me what you mean about Grandma Emmajean's pecan orchard."

Claire turned back to focus on Emma, apparently finally hearing the note of dismay in her voice. Her smile faded as she tilted her head in confusion. "Yes, the orchard." Her voice lowered. "I knew how much you loved the place. So when I found out it was you everyone was talking about in the store yesterday, I knew you couldn't be the porn…*person* building the club. I have to admit, though, I had to wonder why you sold the land."

Sold? Claire thought the orchard had been sold? Emma grabbed the front door handle for support. "Please, Claire, tell me what you're talking about because I have no idea what you mean."

Claire grabbed her daughter, who looked poised to dart back toward the kitchen. She lifted her to her hip, holding her tight in a silent battle of wills and elbows.

"Well," she finally replied, "the club, Joyful Interludes, is being built right there, on what used to be your grandma's land." She shook her head in sympathy. "Didn't you know, honey? The orchard's been pretty much destroyed."

WHEN EMMA saw what they'd done to her grandmother's pecan grove, she began to cry. Each tree missing from the lovely, shady parcel of land was like an ancestor torn from her past. Every piece of lumber on the construction site was a spike through her memories.

She supposed whoever had committed this atrocity had thought they were doing well by leaving several of the trees on the perimeter of the lot untouched. But the very center, where Emma remembered having picnics with her grandmother, had been completely cleared for the building which now stood there.

"Who would do such a thing?" she whispered.

"I don't know," Claire answered, though Emma had been speaking to herself. "Em, did you really know nothing about this?"

Emma shook her head. She remained almost dazed by what she was seeing. "Nothing."

The two of them were sitting in Claire's car, parked just beyond the dirt construction entrance of the pecan grove. Emma had begged her friend to drive her out to the site, needing to see for herself if what Claire said was true. Eve certainly didn't seem to mind missing her dreaded dance lesson.

"But you sold the lot...."

Emma jerked her gaze from the nearly completed building, where once a dozen stately trees had stood, and looked at her friend. "I did *not* sell this property, Claire. I inherited it. I have a copy of my grandmother's will saying it's mine. And I would never, *never* have sold it."

Claire's jaw dropped open. "They stole this lot?"

From the back seat, they both heard little Eve say, "Who stolded a lot? A lot of what? A lot of cookies? I bet it was Courtney Foster, cause she's a bad kicking girl, so she's probably a stealing girl, too."

Emma—whose tears of sadness had begun to dry as a great, thick anger choked her throat—was startled into a half-hysterical laugh. "I don't know who, Evie." She swallowed hard and looked out the windshield at the construction workers busy as frenzied termites destroying something valuable and rare.

She reached for the door handle, the handle of Grandma Emmajean's cane clutched tightly in her grasp.

"But I'm going to find out. Right now."

CHAPTER SEVEN

IN HIS FORMER LIFE as a low-paid grunt on the staff of the District Attorney's office in Atlanta, Johnny had rarely had a Saturday off. Sundays had often been sacrificed, too.

That was one good thing about living in Joyful. There was just enough crime to keep him from going stir-crazy with boredom Monday through Friday. And his weekends finally belonged to him.

"Hey, Walker, you gonna pitch it or jerk off on it?"

Johnny shook his head at Mike Gilmore who stood at home plate, his bat at the ready and a good-natured smirk on his face. They stood on the grassy field at the park by the high school, where he and some buddies met every Saturday for nine innings and some good old-fashioned bull-shitting.

Speaking of which… "You telling me *that* works better than spit on a spit ball? Well, I guess you'd know." He gave Mike a chance to figure out what he meant. When a grin broke over the other man's face, Johnny fired a fast ball across home plate.

"Strike three, Mike," the volunteer umpire said.

"Just in time for the seventh inning stretch," Mike said, obviously not caring that he'd struck out. Tossing the bat aside, he headed straight for the cooler of beer inside the dugout.

For Johnny, eleven-thirty was a little early to be hitting the cooler, unless it was for an icy cold bottle of water. He'd already had his fill of that, not only drinking two glasses, but also dunking his head under the sink at his house to try to cool off after his interaction with Emma Jean.

Eighteen hours. She'd been back in town eighteen hours and she'd thrown his entire world off-kilter. How on earth he was going to survive having her here for days…or even weeks…he had no idea. But he had the feeling he was going to be taking a lot of cold showers. Or working off a lot of tension with aggressive ball games in the park.

"Ahh," Mike said as he popped his beer bottle open. "Hair of the dog, just what I need after last night."

Most of the guys on his Saturday baseball team were sticking to the water cooler, like Johnny. But Mike was a twenty-three-year-old bachelor who partied from Friday at 5:00 p.m. until early Monday morning.

The players were an odd mix. Eleven years ago, when he'd gotten out of Joyful to go to college, Johnny would never have pictured days in the park with guys as varied as these. He now counted among his good friends the town's new mortician, the local OB-GYN—he took a lot of bashing, that was sure—and a former class president turned CPA. There were also, of course, some of those fun but disreputable Walkers in the bunch. Like Virg.

Joyful had come a long way in the past decade. He wondered exactly when the wrong side of the tracks had stopped meaning anything in Joyful, at least to his generation. Probably for himself, he conceded with a hint of amusement, it had happened when he'd come back to town with a law degree in tow and a much smaller chip on his shoulder.

"Johnny, your pager's going off," someone called from the dugout as he headed toward the cooler.

As he passed home plate, he saw Tim Deveaux, Claire's husband, straighten up and flip off his catcher's mask. He gave Johnny a thumbs-up for the three up, three down inning, and Johnny attempted a weak smile in return.

Hell, he could barely meet the guy's eye this morning. He couldn't stop wondering what Tim could do that would have made him such prime marriage material, according to that magazine Claire and Emma had read back in high school. It could be anything from knowing how to give a woman an orgasm in public when she was fully clothed—which, to be honest, Johnny *did*—to knowing how to sit through a chick flick without falling asleep—which Johnny did *not*. Some day, when they'd downed a few beers too many at the Junctionville Tavern, Johnny was going to ask the man.

"Hey, I thought this was guys' morning," someone called when a cell phone began to ring from the gym bags piled on the bench. "Phones, pagers, you guys wimping out?"

"Always on call," Johnny explained, reaching for his beeper.

Tim's was the phone ringing. "Just want to make sure Claire can reach me in case there's any problem with the baby."

Johnny hid a laugh. No question about it, belligerent little Eve was the apple of her daddy's eye.

After scanning the message on his alphanumeric pager, his jaw dropped. "Assault with a deadly weapon?" he mumbled, not sure he was reading right. Usually when he was called down to the police station for an arrest, the message read something like, "Mooned old ladies outside

Bingo Hall," or "D&D tipping cows at Able farm," the D&D standing for drunk and disorderly. There were a lot of those types of calls, quite often involving a Walker.

Johnny would show up, do his tap dance around Chief Brady, work out a plea involving an apology and compensation to the cow owner…or the scandalized—but secretly titillated—old ladies. Close book, end of case.

But in the eighteen months he'd been back in Joyful, he'd never seen an assault case that didn't involve two drunks armed only with their fists and too much liquid courage. "Assault with a deadly weapon," he mused again, shaking his head in disbelief. "What's good old Joyless coming to?"

"Did you say assault with a deadly weapon?"

Hearing the note of concern in Tim Deveaux's voice, Johnny dropped his pager into his gym bag and turned around. "Sorry, talking out loud. I just got paged to go down to the police station."

Tim's expression was as worried as his tone. "Claire just called. She needs me to come to the police station right away, too. She and the baby are there. She wouldn't say why."

"I'm sure she's okay…."

"What if this assault was some sicko attacking her or Evie? What if they're hurt?"

Johnny watched the worry on Tim's face segue into near panic. Before the man could go any further visualizing horrendous scenarios involving his family, Johnny put a hand on his shoulder. "Calm down. I'm sure they're fine."

Tim didn't look convinced. "But…"

"If they were hurt, she would be calling from the clinic, or the hospital down in Bradenton." He forced a dry laugh. "Deputy Fred probably got a little bossy with his ticket book. And knowing your Claire, she's down there at the police station raising a ruckus about it."

Tim's stiff stance eased a bit. The explanation made sense, and they both knew it. Given Claire's reputation as a fighter—who'd once, as a teenager, publicly called the members of the town council a bunch of Nazis because they were considering a teen curfew—Johnny could easily picture her complaining to Sheriff Brady about one of his deputies.

"Listen, why don't you hitch a ride with me down to the station. The last thing you need is to get into an accident because you're driving like a maniac. Or to get another speeding ticket from Deputy Fred."

Tim frowned. "Will *you* drive like a maniac?"

Johnny chuckled and led the way to his car. "Yeah. I get to do that whenever I'm paged by the police."

Johnny didn't drive recklessly during the three-mile trip from the park to the station. But he did move fast enough to satisfy Tim, who leaned forward in his seat, a sheen of sweat on his brow as he mumbled under his breath. Johnny thought he caught the words "please be okay."

That got him thinking. About Tim and Claire. Other couples he knew. Even, just a little, himself.

Tim and his wife seemed to epitomize everything the textbooks said marriage ought to be. They were crazy in love, anyone could see that. But it seemed to Johnny that they were a rare breed. Like Virg and Minnie. The exceptions, not the rule.

Most marriages seemed to be more like carefully balanced monogamy zones, where each partner tried to keep cool and faithful, figuring stability was better than being single again. And some…some were worse. His own parents' marriage had been a battlefield. His brother's attempt at matrimony had lasted less than a year and had ended in a ton of anger.

All in all, marriage seemed like one risky proposition. Especially for a Walker. Good thing he wasn't interested in it. And he hadn't been, not for a long time.

Oh, sure, he'd thought about it once. About ten years ago. With the girl who'd ripped his heart and his guts out on the very same night he'd finally been sure they'd started something perfect. The night he'd made love to her under the stars. Heard her whispering his name. Watched her beautiful face bathed in moonlight as she looked at him with an emotion he'd incorrectly interpreted as love.

Not love. How could she love him when she'd obviously been in love with Nick? Not only in love, but planning to *marry* him.

"Hell," he muttered, unwilling to even consider the thought of Emma as his sister-in-law. The idea had given him nightmares for months after she'd skipped town. He'd never have been able to survive. Not given the way he'd felt about Emma Jean Frasier from the first time he'd sat in her car with her, smelling her fruity perfume and hearing the husky, sexy note in her voice that all her golden-haired sweetness could never fully hide.

Unfortunately for him, she'd only looked at him as a savior. Someone to lean on. Someone to take care of her.

Seemed like things hadn't changed too much.

"You okay?" Tim asked.

Startled, Johnny yanked his attention away from the painful past and back to the confusing present. At least, it had been confusing since yesterday, when she'd waltzed back into town with her short skirt, short hair and riding a wave of porn rumors.

"Yeah. Sorry."

Tim's frown eased for the first time since he'd answered his cell phone back at the field. "Woman."

Johnny just grunted. Guys always knew. He sure as hell always did, whenever one of his buddies was wearing that sappy, stupid, "who am I and how did I get here?" look that always accompanied a fascination with a new woman.

Of course, Emma Jean wasn't new. She'd owned a chunk of his heart for going on eleven years now.

"If you need to talk…"

Johnny briefly thought about asking Tim about the whole eyebrow licking thing, but figured it wasn't the time. Actually, he wasn't sure there was *ever* a good time to ask a guy that kind of question. At least not while they were both sober.

They arrived at the police station, and Tim was opening the car door before Johnny'd even had a chance to put the SUV into Park. Once inside the station, Deputy Fred Willis—who was Johnny's main contact here at the sheriff's office since Johnny and the sheriff loathed each other—nodded from behind the desk. Handing Johnny a police report, he jerked a thumb over his shoulder, toward the holding cells. "I don't know any of the details. Sheriff brought 'em in himself."

Typical. No details, probably no proof, just Sheriff Brady throwing his weight around and sticking somebody in a cell for one of his infamous "cooling off" periods. Same old routine.

"My wife is here," Tim said, placing his hands flat on the front desk. "She called me. Is she all right? Where is my daughter?"

Willis merely nodded impassively, and jerked his thumb in the same direction. Johnny didn't quite understand. At least not until he pushed open the door and walked toward the holding area.

Inside a locked cell were Claire and Eve Deveaux.

And a fired-up-looking Emma Jean.

ARRESTED. Emma Jean Frasier, arrested, hauled off to the police station in handcuffs, and locked inside a cell.

God, wouldn't Ginger Devane, president of the Junior League in Manhattan, just rock in her Emil Leblanc's and fall flat onto her twice-lifted-by-the-hottest-doctor-on-Madison-Avenue butt if she heard about this one?

Not that Emma had ever much cared for the Junior League set. When she'd first moved to New York and had lived for a while on her trust fund, she'd dabbled in that lifestyle. It had quickly bored her. That's why she'd started exploring a bunch of different interests—cooking classes, archeology lectures, art appreciation. It had led her to fund the art show for the erotic artist.

But her fund-raiser and art show days quickly grew stale, too. Once she'd decided to work for her money, using her natural talent with numbers and her accounting degree to get in with an investment firm, Ginger and her cronies had turned up their collective noses at the stench of the blue collar they thought she'd embraced. That hadn't, of course, stopped them from asking for free investment advice on occasion.

Yes, her Junior League days had been long behind her even before she lost all her trust fund money—and her own hard-earned savings—when the company went bust.

Don't even go there. She couldn't think about the troubled times then, not when she was facing quite a horrendous time now.

Arrested was bad. Arrested and penniless was too pathetic for words.

Another day like this and it was straight to Jerry Springer'ville for Emma Jean Frasier. Life in a trailer park with a next-door neighbor pregnant by her mother's ex-husband's son-in-law's brother. That was where she was headed. And, of course, there'd be a transvestite around somewhere. *The Jerry Springer Show* seemed to love transvestites.

Yep. One little penniless, jobless, futureless, jailed, former princess dressed in rags would fit right in.

She couldn't prevent a tiny hitch in her throat as her eyes grew hot. Having an urge to throw herself down on a flat surface and pitch a first-class fit or just bawl her eyes out, she willingly refrained. The cot in the cell was filthy and probably loaded with lice or worse. The floor looked the same. She remained standing, leaning against the bars to take some of the stress off her sprained ankle, which had begun to ache again.

"It's not bad enough to get arrested. But did I have to do it looking like this?" she muttered in disgust. "I slept in these clothes last night."

"Your Grandma Emmajean is likely rolling over in her grave," Claire added mournfully.

"If I had to be hauled off by the police and locked in this tiny cell, I ought to at least be dressed like I frankly don't give a damn. Not like I *belong* here!"

"I don't think the clothes are the main problem, sweetie," Claire said as she sat on the far outermost edge of the bunk, daring because she, at least, was wearing pants. "The fat lip looks downright disreputable."

"That daughter of yours has some hard head."

"Not to mention your cheek is all red and swollen."

"And her mama's still got one heck of a punch."

The two of them stared at each other for a second then

burst into laughter. The lip had been an accidental gift from Eve. The cheek from a wild swing by Claire.

The pain in her wrist, though, had been all hers. But ooh, remembering the way that foul-mouthed construction foreman had gone down for the count made it all worthwhile.

She couldn't believe that he'd pressed charges. She was the wronged party! She was the one whose property had been stolen and desecrated. Every minute she spent in this jail cell was another minute for those bastards to ruin another piece of the grove.

"I gotta go potty."

Emma and Claire exchanged one horrified look at the thought of little Eve using the facilities in the cell. Joyful might not have much of a criminal element. But those they did have obviously had never heard of things like keeping the seat down for a lady. Not to mention the fact that Chief Brady and his crew had apparently never heard of things like scrub brushes, 409 or even clean water.

Terrorist camps probably had cleaner facilities.

"We'll be out of here soon, honey, then Mama will take you to the potty. And we'll get you some ice cream with sprinkles."

Their jailer—a mile-mannered guy they'd gone to high school with—had offered to keep Eve out in the front of the station with him, but the little girl had refused to be separated from her mother. She'd relished the chance to inspect every square inch of the cell, asking an endless stream of questions about what people had to do—other than hitting bad men on construction sites—to get arrested.

By the end of Claire's explanation, Eve had been muttering under her breath about Courtney Foster. Courtney, Emma decided, had better never let Eve Deveaux catch her anywhere near the police station. Or in a dark alley.

Eve also took great delight in showing them how easily she could slip through the bars. Emma just wished Fred Willis, who she'd had homeroom with in senior year, had left the keys nearby. Escape would have been startlingly easy.

"But I have to go now, Mama. Why can't I use this potty?"

"Over my dead body!"

Emma didn't recognize the voice, but she recognized the tone. Worried Daddy.

"Tim. Thank heaven," Claire said. Though, to be honest, combined with her thankfulness, Emma detected a note of genuine trepidation in her friend's face.

Definitely the husband.

"I, uh, guess you're wondering what's going on."

Claire sounded like Lucy greeting Ricky after he'd caught her doing something really stupid. Emma almost laughed, wondering if Tim was going to tell Claire she had some 'splaining to do when she realized that he wasn't alone. Seeing the person who'd accompanied Tim, her laughter died on her lips. Johnny.

"Oh, shit," she whispered, unable to help it.

"I suppose the language is appropriate, given your current address, but maybe you should watch it in front of the kid."

Emma winced at the rebuke. Then winced again at the realization that her first lover was standing there, watching her, when she looked like the poster girl for Blondes Gone Bad.

"Hello, Johnny," she said, forcing her voice to remain steady. "Fancy running into you here."

"Oh, I love spending my Saturdays at the police station. After all, it's my job."

His job. Oh, good lord, his job. As prosecutor. "Those charges are bogus."

Claire, who'd been talking to her husband as he held their daughter protectively in his arms, nodded. "Entirely bogus."

"Yep. Bogus," Eve echoed with a vehement nod.

Claire's husband's frown deepened. "Johnny, what do I have to do to get Claire out of here?"

"Go right now," Johnny murmured, not even hesitating. "I'll get the story from Ms. Frasier here." He gave her a look that said *she* was the one who had a lot of 'splaining to do. "I know where to find you if I need to talk to Claire."

Then Claire and her family left, but not before her friend gave Emma a weak little nod of encouragement.

Once they were gone, Johnny met her stare, shaking his head and tsking under his breath. She'd swear a sparkle of amusement shone in those wicked blue eyes of his. If he laughed at her, she was gonna launch at him. She was already in jail. What else could they do to her if she assaulted the D.A.?

"Sit down."

She pointed to the cot. "Not on that thing I'm not."

Johnny followed her stare and frowned. "You're right. Let's get out of here."

Hope rose in her chest.

"We can use the sheriff's office."

Okay, so he wasn't just letting her go as he had Claire. Funny, she'd have expected him to assume Claire was the one who'd caused all the fuss, given the other woman's, umh, renowned temper. But he hadn't. He'd zeroed in on Emma. Correctly so. She wished she knew how. "I don't suppose you could just let me go home?"

He shook his head. "Come on."

But Johnny seemed to have forgotten her ankle, which was positively screaming because she'd been standing in the cell for so long. They'd confiscated her cane. *Deadly weapon my ass.*

He turned to leave, expecting her to follow. She could, if she wanted to hop after him like a deranged, one-legged Easter bunny. But her dignity, already in shreds, couldn't handle it. So she stayed still.

"Am I going to have to have Deputy Willis come in here with handcuffs to move you?" Then he lowered his voice. "Or do you expect to be carried out of here like some high-flung princess too good for your surroundings?"

The disgusted tone got to her. Got to her like nothing else had since the minute she'd been handcuffed and stuck in the back of a squad car with a sputtering Claire and a chattery Eve.

She tried to stick out her chin and blinked quickly. She'd sooner shave her head bald again than let Johnny Walker see her in tears. Those she'd save for later.

"It so happens," she replied, wishing her voice sounded lofty, as she'd intended it to, rather than quivery with emotion choking her throat, "that the officer confiscated my cane. I am not able to walk very well, in case you've forgotten."

The sudden flash of remorse on his face told her he *had* forgotten. He instantly dropped his gaze to her bandaged ankle.

"I'm sorry," he murmured. Then he strode over and slid an arm around her waist. "Lean into me."

Lean into him. Into his strong, hard body that had once made her feel cherished and adored. How tempting the thought was, in more ways than he could possibly know.

She hadn't had anyone to lean on in a long time. Not through the loss of her job, her apartment, her home or her savings. No one to help her deal with coming back to Joyful, not to mention what had happened since she'd arrived. She'd been alone. Completely alone, relying on false bravado and her hot pink wardrobe to get her through the nightmare of the past few weeks.

Since she still wore the ratty shorts and T-shirt she'd slept in last night, the clothing column of support was gone. And after the horrible episode at the pecan grove, her bravado was just about shot, too.

Which was why she went all girly and sniffled.

"Em…"

"If you could bring a chair in here, maybe we could sit down and talk," she mumbled, wanting him gone so she could pull herself together. But even as she said it, she knew she didn't want him to go. She didn't want him to leave her alone here in this smelly place with its stained, graffiti-covered walls and fuzzy ceiling where heaven only knew what was growing.

Not now. Not when she'd had a few moments to sink against all that male heat and strength and feel safe for the first time in longer than she could remember.

He was tall and hard and wonderfully warm against her. Johnny's clothes were slightly damp, a sheen of sweat evident on the dark hair at his temple. He wore shorts and gym shoes, and a sleeveless muscle T-shirt that hugged his broad chest and displayed his thick arms. Very thick arms. Lordy, he did *not* look like the kind of man who worked behind a desk all day. He made the pale, suit-wearing brokers she'd been working with in New York seem like prepubescent boys.

Johnny had obviously changed clothes and done some serious physical activity after he'd left her house this morning, judging by the glisten on his muscles and the way his clothes clung to his body. *All* of his body.

Her mouth went dry thinking of the *all* part.

The confident, secure Emma would have pulled away, never admitting for a second—even to herself—how nice it was to lean against Johnny. But that Emma was long gone. She'd bailed the minute the cuffs had snapped shut on her wrists at the construction site. Or maybe a few weeks ago when she'd found out she'd been duped, robbed and used by her former employer.

"Are you crying?"

She shook her head. "It hurts a little," she whispered, which was true, though it wasn't the reason for the hot moisture in her eyes. In truth, it was her life making her misty-eyed. Her life which, right now, basically sucked eggs.

She heaved in a breath, trying to force the fear and hurt and anger and insecurity away. But she couldn't quite manage it.

"Aww, hell, Em," he whispered, turning so he faced her. He tilted her chin up with the tip of one finger. Emma tugged her lower lip into her mouth, not wanting him to see how it quivered.

But it didn't matter. Judging by the moisture on her cheeks—and the look of tenderness on his face—she hadn't succeeded in hiding her tears.

Without another word, Johnny hauled her into his arms, hugging her close.

And Emma began to bawl.

CLAIRE WATCHED her husband hug Eve yet again as he stood next to the rear passenger door of Claire's car, which had been towed to a nearby lot by the police. He cuddled their daughter close, being the concerned, loving father he always was. He wasn't, however, acting much like the concerned, loving husband.

"Oh, for heaven's sake, she's fine. It was an…adventure."

Tim frowned. "An adventure a four-year-old doesn't need."

Well, maybe not a four-year-old. But Claire hadn't minded having it. She hadn't had so much fun in years.

Certainly not with Tim, who, though he was still the man she loved with all her heart, had settled almost too firmly into his role of family man. Somewhere along the way, he seemed to have lost the spark of irrepressible spirit that had so drawn her to him in the first place.

"We'll talk about this at home," he said as he buckled Eve into her booster seat. He shut the door, blowing their daughter one more kiss, then turned to Claire.

She wanted to fall into his arms, to suck up his strength, to get some of the sweet comfort he'd given to Eve. But he wasn't offering it.

"I don't want Eve around that woman anymore."

Claire's jaw dropped open. "Emma Jean?"

"Is that her real name?"

"Of course. I've known her for years, she's my friend."

Tim just shook his head, looking disapproving. Cold. Unlike himself. "Maybe she was in the past. But her profession makes her someone I don't want Eve—or *you*— associating with."

Claire nearly snorted, knowing Tim had heard and believed the ridiculous porn star rumors. "Emma is not who everyone is saying she is."

Her husband didn't look convinced. "Whatever the case, she's trouble. Back in town one day and she gets you arrested."

"No, that obnoxious pig of a construction foreman got me arrested because he's a jerk and he yelled at Eve."

Tim's eyes widened. "He *yelled* at her?"

Claire nodded. Sure enough, mention Eve and Tim would get defensive and irate. Once upon a time, he'd been protective of her. God, that sounded terrible, as if she was somehow jealous of her own little girl, whom she adored. She wasn't jealous…she just wondered why her husband hadn't learned yet that there was enough love for all of them to share.

Since Eve had been born, the little girl had been number one, leaving her mother often feeling very much second-best. Claire had fallen into a routine, telling herself it was right he should put their child ahead of everything else, including their marriage, their alone time.

Their sex life.

Which probably explained her recent love affair with Snickers bars. She'd been getting most of her fulfillment from chocolate these days.

Now, though, she sensed she wasn't going to be satisfied with the status quo. Emma Jean's return had sparked something in her. It had reminded her of the girl she'd once been. A pretty girl. A girl with ambition. A girl who could flirt and laugh, who had drive and spark. More than just Tim's wife, and Eve's mama. She wanted to be Claire again.

Tim seemed to see something come to life in her eyes because as he walked around the car to get into the driver's seat, he kept giving her questioning, sidelong glances. When he got in, he immediately turned to glance at Eve, who sat in the back seat, muttering under her breath.

"What'd you say, honey bun?"

"I said I wish Aunt Emma had bonked her cane on that nasty man's head instead of knocking it against his leg."

Claire bit her lips to keep from laughing.

Tim flushed red, then went on to say hitting anybody with a cane was a bad idea. "Ms. Frasier shouldn't have even been there, and she definitely shouldn't have brought you and your mama out to a construction site."

"Mama drove."

Claire couldn't hide the little snort this time, earning a glare from her husband.

"In any case, you and Mama aren't going to get in any more trouble because of Ms. Frasier," Tim said, giving Claire a steely-eyed stare that she barely recognized as her husband's. "You won't be seeing her again."

After he'd finished and turned his attention toward driving them home, Claire frowned and crossed her arms. Tim had gotten used to having a nice, quiet housewife who always aimed to please. The one who subdued the wild, rebellious part of herself that had gotten her into trouble in her younger years.

It might be time to reintroduce him to that girl…the one he'd *married,* whether he wanted to acknowledge her or not. Claire only hoped she could find her after all this time of being wife and mommy.

Somehow, today seemed like a good start.

Smiling to herself, she turned around and gave her daughter a conspiratorial look. Her precocious little girl grinned, knowing exactly what was going on in her mother's mind.

No way were they going to stay away from Emma Jean Frasier. No way at all.

CHAPTER EIGHT

JOHNNY HAD INTENDED to get Emma out of the dirty jail cell as soon as possible, and bring her into the sheriff's office to get to the bottom of the whole ridiculous assault charge. But no sooner had he disentangled them from their completely unexpected embrace than they'd been interrupted by Deputy Fred.

The charges had been dropped. The construction foreman out at the Joyful Interludes site had decided the whole thing had been a misunderstanding, after all. And that the cane incident had been a complete accident. Meaning Emma was free to go.

Emma hadn't looked relieved when she found out she wasn't facing charges. In fact, she'd barely seemed to hear Willis, who'd entered from the front of the jail only a few seconds after Johnny had released Emma so she could wipe away her tears.

Then again, maybe it wasn't so surprising that she'd been a little...distracted. They'd both been slightly uncomfortable after their unexpected closeness, with him rubbing her back, whispering softly against her hair, and her clinging to him like he'd rescued her from a burning building.

If someone had asked him twenty-four hours ago if he'd even consider holding Emma Jean Frasier in his arms so she could cry her eyes out, he'd have replied that he'd rather eat one of Virg's mayonnaise-and-onion hot dogs.

But the embrace had happened. She'd been in need, and his arms had opened to her before his brain had given it any conscious thought.

She'd felt good. Too good, dammit. Sweet and curvy and vulnerable and soft. And he'd started to fall again, into the crazy place he always went when Emma Jean was close enough to touch, to taste, to smell.

It'd taken the moisture of her tears on his neck to remind him they weren't sharing the kind of embrace they'd experienced in her kitchen this morning. Yeah, there'd been attraction. As always. But also kindness, a sweetness he hadn't wanted to explore with anyone in a long, long time. If ever.

Her. Why is it always her?

Maybe it wasn't. Em had reminded him of an abandoned puppy. Johnny had a long track record of being the stand-up guy who helped out anybody in need. He'd have done the same for any woman who looked like Emma had and would be feeling exactly the same way about it.

Made sense. But deep in his own mind, he called himself a liar.

In spite of being out of the jail, Emma still looked dejected. Exhausted. Not to mention completely awful. "You know you have a fat lip?" he asked as he drove her back to her place. He hadn't bothered asking if she needed the ride. He'd just led her to his SUV as soon as they'd left the jail.

She nodded.

"Want to explain it?"

"The foreman bent over to yell at Eve for trying to kick him. I saw Claire winding up to swing, so I grabbed Eve to get her out of the way. Her head kind of bumped against my mouth."

Tsking, he shook his head. "Claire took a swing?"

"Yes, but I deflected it."

"With your cheek?"

"Uh-huh."

That explained the redness, which he'd wanted to kiss away earlier when she was crying in his arms.

He shook off the thought. Those kind of impulses needed to get the hell out of his head.

"Where did 'the foreman getting whacked with a cane' come in?"

She blew out an exasperated breath. "Between my cheek and my lip and a squirming four-year-old, I lost my balance. The cane really *was* an accident." Then, with heat in her voice, she added, "If I'd wanted to hit that awful man, I wouldn't have aimed for one of his legs, I'd have aimed *between* them."

"I don't think he'd have dropped the charges if you had," Johnny replied dryly.

"I don't think I'd have cared." She straightened in her seat, her spine growing stiffer as some of her spirit began to return.

He was glad to see it. Emma Jean had never been the type to let anybody keep her down for long. "Bloodthirsty, aren't you?" Speaking of blood…her clothes were sprinkled with a few drops. Probably from the fat lip. She was quite a sight. "What'd you do, take off the minute I left your house this morning?"

"Almost. Claire told me what was going on out at Grandma Emmajean's pecan grove and I talked her into driving me out there."

He figured as much. "You mean the construction site."

"Yes. How could this have happened? The land is decimated."

He shrugged, turning the SUV down an all-too-familiar street. *Hers.* "What'd you think the new owners were going to do with the place after you sold it? Have picnics in the summer?"

The smack of her hand against his dashboard startled him so much he almost swerved off the road. "I did *not* sell the place."

The fury in her tone told him the sad, beaten-down Emma was long gone. In her place was one enraged, raggedy-looking blonde with fire in her stare and a curl on her lips.

He pulled into her driveway, cut the engine and turned to face her. "I figured you must have sold it after your grandmother died."

She gave a fierce shake of her head, which sent those wild, untamed curls of hers rioting onto her forehead, almost covering her eyes. Unable to resist, Johnny reached over and brushed them back, fingering the silkiness for a brief second before letting the curl go. "Did you even brush your hair today?"

"No, I didn't," she snapped, not looking like she cared one bit. "And I did not sell the lot, either. I inherited it, along with the house."

Interesting. She sounded completely sincere. But there had to be some explanation. Maybe Emma's parents had dealt with it, sold the land themselves…wanting to "help." Or maybe her grandmother had unloaded it.

Something had happened back when Emma was recovering from her accident. She just didn't know, or didn't remember. But he wasn't about to tell her that. He had the feeling if he did she'd slug him. She was too riled up, full of righteous indignation to listen to reason right now.

"I believe you," he murmured. "But charging out there probably wasn't the best way to handle it."

"What would you suggest?"

"Maybe just calmly calling the construction company?"

"I didn't have their number," she replied with a lofty little shrug.

He chuckled. "Well, sugar, they now appear to have yours."

"As in one angry wronged party?"

"More along the lines of crazy lady with a cane and a dark-haired little pit bull named Eve."

Emma snorted a laugh. "That apple didn't fall far from Claire's tree, that's for sure."

Suspecting she was right, he began to feel sorry for Tim Deveaux, who had yet to see his angel for the hell-on-wheels kid she'd someday become. Kinda like her mama had been, as he recalled.

"Are you the only attorney in town now?" she asked, her voice growing serious again.

He shook his head.

"Because I think I need one."

"Charges were dropped."

"I mean a property attorney," she said. "I'm going to call one right away. And Jimbo Boyd, because he was supposed to be looking after my interests."

"I'll write down a couple of names for you," he said, glad she hadn't asked him for his help. He didn't want to get involved with her any more than he had to. He'd already broken his silent promise to stop being Emma Jean's savior.

Not when he'd long ago wanted to be *so* much more.

Emma let him help her into the house. She didn't have much choice since she could hardly walk. Her entire body was tense against his, though, he had to admit, she still felt good. Soft and curvy and welcoming. Which sent his thoughts where they had no business going. South.

Shit.

Emma always had fit him better than any woman he'd ever known, and he'd known more than a few in his day. Not recently, though. He'd been going through a dry spell in his personal life. Not to mention his sexual one.

For some reason, he just hadn't been able to muster much interest in any of the women he knew. Nor had he much cared to get to know any new ones. In the year and a half since he'd moved back to Joyful, he'd dated a handful of women—none from here in town, of course, he wasn't that stupid. The Joyful gossip lines had quite enough to talk about without adding this Walker's sex life to it. But he hadn't gone much beyond dating.

Apparently his dry spell had ended. Because if putting his arm around the waist of a bedraggled, bloodied, unshowered, unbrushed blonde was getting under his skin like an itch that needed scratching before it drove him stark-raving nuts, he definitely needed to get laid. By just about anyone but her.

Too bad she was the only one he wanted.

Emma continued to mutter under her breath, not noticing the way he'd stiffened against her...not to mention his zipper.

He needed to think of something else, something quick to kill his out-of-control libido. *Control. Think of old lady Dillon. Castration. Having to ride the Small World ride at Disney World for twenty-four hours straight.*

Anything except backing her up into the porch swing and taking them both for one wild ride.

Once inside, she slammed the front door shut, pulling

away from him to lean on the inside wall. "I can't believe they wouldn't give me the cane back."

"I'll get it for you," he muttered, his throat tight. But not as tight as his pants.

"After I no longer need it?"

"What happened to the silver lining girl?"

"She's pissed off," Emma shot back. "Tired and grungy and sore and ready to fight."

"So you're done crying?"

"You would have to remind me of that." She clumped into her grandmother's front room and dropped to a chair. "You caught me at a weak moment. It won't happen again."

"Lots of those weak moments going around," he murmured, remembering the one in her kitchen that morning.

She met his even stare and her face flushed pink. The heat of anger slipped away, replaced by hot memory. What a double-edged sword, bringing up that intense outbreak of passion they'd shared. Because just thinking about it affected him every bit as deeply. So much for gaining control—his had taken a big flying leap. His heart rate kicked up and his stomach rolled over as he thought of how crazy they'd gotten on her kitchen table.

Now he began to suspect why it was he hadn't had much interest in other women lately. Because never, not once with any other woman, had he ever felt as sexually hungry as he did whenever Emma Jean Frasier was within a hundred yards.

They were alone again, staring at each other with awareness and intensity, their eyes locked together. Hers were molten gold, full of fire. He felt the same way. On edge. Ready. Waiting for a spark to set them both ablaze.

As if not even aware she was doing it, Emma slipped

her tongue out to moisten her lips. His whole body clenched. The lip-licking move could've been the spark. It sure had been this morning in the kitchen when she'd been kissing him like she needed his breath to survive.

But it was also accompanied by a slight wince when her tongue brushed against the lump on her bottom lip. So, as much as he wanted to haul her up outta that chair for another brain-zapping kiss, he was able to resist.

Kissing the taste out of her mouth would hurt her. Not to mention further rip his guts out when she did her pretty little song-and-dance as far away from him as she could get once their lips were unlocked and her defenses firmly back in place.

"I'll be right back," he muttered, needing to get away. He headed for the kitchen, to get her some ice. Maybe he could throw some down the front of his shorts while he was at it.

The kitchen was a mess. Lumps of powdered sugar doughnuts were strewn like little mummies across the table, and white powdery fingerprints all over the fridge and pantry door. Tiny fingerprints. He chuckled, thinking the construction foreman had been lucky Eve's kick had missed its target. The kid was a terror.

While in the kitchen, Johnny grabbed a pen and paper and wrote down the names and numbers of a couple of good attorneys in Joyful and Bradenton, the next nearest town. Then he filled a bag with ice and wrapped it in a towel. Returning to the other room, he held it out to her. "Here. It'll help the swelling."

She took it gratefully and brought it to her mouth, hissing when the coldness touched her skin. But her hiss quickly turned into an appreciative sigh. When she rubbed the moist bag back and forth over her lips, the condensation made them slick and shiny.

Johnny closed his eyes against the sight, fighting the urge to kiss her again. She was hurting; it would be downright ungentlemanly to kiss her. Not that he was a frigging gentleman. No one had ever accused him of that, any more than they had any other Walker.

Still, he was decent enough to see when a woman was in pain. Physically as well as emotionally. And Emma seemed overloaded on both. So he stepped a few feet away, maintaining a careful distance.

The space between them didn't stop him from idly trying to remember whether or not she was wearing a bra under the loose T-shirt she wore. His hands remembered better than his brain. *Nope.*

She looked up, curious, obviously not noticing the testosterone level in the room had gone way, way up.

He'd sure noticed. The continued tightness in his shorts told him his brain had lost the battle with his groin when it came to Emma Jean. At least for now. She was about to realize that, too, unless he got the hell outta here.

He headed toward the door. "Go take a shower, Em. Get dressed. Have something to eat."

She mumbled something about her cane. But even knowing she was going to have a rough time getting around by herself didn't make him pause.

He had to get away. Lusting after a woman with a fat lip and a sprained ankle was bad. That the woman was Emma Jean made it a million times worse.

Their kiss that morning had proved they still shot incredible sparks off one another. Those kind of sparks had left his ass fried the last time she'd been around. He didn't know if any man was capable of being so badly burned twice in a lifetime. "I've gotta go."

"Johnny," she called as he reached for the knob.

He looked over his shoulder, seeing her watching, her eyes wide and curious over the bag of ice clutched to her lips.

"Thanks," she mumbled. "For everything."

He shrugged it off. "No problem. I left you the names and numbers of some lawyers. They're in the kitchen."

She thanked him again.

"Just try to stay out of trouble." He opened the door, but before leaving, he had to caution her about one more thing. "And stay away from the construction site." Seeing her frown, he quickly added, "At least until you get all the facts."

She sighed and her lip popped out a little more, probably from more than mere swelling.

"Em," he said, a warning tone in his voice, "I don't want to have to meet up with you in a jail cell again." She didn't respond, or even meet his eye. "Emma Jean…"

"I know, I know."

Her response didn't sound exactly enthusiastic. He stared at her until she met his eye. "Don't do it," he bit out.

He wasn't leaving until she agreed. She seemed to realize that because she finally sighed and mumbled, "I won't."

She'd said what he wanted. Somehow, though, he had the feeling Emma might have had her fingers crossed behind her back.

"I won't bail you out next time."

She smiled. "You didn't bail me out this time. The charges were dropped."

"You know what I mean."

Crossing her arms, she leaned back and frowned. "I've learned my lesson, Johnny. Cross my heart and hope to die, you will never see me sitting in a jail cell facing assault charges again."

ON MONDAY MORNING, Emma was arrested for trespassing.

She'd kept her word, at least. She hadn't assaulted anybody. Though she'd certainly felt like it when the stupid foreman had insisted the sheriff take her into custody for refusing to leave the construction site.

She'd gone out there, all reasonable-like, politely but firmly asking to see the building permits, or to talk to someone in charge. Anything to find out just who was behind this nightmare.

Instead, she'd immediately been ordered to get back into her car and leave.

She'd gotten back into her car, all right. But she hadn't left. She'd pulled it dead center in the middle of the site, blocking one dump truck and a half-dozen angry, sweaty construction workers trying to unload a tractor-trailer full of drywall.

For a second there, she'd thought the foreman was going to order the dump truck driver to fill Emma's pretty little car with a few tons of dirt. She'd held her breath, resisting the urge to blink at his unexpected game of chicken by hitting the button to put the convertible top up.

He'd finally backed down, disappearing into his trailer.

The cops had shown up eight minutes later. Sheriff Brady had come out to the site to make the arrest and take her away. He'd been nice about it—the barrel-chested man had always been a nice old guy, except when anyone named Walker was around. But he'd also been stern. When Emma had tried to defend herself, insisting she was the wronged party, he'd merely shaken his head with pure patronization, and told her she didn't know the facts.

Emma hated being told she was wrong. Particularly by a blustery, laid-back old Southern man who thought he knew everything. One who had fathered Emma's high school arch-enemy.

"Why do I get the feeling you're going to claim this doesn't count as breaking your promise?" a voice asked.

She looked up from where she sat perched on the very edge of the cot in the much-too-familiar jail cell. This time, she'd thought far enough ahead to wear long pants, which were going in the wash as soon as she got home.

"Because I didn't," she told Johnny. She'd been expecting him ever since Fred Willis had locked her in this place.

Stiffening her shoulders, she tried to keep her lips stiff, too. Not to mention her voice. She wasn't going to cry on Johnny's shoulder again. "I didn't break any promise. Besides which, it wasn't a real promise. I didn't pinky swear or anything."

Tsking, he shook his head. "You couldn't stay out of trouble for forty-eight hours?"

"I started trying to reach Jimbo Boyd on Saturday and have left a half-dozen messages, but he's not returning my calls." Emma stood and walked over to the cell door, favoring her bad ankle, which had, at least, improved enough so she didn't need a cane.

Johnny had kept his word and left it on her porch sometime Sunday night. But Emma had resisted the urge to bring it with her out to the grove today, figuring there was no point tempting fate. Or depriving the construction foreman of future children.

Not that the world wouldn't be better off without the progeny of foul-mouthed, foul-smelling, foul-tempered jerks like him.

Never taking his eyes off her, Johnny unlocked the cell. When the bars were swung out of the way, and they stood there, face-to-face, she tilted her head back and narrowed her eyes, wanting him to understand. There was one way to get her point across. "Would *you* have just let it go?"

He met her stare, his frown easing somewhat, and she knew the answer to her own question. *No.* In her position, Johnny would have done exactly the same thing.

"At least you didn't hit anybody this time," he offered, with one lip quirked up in a half smile.

"I told you I wouldn't assault anyone." She had to hand it to herself, she'd sounded downright pious that time.

Johnny, of course, saw right through it. "You knew what I meant, though. I warned you to stay away from the site, Emma. Now the foreman is talking about filing a restraining order. You'd be restricted from coming within a hundred feet of the property line."

Groaning, she swiped an angry hand through her hair. "They can restrict me from my own property?"

"According to the tax records, it's not your property."

His words stunned her for a moment. Judging by the sincerity—and the regret—on Johnny's face, he was entirely serious. "But I inherited it…along with the house."

"A company called MLH Enterprises is the recorded land owner and has been since April of last year. I looked it up this morning. I can get you a copy of the tax roll if you don't believe me."

April. The month Grandma Emmajean had died. She couldn't take it in. "That can't be. Grandma Emmajean's will…"

"Did you see the deed?"

Absently shaking her head, she admitted, "My parents took care of everything. Like I said, I was just out of the hospital, still in physical therapy. After probate, I invested all the cash, and left the property in the hands of Jimbo Boyd."

His jaw tightened, as if he didn't like being reminded of her accident. On rainy days, when her healed bones ached, she agreed with him. "Did your parents *tell* you the land was included in your inheritance?"

She had to admit it: no, they hadn't. But it had been a foregone conclusion. Her grandmother had always made it clear what she wanted. Emma's parents didn't have the need, or the ties to Joyful. Though her father had been born in Georgia, he'd become firmly ensconced in Mother's world and currently ran the London branch of her family's electronics company. He wasn't interested in coming back to Georgia and had always agreed that the home place should go to his daughter, who truly loved it.

A daughter who would fight for it. No matter what.

"I'm certain the will said I inherited *everything*."

"Even if it did…she might have already sold the land before changing her will."

"She didn't," Emma snapped. "I know it. You can believe me or not, but one way or another, I intend to prove it."

DANEEN HAD GIVEN Jimbo the messages from Emma Jean Frasier every time she'd heard another one on their office answering machine. Each time, Jimbo had barely spared them a glance before shoving them into his desk drawer.

Interesting. He was avoiding the woman. Daneen had seen that kind of behavior before. Usually, though, Jimbo only avoided the stupid, brainless women he'd done then dumped whenever he and Daneen were on the outs.

There'd been more than a few of those over the years.

Jimbo worked fast, but he sure couldn't have worked fast enough to have done anything with Emma Jean. Not with her only having been in town a few days. And not with Jimbo having spent all of his sexual energy with Daneen right here in the office. So she wondered why he wasn't calling Emma Jean back.

"Is that something I can take care of?" she asked, after giving him the last message Monday evening.

He shook his head. "Nah, sweet pea, she's just being a northern pain in the ass. Always gotta have everything right now."

Hmm…sounded like some men she knew.

"I hear she caused a commotion out at the site of the club. Not once but twice."

Jimbo pushed his chair back from his desk, leaned back and laced his fingers together over his chest. "Did she now?"

Jimbo knew darn well she had. Daneen's father had been in here earlier telling him all about it. Daneen hadn't heard all their conversation through the closed office door, but she'd heard enough to know her daddy hadn't been happy with Emma Jean.

"I woulda paid money to see her tossed into jail," Daneen said with a grin.

"It was all a misunderstanding," Jimbo murmured, still watching her from across the desk. "But do me a favor, will you?"

She nodded.

"Keep an ear out. Let me know if you hear anything else about her, okay?"

Daneen assumed he meant anything *other* than the porn star story, which was garbage and she knew it. So she nodded, then turned to leave his office. But as she returned to her desk, she had to wonder why Jimbo cared so much. Which also made her wonder about who else seemed to care too much about Emma Jean's presence in town.

Johnny.

She still hadn't been able to get a minute alone with him

since Friday. She'd seen him Sunday, at his mama's place, when she'd taken Jack out for a visit. But she hadn't had a chance to grill him on Emma.

She wanted to know why the other woman had come back. How long she planned to stay. If there was anything Daneen could do to make her hurry back out of town.

And just how Johnny felt about it.

Daneen wanted things to get back to normal, with her being the only local woman Johnny gave the time of day to. She knew it was only because they were family, but that was better than being ignored, like the rest of the female population in Joyful.

Johnny could have had any woman he wanted. Rumors said he wanted a *lot* of women. From down in Bradenton. Or up in Lawton. Not in Joyful, though. Never.

She'd long since given up on thinking she'd ever actually get him. Johnny had made it pretty clear years ago that even their friendship would disappear if she didn't back off. It'd been hard to do, considering he was darn near the sexiest man she'd ever seen. But she'd done it, knowing she'd never be able to hold on to him. And she'd certainly never be able to get him to marry her. The chance of that was even lower than the chance she'd ever been able to get a commitment out of Jimbo.

Because Johnny was a loner. He'd never fall in love, never settle down, never commit to one woman. He didn't believe in any of it. His parents' marriage had done something to him and he seemed content to be alone during the day.

As for the nights? Well, they were another story. But as long as she didn't have to hear about who in town he was spending them with, Daneen found it in herself not to mind so much that it wasn't her.

CHAPTER NINE

As MUCH AS she wanted to deal only with the pecan grove, Emma realized by Tuesday morning that a job was going to have to come first. She didn't have a penny to spare to hire a lawyer, not yet anyway. And until she could reach her parents—who were traveling somewhere in Spain this week—she couldn't get a copy of her grandmother's will or find out where the rest of the paperwork was. So there didn't seem to be much she could do, except risk arrest.

Which was getting a little tiresome.

However Emma fully intended to show up at Jimbo Boyd's office if he didn't call her back soon. She'd plant herself on his doorstep and get some answers. The one reason she hadn't was that, honestly, she hated the thought of seeing Daneen. She couldn't handle the other woman yet. Her nerves were stretched too thin. The way she was going, Daneen would set her off and she'd end up in jail again. Or a blubbering, sobbing mess. At this point, she couldn't say which was worse.

If Johnny was around, the blubbering part probably would be the way it ended up. With her luck, she'd wind up in his arms again, which was about as tempting—and as bad for her—as a Krispy Kreme doughnut was to a woman on Atkins. She'd been held by him practically from the minute she'd arrived back in town Friday afternoon. When she'd fallen, when she'd cried. When they'd kissed.

Oh, God, when they'd kissed.

Just a kiss, it was just a kiss.

And the Golden Gate was just a bridge.

Enough. She couldn't think about him anymore, couldn't speculate on the things she'd learned—that he was single, eligible, sought after and could get it up five times a night.

Darn you, Claire!

She couldn't allow herself to admit that he'd been truly nice to her, in spite of his teasing, when she'd expected the opposite. Couldn't acknowledge that all those crazy things he'd made her feel when she was young and foolish were ten times more potent now that she was older and experienced.

She was immune to him, she really was. At least, she would be, as long as she stayed away from him. *Forever.*

Dressing carefully in a brightly colored sundress she'd picked up at Bergdorf Goodman earlier in the spring, Emma set out early Tuesday on her job hunt. Luckily, she had at least one pair of low-heeled sandals, since she didn't want to end up back in Ace bandages. She wore a bright yellow scarf tied loosely around her neck, needing the confidence of something hanging down the back of her neck, like her hair used to.

The dress was cute. The scarf was bright. Her makeup was carefully applied. And she was no longer limping. But even wearing all her feminine armor and looking healthy and in control, she confronted some really strange reactions in town.

"You're her, ain't ya?" This came from a young man tinkering under the hood of an old Ford Fairlane in the downtown parking lot where Emma parked her car.

"Her?"

"You're *the one*."

The one. Right. The one who'd been arrested for assaulting a local construction worker. Who'd had a screaming match with him. Who'd landed in jail looking like a homeless drunk picked up on the street during a late-night episode of *Cops*. The one who'd delayed an entire work crew with her bright red convertible yesterday morning.

Yeah, she was the one all right.

"Can I have your autograph?" someone else asked.

Emma stared past the mechanic toward a second young man sweeping the sidewalk in front of a pawnshop. His broom managed only to swirl up some dust and tree pollen on this hot June day, but his earnest expression said he wasn't going to give up his job. Nor give up talking to her.

"I saw her first," the first guy said. "I get an autograph."

"I'm nobody famous," Emma murmured, trying to step around the broom, and the pathetically small pile of dust the second man's efforts had garnered.

He didn't budge. "Sure you are." Then he looked around, as if to avoid being overheard, and lowered his voice. "Are you just, you know, in…in-congenital?"

"*Excuse* me?"

"It's incognito, dipshit," the first guy said with a snort. Then he turned to Emma. "And you don't have to be in disguise. Because I think it's too late. Everybody knows."

Everybody? Great. The whole town knew she had a record. She wondered how prospective employers would look on felons in the workplace. "Look, it wasn't a big deal. You don't know the whole story. I didn't do anything illegal and I'm sure the whole fuss will die down soon."

The broom-holder didn't look dissuaded. In fact, his

gaze was downright worshipful. "I think it's a big deal. Things like this don't happen very often in Joyful."

"He got what was coming to him. He deserved it."

Four eyes widened. The men asked in unison, "Deserved it?"

Emma nodded. "That foreman was begging for it."

"Begging…"

"He needed to be laid low. I happened to be the one to bring him down."

This time the sweeper dropped his broom, and the other guy his jaw. "*Laid*…low…" one of them whispered.

"Brought down flat," Emma added, wondering if the young men were on the slow side.

"He was flat?"

She nodded.

"On his back?" the other asked.

She nodded again.

They glanced at each other. "In *public?*"

"Yes, in public. Are you two hard of hearing or something?"

One whistled as the other slammed down the hood of his car.

"I gotta get me a camera."

"I gotta get me a pen."

"I gotta get my brother on the phone."

Emma clenched her jaw, really annoyed at the fuss these two were making. It didn't say much for how the rest of her day was going to go. "I barely touched him," she muttered.

"Who?"

"The foreman. I mean, I sort of ended up on top of him, but that was only because I lost my balance."

Wide-eyed? Now the two young men wore almost cartoon expressions of shock, with eyes bugging out of their sockets. Emma's explanation about how she'd flattened a construction worker was making things worse instead of better.

"Was this here, in town?" the sweeper asked in a whisper.

She nodded. "Yes, but honestly, there was no harm done. He was fine. I expect he's used to rough-and-tumble experiences in his job."

Mechanic boy jerked upright. "So do I. I'm rough. I tumble."

Sweeper elbowed him away. "I'm rougher. I can take anything. Right here on the hard concrete, or anywhere else. Tumble away."

Okay, she hadn't left home. She was still in bed, asleep, dreaming she'd fallen down Alice's rabbit hole and was having a conversation with Tweedle Dum and Tweedle Dumber.

"Land on *me*," the sweeper ordered. "I'm soft."

"She don't want *soft*, ya moron." The greasy mechanic gave her a salacious smile. "Do ya, sweetheart?"

Oh, lord, now she got it. They were *hitting* on her, not accusing her of being a criminal. They were trying to pick her up. Emma had just been so focused on the ridiculous arrest thing and how it would affect her job search that she hadn't been paying proper attention. "Thanks anyway, guys, I've got business to do today."

"Can I watch?" the mechanic said. "I won't say nothin', I'll just, uh, you know, be there."

Mercy, things must be boring in Joyful if amorous young men got their kicks out of watching women job-hunt.

"Why don't you go home to your wife?" the one who'd been sweeping said, his face growing red.

"Why don't you go home to your mama?" he got in return.

Ahh, such a proud display of Joyful's male population. They looked ready to start bitch-slapping one another at any minute.

The two men's voices escalated as they focused their attention strictly on each other. One called the other a soft-kneed, whipped sissy boy, which inspired the sweeper to step off the curb, swinging his broom in a threatening manner. Emma almost warned him about the broom swinging—given her recent experience with the cane—but refrained, since their distraction helped her escape.

They didn't even notice as she hurriedly ducked into the closest store—a dress shop. Hiding behind a rack of clothes near the front window, she peeked outside, noting the exact moment they realized she'd vanished. They both looked around, frowned, then started to yell at each other again.

"Bizarre," she whispered, wondering if there was a dearth of women in Joyful. Sure, she was cute and she got her share of male attention, but she had never inspired brawling on a public street. The closest she'd come to driving a man crazy with lust lately was when she'd told a Manhattan businessman that one of her investments had garnered a thirty percent return. It hadn't been her body he'd lusted for, just her brain. And her portfolio.

Correction, her *former* portfolio.

"You're her, aren'tcha?"

Oh, God, no. The news of her arrest must have been shouted from the pulpits of local churches yesterday. Giving her attention to the woman who had spoken, Emma said, "Good morning."

The woman—girl, really, she appeared to be a teenager—gave her a big toothy grin. "Mornin'. Don't pay any attention to them," she said, nodding out the window. "Tony'd never cheat on his wife, fr'fear she'd cut off his dick while he slept."

Emma raised a brow.

"'Cause, you know, that's what she tried to do when she caught him tinkering with Suellen Gantry's *tailpipe* when he was supposed to be working on her transmission."

So, Mr. Mechanic was named Tony. And he might very well have only a partial penis. She tucked the information away for future reference.

"And Bobby, well, he wouldn't know what to do with a girl if one landed in his lap. Naked." She lowered her voice. "I should know. He started looking mighty good after I'd helped empty a pony keg of beer at a grad night party last year." She gave a rueful shake of her head. "Me, naked on his lap and he passes out. Can you believe it?"

Emma didn't know whether to laugh or merely drop her jaw as this teenage girl with puffed up blond hair, big blue eyes and freckles rattled on like they were long-lost friends.

"Can I ask you a question?"

Here it comes.

"Uh, if you must," Emma replied slowly, hoping the girl could pick up on the unspoken "no" in her voice.

"How'd you get your start?"

Obviously subtle nuances in voice and speech were lost on the Joyful crowd. "Start?"

"You know…"

Emma rolled her eyes. "On my life of wickedness?"

The other girl didn't notice her sarcasm. She nodded so hard her hair flopped into her eyes and she had to reach up to sweep it away. "Yeah, how'd you know you were, you know, doing the right thing? That you could handle it?"

Emma sensed the girl would be bored stiff if she started telling stories about picnics in the grove, and summer vacations, and her grandmother's pecan pie. So she went straight for the good stuff, the *important* stuff, trying to impress on the girl how important it was to stand up for what you believed in.

"I'm not one to take things lying down."

The girls eyes widened. "You like it standing up? Lying down's no good?"

Letting out an unladylike snort, Emma shook her head. "Only if you want to get screwed."

When the girl's mouth dropped open, Emma nibbled her lip. "Sorry. What I mean is, a woman's got to be in control."

The girl nodded. "Yeah. In control." Then she cocked her head. "Uh, how?"

"Well, by being in the driver's seat. In charge."

"Like, on top, you mean?"

"Exactly. On top of things at all times," Emma replied.

The girl didn't look too enthused. "I'm not much good on top. I tire out. And things tend to jiggle around too much."

Emma almost laughed at the girl's unusual description. But it made sense. She sometimes got weary and her own emotions often "jiggled around" when she fought too hard for something she believed in. That didn't make it any less important to keep trying. "You just have to try harder. I've always believed in coming out swinging."

"You were a *swinger?*"

"Not literally. What I mean is, when I see something I want, I go after it. I'm not afraid and I can go head to head with anybody."

At least, the Emma she *used* to be was like that. Lately, she seemed to be more the blubbery, sad-sack, arrested type. But not anymore, dammit. Emma Jean Frasier had steel in her spine.

She'd been a hard-hitting New York financier for the past three years and it was about darn time she started acting like it again. Broke, jobless, arrested—so what? She was alive and healthy and she had her grandmother's beautiful house. That was a lot better off than some people had it.

She began to feel better than she had in days.

"So, you, uh, like going head to head," the girl was saying, looking shocked. "With *anybody?* Is that how you decided what you were going to do? Because you liked the, uh, head stuff?"

Emma nodded. "I've never backed away from something just because I thought it was too big or too hard for me to handle."

The girl's gulp was visible. "You have to be able to handle a lot of big heads, huh? Are they really big? Really *really* big?"

"There are definitely some big-headed men out there," Emma replied, thinking of the construction foreman and of her former boss at Parker Securities. "But I can give as good as I get."

The girl's jaw dropped. "Have they *told* you that? I mean, how'd you know you were good at giving the head stuff?"

Emma was barely listening. The more she talked, the better she felt, until she was pepping herself up, more than the teenage girl, who was positively goggle-eyed by this point. "It takes practice. Confidence. And a willingness to bite off as much as you can chew, without swallowing anything."

This time the girl started to cough into her fist. "Don't swallow anything," she mumbled when she could speak again.

"You okay?"

She nodded weakly. "Uh, yeah. I umh…well, I'm not much into swallowing, so that's not a problem. But I didn't even know there was biting and chewing involved."

Emma didn't entirely follow the girl's train of thought, but gave her a friendly smile, anyway. "It's okay. You're young. You're starting out right." Then she frowned. "Just remember, don't sell yourself short. You're worth a lot, don't go offering yourself up for free on guy's laps at parties."

"I won't," the girl said vehemently. "No more freebies."

They stared at each other for one moment, and Emma had to wonder if her makeup was smeared or if she had lipstick on her teeth. Because the teenager just stared and stared. "Is everything okay?"

The girl shook her head, hard. "Sorry. Fine. Uh, now, I know you came in here to hide, and you probably don't do your shopping at a place as boring as this, but can I help you anyway?"

Emma looked around at the small shop, with clothes racks only half-full and Giant Colosul Sale signs everywhere. The place looked like it was about to go out of business. If the bookkeeping was as bad as the spelling, she could see why.

Too bad she didn't have any money because she saw some really cute things hanging within reach. Well, within reach of her fingers. Not of her empty wallet.

"Do you like working here?" she asked, pulling her attention off an adorable beaded black cocktail dress.

The girl nodded so hard she almost smacked her chin on her collarbone. "Yes. Love it. I am *not* looking for another job."

"Good," Emma murmured. "I don't suppose you're hiring?"

The girl snickered. "Funny."

Emma had figured as much. Her luck couldn't possibly be good enough to have her ducking into a hiding spot and coming out with a job. No matter how much the store might need someone to do their books…or heck, dress their mannequins. Emma couldn't afford to be picky right now.

"I figured as much," she murmured to the girl, then peeked outside to see if the coast was clear. It was. Thank heaven.

So she'd struck out on her first try. She wouldn't give up. The day was young. The guys were gone. She had two good ankles.

How hard could it be to find a job in a small, friendly town like Joyful, Georgia?

JOHNNY ALMOST didn't recognize Emma when he spotted her, trudging up Bliss Avenue, late Wednesday afternoon. He hadn't seen her since Monday, which was fine with him. But now, the bright blond hair caught his attention, as did the hot pink dress that pressed against some illegally fine curves. The shoes dangling from one hand, the bright pink scarf trailing the ground, and the slumped shoulders, however, just didn't scream Emma Jean.

"Hey!" he called out when he realized the blonde was about to step into the street, onto the hot black pavement, in her bare feet. Not to mention into the path of J. R. Brandon's pickup, which had turned out of the post office parking lot.

His cry caught her attention and the woman turned around.

Yeah. It was her.

He shoulda stayed where he was—in the open doorway of the diner where he'd bought himself a sandwich for dinner. Or kept right on going where he'd been headed—back to his office to consume that sandwich during a rare late-night working glom.

Instead he walked down the block. Toward Emma. She watched him approach, saying nothing.

"Em," he said with a nod.

"Hello, Johnny."

"You out to break your head open again by stepping in front of a truck?"

She gave a disinterested look over her shoulder at the late-afternoon traffic. Not that the few cars chugging up the avenue could be considered traffic. But hit by a truck was hit by a truck. It didn't really matter how many cars were on the road in the meantime, did it?

"Guess I wasn't really paying attention."

"Anyone ever tell you how to cross a street."

She frowned. "Are you on safety patrol duty this week? Don't tell me, when you're not working as D.A., you're a substitute crossing guard?"

Testy, testy. But there wasn't any real heat in Emma Jean's words. She looked uninterested…distracted. "What's wrong?"

"Nothing."

"Bullshit."

"Tsk tsk. Such language."

He grinned. "Eve's not around. Besides, I have the feeling that kid has a heck of a vocabulary of her own."

For the first time, a real smile appeared briefly on her lips. "I think you're right."

Seeing the way Emma eyed his foam cup, from which he'd taken only a sip of his Coke, Johnny held it up. "Want some?"

She grabbed the cup with a grateful nod, and took a sip.

Johnny watched, the strangest heat filling his gut as her lips curled around the straw. When she pulled it away from her mouth, she left a smear of bright pink lipstick there.

He swallowed. Hard. Unable to tear his eyes off of that pink smear. Finally, though, he cleared his throat and gave himself a good mental kick. "Better?"

Nodding, she fanned herself with her free hand while she passed his drink back to him. "I've had yet another long day, just like yesterday. God, people in this town are so strange."

"How so?"

"They're either rude to my face or they ask a bunch of weird questions. Or they try to pick me up."

There was a perfect opening to bring up the whole porn star rumor, which was still flying around town like a spastic hummingbird. But Johnny didn't particularly want to get kicked in the nuts on a public street in broad daylight for asking a woman if she had sex for money.

Besides which, it didn't exactly seem polite.

"But nobody, *nobody* in this town is hiring."

That thrust the Emma-as-porn-star out of his mind, even though the image of Emma-having-sex was never far away.

"Hiring? What do you mean?"

"You know, the regular old kind of hiring. Cashier at the drug store. Teller at the bank. Popcorn maker at the movie theater." She gave a humorless little laugh. "Ditch digger. Anything at this point."

He just stared, until Emma's face pinkened and she drew in a few deep breaths. Her frustration had made her reveal more than she'd probably intended. Like the fact that she was staying. Here. In Joyful.

"This isn't a social visit for your ten-year reunion, is it?" he asked slowly, hearing the dread in his voice.

She shook her head.

"You're staying."

She nodded.

Staying. Christ, she was staying. This wasn't a week or ten-day-long game of let's-torment-Johnny. This was a frigging nightmare straight from the most tortured part of his subconscious. Emma Jean was moving back to Joyful for good. "You *can't* mean it."

She crossed her arms, the pose doing wicked things against the low neckline of her silky dress. The skin there was pinkened. She'd apparently forgotten the danger of the Southern sun, and he had the most ridiculous urge to yank her dress up.

Only to protect her from sunburn. Not to, uh, cover anything, which would imply that he was affected by the way she looked. *No sir. Not this boy.*

"I do mean it. I'm here to stay. At least for a while."

Her words shook off his lapse into horndog land. "Why the hell would you want to move back to Joyful?"

"Why the hell did you never leave?"

"I *did* leave," he shot back.

"For college. Then you came right back here to drop into your role as wicked Walker man. Why? Did you figure you couldn't make it anywhere else?"

Direct hit. It wasn't precisely true, but Emma's accusation had crossed his own mind once or twice in the past. Leave it to her to zero right in on it.

Coming back here to the familiar faces and the familiar pace and the all-too-familiar lifestyle had been almost too easy. He'd sometimes thought about things he might have done, places he could have gone, if he hadn't felt the need to come back here and…what? Live up—or *down*—to the Walker name? Play devil's advocate to the lousy sheriff? Enable his mother to hold her head up high? All of the above?

Yeah. He'd sometimes wondered if moving back to Joyful had been one big cop-out. But damned if he wanted Emma Jean Frasier to be the one throwing that in his face.

He stepped closer, crowding her, suddenly angry with her for accusing him of nothing more than what he'd thought of himself. "We're talking about you. Not me. Why are you looking for work?"

She inched a step back. "For the usual reasons."

"Like?"

"Gee, a paycheck? Benefits? A regular meal once in a while?"

He'd become used to her sarcasm in the few days she'd been back. He'd even begun to like it, though he'd never have expected it from the sweet angel he'd known in the old days. But he sensed that beneath her smart-ass bravado, she was all-too-serious. "Since when does the spoiled rich girl need to worry about a regular meal?"

She countered with a question of her own. "Since when is it any of your business?" Then, as if she knew he was going to argue the point, she quickly changed the subject. "I don't suppose you've given any thought to looking into the construction of the club. Or gotten me a copy of the tax record?"

The mulish expression on her face told him it was point-less to go back to the issue of her job. She'd changed the subject, end of story.

Northerners.

"Well?" she prodded. "Have you learned anything?"

He had. He'd just been trying to figure out how to tell her what he'd found. She wasn't going to like the answer, not one bit. But she also didn't look like she'd have the patience to keep waiting.

Sooner or later, she'd go back out to the construction

area. He couldn't stand to ever see her in that dirty little jail cell again. And he'd sooner cut off a limb than have to console her while she cried her eyes out one more time.

Or see her get all fired up and spitting mad until his blood was boiling right along with hers. For all the wrong reasons that had nothing to do with the strip club and everything to do with wanting to strip her and take her up against the closest wall.

"Yeah. I did," he bit out.

"Well?"

He didn't want to have the conversation here on the corner. Taking her arm, he said, "Let's go to my office and talk."

She shook her head. "Just tell me what you learned, okay? I'm tired and I haven't had a very good day."

Seeing the determination on her face, he did as she asked. "Your grandma sold the lot right before she died, Emma Jean."

She sucked in a shocked breath, her eyes widening.

"I'm sorry to tell you this, but it's true. I looked up the records myself."

"I don't believe it," she said.

His jaw tightened. "I'm not making it up."

She shook her head, looking dazed. "I'm sure you're not…I just…I can't believe she went ahead and did it."

"You mean, you *knew* she was thinking about selling out?"

"She told me she was considering it." Emma met his stare, her amber eyes glassy and punctuated by dark circles beneath them. "But I never thought she'd really go through with it."

The tremor in her voice confirmed the one question he'd had. A part of him had wondered if Emma, herself, had bought the property from her grandmother, not wanting the truth known because of the kind of business now being built there. Obviously not. "So you really have nothing to do with Joyful Interludes?"

She raised a curious brow.

"The club."

"That's the name of the place?"

He nodded.

"And it's really a…a strip club?"

"Yeah, from what I hear."

"Joyful's gotten big enough to need a strip club?"

"Back to that naked woman issue, hmm?" he asked, remembering their conversation Friday in his car.

"I can't believe quiet little Joyful is allowing this to happen. Where are the protestors? Why hasn't anyone raised a fuss? It's like everyone in this town is asleep!"

It had surprised him, too, though he expected things were heating up in the church meeting rooms and at the local bridge games. Just because nobody had shown up with the picket signs didn't mean nobody was painting them in their garages.

Doing the groundwork for Emma had aroused his own curiosity. Funny how quiet—and how fast—the whole deal had been…from old Mrs. Frasier selling her land to an out-of-state corporation, who then put through some slickly worded paperwork to get the zoning and land use applications approved. He wouldn't go so far as to call the deal a dirty one, but it didn't seem to be entirely clean and aboveboard, either.

Then again, here in Joyful, nothing ever was.

"I can't believe the residents aren't in an uproar," she mumbled, still looking dazed over what she'd learned. The late-afternoon breeze wisped a strand of her short, silky hair across her face, but she didn't seem to care enough to brush it away.

"I imagine there's some talk," he admitted, forcing himself to focus on the issue. Not on her hair. Not on her lips. Not on that sassy little smear of pink lipstick on his straw.

It was the color of a ripe strawberry. His favorite fruit.

"Nobody found out anything until last week when the billboard went up," he finally said.

"So it was very hush-hush. Isn't that unusual for this place, where everybody whispers about every kid who's ten minutes late for his curfew or they discuss what color underwear the new Sunday school teacher's wearing?"

He could have defended Joyful's gossip line as being fully up to date and functional. But he didn't figure now was a good time to mention the leopard-spotted thong rumor. Or the whole porn star thing.

"Yeah, I guess it is," he said with a nod. If he gave a rat's ass either way about this pitiful town he called home, he might have cared enough to investigate. But he didn't. Joyful could get as corrupt and nasty as any other town and he wouldn't go out of his way to reread a single zoning law.

Unless…

"Johnny, isn't there anything you can do about this?"

Damn. Unless *that*. Unless someone—like *her*—asked him to.

"What do you mean?"

"I mean, it's bad enough my family land has passed out of the family. I can't imagine it turning into some tacky roadside strip club. Is there some legal way around this?"

She was asking for his help. Doing the one thing guaranteed to get him to do what he sure as shit didn't want to do. One more word, and he'd be a goner. If Emma Jean said "please," in that sweet, soft way, with her pretty pink lips, he'd promise her just about anything. At least, that's how things had gone in the past.

Not this time.

Tsking, he shook his head and gave her what he hoped was a salacious smile. "You asking me for another favor? Better watch out, Emma Jean, associating with the likes of a Walker. Don't you remember? You lie down with dogs and one day you may just get bit."

His choice of words probably hadn't been wise, considering the way he'd nibbled on her neck, memorizing the taste of her skin, leaving his mark on her that night in the gazebo. But they had obviously done the trick.

Because she remembered, too. Her lips parted as she sucked in a quick breath. Suddenly it didn't seem to matter that they were standing outside, on a public street, in plain view of anyone in the diner, or the courthouse, or the hardware shop across the street. They seemed very much alone for a long heady moment, full of memory and expectation. And a sultry kind of want he didn't think either one of them had ever fully gotten over.

Want. Need. Hunger. Sweetness. Craziness.

Her.

"Are you threatening to bite me?" she whispered, her voice husky and filled with innuendo.

"You never know what a Walker is capable of." He reached up and toyed with the neckline of her dress, unable to resist upping the stakes in this challenging game. He ran his fingertip back and forth. Back and forth. Brushing her skin and pushing the sleeve farther off her shoulder. No bra strap blocked the way. The realization made him hiss out one long breath.

She closed her eyes, then opened them. "Maybe you should be the one who's careful. Because maybe I know how to bite, too."

Oh, wouldn't he love to find out. He'd love her nibbling

on his chest. His arms. Using her wicked mouth and her perfect lips and her hot pink tongue and her sharp white teeth on him. Every bit of him. Then he saw the look in her eyes and realized she'd been getting even, paying him back for what he'd said.

"You don't want to start this game with me," he replied, his voice low and intense as he strove for control.

He meant it. Emma Jean was reaching into the fire here, like she never had before. Putting dangerous thoughts in his head. Dangerous, sensual thoughts he had no business thinking. Not here, not now. Certainly not about her.

"Who says it's a game, Johnny?" she whispered, her eyes sparkling with challenge. "Besides, you're the one who started it."

"Yeah, and you'd better be careful I don't finish it."

They both knew what he meant. Both knew that if he tried, he could back her up against the closest tree, and do pretty much whatever he wanted to her. Flip up her dress and take her higher than she'd ever been. The rest of Joyful be damned.

Unfortunately, he wasn't the only one who held that power. Because if Emma reached for him, he'd be a goner. At her mercy. Up for anything she wanted, any time she wanted it.

Like now.

He knew she was going to stoke the flames about two seconds before she rose on tiptoe, slid her arms around his neck and pulled him down to meet her lips. Her kiss was hot and wet, openmouthed and carnal. Sinful, even, on such a bright, sunshiny day.

And it blew his mind.

She tasted so good. So luscious he had to pull her closer,

then tilt his head so he could truly devour her. Their tongues met and tangled in a brief power play until they settled together in a sweet, languorous thrust that both gave and took.

Then, finally, after he'd completely lost his sense of time and place, she pulled away and took a step back. Her chin up, she tried to look steady and calm, but he saw the way her whole body swayed and knew she was as affected as he.

"Maybe *you're* the one who should be careful," she finally said through deeply inhaled breaths. "Because sometimes good little girls do know how to bite back."

CHAPTER TEN

ONCE CLAIRE had decided to make some changes in her life, she didn't waste any time. She was fired up, excited, energetic, feeling like someone who'd just woken up after a long nap.

She'd thrown away her secret stash of chocolate and made an appointment to get a real haircut. Pitching her sweatpants and long T-shirts in the trash, she'd dug out some of her business clothes to see how much weight she'd have to lose—or how big a girdle she'd have to buy—to get back into them. She'd even skipped her favorite soaps two days in a row.

No more soaps. No more 2:00 p.m. chocolate and potato chip binges. No more naptime for baby and mommy. No more shopping trips with flip-flops and ponytails and not one speck of makeup on her face.

No more nights in white cotton nightgowns, lying next to her husband, wondering if he was going to turn off the news, give her a nice peck on the forehead, then roll over to go to sleep. As usual. Or if tonight might actually bring a return of intimacy to her marriage.

Claire was done laying around waiting to see if she was gonna get screwed, literally or figuratively. It was time to take life by the balls and live it again.

"What balls?"

Claire hadn't even realized she'd been muttering aloud until she heard Eve's voice from the back seat of the car.

"Nothin', honey, I was just talking to myself."

Eve shrugged, not asking a million questions for a change. Claire knew why. Her confident, tough little girl was a wee bit nervous about today.

"Mama, are you sure about this day-care stuff?" Eve asked for about the dozenth time since they'd left the house.

"Yep, honey, I'm sure. It's only for three mornings a week. It'll be fun for you."

Eve scowled. "What if Courtney Foster is there?"

"Well, then," Claire said, casting her daughter a stern look in the rearview mirror, "you'll have more chances to try to make friends with her."

She'd contacted a local preschool about getting a spot for Eve in the fall. But in the meantime, she was putting her in her church day-care center three mornings a week, where Eve already knew the teachers and many of the children. Three mornings during which Claire could do whatever she pleased.

It wasn't just good for her, it'd be good for Eve, too. At the very least, it would teach her how to get along with other kids—rather than beating them up—before she started kindergarten.

Eve made a disgusted face. "I don't want to be her friend."

"Hmm…that sounds like another little girl I know. A girl named Angelica," Claire said, knowing Eve's hot button and pushing it.

Her daughter stuck her lip out. "I am not like Angelica on *Rugrats*. She's a bad girl."

Claire caught her daughter's eye again and winked to

let her know she was teasing. Eve responded with a giggle, but that spark of devilment remained in her pretty eyes.

Lordy, her daughter was holy terror. And she loved her like mad. She had since the first moment she'd felt her child flutter around in her stomach when she'd been four months pregnant. Claire would miss the munchkin, but Eve would be better—*happier*—if she was raised by a mother who didn't resent everything around her because she hadn't grasped at a chance to do something more with her life.

"Why didn't Daddy come with us today?"

She couldn't tell her daughter the real reason: because Tim didn't know. She, uh, hadn't told him yet. But he'd find out soon enough. It might take him a couple of days before he noticed she wasn't in the house as much. Sooner or later—probably when they ran out of Eve's favorite ice cream and he came griping to Claire about it—he'd figure it out.

She wasn't doing anything wrong. She and Tim had agreed before she ever got pregnant that she'd be a stay-at-home mom for at least the first year or two of their child's life. They'd *never* agreed that she'd become a drone. A quiet, overweight woman whose entire life revolved around her husband's work schedule and her four-year-old's play dates and temper tantrums.

Four years. Quite long enough. It was time for Claire to do some living outside her nice house on her nice street in her nice town.

She'd tried talking to Tim about it in the past. But every time Claire mentioned going back to work at the newspaper, he came up with a reason why she shouldn't. Okay, so her job with the *Joyful Gazette* hadn't made her much money. And it certainly hadn't been Pulitzer Prize stuff. She'd covered everything from high school football games to garden club fund-raisers. She'd interviewed farmers who grew gourds shaped like Elvis, and local politicians who always said the same thing: "I'm a good ol' boy, vote for me."

But she'd loved working, really loved it. Apparently, Linda Whitaker, her old boss who'd hired Claire right out of high school, had loved her work, too. Because the minute she'd heard Claire's voice on the phone Monday morning, she'd asked her if she was finally ready to come back to work.

The answer was yes. Part-time at first, but definitely yes.

"Mama?"

"Yes, honey," she murmured, smiling at how enthusiastic Linda had been about her return.

"Let's make a deal," Eve said in that singsong voice that Claire knew only too well.

Uh-oh.

"If you don't tell Daddy I acted like Angelica, I won't tell him you said balls."

Claire sucked her lower lip into her mouth and slowly began to shake her head, trying not to laugh. Eve had no idea what Claire had meant, but she'd obviously zeroed right in on the tone and recognized a naughty word when she heard one.

Then she nodded. "Deal."

Eve's smile was decidedly self-satisfied.

God help her, it was definitely time to get back into the workplace. If only so she could get back some of her negotiating skills. Because she was definitely going to need them to raise her precocious daughter.

CONTRARY TO her confident predictions to Johnny about being able to deal with the club issue on her own, Emma needed help. She'd tried going down to the courthouse and looking up the tax records, to no avail. The county workers there were about as fast-paced as everyone else in Joyful. Meaning, they didn't wind up to start their days until about ten minutes before lunchtime. And they mentally called it quits a half hour after they got back.

She imagined prison guards were more helpful and friendly.

To make things even worse, her search for employment hadn't been any more successful. By the time she got back to the house on Friday afternoon, she was tired and annoyed. Frustrated. And still jobless.

"I can't believe nobody in this town is hiring," she muttered aloud as she kicked off her sandals to pad around in bare feet. The smooth, polished oak floor felt cool against her toes, a relief after yet another stifling hot June day.

Since she wasn't sure she'd be able to afford to pay the electric bill next month, she'd been getting by without using the window air conditioners Grandma Emmajean had had installed sometime in the past ten years. Today, however, she couldn't stand it. She walked over to the one sticking into the room from the front window and jerked the switch on. Rewarded by a blast of cold air, she closed her eyes and reveled in it, letting it cool off her overheated skin. And her temper.

Emma certainly hadn't expected to land in a permanent job, one suited to her qualifications. There weren't any brokerage houses in Joyful, as far as she knew. But jeez, she couldn't even get work as a bagger at the Joyful Grocery Store!

Of course, she hadn't actually applied there. The memory of the faces of those girls at the checkout counters the day she'd hit town had made her pass by the store. Still, she'd sure tried a number of other places, and had gotten the same odd reactions: either gawking shock, laughter or rudeness.

Apparently everybody in Joyful still thought of her as the rich outsider. Maybe they considered her job hunt a joke. The woman who ran the Let Your Hair Down salon certainly seemed to think so, since she and her clients had laughed uproariously when Emma had tried to apply for the wash-girl position.

With the exception of last year when she was bald, she'd been washing her own hair for a long time. How much skill did it take? Apparently, according to the salon owner, more than Emma possessed. Though, she had laughingly said that if Emma showed up bearing one of her grandma's pecan pies, she might reconsider the matter.

Speaking of which…Emma still hadn't found the recipes. Not that she had time to start baking—or the money to buy the ingredients.

Glancing at the answering machine, she sent up a quick, silent prayer for messages. The red light wasn't blinking…but maybe the bulb was out. Half holding her breath, she punched the play button.

Nothing. Not a single, "We got your application and will let you know when we have an opening." Not even a "Hey, heard you were back in town and look forward to seeing you at the reunion."

Nobody had come knocking on her door bearing muffins or anything else. No calls all week, except for two from Claire. No word from Jimbo Boyd, in spite of her numerous messages.

Emma was beginning to wonder if she'd turned into the invisible woman.

She knew better than to even try turning on her laptop to see if she had any e-mails responding to the résumés she'd sent out. Until the SEC investigation was over with, she and all her former co-workers were on the outs in the financial world. She'd known sending out the résumés had been nothing more than flinging hopeful coins in the World Wide Web fountain, praying her wish would come true.

She had to admit the worst part, what had really been bugging her: no Johnny. She hadn't seen or heard from him since Wednesday when she'd given in to some sadomasochistic impulse and kissed him.

Kissing Johnny always got her into trouble. This time it'd left her shaking, empty and confused for forty-eight hours.

She might not have seen him, but she'd sure heard about him. The women in this town seemed to enjoy talking about their hunky D.A., particularly when Emma was within earshot. She'd overheard two tellers at the bank gossiping about him. The waitresses at the diner, the women at the beauty parlor, they'd all somehow managed to bring up his name whenever Emma was around. It was a wonder nobody came right out and asked if the sex had been any good on prom night.

Uh, yeah, that'd be a big 10-4.

It was her own fault. She figured a bunch of people had to have seen—and gossiped about—the kiss she'd laid on him in the town square.

Laid. Hmm…

No.

Smothering a sigh, she went into the kitchen and got down Grandma Emmajean's coffee can. The pile of bills was still sizeable, mainly because Emma had been down-right thrifty this week, living primarily on lettuce and cof-fee.

Which was why she was about to lose her mind with a craving.

Chocolate. She needed it. Needed it bad. Needed it now. Sex might have done as an alternative, but she couldn't guarantee it.

Unfortunately, there was no sex to be had, *Johnny Walker get out of my head,* and no chocolate, either. Noth-ing. No stale candy bars, no dried out Kisses floating around in the bottom of the candy jar. Not a sticky fudge pop in the freezer or a bottle of Hershey's syrup in the fridge that she could squirt straight into her mouth.

It seemed utterly pathetic to get in her car and drive back downtown for a Baby Ruth bar, but she was seriously con-sidering it. Then she spied the chocolate baking squares up next to the baking powder and vanilla up on a shelf in the pantry.

It'd do.

Grabbing the box, she tore it open and eyed the waxy hunk of black stuff inside. "Chocolate chips," she mut-tered. "It'll taste like chocolate chips."

Only, it didn't, which she realized after she took one tentative nibble on a corner. *Unsweetened.* "Blech."

Grandma Emmajean had had some sugar left in her pantry when she arrived, but one of the first things Emma had done was to make a pitcher of sweet tea. It'd been pure heaven after drinking the stuff Manhattan called iced tea for ten years. But she'd used up all the sugar. Inside the pantry, however, was a box of sweetener packets. Desper-ate times...

"What the heck?"

She went to work, and soon discovered that chocolate baking squares coated in sprinkled-on sugar-substitute weren't going to kill her. They definitely weren't orgasmic. They weren't even entirely palatable. But they were cheap, and at hand. And they contained cocoa.

After she finished as much as she could stand of one, though, she still felt…hungry. Ravenous. In need of—*craving*—something. Lousy chocolate hadn't even come *close* to making her feel better. She wasn't sure Godiva would have, either.

"It's the heat," she whispered. This heat was making her itchy and restless and tense. That's all, she just needed to cool off. More sugar wouldn't hurt, either.

She grabbed the pitcher of tea out of the fridge and poured a big cup, filled to the top with ice. The coldness of the glass provided sweet relief to her fingertips, so she lifted it to her face. When the condensation touched her temples it brought instant delight.

Sipping her tea, she returned to the front room, toward the air conditioner. Lord, it was hot. New York City could be stifling in the summer, particularly with millions of tourists everywhere. But Georgia was downright wicked.

That had to explain why she was feeling this way. Hot and uncomfortable.

"And wicked?" she mused aloud.

Maybe. Just a little.

Before she could prevent it, an image of Johnny's face flashed through her mind. She sipped from her glass again, remembering that moment right here in her living room the other day, when he'd driven her home. She knew what he'd been thinking…because she was thinking the same thing.

About their kiss. The insane way they'd lost themselves

in each other on her kitchen table. At the gazebo. In the square Wednesday when she'd threatened to bite him.

Anywhere. Everywhere.

"Stop thinking about him," she muttered, knowing it was simply heat and frustration and, yes, loneliness making her so jumpy and restless. What a pathetic picture she made. All alone, devouring pseudo-chocolate and sugar, and sidling up to an air conditioner to give herself some satisfaction on a lonely Friday evening.

She stepped closer to the vent, turning the unit up to full-blast and letting cold air stream onto her neck. If she was going to get some relief, she might as well go all out to enjoy it. Reaching up, she unfastened the top few buttons of her scoop-neck dress. It fell open and the frigid air touched the curves of her breasts.

"Mmm." She sighed as she brought her glass to her lips and sipped again.

But she still wasn't cool enough. She wanted to strip off her clothes, to dive into a pool of icy water. Or to go out to the lake at a nearby state park and swim naked, like she and Claire had done once or twice in high school.

She wanted raw physical pleasure.

Joyful, however, had seen enough of her naked for one lifetime. Her skinny-dipping days were over. She had no pool, and the sprinkler was a poor substitute. So the A.C. and the icy glass would have to do.

Reaching down, she pulled the bottom of her short dress higher, until her legs were bared all the way up to her tiny pink panties. Grandma Emmajean had probably never envisioned her A.C. being used like this when she'd had it installed at hip-level in her front window. But to Emma, it was pure heaven.

Her thighs were damp with sweat, and her skin instantly

An Important Message from the Editors

Dear Reader,

Because you've chosen to read one of our fine romance novels, we'd like to say "thank you!" And, as a **special** way to thank you, we've selected <u>two more</u> of the books you love so well **plus** an exciting Mystery Gift to send you — absolutely <u>FREE</u>!

Please enjoy them with our compliments...

Pam Powers

Lift here

Peel off seal and place inside...

How to validate your Editor's *"Thank You"* FREE GIFT

1. Peel off gift seal from front cover. Place it in space provided at right. This automatically entitles you to receive 2 FREE BOOKS and a fabulous mystery gift.

2. Send back this card and you'll get 2 brand-new *Romance* novels. These books have a cover price of $5.99 or more each in the U.S. and $6.99 or more each in Canada, but they are yours to keep absolutely free.

3. There's no catch. You're under no obligation to buy anything. We charge nothing—ZERO—for your first shipment. And you don't have to make any minimum number of purchases— not even one!

4. The fact is, thousands of readers enjoy receiving their books by mail from The Reader Service. They enjoy the convenience of home delivery...they like getting the best new novels at discount prices BEFORE they're available in stores... and they love their Heart to Heart subscriber newsletter featuring author news, special book offers, book reviews and much more!

5. We hope that after receiving your free books you'll want to remain a subscriber. But the choice is yours— to continue or cancel, any time at all! So why not take us up on our invitation, with no risk of any kind. You'll be glad you did!

GET A *Free* MYSTERY GIFT...

SURPRISE MYSTERY GIFT COULD BE YOURS **FREE** AS A SPECIAL "THANK YOU" FROM THE EDITORS

▼ DETACH AND MAIL CARD TODAY!

Yes! I have placed my
Editor's "Thank You" seal in the
space provided at right. Please
send me 2 free books and a
fabulous mystery gift. I
understand I am under no
obligation to purchase any
books, as explained on the
back and on the opposite page.

**PLACE
FREE GIFT
SEAL
HERE**

393 MDL D39E   193 MDL D39F

FIRST NAME

LAST NAME

ADDRESS

APT.#

CITY

STATE/PROV.

ZIP/POSTAL CODE

(ED2-HQ-05)

Thank You!

The Reader Service — Here's How It Works:

Accepting your 2 free books and gift places you under no obligation to buy anything. You may keep the books and gift and return the shipping statement marked "cancel." If you do not cancel, about a month later we'll send you 3 additional books and bill you just $4.99 each in the U.S., or $5.49 each in Canada, plus 25¢ shipping & handling per book and applicable taxes if any.* That's the complete price and — compared to cover prices starting from $5.99 each in the U.S. and $6.99 each in Canada — it's quite a bargain! You may cancel at any time, but if you choose to continue, every month we'll send you 3 more books, which you may either purchase at the discount price or return to us and cancel your subscription.

*Terms and prices subject to change without notice. Sales tax applicable in N.Y. Canadian residents will be charged applicable provincial taxes and GST.

loosened in relief. Lifting one foot, she placed it on the closest chair, and dropped her head back, letting all that coldness touch her where she was so very hot.

Her face. Her chest. Her throat. Her thighs. Between them.

That brought *his* image back to her mind and she grew even hotter. Moister.

It was Johnny's fault she was in this state. Because thinking of him moments ago had flooded her with the kind of want no air conditioner was going to relieve. Even when he was nowhere around he left her hungry and needing.

She lifted her glass again, touching it to her cheek and her throat, letting one drop of condensation fall to her chest, where it trailed away between her breasts. And she finally began to cool off, to relax, to loosen up and enjoy the sensation.

God, it was glorious. Decadent, almost. So delightful she simply had to close her eyes and revel in it, focused purely on the pleasure of the coldness on her skin, the whoosh of the air and the hum of the A.C. unit drowning out every other sound.

Which was why she didn't hear anything other than the pounding of her own pulse surging through her veins.

Not until she opened her eyes and saw Johnny Walker standing inside her house.

JOHNNY HAD NEVER imagined when he decided to swing by Emma Jean's place to talk to her about her grandmother's property Friday evening that he'd be walking into his own private version of heaven. Or hell. He hadn't yet decided which.

It kinda depended on what happened in the next ninety seconds.

He couldn't tear his hungry gaze off Emma, hot and glistening and almost purring in satisfaction as she cooled herself in front of the air conditioner. She was toying with the moisture on her glass, rubbing it between her fingertips, then touching her pulse points—her throat, her wrists, behind her ears—as if applying a heady perfume.

Not that she needed it. Emma'd always smelled sweet. He knew if he stepped closer and inhaled, his head would fill with all that sweetness. Not to mention the intoxicating, musky scent of aroused woman.

Because she *was* aroused. From the way she rubbed the wetness against her skin, to those sultry lips parted to allow a moan of pleasure, she was the very picture of a woman in heat.

The moment was intensely personal. Sexual, though she was alone. He had the feeling if he stood here long enough, she was soon going to touch herself the way he'd been wanting to touch her since she'd walked back into his life a week ago.

Intimately. Erotically. Thoroughly.

He should have walked away a few minutes ago. Should have turned around and stepped off the porch when she didn't answer the bell or his knock. But he'd caught a glimpse of her through the small window in the door, and had grown worried when she didn't answer.

So he'd had to play her frigging hero once more.

He'd opened the door, just to check on her. And had stumbled onto one of the most erotic moments he'd ever witnessed. Lord have mercy he had never seen a more sensual sight.

Remaining frozen in place, he watched her, knowing she was unaware of his presence. Emma's hair was wildly tangled around her face, the short curls dancing at her temples and blowing across her pinkened cheeks. Her head was thrown back, a look of pure satisfaction on her face. Her parted lips glistened as she moistened them with her little pink tongue.

Another iron band of his control snapped.

Emma's eyes remained closed. Looking at the tempting sheen of sweat on her throat, his mouth went dry. He wanted to taste that spot, to indulge in the salty flavor of her body.

There. And everywhere else.

When he finally managed to tear his eyes off her lips, her throat and her neck, his whole body grew taut with anticipation.

He looked lower.

Torture. God, this was torture.

She was clothed, but only barely. Her dress was unbuttoned. Given how much it revealed, she might as well not have been wearing it at all. One side of the flowered fabric fell away low enough to reveal the lacy edge of a pink bra which barely covered the curve of her breast.

The other side had fallen even lower, into downright sinful territory. His hands clenched at his sides with the need to cup her, touch her, hold her. One dark, puckered nipple pressed against the pink lace in sweet invitation and his lips parted as he imagined encircling it. Tasting it. Sucking her until she wrapped her fingers in his hair and begged him never to stop. Like she had that night.

When she lifted a hand, he knew what she was going to do. Silently, he watched her trail her hand over her body, from hip to neck, grazing her breast with the tips of her fingers. A light touch. A brief caress. But so utterly, heartstoppingly seductive he nearly echoed her deep, throaty moan of pleasure.

Johnny's mouth, which had gone dry, suddenly grew wet with hunger. Ravenous, insatiable hunger. But it was when he finally dropped his gaze to *really* look at the rest of her that he truly lost his mind.

Even from a few feet away, he could see every bit of her legs, from the tips of her pink-tinted toenails, all the way up the endless length of her thighs. He groaned softly when he saw how the pale skin there had risen into goose bumps under the chilled flow from the vent.

Then he looked higher. God almighty, higher. To the pale pink panties which did absolutely nothing to shield her soft curls from his stare. To that place where he'd found heaven on earth for a few hours ten years ago.

One leg was bent, raised, exposing her secrets. She looked pagan. Open. Willing. Damp. Taking pleasure any way she could get it, from the top of her head to the bottom of her feet. And every luscious inch in between.

Right now, he wanted her more than he wanted to live to see another day.

"Johnny?"

He didn't realize she'd opened her eyes until she spoke. Pulling his attention back up to her face, he let his expression speak for him.

She understood. She didn't say another word, she merely stared at him. Not moving. Not smiling. Just watching with a heavy-lidded intensity that told him she was every bit as aware of what could happen here in the next few seconds.

Her lips remained parted as she sucked in deeper breaths, her chest heaving. But she made no effort whatsoever to cover herself.

She was wanton. Open eyes. Open dress. Open legs.

And issuing one hell of a silent invitation.

"Do I go or do I stay?" he asked, his voice nearly a growl.

If she told him to go, he would, but not without one taste, one hot, sweet taste of her.

If she told him to stay, he'd be tasting her all weekend.

"Stay."

STAY.

Emma knew what she was really saying with that one little word, knew full well what kind of bridge she was crossing here, but she couldn't bring herself to care.

She wasn't asking him to merely remain in her house. She was ordering him to satisfy her craving. Give her what she needed. To take her. Hot and hard and fast and now.

Right now.

Johnny dropped the papers he'd been holding. The pages rode the current of air to the floor, landing beneath the coffee table. He ate up the distance between them in two large steps, and had her in his arms in the time it took her to take one deep breath. His hungry mouth devoured hers, his ravenous kiss telling her just how thin the last thread of his restraint had been.

Hers had snapped completely when she'd opened her eyes to see him watching her with pure, undiluted want. She'd never seen such a look on a man's face. A look that said he'd rather lose an arm than wait one more second to touch her. A frenzied expression saying his mind had completely given over control of his actions to his body.

That body. Lord have mercy....

That it was *this* man—the one she wanted beyond all reason and against her own better judgment—made it even more potent.

She wanted so much. Everything. As much as he could give her as many times as she could get it.

One of his hands was twined in her hair and he cupped her head while ravaging her mouth with his own. Their tongues met and danced and gave and took as their bodies melded together to form one fluid shape.

Here, *here* was what she'd been hungry for, what her body had been crying out for when she'd foolishly tried to sate her appetite with chocolate, sugar and cold air. She didn't want sweet, she wanted dangerously spicy. Didn't want cold. She wanted sizzling hot. Frenzied. God help her, if he was the least bit kind or tender, she might have to bite him as she'd threatened to the other day.

He seemed to know, because he wasn't gentle and careful as he'd been so many years ago. His groans were guttural, his mouth, his lips, oh, lord, his *tongue,* were unrelenting, demanding, holding nothing back. His kisses were strong and wet and deep as if he wanted to eat her up. Gobble her down. Take her inside him.

But that was her prerogative.

"Touch me," she ordered, against his open mouth, almost whimpering with her need for more.

His free hand moved instantly to the sleeve of her dress. She heard it tear as he pushed it away but didn't care.

"Tell me what you were thinking before you saw me standing there," he muttered as he moved lower to press kisses against her jaw, her throat, her neck.

She could barely think to answer. "I was hot…"

"Steaming," he hissed, his breath tickling her ear as he nibbled around her small gold earring.

"Uncomfortable."

"Aching."

"I was aching for *this,*" she managed to whisper when he nipped at her neck.

"I know."

Then he shut up and focused on ripping her dress the rest of the way off her body, until it fell apart and landed on the floor at their feet. She'd barely kicked it away when he ran one strong hand down her side, lingering along the curve of her backside, but not removing her panties. He stroked her thigh, then lower, until he could grab her leg at the knee. Lifting it, he hooked it over one of his lean hips, until her lower body arched into him.

"Oh, yes," she groaned as that hot, hungry, empty part of her met the thick erection his zipper could barely contain.

With his arm supporting her around the waist, she leaned back, grinding into him, torturing them both. He responded with a groan before bending low over her, covering the tip of her breast with his mouth. The wet warmth of his tongue against the lace of her bra did crazy things to her nipple and sent sparks shooting down her body. Lower. Until she had to jerk against him to try to gain some relief from the ache between her legs.

"You gonna come against me or with me?" he muttered before nudging her bra away from her breast with his mouth.

"Both?" she asked.

He chuckled, deep and evil-like, then sucked the sensitive tip of her breast, hard, flicking his tongue over her and drawing deep.

Oh, mercy…she was being completely devoured. The pressure began to build to a fever pitch. Just his touch, his hands, his lips, and the feel of all that male heat hidden behind his clothes made Emma start to shake and quiver.

Her response to his sexy question hadn't been off the mark.

Johnny let go of her leg long enough to unzip his pants

and free himself from them. He tore her panties to the side, and when wet, moist flesh slid against hot, hard skin, Emma's entire body shuddered with rolls and waves of pleasure. Endless, moan-inducing pleasure.

"Do it," he ordered.

And she did.

Returning his lips to hers, he took her orgasmic cries into his mouth as if tasting them, consuming them.

Emma's legs were rapidly turning to jelly, and he seemed to know it, because he pushed her back, until her calves met the sofa. Then farther, until she fell down upon it. She lay there, still gasping for breath as she recovered from her orgasm, and watched him strip off his shirt.

Though it had just been sated, the intense need began to rebuild as more of his incredible body was revealed. The hard chest. Those arms. Strong, roped with muscle, like the rest of him. Her fingers tingled with the need to touch him, and her mouth grew dry wanting to sample the way his skin tasted.

She lowered her gaze, her mouth falling open on a hitchy little cry as she saw him—*that* part of him—for the first time in the light of day. She'd lost her virginity to this man. But she'd never seen all he had to offer. "Oh, my God."

He was utterly delicious, hard and thick, protruding from his unzipped trousers, all that throbbing male heat within her grasp.

So she grasped. Ignoring his groan, she cupped him, stroked him, squeezing his shaft until his groan turned into crazy, frenzied mutterings. He dropped his head back, his entire body growing tense, cords of muscle throbbing in his neck, his fists clenching at his sides. "Enough, Emma. Stop."

She knew what he was doing. Knew how close she was bringing him. That knowledge drove her nearly out of her mind. "Now, Johnny. I want it now."

He looked down, watching her through half-lowered lashes as he drew in several ragged breaths. Giving another of those wicked laughs, he reached for his belt. "You want *it?*"

"Yeah. It. You. Everything. Right now."

"You've gotten mighty bossy, Emma Jean."

"And I'm about to get violent," she said with an impatient growl as she reached for him again, helping him shove his pants and briefs down to his knees, not wanting to waste the few precious seconds it would take for him to get them all the way off.

She began to shake in anticipation. Trying to pull him down, she reached for his hips and curled her legs open in invitation.

"Wait, I don't have…"

"I'm on the pill," she snapped.

"Thank heaven," he murmured.

Then, instead of falling onto her, as she silently demanded, he knelt on the floor in front of the sofa. He pulled her up so she was sitting, facing him, then tugged her mouth toward his again. They exchanged another frantic kiss as he hooked his hands below her knees and pulled her closer, inch by inch, to the edge of the couch. Until finally she was within reach, not sitting on the seat, merely perched on the edge with her feet on the floor. Her thighs were wide, her sex open and wet and waiting.

When he finally plunged into her, filling her to her very core, she let out a tiny wail. She closed her eyes, holding her breath, focused on the incredible sensations racking her body.

He held her around the hips, supporting her above him, then began to move them both—pulling her down and pushing up to meet her until she caught his rhythm and began to meet him thrust for thrust. "Johnny, yes," she said, dropping her head back and arching harder against him.

"Satisfied? Now that you got *it?*"

"It's a start," she mumbled, then moaned when he jerked into her again. Hard. Touching her so deep she didn't know if he'd ever be able to find his way back out again.

It continued like that. Fast, hard, intense, with her arms around his neck, his hands on her hips and thighs. The cold air coming from the window unit did nothing to cool them off as their bodies strained together, but Emma suddenly found she didn't mind the heat now. Tasting the salty sheen of sweat on his skin, feeling the slickness growing between them, she decided she liked it. Liked it very much.

"Is this what you were thinking when you were standing there touching yourself?" he asked, his voice thick and hoarse.

She nodded, unable to lie. "I wanted you to fill me up completely."

"What would you have done if I hadn't shown up?"

She gave him a catlike grin and squeezed him, deep inside her body, wringing a groan from his lips. "Wouldn't you like to know?"

Nodding, he slid a hand into her hair, cupping her head and drawing her mouth to his for a wet kiss. He slowed the pace, kissing her languorously, matching the slow, deep thrusts of his tongue with slow deep thrusts of his body. Then, when they drew apart, he whispered, "Yeah, I would like to know. You'll have to show me sometime."

Oh, lordy, yes, she'd show him anything he wanted if only he didn't stop, didn't let this wonderful pleasure end.

She mumbled something incoherent, then wrapped her legs tighter around his lean hips, rubbing her calf against that hard backside to tug him deep again. Oh, *so* deep.

Emma began to shake, to moan and to quiver as another orgasm washed over her. She dug her fingers into his shoulders, and he held onto her while she shuddered through another intense climax.

Then Johnny seemed to let go of his last bit of control because he thrust up into her, hard and insatiable. Capturing her mouth in another wet kiss, he stroked her inside out, finally groaning his own completion against her lips.

CHAPTER ELEVEN

CORA DILLON had been thinking about it all week, but she still hadn't come up with a solution to her problem. She'd stewed and prayed, she'd talked to Bob, knowing, of course, that he wasn't listening, so she didn't have to worry about him actually trying to tell her what to do.

She was fretting over her knowledge of Jimbo Boyd's latest shenanigans, and cursing her own ability to ferret things out. Sometimes it caused too much confusion.

Cora liked knowing things, liked sitting quietly in the diner listening to the conversations of the people behind her. Or at the hair salon, pretending her head was all the way up inside the dryer hood, but secretly hunkering down so she could pay attention to the stylists as they chatted back and forth.

It wasn't that she meant to *do* anything with the tidbits of knowledge she found out. She just liked to hold on to them, like sparkly pebbles she could hoard in her pocket and take out and giggle over when she was alone.

At least, usually. Sometimes, as in the case with the Frasier girl, the things she learned deserved to be told. And hadn't she been proved right? Look at what the truth had turned out to be—the girl hadn't only *sold* dirty pictures up north, she'd been *making* them! Clara'd heard the story from a very reliable source at her church prayer meeting Wednesday night.

But this Boyd information troubled her. Yes, indeedy, it troubled her mightily. Because though the daughter was a cheap bit of goods, Daneen Brady's mother had been one of Cora's closest friends. She couldn't imagine what Lila would think of her little girl having a desktop affair with Mayor Jimbo Boyd.

"I do appreciate you coming over at the last minute, Mrs. Dillon," she heard from behind her as she finished waxing the tiled foyer floor of the Boyd house. "Especially on a Friday."

Straightening, she put a hand to the small of her back and looked at Hannah Boyd, Jimbo's wife, who stood at the bottom of the stairs in the Boyd mansion. Well, not a mansion, but pretty dang big for this place where the average folks lived in 3/2 tract houses.

Hannah was all trim and tidy, dressed in a decent, respectable gray dress with a tasteful strand of pearls around her neck. Ladylike. That described Hannah Boyd. She fit in here all right, into this house her daddy had left to her.

Unlike her husband. The miserable cheater.

"Friday night's the same as any other," Cora replied. "With the kids gone, me 'n Bob usually eat frozen TV dinners on Friday nights, anyway.

Hannah gave her a small smile that softened up her tight face a bit. The first lady had been a pretty girl when she was young, back before Jimbo'd gotten his beefy paws on her.

"How very sweet, Cora. I didn't mean to make you late for your date with your husband."

Cora merely shrugged. She hadn't been about to turn down the extra work when the first lady of Joyful had called in a tizzy earlier today. Seems her regular housekeeper had come down sick and there was a speck of dust on Hannah Boyd's dining room table. Or a smudge of a thumbprint on the mirror over her sofa. Heaven forbid Hannah not keep a perfect house.

Cora had a feeling one'a them shrink fellas would say it was because Hannah couldn't keep a perfect husband.

"The mayor and I are hosting a prayer breakfast in the morning, you know," Hannah said, folding her hands in front of her.

Cora pursed out her lips. She could imagine the kind of praying Jimbo'd been doing with Daneen at work today. She'd bet anything *he* hadn't been the one on his knees.

"Well, you're all ready then," Cora said as she gathered up the cleaning supplies.

As she prepared to leave, Hannah followed her into the kitchen, chatting about the weather and Cora's grandchildren. Not for the first time—not for the twentieth—Cora felt sorry for the woman. She wondered what Hannah would do if she heard about Jimbo's office wickedness.

She also wondered what Chief Brady would say about his little girl being part of it.

She wondered what Johnny Walker would do if he knew his brother's boy was around such sordid goings-on. And if his brother might come to town to do something about it.

She wondered what Daneen would have to say for herself.

She wondered what Jimbo might offer to try to get her to keep quiet.

And, most of all, she wondered which of them she was going to tell first.

JOHNNY WAS the first to hear the knocking. After he and Emma had both gone as high as they could go, they'd sagged together onto the sofa, still joined. She lay limply beneath him, he half-knelt, half-lay atop her.

At first he'd figured the knocking sound was just his heart banging against the walls of his chest. Or maybe his nuts cracking, wrung completely dry as he spent himself inside her.

But no. The sound came from the front door.

"Emma? Someone's here."

Her eyes flew open immediately. "Oh, my God."

"Shh," he replied, kissing the expression of panic off her lips. "We won't answer."

He didn't think he *could* answer. Or even move. Except, maybe, to pick her up and carry her to her bedroom. It was about damn time he and Emma Jean made love in a bed.

He hadn't come over here expecting this…nothing like this. But it had happened. Ten years of wondering and waiting and hungering had reached this explosive climax, and he wasn't fool enough to question it.

Johnny didn't quite know what it meant, other than the fact that having had her once, he wouldn't rest until he had her again. Beyond that…who knew? But they were different people now. They weren't stupid teenagers acting on hormones and hurt feelings. No other people were involved.

The future seemed…well, not bright, but at least possible. Emma Jean was back in Joyful. She'd come home of her own free will. Maybe, he had to wonder, because she, too, had realized she had some unfinished business to attend to.

Whatever the reason, they were both responsible adults. Free to make their own choices. That she'd chosen Joyful…and him…said a lot about the way Emma had changed. She wasn't the spoiled teenage kid anymore, hiding out from her parents, biding time until she could get away and be on her own.

Which made him suddenly feel very positive.

He didn't have much opportunity to feel positive, however, because a moment later, he heard the knocking again. Apparently the person at the door didn't much care if they answered or not. Before he could even think to suggest they get more comfortable—like, at least letting him take his pants all the way off—he heard the click of the knob as it started to turn.

He hadn't locked the door.

Someone was about to get quite a sight. His bare ass, with her legs wrapped around him.

Johnny leaped to his feet, yanking his pants up with one hand and grabbing for Emma with the other. He hauled her to her feet, feeling like a kid about to get caught making out by his parents.

"Go," he ordered, pushing her toward the hall as he got his pants in place and yanked at the zipper. That could've been dangerous considering his cock still felt like it was ready to explode. He had the feeling if they hadn't been interrupted he could have started right back up again, without ever leaving Emma's sweet, tight body.

"Em, I know you're here, I have to see you," he heard a voice from behind him.

He swung around just in time to see the front door open and Claire Deveaux enter the house, accompanied by her daughter.

Claire's pretty face was puffy, her eyes suspiciously bright. But the redness in her cheeks, he'd have to say, came *after* she realized what she'd walked in on. Her eyes grew to saucer proportions and her jaw dropped open.

"Oh, my goodness," she whispered, drawing a shaking hand to her mouth.

Yeah. That about summed it up. Him shirtless, Emma's torn dress on the floor, her bra hanging from the arm of the couch and her panties God only knew where. The room smelling like hot sweaty bodies and sex.

Nope. There wasn't much chance she was gonna mistake this for anything but wild monkey sex in the living room.

"I'm so sorry," Claire whispered, immediately backing toward the door. "I didn't think…"

"Give Emma a minute, okay?" he bit out, turning his attention to Eve, who was looking around the room with curiosity.

If the kid found Emma's panties, he was gonna croak.

"No, no, just tell her I stopped by." Then Claire sucked her lower lip in. "Uh, tell her I'll come back later."

"Mama, are you gonna get our suitcases out of the car soon? I want my Dora the Explorer doll."

Suitcases. Holy shit, suitcases? And that teary look on her face?

Uh-oh. This was a marital crisis. He'd seen it enough to know. As much as he wanted to usher Claire out, making sure she took her wide-eyed, inquisitive daughter with her, he knew he couldn't.

Bending over, he grabbed his shirt off the floor and yanked it on. "Emma will be right back. Don't go anywhere," he ordered the other woman.

Claire didn't look ready to argue. She just continued to stare around the room, wide-eyed, particularly when her attention turned toward Emma's torn dress.

"Uh…"

"I'll be right back," he snapped, grabbing for the dress and the bra as he headed for the doorway. He only hoped Emma'd had the presence of mind to shove her underwear under the cushions of the sofa because he didn't see them.

"Who was it?" Emma asked as soon as he found her standing at the top of the staircase, wearing a pink robe.

Her embarrassed expression couldn't entirely hide her amusement. "Tell me we didn't get busted by somebody peddling religion."

He grinned. "Nah, though maybe it would've helped that you were crying out to the lord for mercy."

She lifted one lofty brow. "I think that was *you.*"

"No, I was the one singing hallelujahs for window air conditioners and Georgia summers."

The smile slowly faded from her face and she shook her head in bemusement. "Oh, Johnny, what on earth have we done?"

He quirked a brow. "You want the technical term?"

"You want a black eye?" She ran a hand through her mass of curls, sending them tumbling all around, just begging to be touched and played with again.

"We beat the heat," he finally admitted. "And answered some questions that'd been floating around out there for the past ten years."

Like could it really have been as incredible as he remembered? Could she possibly have been that sweet, that tight, that good?

Yeah. Yeah. And ohhhh yeah.

Emma was shaking her head. "I never intended...this doesn't mean..."

His jaw stiffened. "It is what it is, Emma Jean. To hell with intentions or regrets."

"I don't regret it," she replied, her admission surprising him. He'd have figured she'd sooner slip and fall in the Joyful Grocery Store again than be so honest. "But hooking up with you again sure wasn't what I had in mind when I came here to hide out."

Her words took him by surprise. "Hide out?"

She tugged her robe tighter around herself and looked toward the floor. "No, I'm just kidding."

Sensing she was close to coming clean about why she'd really come to Joyful, and why she planned to stay, he took her chin and lifted her face. When they were eye to eye, he ordered, "Tell me."

With a heavy sigh, she admitted, "I lost my job. My life savings. My best friend. Everything. I'm destitute and broke and unhirable. So I came to Joyful to…I don't know…wait out the storm?"

His jaw dropped open. He had not expected this. Emma'd been raised with not only a silver spoon in her mouth but an entire tea service at the ready. How she could have reached such a state truly baffled him.

She seemed to see his disbelief. "It's true." Then she turned her face, curling her cheek into his fingers. "But today, now…well, let's say I'm feeling better than I have in a long time. I'd been feeling lonely and lost and afraid." She gave him a saucy smile. "Not to mention *hot*."

Her suggestive comment didn't have the effect she'd probably been going for. Emma's sexy teasing couldn't refill the part of him that had suddenly been sucked empty by what she'd admitted. By what it meant.

She was down and out. She needed a savior, someone to make her feel better, someone to lean on.

Same old story. Once again, he'd played the hero for Emma Jean Frasier. No, this time he hadn't given her flowers and an arm to lean on while walking into the prom. Instead, he'd given her a mind-blowing fuck to help her forget her troubles for a while.

Closing his eyes, he took a deep breath and pulled his hand away from her.

She didn't seem to notice his distraction, because she

sounded very casual when she asked, "So who *was* at the door, Johnny?"

He finally remembered why he'd come looking for her. Just the sight of her in her silky pink robe had made him forget they were no longer alone in the house. And her confession about what she was really doing here had made him forget everything except how empty and furious and used he'd felt the last time he'd been stupid enough to get involved with Emma Jean.

She hadn't wanted him back then, she'd wanted Nick. And this time, she hadn't wanted him, either. She'd wanted a hard body to comfort her.

If this were a normal situation, he'd probably have figured what the hell and taken her to bed again as many times as she needed until she felt better. But not with her.

He couldn't do this again. She'd torn him up when he'd been a young, stupid kid. He couldn't imagine the damage she could do now that he was a grown man.

No more.

"It was Claire," he finally responded, keeping his voice even and his breaths steady. "She's, uh, still downstairs. I think she's in trouble and she needs a friend."

Thank God for Claire. No way could he stay here and not let Emma Jean know exactly what was going on in his head. Which would do nothing but leave them snapping and shouting at each other as they had on prom night.

He was older and wiser now. He didn't need to fight with Emma Jean. He just needed to get away from her.

EMMA KNEW THINGS had to be bad with Claire because for the rest of Friday night, and all morning Saturday, her friend never asked for the dirt on what she'd interrupted between Emma and Johnny. That would have been easy to answer: the most incredible sex of her life. Or, at least, the afterglow of the most incredible sex of her life.

She was still slightly stunned by it. By the suddenness and the intensity. Like a wicked summer thunderstorm, what they'd shared had been shocking and powerful and then suddenly gone.

Gone. She sensed Johnny had been gone even before he'd left the house the previous night. *Something* had certainly been gone—his warmth? The lazy-sweet look in his eyes that said he wanted to take her to bed and never get up?

Something.

He'd been almost tense. Not cold, but somehow, as crazy as it seemed, reserved. Ridiculous given the intimacies they'd shared in her living room, but it was true. Something had made him grow distant.

It's for the best.

She'd been repeating those words in her brain all morning. Getting involved with Johnny would be a mistake of gargantuan proportions. She was in town for one reason—to wait out the firestorm and controversy until she could get another job and go back to her real life in New York.

Not to stay. Not to turn into a small-town girl involved with the local stud. No matter how good that stud was in bed. Or on the floor. Or any flippin' place.

Johnny had chosen Joyful. He'd gotten out once, had tried living in a big city, with a good job, far away from the stigma of being one of "those Walkers." But he'd come back. His choice said a lot about where his head was and what he wanted out of his life.

They were on two different roads, going in two different directions. They'd both been caught in the same summer storm, that was all. It *had* to be all.

She just had to stop the whispers in her brain that kept reminding her it was the stormy season.

"So, you're sure you want to go to this reunion?" Claire asked from the doorway.

Emma looked up from her bed, where she sat painting her toenails a screaming fuchsia, and nodded. "Yes. I'm sure. It's about time this town realizes I'm not hiding because of what happened on prom night. And you're coming, too."

Claire entered the room and sat down on the bed. Reaching into Emma's giant cosmetics case, she sorted through the nail polish and selected a bloodred shade.

"Umh, honey, that shade is *so* not you," Emma said.

"Why not? I'm through being safe and sweet."

Emma couldn't help it. She snorted. "You? Safe and sweet?"

Claire simply glared. "I *am.*"

"If you say so."

Emma still couldn't believe the reason Claire and Eve had shown up on her doorstep. Claire's husband, Tim, had apparently gone all caveman on her because Claire had decided to go back to work. He sure didn't sound like the loving husband Claire had spoken of.

"I still can't believe you walked out," Emma murmured.

"What was I supposed to do when he practically accused me of being a lousy mother?"

"I'm sure he didn't say such a thing."

"He didn't have to," Claire replied with what looked and sounded like a harrumph. Emma couldn't be sure, since she'd never actually witnessed one, but that disgruntled, groaning, frowning thing Claire had just done probably qualified.

"Whose side are you on?"

"Yours," Emma said without hesitation. "And you're right. You do deserve to live your life and feel free to be who you really are."

Claire nodded. "Yes, I do."

"But…"

The harrumphing thing happened again.

"But, you should at least expect your husband to react when you don't tell him about things like getting a job or putting your daughter in day care."

Claire had told Emma about her drastic lifestyle changes, and her husband's less than enthusiastic reaction to them. What she hadn't been clear on was what had fired her up so much to go roaring out and make those changes without a word to Tim.

Claire swiped some red nail polish on her index finger, and looked at Emma through her curly brown bangs. "I got his attention."

"Yeah, you sure did."

"He knows I'm serious."

"Considering you packed your bags and your child and left, I'd say he does." Then Emma gave her friend a gentle smile. "But don't you think it's time to talk to him about all this?"

Claire frowned. "I'm not sure he's ready for talking. Besides, I think he needs more than one night alone in our bed to realize I actually *was* there, sleeping beside him, for the past few years."

Whoa. That sounded more serious than a spat over a job. Though she didn't want to pry, she sensed her friend needed to talk. "Um, problems there, too?"

Claire frowned. "Closest thing I've had to a sexual experience this month was when the guy fixing my bathroom sink bent over and gave me a plumber's smile." Tapping her finger on her cheek she added, "I think I had my last nonchocolate-induced orgasm right before the turn of the century."

"You're exaggerating." She *hoped*.

"Maybe. But not by much." Claire grabbed a bottle of nail polish remover and began to methodically remove every bit of the polish she'd just applied.

Emma nodded toward her supply of polish. "Go for something softer this time."

"You're the one who had the screaming hooker red in your makeup kit," Claire shot back.

"Gift with purchase."

Claire nodded, understanding instantly, as would any woman who glommed up every gift with purchase at the makeup counter. Even though the colors in said gifts were ones that would usually only look flattering on a corpse. Or a transvestite.

Emma reached for the bottle, intending to tuck it away in case she ever needed to bribe someone on the set of the *Jerry Springer Show*. Not that she'd been arrested, for, oh, a few *days* now.

"I don't know why I'm bothering," Claire said, looking with disgust at her short, neatly trimmed nails.

"Because you're beautiful," Emma replied. She'd waded in this deep, so she figured she might as well head all the way in. "Get back to your orgasms."

"What orgasms? You mean the ones I'm not having because of the sex I'm not having?"

No sex. That'd been Emma's lot…until yesterday…but as a single woman who hadn't dated anyone even casually for over a year, she had an excuse. Claire did not. "Why not?"

"Well, I've never been a vibrator kind of gal…."

Emma snorted a laugh. "I meant, why aren't you having sex?"

Claire's grin faded and she absently reached for a bottle of pale pink polish. "I look awful."

"Oh, puh-lease..."

"No, I know I've let myself go. It was hard enough losing the first twenty pounds I packed on when I was pregnant. These last twenty are a bitch. I don't think they could be blown off my butt with an explosive device."

"So what? You're beautiful, Claire. Voluptuous. Gorgeous."

Her friend didn't look convinced, though Emma was serious.

Pointing to her breasts, Claire muttered, "Then there's *these* things."

Emma sucked her lip into her mouth to prevent a laugh. Claire looked as disgusted as if two dead rats were hanging from the front of her dress. "Uh, honey, in case you hadn't heard...men like big breasts."

"These have moved past big and gone to the watermelon stage. When Eve was a baby, I was afraid to bring her into bed to nurse her at night because I thought for sure I'd suffocate her with one of these puppies. They were about four times the size of her head."

Emma was snorting by this point, and Claire's grin had returned. Then she softly admitted, "I guess that was part of the problem. Suddenly they turned into milk machines instead of..."

"Playthings?"

Claire nodded.

"I think there's a name for that."

"Elvis Presley syndrome?"

"Something along those lines."

Emma thought about Claire's problem. So much for perfect, blissful marriages. If someone as kooky-sweet and loveable as Claire couldn't make it work, how could anyone?

What an utterly depressing thought.

"So you see why I'm not totally thrilled about going to this reunion tonight. I'm already feeling bad enough about my life. I don't particularly relish spending an evening with a bunch of people who've probably already heard through the grapevine that my husband's thrown me out because he wants a younger, skinnier, *nicer* woman."

Emma rolled her eyes at Claire's exaggeration. Though, honestly, experience told her the gossip chain probably would distort the truth in such a manner.

"Personally," Emma said, "if it were me, I'd want to dress myself in something drop-dead gorgeous and show up at the party making every man there drool."

"Drool? I think you mean gag."

Emma groaned. "Drool! Now, Tim is coming, right?"

"I'm sure he will. If only to see if I show up." Then Claire snickered. "Drop-dead gorgeous, huh? Got any big giant canvas feed bags floating around?"

Emma glared at her friend, getting tired of hearing her rag on herself. "You're buying into the stereotypical b.s. that has screwed up so many American woman. Have you seen some of the new, more normal-sized supermodels?" Determined, Emma rose to her feet, walking carefully with toes spread and upraised to avoid any smears, and pulled a dress out of her closet. "You've got to pull a Scarlett in *Gone With The Wind*. Show up in a wicked dress and act like you don't give a fiddle-dee-dee what anyone thinks."

She pointed to her own red dress, which was short, tight and low enough to stop traffic. She'd only worn it once and had immediately decided upon it when thinking about the reunion.

Claire's eyes bugged out. "You must be crazy if you think I can fit into that!"

"No, this is what I'm wearing." She hung the dress back up and carefully waddled back over to take Claire by the hand. Pulling her to her feet, she said, "Let's drop Eve off at your mom's. Because you are going to get a new dress. And I know just where we're going to look. A shop that's having a huge col-o-sul sale."

CHAPTER TWELVE

JOHNNY HAD absolutely no interest in attending the ten-year reunion of his brother's high school class. He'd gone to his own last year and had been bored to tears. This would be much worse.

Unfortunately, he couldn't get out of it. He'd agreed to be the alumni speaker. A former Joyful High grad who'd somehow done something to aid the residents of this town was always invited to address the party. Usually it was an alumni from the same class. But apparently Nick and Emma's graduating class had been kinda thin on suckers... er...local success stories.

Lucky him.

Of course, he'd agreed to it weeks ago, long before Emma Jean had ever come back to Joyful. Certainly before he'd done the unthinkably stupid and had sex with her again. This party would have been bad even before what had happened between them last night. Now, he couldn't imagine how tough it was going to be, knowing what they'd shared the day before. And knowing there was no way they were ever going to share it again.

He'd rather be tied to a chair and forced to watch *Gigli* a dozen times than attend tonight's big to-do. But he'd promised.

Arriving at the hotel in Bradenton where the reunion

was being held, he couldn't help casting a quick eye at the people entering the place. He recognized a few faces. Guys he'd played football with, some he'd shared detention with. A former bully he'd punched for beating up one of his younger Walker cousins.

But no Emma. And, he found himself acknowledging, no Nick.

Not that he expected his brother to show up here. No way would Nick come back to town, for this event of all reasons. If he'd been coming, he would have told their mother, and she would have told Johnny.

Still, he couldn't help looking at every guy entering the place, wondering if he'd see and recognize his brother's lanky form or familiar cocky grin.

Dammit, he'd missed him. Missed their friendship, the relationship they'd once had.

Sometimes Johnny wished he'd handled things differently. He'd just been so furious with Nick after he'd run out on Daneen. Truthfully, he'd been furious with him since he'd run out on Emma. But it had only been when Daneen had come back to Joyful with her baby son that he'd confronted his brother. Once the family had found out where Nick was—in the Marines—Johnny'd written him to express his opinion. He'd pulled no punches in his letter, expressing every bit of anger and disappointment he felt for his only sibling.

Nick had never replied. And the only time they'd seen each other since was when they'd stood on either side of their mother, watching their abusive prick of a father being buried.

"Penny for your thoughts?"

He immediately looked up and saw Daneen standing right outside the door of his SUV.

"They aren't worth a wooden nickel."

She shrugged, then stepped back to let him open the door and step out. "I heard you were the guest speaker tonight."

"Your class wasn't exactly full of overachievers, was it?"

She swatted his arm. But before she could say another word, they both saw a little red convertible pull into the parking lot and zip into a space close to the entrance.

He'd recognize that blond head, not to mention the shrill squeak of her brakes, anywhere.

"Emma," he murmured.

"So she showed up after all," Daneen muttered, not sounding pleased by the development. She said something else, but by that point, Emma had stepped out of her car, and Johnny was completely incapable of focusing on anything else.

Red. Oh, God help him, her dress was red and short and glittery and tight enough to reveal every delectable curve of her body. Low-cut with thin shoulder straps the only thing holding everything in place.

"Have you seen much of her since she's been back?"

Johnny smiled inwardly, thinking of just how much he'd seen of Emma Jean recently. Particularly last night. "I've seen her."

"I hear you've been seen *with* her," Daneen said, sounding deceptively noncommittal.

He knew his sister-in-law. She was very interested, but knew him well enough not to start hitting him with questions. Because she knew he'd never answer them. "We're old friends."

She snorted. "But apparently you were more than that before she left town." Shaking her head, she tsked, then gave him a wicked smile. "Who'dve thought it of good girl Emma Jean Frasier. And *you*."

He took a second to close his window and get out of the car. When she still waited, expectantly, he gave her a pointed look. "Yeah, who'da thought it? But then, *or now,* what happens between me and Emma Jean is nobody's business."

Daneen merely nodded, obviously realizing she was pushing too hard. "Be careful. You know there are some wild rumors floating around about her." The expectant sparkle in her eyes told him she was dying to tell all she knew.

"Yeah, I know. They're pure bull. I'd like to find out how they got started." Then he narrowed his eyes. "I'd also like to talk to your boss about a few things. Emma came to town under the impression she still owned the land where the new club is being built and I've been looking into the records for her."

That reminded him of the papers he'd dropped the previous evening. He'd meant to grab them on his way out, but had completely forgotten. Considering how distracting his visit had been, he couldn't be too hard on himself.

Daneen's brow shot up in unfeigned surprise. "You're kidding! I don't see how she couldn't know about the lot. Jimbo's been working with the new owners for more than a year." Then she looked past him, again toward where Emma had parked her car. "Wow. *She* looks good."

Daneen's comment surprised him, since he knew how much she and Emma disliked one another. Then he realized she wasn't talking about Emma. No, his ex-sister-in-law was entirely focused on the other woman who'd been in Emma's convertible. The one he'd barely even noticed since no other female seemed to exist whenever Emma Jean Frasier was around.

"My God, is that Claire?" he asked, his jaw dropping open when he finally took a good look at the woman in black.

"Yeah. I wasn't sure she'd show up since she walked out on her husband." Daneen whistled. "She's obviously out to show him what he's missing."

He hadn't heard the full story of Claire's unexpected arrival on Emma's doorstep the night before, but Daneen's comment came as no surprise. The suitcases had been a dead giveaway about problems in Deveaux land.

So much for true love and great marriage. The next time he saw Virg and Minnie, he was going to make them swear to never break up. It was too frigging depressing for the rest of the loveless suckers to watch the few lucky ones fall apart.

He was glad for Claire in one respect, though. The town of Joyful had grown used to seeing her in ratty sweatpants and T-shirts. Now she wore one of the slinkiest black dresses he'd ever seen. There was no baggy fabric to cover up the few extra pounds she'd obviously put on since having her kid. No, she was flaunting what she had, and damn if she didn't look fantastic—in a buxom, Mae West sort of way—while doing it.

"Ready to go in?" Daneen asked, giving him a cheerful smile. Daneen looked younger, prettier when she smiled, without the hard, angry look she often wore. He attributed her good mood to the fact that she was about to waltz back into her high school element, where she'd once reigned supreme.

"Sure," he said, locking his door and dropping his keys in the pocket of his sport coat.

"You look very yummy tonight," Daneen murmured as she walked beside him. "I just might have to be your bodyguard to keep all the horny Joyful women off your back."

He didn't imagine a man's back was where a horny woman typically wanted to be. But he wasn't about to argue the point with her.

Johnny truly didn't think about how it looked for the two of them to be walking to the front door together. They'd arrived at the same time, parked near each other. It was natural for them to fall into step together.

Obviously Emma didn't see it that way.

She and Claire had come around from behind a large van parked between Emma's convertible and the entrance. They reached the sidewalk as Johnny and Daneen came around the other side of the van.

Emma's face went pale, and her eyes round. And he suddenly realized what this looked like. Taking one step to the side, to distance himself from Daneen, he met Emma's stare without flinching. He hoped.

Then he crossed his own arms in front of his chest and focused on the one woman who *wasn't* glaring daggers at him. Claire. "Girl, you look downright scrumptious tonight."

Claire's bright smile almost made it worth the uncomfortable moment. "Why sir, I declare, you could turn a girl's head. Emma and I went shopping."

"Tim's gonna have to beat off other men with a stick."

"Or just beat off, since I have no intention of going home with him tonight," she replied with a saucy toss of her head.

He almost choked. Coming from any other woman but Claire, and he would have. But this was the girl who'd responded with a resounding, "Eat me," when another kid had accused her of being white trash back in junior high. As someone whose family ranked even lower than white trash on the socioeconomic scale of Joyful society, Johnny had found himself liking Claire ever since.

"Why do I suddenly feel sorry for Tim?"

"Because you have a penis and those tend to stick together?"

"Disgusting."

She chuckled. "I meant those *people* tend to stick together."

Finally, Johnny worked up the nerve to turn his attention to Emma, who stood quietly beside her friend. She looked torn. Ready to commit murder on him, but also staring at her friend with a look of approval and warmth. He had the feeling Emma'd had something to do with Claire's transformation tonight.

God, she looked beautiful. His gut clenched and his heart picked up its pace in his chest as he thought about what they'd been doing round about this time the previous night.

Going absolutely insane.

"Hello, Em."

She looked up at him and met his even stare. "Johnny."

"You're beautiful," he admitted, the words low and thick, meant only for her ears but obviously overheard by her friend.

Before she could reply, Claire cleared her throat and tapped him on the shoulder. "I gotta say, boy, you look nice, too. I like the outfit. But, uh, I think you probably looked better in what you had on at Emma's last night right before I showed up."

She scrunched up her brow in thought as Emma and Johnny both shot her looks that told her to shut up. Then she grinned. "Oh, yeah, now I remember, I think it was nothin'?"

Johnny closed his eyes as he practically heard Daneen's spine snap straight. Shaking his head in half-amusement, half-dismay, he didn't even turn around to watch his ex-sister-in-law walk into the hotel without another glance for any of them.

"Oh, right, so she knows you're just brotherly, huh?" Emma snapped. "In case you didn't notice, your date went inside without you."

He gave Claire a look and without a word, she scooted away, leaving them alone. Emma appeared ready to follow her, but Johnny stopped her by putting one hand on her shoulder. "We showed up at the same time. *Separately.* By coincidence."

Nibbling her lip, she stared at him as if gauging the truth of his words.

"That's her blue car right next to mine," he added, tilting his head toward the parking lot. "No matter what you might think of me, there's no way in hell I'da shown up here tonight with Daneen after what happened between us yesterday."

She looked around, as if making sure no one was within earshot. Then she frowned. "What did happen between us yesterday, Johnny?"

A wicked smile crossed his lips before he could prevent it.

"I mean *after* that. I thought I knew, but something seemed…different when you left."

So she'd picked up on his mood change. Not surprising, really. Forcing nonchalance, he shrugged. "Everything was fine. We went a little crazy, Claire interrupted. I left. End of story."

"What if Claire hadn't interrupted?"

Then we'd still be naked in your house and I'd be breaking world records for the number of times a man can get it up in a twenty-four-hour period.

"She did" was all he said.

Emma stiffened slightly, then gave him a brief nod. The tilt of her chin told him she was going for bravado. The tiny quiver of her lips said she couldn't quite manage it.

"Look," he said, unable to leave things this way, "it was wild. Incredible. But it didn't mean anything more than a great time. For either of us."

He was going to join the Screen Actor's Guild, because he'd just pulled off one amazing performance.

Finally, the lip thing stopped as her mouth drew into a tight line. "Fine. You're right," she bit out. Then she turned toward the door. "Claire will be waiting."

"Emma…"

She'd already started to walk toward the entrance, and didn't even pause as he softly said her name. It was only after she'd gone inside, the glass door swinging silently shut behind her, that he admitted, "I lied. It meant something."

CLAIRE DIDN'T KNOW when that sassy, foul-mouthed creature had taken over her body, but she couldn't bring herself to much care. She liked her.

It felt good to be bad. Good to be shocking. Good to have a guy like Johnny Walker—or some of the other men she saw every day who now stared at her like she was a complete stranger—give her appreciative looks. God, it'd been a long time since she'd felt like this.

Attractive. Desirable. Sexy.

Too bad not one of the guys making her feel that way was the one she was in love with.

Standing near the bar in the crowded banquet room where the reunion was underway, she nursed a glass of wine. Three guys she'd graduated with had come up to chat. All three of them probably had walked past her a dozen times on the street in the past year and had never given her the time of day.

Men. Bizarre how they went to pieces over women's breasts. All except her husband. She had the feeling he viewed them as pure milk-producing udders. Maybe she'd greet him with a "moo" if he showed up.

Watching over Emma's shoulder, Claire paid close attention to the door. Each new arrival made her tense a little, though she knew he might not come at all. This wasn't his reunion. He hadn't moved to Joyful until after Claire had graduated high school. Considering how mad he probably was at her for leaving, she suspected he might stay away.

She still couldn't believe she'd packed up and walked out yesterday. Wow. He'd been surprised. Stunned. Nice wifies didn't do such things.

Claire wasn't a fool. She'd been fully prepared for Tim to be upset about her going back to work. She'd been holding her breath all week, waiting for Eve to say something to her daddy about going to day care. But for some reason, her daughter hadn't. In fact, she'd been awfully quiet about it the two times she'd gone. Claire very much feared her daughter was learning a hard lesson: she really *wasn't* the center of the universe.

Eve's silence had stretched things out, until Claire was going crazy. That was why she'd asked Tim to come home from work early Friday, while Eve was at Claire's mother's. They needed to talk things out.

She'd talked. He'd listened. At the end of her explanation, when she'd waited for him to ask reasonable questions or voice reasonable concerns, he'd done the unthinkable. He'd practically accused her of not loving their daughter, or him. Then he'd stalked out, slamming the front door so hard their wedding picture had fallen off the wall in the living room.

It had seemed like an omen.

So she'd gone to her room, packed a bag, grabbed some of Eve's things and left. She could have gone to her mother's, but she'd gone to Emma instead. Emma, who'd faced the worst this town had to offer and had still come back here with her head up high. In spite of the rumors.

The rumors... She'd really meant to tip Emma off about them, since someone was sure to say something odd tonight. Then again, it wasn't the easiest topic to bring up. Hopefully it'd died a natural death, anyway, and Claire could fill her in on it late tonight when they gorged on ice cream after the reunion.

"So did your mom say whether Tim has called again?" Emma asked.

"No, not since the first time."

Her mother said he'd called last night to make sure she was okay, but he hadn't come looking for her. Hadn't gone all Brando on her and stood in the middle of the street screaming her name. Not that "Claa-aire" would have sounded quite as good as "Stel-la." But it would have been nice to think he cared when she was coming home. At the very least she'd expected him to call to ask how to operate the stinkin' microwave.

So maybe he won't show up tonight. Maybe he didn't miss her at all. Maybe he'd already decided he was better off. Maybe he *did* know how to heat up a frozen dinner. Maybe...

Oh boy...no maybe. She saw him walking through the door of the room, recognizing his sandy-blond head anywhere.

"He's here," she hissed.

Emma didn't even flinch, she just continued to sip her martini, cool as could be. "Oh? Be sure to give me a proper introduction, if you start speaking to him again."

Claire continued to watch her husband as he nodded some hellos, and scanned the crowd. His eyes moved right past her not once but three times. "He doesn't even recognize me, the jerk."

Then he did. Tim's hazel eyes widened and he stopped talking to Joe Brown, their neighbor. Joe followed Tim's stare, did a double-take of his own, then gave Claire an obvious wink.

When Joe nudged Tim to approach his wife, Claire had had enough. "He has to be pushed over here to talk to me," she whispered. "Boy I wish I had somebody to drag onto the dance floor."

She gave a frantic look around, saw no male bodies close enough to do any good, and almost groaned. Tim was within ten feet now.

Finally, stiffening her jaw, she grabbed Emma's drink out of her hand. "Come on."

Emma snickered. "We're not going to do the pathetic two girls dancing together thing, are we? I mean, we used to make fun of girls who did that in high school."

Claire didn't care. She strong-armed her friend out to the middle of the small parquet dance floor, where a deejay stood alone, sorting through CD's and looking completely bored.

She supposed she and Emma made quite a picture, two snazzily dressed women alone on the dance floor, doing their white-girls-can't-dance moves to Hootie and the Blowfish while the rest of their former classmates looked on.

"Can I cut in?"

She'd braced herself for Tim. Not Johnny. Yet that's who stood there, giving Claire a look of understanding and sympathy, before shifting his gaze to Emma.

When she saw who stood behind Johnny, she understood why.

"Hello, Tim."

He didn't say a word, merely stared at her. She stopped dancing, hardly noticing as Johnny led Emma away. Her friend gave her a reassuring glance over her shoulder before she left.

"You look amazing," Tim finally said, his voice sounding shaky.

"Thank you."

She ran her hand across her chest, as if smoothing her dress. He didn't need the prompting to focus on the low neckline; he'd been less than discreet about staring her up and down.

Finally he frowned. "Don't you think you need to put on a sweater or something?"

"I'm not cold."

He looked so darned uncomfortable, so uncertain, and unhappy. Claire's heart clenched a little. Then she reminded herself of what was at stake. Her future. Her happiness. Her marriage. Everything. If she couldn't make him see that they needed to work together to find a solution to satisfy them *both*, they were doomed to fail.

Claire had come out of her box. She didn't think a crowbar and a chisel were going to be able to shut her back in. Tim had to make her believe he could still love the girl he'd married. Not the one he and motherhood and life had made her become.

"Want to dance?" she asked when the song changed to something slow and mellow.

Giving her a relieved nod, he tugged her into his arms, pressing his cheek into her hair. "God, you feel so good."

He couldn't have feigned the emotion in his voice. And Claire began to feel hope bubbling up inside her.

"Almost as good as the hug and butterfly kisses I got from Eve when I stopped by your mama's house to see her on my way here tonight."

And just like that, the hope bubbles popped.

EMMA DIDN'T KNOW exactly when she became aware of the strange whispers and looks. But within a couple of hours of her arrival, she began to feel like she was missing something. Like a big joke had been told and she was the only one who hadn't gotten the punch line.

The evening had been going okay. She'd recognized several faces, and engaged some former friends in conversation. Still, people hadn't reacted as she'd expected. Nobody shrieked and hugged her. Nobody chatted a mile a minute, asking her where she'd been and if she was married or why she'd come back.

This was Joyful, so she knew better than to expect any former football stars to come back as women. The crowd seemed pretty much the standard. Geeks who were now computer programmers. Beefy jocks turned truck drivers who liked to relive their glory years. Lots of high school sweethearts who'd gotten married, bought a tract house, had a kid or two—or six—and never dreamed about leaving town. She could have predicted it.

But she'd expected at least a *few* people to seem genuinely happy to see her again. So far, they weren't.

It's Johnny. She cursed the luck that had brought him here tonight. Because with the two of them both present, there was absolutely no chance of anyone forgetting about prom night.

She almost told them all to get a life. Really, what was the big hairy deal about two teenagers doing what millions of other teenagers did on prom night? It was only because he'd been the brother of her boyfriend that her situation was the least bit unique. And it still didn't seem nearly important enough to warrant the arched brows and the strange looks she'd gotten tonight. Two blondes whose names she couldn't remember had made some weird comment about how "demure" her dress was, then giggled as they walked away. And then there were the obnoxious pickup lines a couple of former classmates had used on her.

It seemed to go deeper than teasing or suggestive comments. She'd expected those, since a bunch of them had glimpsed her naked in the gazebo that night. But she'd anticipated flirtatious, not salacious. Two guys, Jason Michaels and Kevin O'Leary, whom she remembered from her Algebra II class, had actually made her a little uncomfortable when they'd cornered her coming out of the ladies' room.

The sheepish looks on Fred Willis's face whenever she'd met his eye made things even worse. Sharing an evening with a guy who'd locked her up twice in the past week wasn't her idea of fun.

Something else was bothering her. Johnny. He hadn't been cold, hadn't even been unfriendly. He'd been…distant. Like they were just two old high school friends who'd run into one another at this reunion. As if he hadn't been naked and panting and groaning with her the day before.

She was half-tempted to go to the ladies' room, take her panties off, then come back and hand them to him. That would get a rise out of the man, figuratively speaking. Although, literally might have been nice, too.

Might? Who was she kidding?

If he was anyone else, she would have fumed and written off his aloofness with a disgusted "men" grunt. But she knew Johnny too well. Their out-of-control sexual encounter yesterday had meant something to *both* of them, not only to her. She'd bet her last dollar—which she was pretty close to reaching—on it.

It's for the best.

She kept telling herself that. Whatever the reason, it was just as well they'd cooled things off…no matter how much it hurt to constantly look around the room and see him chatting easily with one woman or another.

Unfortunately, her mental pep talks weren't working. The only things that helped were the martinis.

She didn't think Claire was having a very good time either, in spite of her brief dance with her husband. Something he'd said had set Claire off, and she'd pulled out of his arms, stalking out of the banquet room. Claire and Tim hadn't exchanged a private word since, though he'd hovered nearby for the past hour. Which was darned uncomfortable, since he'd been giving Emma hard looks all evening. Tim apparently hadn't forgiven her for the arrest incident.

"So, Emma," said a girl Emma had known from gym class, who was sitting across from her. "Seen any good *movies* lately?"

The guy sitting next to her—her high school boyfriend now chubby-faced husband—snorted a laugh. So did his former football buddy who sat with them.

Emma shrugged, surprised by the question, but glad someone other than Claire had tried to engage her in conversation. "No, not really. I don't have much time for movies."

The woman raised a brow. "Really? How…strange."

Beside her, she heard Claire make a funny noise. She glanced at her friend, who was actually trying to cut into the rubbery chicken and overcooked broccoli they'd been served for dinner. For some reason, Claire frowned across the table.

But that didn't deter the woman who, Emma remembered, was named Melanie. "You must find Joyful pretty slow compared to the life you've been living."

A normal sentence. But there was something hard in it that got Emma's hackles up. Once again, she had a feeling of not being in on the joke. It was starting to tick her off. But before she could reply, she felt someone's hands drop to her bare shoulders.

She didn't have to turn around to recognize the touch. Her entire body tingled, not just from the warmth of his fingers on her skin, but from the spicy scent of his cologne, and the brush of his jacket against her back. It was all she could do not to close her eyes, sigh and lean back into him.

Johnny.

CHAPTER THIRTEEN

"DANCE WITH ME, EM," Johnny said, not asking but ordering.

Emma pushed her plate away, and rose from her seat, glad to get away from these giggling people. Every set of eyes at the standard eight-person round banquet table was glued to her. Claire's were the only ones that looked the slightest bit warm. The others were all anticipatory.

"Thank you," she murmured as he took her arm and led her to the dance floor, where a few couples were gyrating. But once they got there, she found she wasn't much in the mood for dancing. The floor was the tiniest bit spinny.

Three martinis. No food. Not good.

"I don't feel much like dancing right now," she admitted. "Will you take a rain check? I think I'll go outside for some fresh air."

"Come on," he said, not giving her a chance to argue. He slipped his arm around her waist and led her out of the banquet room, and down a short corridor. They stepped outside, into the night, and found themselves beside the dark swimming pool.

Emma sucked in a few deep breaths, grateful for the chance to clear her head. "Thank you," she said. "I didn't realize how much I needed to be rescued from that crowd."

Though he said nothing, she felt his entire body grow

stiff against hers. But she couldn't, for the life of her, think why.

"Your speech was nice," she offered, trying to keep things normal and cordial when what she really wanted to do was throw her arms around his neck and her legs around his waist and beg him to take her again.

"Thanks." He stepped away, closer to the pool, glancing into its blue depths.

Emma didn't follow. Her heels were high and wobbly. And her head was still a bit dizzy. With her luck…and her weak ankles…she'd likely trip and fall right into the water.

"You all right?" he asked, his voice low and noncommittal.

"Nope. Pretty rotten."

"I can tell. Not having a great evening?"

She shook her head. "High school reunions really are torturous. Whoever made up the reality show had the right idea. Because of all the people in the world I would *not* want to get stuck in a big house with, it's that crew."

He grinned. "They're not *all* bad."

"Oh, no, they've all been so friendly and cordial. Why, I swear, if Daneen smiled at me one more time, I was just gonna faint from all the sweetness in the room."

He rolled his eyes at her sarcasm. Then he crossed his arms and stared at her. "Tell me about your job."

She had the feeling he wasn't referring to the nonexistent one here in Joyful. But, rather, the nonexistent one in New York. "I don't have one." She'd been going for flip, but, even to her own ears, her voice had sounded a little tense.

"Why not?"

Ooh, there was an interesting story. But not one she could tell after having had a few martinis. At least not tell and still maintain the illusion that she was something of a lady. Because in this slightly inebriated condition, her language was apt to approach sailor level.

Then again, she *would* be talking to the man who'd seen her playing with herself in front of an air conditioner twenty-four hours ago. So she didn't suppose she could shock him much.

"Short version, the company filed for chapter eleven after one of its executives and one of its accountants—who, by the way, was my best friend at the time—made off with several million dollars of our clients' assets." She shook her head in disgust. "Not to mention the contents of the mutual fund accounts of several employees. Including mine."

He whistled. "Nobody ever suspected?"

"Not until it was too late."

"Guess your friend won't be on your Christmas card list this year."

"More like my personal hit list."

"I don't think I'd want to hear who else is on that one," he said with a visible wince.

"Don't worry, you lost your original slot a while back. The guy at the FDA who insisted the sponge had to be taken off the market knocked you out of first place years ago."

Johnny chuckled. "Remind me to add him to *my* Christmas card list."

"Why? Because it knocked you out of first place? Or because you think that stopped me from having sex?"

"Did it?" he shot back, suddenly looking less playful. He stepped closer, reaching up to toy with the thin strap of her dress. His fingertips sizzled on her skin and Emma had to think for a moment to remind herself to breathe.

"Well?" he asked, his voice husky. Low. Sweet and sexy and as intoxicating as a hot summer night.

If she'd been a little drunker, she would have thrown caution out the window and kissed him like he'd never been kissed before.

If she'd been more sober, she would have tormented him as repayment for his aloofness all evening.

But she was neither. "Actually, I was kidding. The sponge thing was a little before my time." Then, just to goad him a bit, she added, "It was taken off the market in 1995. Which was, if you recall, the year you and I went to the prom."

His eyes narrowed, glittering in the semidarkness, and he stepped even closer, until his breath touched her cheek and his trousers brushed against her bare legs. "We back to talking about the prom, Emma Jean? You ready to hash that out?"

"Uh-uh. I don't want to fight with you tonight. I'm finally feeling relaxed and actually enjoying myself."

"Chicken."

But he respected her wishes, because he stepped back, far enough so she could breathe without inhaling his cologne and so her heart could try, at least, to return to its normal rhythm.

Then he tilted his head in concentration. "I think I read about your company. Or saw it on CNN or something."

"I'm sure you did."

"I guess I know now why you came to Joyful."

She nodded.

"You lost everything?"

Another nod.

"Damn, Emma, I'm so sorry."

Wow. This was the first time anyone had said that to her

since the whole thing began. Even her attorney, who'd been awfully nice and supportive, had never tried to empathize and let her know how sorry he was about what had happened.

Only Johnny.

"Thanks. I'll be okay. It just might take a while for me to get another job in my field."

"Your field being?"

"Anything related to being trusted with other people's money," she said with a dry laugh.

"I'd invest with you. If I had a job which actually paid enough for me to live beyond paycheck to paycheck."

She saw the teasing sparkle in his eye, but knew he probably wasn't exaggerating by much. "So, we're both sad sacks when it comes to our employment." She looked away, gazing at the water, wanting to suck up some of its tranquility and smoothness. Because beneath her surface, Emma felt the emotion building and building.

She was alone, outside, laughing quietly and enjoying a conversation with someone she wanted to jump on.

Get a grip. The class of '95 does not need to see you naked again!

Before she could think of what to do—whether to jump or retreat, keep talking lightly or beg him to tell her why he'd withdrawn the night before, she noticed someone approaching from the other side of the pool. She hadn't even realized they weren't alone outside until the old man made his way closer.

"Oh, no," Johnny mumbled.

"I thought that was you," the man said. He actually clapped his hands together, looking inordinately pleased. "Who'da thunk it? I been lookin' for you all week, little lady, and here I stumble on ya thirty miles from town just when I'm cursin' about havin' t' come to this family reunion."

Now Emma remembered. He was the old man who'd been in the grocery store the day she'd arrived. The dirty old man. Who was now leering at her dress and giving Johnny a very obvious thumbs-up.

She cleared her throat. "We're here for the same reason. A reunion. Joyful High class of '95."

He didn't appear convinced. Instead, he leaned closer to whisper, "Sure, sweetie. Tell me true, are you the entertainment for the bachelor party goin' on in the bar?"

Johnny stepped closer, putting his arm around Emma. "You're way off base, Mr. Terry."

The man reached into his pocket and fiddled around. Emma wondered what he was up to, then had the sick feeling she knew. She instantly pulled her gaze away, staring up at Johnny, wondering if the nasty old thing was doing what it *looked* like he was doing. When he finally made a triumphant "aha" sound and pulled a pen from his trouser pocket, she breathed a quick sigh of relief.

It was short-lived.

"Here we go. Now, I want an autograph."

Autograph?

"That's enough, Mr. Terry," Johnny said, smoothly stepping between them and taking the old man by the arm. "You need to go inside now." Then he lowered his voice and looked around as if to avoid being overheard. "I think I saw Joe Bob Melton in there and he looked to be talking to Mrs. Kerrigan."

The old man dropped the pen and stuck his chin out. Then he made a raspy back-of-the-throat kind of sound. God, Emma hoped he wasn't about to hawk a spitball right out here by the pool. If so, she pitied tomorrow's swimmers.

"What's he doin' here? He's not a relation. And he knows I got my eye on her," the old man said, completely distracted, as Johnny had obviously intended. And without another word, he beelined for the door and disappeared inside the hotel.

Once he was gone, Johnny tried to shrug it off with a laugh. "Crazy old guy. He and Joe Bob have been competing for women since the forties when they both fell for some French singer during the war."

Emma wasn't distracted. Crossing her arms, she tilted her head back and met Johnny's stare to convince him she meant business. "Okay, what am I missing? Tonight he asks for an autograph. The day I hit town, he said something about a star." She ticked off point after point on her fingers, her voice growing in volume and in heat as everything came together. "Two guys almost brawled in the street over me." That one made his jaw go tight. But she rushed right on. "Every person at this reunion is acting so strange you'd think I'm an ex-con."

She stepped closer, and he took a step back. She followed, crowding him until their bodies nearly touched and he had nowhere else to go but backward into the pool. Then he finally stopped.

Emma ignored the sparks shooting through her from the tips of her breasts, which touched his chest—to the tips of her toes, which touched his shoes. "Give it to me straight. I want to know what is going on here. I know you know, so don't try to pretend otherwise. What exactly has the town of Joyful been saying about me?"

She held her breath, wondering if he'd laugh her suspicions off, if he'd walk away, if he'd leap in the pool.

He did none of the above. Instead, he did something even more shocking.

Johnny Walker told her the truth.

DANEEN WOULD have been having a grand old time tonight catching up with old friends and reliving the glory days of her teen years if not for two things: Emma Jean Frasier was here, and Johnny Walker was with her.

They'd disappeared outside a little while ago, and though Daneen had put her head together with friends to keep talking over the outrageous Emma-as-porn-star rumors, she watched every step they took out of the room.

They look good together.

She hated to admit it, but it was true. She hadn't seen her ex-brother-in-law looking so interested and protective of a woman in, oh, forever. Wherever Emma Jean had gone all evening, Johnny's stare had followed. He'd tossed back a few drinks, though he wasn't a drinker. He'd talked with people she knew he loathed. And he'd grown more and more tense as the evening wore on.

Because he was in love with Emma Jean. Any fool could see it, and Daneen Brady Walker was no fool.

"He loves her," she muttered as she sipped her beer, wondering why that left such a strange, achy feeling inside her.

It wasn't that she wanted Johnny for herself. She didn't. Well, she wanted to have sex with him, at least once before she died. He was at the top of the "want to have sex with before I die" lists of a *lot* of women in Joyful. Him and Brad Pitt.

But she didn't love Johnny, didn't want him as a husband or anything. For better or for worse, she'd lost her heart to Jimbo Boyd years ago and it wasn't big enough to love another man.

There was, however, still enough resentment inside her to not want Emma Jean to have him.

It was silly. She didn't resent Emma being involved

with Johnny, it was her involvement with *Nick* that still rankled.

Nick. Her all-too-brief, all-too-absent husband. He was her first love, the one she'd thought would last forever. At least until he'd walked out on her during her eighth month of pregnancy. He'd enlisted in the Marines, preferring to go get his ass shot up in Bosnia—to play *hero*—than staying in their crappy little one-room efficiency apartment in Savannah with her.

On dark nights, when she was alone with Jack sleeping in his room right down the hall, she wondered how different things might have been if Jack really had been Nick's son. She could have made him love her, she *knew* she could.

She hadn't lied on purpose. Not really. When she'd told Nick she was pregnant, she'd known it was at least possible he was the daddy. Daneen had been very sure of who the possibles were, and Nick was one of them.

The two of them had hooked up after a party during spring break, when he and Emma had been quarreling. He'd been drunk. She'd been, well, not drunk, but intoxicated enough not to care that she was having sex with a guy who was almost passed out in the backyard of a friend's house.

So, yes, he could have been the daddy. If she'd only been two months pregnant, as she'd hoped, instead of four months pregnant, as he'd quickly figured out.

Her insides grew tight and achy as she thought about Nick, whom she'd had a crush on since seventh grade. When Emma Jean had waltzed into town and grabbed him for herself in senior year, Daneen had been devastated. Truly hurt. Denied something she'd really wanted for the first time since her mother had died and her father had decided to spoil her rotten to make up for it.

Yet Daneen was the one everyone had thought of as the bitch for running away with Nick the night before Prom.

Not anymore, though. Because tonight, Emma was the subject of conversation. The room was nearly buzzing as the rumor floated about from person to person like a busy bee.

"Porn star," she muttered, shaking her head in disbelief. "Ridiculous."

For the life of her, she could not understand this whole thing. It should be clear to anybody that the woman was too stiff and proper to ever get naked in front of strangers, much less have sex in front of a whole entire camera crew. Plus, she didn't have the body for it. Those boobs on the billboard were three times the size of Emma's...or of any unsurgically enhanced woman's. Nope, Emma was cute, but too normal-looking to be a man's fantasy woman.

Except Johnny's.

Yeah. She apparently was his. And had been for a very long time.

A part of her—the part that appreciated his many kindnesses and the support Johnny had given her and Jack over the years—wished him luck with his fantasy girl. He deserved to be happy, if any man in this lousy town did.

The more spiteful part of her wished Emma would leave Joyful as soon as this reunion was over and never come back.

Thinking about Johnny reminded her of what they'd talked about earlier in the parking lot. About how he was helping Emma by looking into the sale of the property where Joyful Interludes was being built.

Glancing at her watch, she decided to take a chance and call Jimbo. If Hannah answered, well, she had a legitimate reason for calling at this time on a Saturday night. Jimbo had asked her to keep him apprised of anything she heard relating to Emma. This definitely qualified.

Ducking out of the room into the hallway, Daneen stood in a quiet alcove and pulled her cell phone out of her purse. Fortunately, Hannah didn't answer. "Hey, it's me," she said when she heard Jimbo's voice.

"Daneen…" Jimbo sounded distracted. And his voice was slightly slurred. "Why are you calling me at home?"

"I heard something tonight I thought might interest you." She quickly filled him in on her conversation with Johnny.

For a long moment, Jimbo stayed quiet. Then he said, "Johnny told you he's personally looking into it?"

"Yes."

Jimbo cleared his throat and fumbled with the phone. Daneen waited patiently, then heard him talking to someone else. *Hannah.* When he got back on the line, he was using his blustery, mayor-type voice. "Well, yes, thank you so much for calling to let me know, *Dan.*"

Oh, great, now her own father was being used as a cover for her illicit affair. God, wouldn't that give him a heart attack if he found out? As would this whole mess.

"You're welcome," she said. Then she ran a weary hand over her eyes, wondering why she continued to do this to herself. She disconnected the call, suddenly feeling all her earlier happiness over the evening dissipate.

Dropping her phone into her purse, she thought about reaching for her keys and going home. She and Jack could stay up late watching a scary movie and eating popcorn. That sounded much more appealing to her than hanging out with a bunch of gossipy people who hadn't changed a bit since high school. Or dancing yet again with Fred Willis, who'd tagged along after her all evening.

Before she could turn to leave, however, someone came storming down the hallway from the direction of the pool exit. She froze, watching Emma Jean Frasier practically march into the banquet room.

Right then, Daneen decided to stay. Because, suddenly, things looked like they were going to get interesting again.

JOHNNY HADN'T TAKEN Emma outside with the intention of telling her what people were saying about her. He'd wanted to act as a buffer—as Claire had been doing—between Em and anyone ignorant enough to confront her with the ridiculous stories. When he'd seen Claire glaring daggers at Melanie Forsythe, another woman at their table, he'd figured the time had come to step in.

He'd intended a dance. One dance to diffuse things, let people get distracted, and get Emma out of their line of fire. When she'd asked him to step outside, instead, it had seemed just as good a solution.

Going outside was *supposed* to be about letting her get some air. It wasn't supposed to turn funny and playful and sexy and personal.

But it had. And for a brief time, he'd forgotten all the decisions he'd made the night before about staying out of Emma Jean's life.

He still couldn't believe what she'd gone through at work. Nor the laid-back, easy way she talked about it. Her personal life had fallen apart around her, yet she'd been casually joking about hit lists and birth control.

Birth control. He hadn't liked the detour his thoughts had taken then. It'd been all he could do not to pull her into his arms and kiss the teasing laughter off her lips. To say to hell with it all, play her hero, let her take whatever comfort she needed and enjoy it for as long as he could.

Emma, however, hadn't seemed to be in need of comfort. In fact, she'd seemed completely in control. So much so that when she'd demanded the truth, he'd had no choice but to give it to her.

All of it.

He hadn't been sure what to expect. Horrified tears? Righteous anger? Hysterical laughter? All three?

The one thing he *didn't* expect was what he got. Silence. A long, silent moment when her pretty gold eyes grew wide, her mouth fell open and she stood there staring at him.

"Are you okay?" he'd asked. "It's silly gossip, it'll die down."

She hadn't said a word. She'd just whirled around and marched back inside. After one second's consideration, he realized exactly what she was going to do.

Oh, boy.

"Emma," he called after her, not sure whether he should try to change her mind. Or tell her to go for it.

"What's going on?" Daneen stepped out from a mirrored, recessed alcove, watching with him as Emma disappeared inside the banquet room.

"I told her the rumors."

Daneen whistled. "Is she doing what I think she's doing?"

"Uh-huh."

"This I gotta see."

The two of them entered the room where the reunion was still going strong. His gaze immediately scanned the crowd for Emma's bright blond hair and her bright red dress.

The crowd had finished dinner, and the drinks had begun to flow a little heavier. Loud nineties music blared from the deejay's speakers and a bunch of people crowded the dance floor, moving in one big, intoxicated mass.

In one corner of the room, Chuck Stubbins was posing for pictures with some of his football buddies, all of them trying to look young and tough instead of thirtyish and balding. In another, Gloria Gilmore, who'd been the class president, was operating a slide projector. Who was it that said pictures from the old days *had* to be dragged out of closets for these things? As was typical, the projector flashed pictures from the yearbook up onto a huge screen, just to remind everyone, in case they'd forgotten, that they were no longer those young, carefree kids.

Close by, he saw Sue Ann Tillman Todd. According to one of the pictures on the screen, she'd been named Girl Most Likely To Succeed in the class superlatives. Since she now seemed to be gleefully regaling some of her former classmates with the details of her divorce settlement, during which she'd ruined her dentist husband, he figured she'd succeeded all right.

He continued to check out the room. At the middle table, a former cheerleader—who looked like she couldn't stand up straight unless someone stuck a pole up her ass— wobbled on top of a chair. She held two fistfuls of flowers, obviously taken from the massacred centerpiece, and was shaking them like pom-poms. Around her were a few former jocks who looked ready to catch her if she fell. Who'd catch *them,* he had no idea.

Then he spotted her. Right through the middle of all the madness marched Emma Jean. She beelined for the deejay, exchanged a few words with him, then gratefully accepted his microphone. "Excuse me, may I have your attention?"

Johnny closed his eyes briefly, and took in a deep breath, almost feeling sorry for the Joyful class of 1995. Because they were about to get some payback.

"I'm sorry to interrupt the music," Emma said with a big smile for the deejay, who looked ready to fall down to his knees in front of her. Johnny'd been on the receiving end of that smile, so he understood completely.

The room slowly grew quiet. Conversations died down, laughter stopped midjoke and the few people still eating put down their forks. Finally, the only sound in the room was the mechanical swish of the slide machine, still flashing black-and-white photos from ten years ago onto the wall.

How appropriate that the slide now splashed up there for all to see pictured Emma Jean Frasier...Nicest Girl.

"I just want to tell you all how thrilled I am to be back here in little old Joyful," Emma said into the microphone, her honeyed voice holding a hint of southern accent. "Wow, my life has changed so much since I lived here, I can't tell you how much fun it's been to see y'all again." Her eyes scanned the crowd. "Why, the friendliness, the sweetness, the *kindness* of this place was something I'd almost forgotten about in all my travels. My varied experiences."

Johnny heard a murmur nearby, followed by a feminine giggle.

Just wait.

"Imagine my happiness in knowing the generosity of spirit, the honesty, openness and goodness I'd always remembered about Joyful, Georgia was still here."

Beside him, Daneen let out a little snort. He cast a quick glance at her and noticed the smile playing about her lips. She knew full well what Emma was up to and was enjoying the hell out of it. One thing he had to say for his sister-in-law, she believed in equal opportunity cattiness.

"My, it seems like everyone here just loves everybody."

Emma looked over at Melanie, the woman Claire had been glaring at during dinner. "And y'all are *so* forgiving. I mean, Melanie, imagine you and Charlie getting married even after what you did when you went down to Florida for spring break in senior year."

The woman blanched. Beside her, her husband's eyes grew round. Emma didn't even appear to notice. "And heavens, Kevin O'Leary, imagine *you* a town council member even though you used to cheat like crazy off of everybody else during algebra exams."

Kevin's face turned red and he gulped at his beer.

"Then there's you, Jason Michaels—how wonderful that you did finally find some girl to marry you. We were all so worried since all your ex-girlfriends used to talk about your—" she lowered her voice as if whispering into the microphone "—size issue."

A couple of men laughed. Everyone else remained silent. While beside him, Johnny heard Daneen sigh. "Oh, boy," she whispered, "I don't imagine I'm going to escape this?"

"Probably not," he whispered back, glad his ex-sister-in-law seemed to be taking Emma's tirade in stride. Unlike the rest of the class, who merely gaped in shock and confusion.

"And Courtney Zimmerman, how wonderful that you and Marie Fox were able to stay friends even after she told everyone you'd slept with fifteen guys during the summer between junior and senior year," Emma said, smiling at a blonde in a black dress, who'd been standing beside a blonde in a blue dress. The two blondes turned on each other and started whispering fast and furious until one's husband stepped between them to pull his wife away.

Emma's smile slowly faded, as if she'd lost the energy to continue with the spite that was so unlike her. She looked over the crowd, shaking her head, looking disgusted with them all. "It's not pretty, is it? Not fun. The rumors and the gossip." Then she snorted a laugh. "The lies."

She walked over to the deejay, and appeared to be about to hand him the microphone back. Johnny sensed a collective sigh of relief from the crowd, who would likely be back to ripping each other to shreds in a few minutes, but for now seemed cowed into silence.

But Emma wasn't quite done. Before giving up the microphone, she turned to face the room again. "By the way, in case you're interested in the *truth,* I'm a financial analyst and stockbroker. I've worked for a major Manhattan firm for the past five years." She laughed softly. "I am *not* responsible for that monstrosity of a building being constructed on what I thought, until I arrived back in town, was *my* property. And believe me, if there's *anything* I can do to put a stop to it, I will."

The crowd seemed to hold its breath, waiting for the punch line they all knew was coming. Then they got it.

"I've never *seen* an X-rated film, much less been *in* one."

Each person in the room giggled, coughed or whispered in reaction to her words.

Emma gave them all one last pitying look, before adding, "I've had sex with a total of three men in my life, one of whom is in this room, as you all know, since you saw us naked on prom night."

Oh, shit, now every set of eyes in the room was on him.

But even as he grew uncomfortable under the stares, another part of him was ready to sing hallelujah at her admission about her rather uninspiring sex life.

"As for who I'm sleeping with now?" she continued. "Well, frankly, that's none of your goddamn business."

Then and only then did she hand over the microphone.

Everyone in the room remained silent, frozen, watching her as she stood defiantly alone on the dance floor, looking ready to rip the arm off anyone who dared approach her. Probably only Claire could have done it, but Emma's friend remained near her husband, just as stunned as everyone else.

Johnny was about to go to her, to take her by the hand and escort her out of this place, whether she wanted him to or not.

Suddenly, however, the silence was broken by a sharp sound.

A clap. Then another. Everyone immediately looked toward the doorway to see who it was who dared to applaud Emma's outrageous performance.

Johnny couldn't see at first, until the crowd shifted. And then, one split second before he saw the man still slowly applauding Emma Jean, he heard Daneen gasp in shock.

Somehow, he knew by that one little sound, and by the sense of inevitability flowing through him, who he was going to see.

And he was right.

It was his brother Nick.

CHAPTER FOURTEEN

ON SUNDAY, while Claire went to church and then to a family gathering at her mother's house, Emma scoured the kitchen for Grandma Emmajean's recipes. She finally found them inside an old, empty box of rock salt that she remembered her grandfather using to make ice cream during long-ago summer visits.

On Monday, after Claire went off to work at her new job, Emma went to the grocery store to buy some ingredients.

Because she was going to bake a pie. She had to keep busy. Had to bake and clean and do laundry and help Claire with Eve and think about absolutely anything else but what she'd done Saturday night at the reunion.

She still couldn't believe it. Not the things she'd said—which, to be honest, had only been the truth—but that she'd said them at all.

It had been petty and childish. If she hadn't had a few drinks, and hadn't been so completely enraged by what Johnny had told her, she would never have done such a thing.

Porn star. Good grief, the entire time she'd been back in Joyful, wondering why people were acting so strangely, everyone had been talking about her wicked life as a porn star. No wonder nobody'd shown up on her doorstep with blueberry muffins. She was lucky they hadn't shown up with sex toys.

She still hadn't entirely forgiven Claire for not telling her the truth about the rumors. Her friend had apologized, and had sworn she thought the silly stories would die on their own.

Now they wouldn't die, they'd merely change. Emma wasn't a porn star, she was the tornado who'd probably managed to ruin a few marriages and destroy a few friendships Saturday night.

"I should've gone to Florida," she whispered as she stood in the kitchen, reading Emmajean's recipe for a perfect, flaky pie crust early Monday morning.

Saturday night had been shocking in a number of ways. Not just the rumors, or how she'd handled them, but also Nick's arrival. She'd certainly been surprised to see her old boyfriend at the reunion—but not nearly as surprised as everyone else had seemed.

Especially Johnny and Daneen. They'd looked stunned, both silently staring at Nick, who, Emma had to admit, had grown into as handsome a man as his brother.

Maybe it hadn't been such a big deal to Emma because she hadn't seen *any* of these people for ten years, Nick included. For Johnny, however, Nick's arrival appeared momentous.

Emma had watched the two brothers approach each other and exchange a few words. She hadn't seen much else, because Claire had soon appeared by her side, offering to drive home. Handing over her keys, Emma had immediately followed Claire out, not giving the rest of her classmates another thought.

They, however, had apparently been giving her some. Because, as bizarre as it seemed, she'd had several phone calls throughout the day Sunday, and already this morning. Nice calls. Apologetic calls. From people she'd considered friends, and those she'd hardly known.

It seemed her tirade had done some good, at least. It'd made the class of '95 take a collective look at itself, at the gossiping and malicious rumors that'd been such a part of high school life…and remained part of their lives today. Some, it appeared, didn't like what they saw in the mirror Emma had held up before them. So far, she had three lunch invitations as well as an offer to come speak to the local ladies' group about stock market investing.

Only in Joyful could she go from pariah to social butterfly with one public meltdown.

Removing the large package of pecans from the grocery store bag, Emma began to sort them out into piles for individual pies. One for her, Claire and Eve. One for Claire's mom. And one for the woman who owned the hair salon. She might have been joking about Emma bringing her a pie if she wanted a job, but Emma was very serious. It was time to get on with her life, and short-term employment was step one.

Eventually, word would spread about what Emma had done at the reunion. The porn star stories would die down, but they'd soon be replaced with ones about Emma's rant. Meaning that while her classmates seemed to suddenly like her again, her job prospects probably still wouldn't be too great.

If it took a pie to get a job, darn it, she'd bake a pie.

So she did. She followed her grandmother's recipe to the tiniest detail, remembering not to overroll the crust, as her grandmother used to caution when Emma watched her bake.

By the time she was done in the kitchen, she had three

pecan pies cooling on racks, and she was covered with sticky syrup and sugar. But it was worth it. Because the smell in the house had done something to her. Calmed her. Soothed her. Reminded her of so many days in this kitchen, of the happiest parts of her childhood. She began to feel better than she had in weeks.

About to go upstairs to shower, she paused when she heard someone ringing the doorbell. She certainly wasn't dressed for company, but it was such a nice change to have some, she didn't bother grabbing a brush for her hair or a towel for her hands.

When she opened the door and saw the man standing there with his back to her, his thick brown hair made her believe it was Johnny. Reaching for her hair, she immediately began to breathe faster. Darn the man for catching her off guard, looking so awful again!

Then he turned around.

"Nick," she said, her brow shooting up in surprise.

"Hey, Emma Jean."

"Hello. Wow, this is unexpected." Glancing at her watch, she added, "You're, uh, ten years late."

He winced. "I deserved that. But can I come in, anyway?"

She nodded, stepping out of the way and ushering him inside.

The years had been kind to Nick—as kind as they'd been to his brother. He was tall and thick-chested, and he stood straight, with a rigidity illustrating his military background. His thick hair was the same shade as Johnny's, but his eyes were brown, like their mother's. And they didn't twinkle the way Johnny's blue ones did. Still, he'd turned into quite a handsome man, though a much more serious-looking one than she'd have expected.

"You sure surprised everyone Saturday night," she murmured, gesturing for him to sit on a chair near the window. She sat opposite him, on the couch.

"You're one to talk. That was quite a speech."

Feeling her cheeks pinken, she defended herself. "You don't know what this town has put me through this past week."

"Someone filled me in."

Emma frowned. "Johnny? He knew all along. Knew and didn't tell me until Saturday. I could kill him."

Nick leaned back in his chair. Lifting a booted foot, he crossed it over his jean-clad leg and stared at her. "No, it wasn't Johnny." Then he added, "And I suspect you don't want to kill him. You and he got awful friendly, didn't you?"

She met his even stare. "Yeah. We did." She didn't add *not that it's any of your business.* It was implied.

He apparently got the message, because he finally smiled a bit. "You sure have changed."

"Have *you?*"

He nodded. "Yeah. I'm not the good-for-nothing Walker kid anymore. You're not the only one who got out and got a real life. I just made detective on the Savannah P.D."

"I'm glad to hear it," she said, meaning what she said. Staying here would have been the worst thing he could have done. It was, however, hard to picture Nick a cop, though she bet the women of Savannah didn't mind having him on the beat.

"Anyway, I figured the time had come to straighten things out with some people here in Joyful. I didn't know you were gonna be one of them until I saw you Saturday night." Shrugging, he added, "I'm glad you are. Because I came over here to apologize."

"For?"

"For not showing up that night."

He was apologizing for standing her up at the prom. Not for cheating on her with Daneen. Then again, that might be asking too much, considering he had to have heard her confession about who *she'd* slept with on prom night.

"It's all right." She curled her legs up and wrapped her arms around them, looking at him over her knees. "I went anyway."

"I heard."

They fell silent for a long moment, during which the only sound was the ticking of the mantel clock and the flick of the ceiling fan above them. Then he finally said, "It was always Johnny you wanted, wasn't it? Even when we were dating?"

Emma had no idea how he could have known such a thing. But he was right. It'd always been Johnny. Since before she'd even *met* Nick Walker.

She slowly nodded.

"I figured. So are you two…"

Emma ran a weary hand through her messy, curly hair, probably smearing Karo syrup into it. "I don't know what we are. Your brother is one confusing man."

"Yeah, he is."

Nick rose to his feet. Emma stood also, sensing he'd done what he came to do and was ready to check her off his list. She didn't think the rest of his meetings with the people he'd be talking to here in Joyful were going to be quite as easy.

"Well, it was good seeing you, Emma Jean. I hope things work out for you, however you want them to."

However she wanted them to? That was anyone's guess.

Walking him to the door, she wondered whether to hug

him, or shake his hand, or kiss his cheek. This was the boy who'd asked her to marry him many years ago. She never would have. But it'd been nice to be asked.

"Take care of yourself, Nick," she said, settling on a friendly smile.

When she opened the door to let him out, she found herself very thankful she hadn't given him the hug, or the kiss.

Because Johnny stood right outside.

JOHNNY HAD WAITED until Monday to go see Emma because he knew Claire would be around all day Sunday. And because he'd figured he'd be dealing with his brother.

To his surprise, though, Nick hadn't come knocking on his door. Johnny finally figured if he was going to end this thing between them, he was going to have to track his hardheaded sibling down out at their mother's place.

He'd planned to do exactly that Monday afternoon. First, however, he'd wanted to check on Emma, to see how she was doing after her big meltdown Saturday night.

Man, what a meltdown. She'd been a sight to see. All fiery and indignant, yet still vulnerable and far too good for the crowd who'd been belittling her.

He'd been so incredibly proud of her. Yet, at the same time, sad, because she'd had to stoop to a level so far beneath her. He wanted to tell her so, face-to-face.

And maybe tell her a lot more. Like how sorry he was for ever imagining she'd used him out of self-pity or weakness. Because, damn, one thing the woman had not been Saturday night was self-pitying or weak!

He was still smiling over it when he reached her house and walked to her front door. Before he could even lift his hand to knock, the door swung open from the inside.

His kid brother stood there. Right beside a smiling Emma Jean.

"What the hell are *you* doing here?" he snapped, before he thought better of it.

"Well, hello to you, too, big brother," Nick said as he stepped out onto the porch. "I just came to say hello, and goodbye, which I have, and now I'm leavin'." Nick's easy tone didn't hide the hard look in his eyes.

"Where are you going?" Johnny asked, trying not to wonder why, and for how long, Nick had been here.

"Back out to Mama's." Nick nodded to Emma, stepped out onto the porch, and stood nose to nose with Johnny. Their stares met and held. Finally Nick added, "When you're finished here, come out and find me. We have some talkin' to do."

Johnny answered with one short nod, then watched his brother walk down the front steps.

Once Nick's truck had roared away down the street, Johnny turned to Emma. She stood in the doorway, looking like anything but a woman who'd just had any kind of romantic tryst, thank the lord. Her hair was a mess— which, he'd decided, really did suit her. And she wore a simple sleeveless T-shirt and shorts, both of which showed evidence of something sticky. Not to mention what looked like white flour fingerprints on her hip.

"Lemme guess," he finally said, trying to hide a smile, "you found your grandma's recipes."

She grinned, looking relieved that he hadn't launched into a million questions about Nick. "Yes, I did."

He had questions, all right. He sure wanted to know why his brother had been here...had he apologized? Had he gone on the attack because of what Emma and Johnny had done on prom night? Had he tried to get her back? But he wasn't about to ask Emma to explain a thing while they stood out here in the eagle-eye view of all the busybodies on the street.

"Pecan?" he asked instead.

"Yep. Want some?"

"You did promise me a piece."

She turned and let him in, shutting the front door behind him. He followed her down the hall, watching the gentle sway of her hips and the supple movement of her long, smooth legs. He had to swallow hard, suddenly hungry for a lot more than pie. But before he could do anything about his crazy, instant hunger—and even he didn't know what that might have been—she started to babble a mile a minute.

"You can't imagine how hard it was to read the writing. Grandma must have written the recipe down fifty years ago and never rewrote it. Plus I had to go get pecans, only can you believe it I had to get them at the grocery store because I couldn't find a single roadside stand?"

"Shut up, Em," he murmured when they reached the kitchen.

She swung around to face him, her eyes wide. "What?"

"You don't owe me an explanation," he added, knowing why she was so nervous and chatty. The realization made his jealous imagination kick into overdrive as he wondered what the explanation really was.

"About the pie?"

"About Nick."

She fisted a hand and put it on her hip. "Oh, I don't, huh? Thanks for being so magnanimous."

"I meant, it's none of my business what Nick was doing here."

Her eyes narrowed as she stared at him from a few feet

away. Her lips pulled into a tight line before she nodded once. "You're right. It's none of your business."

None of his business. That's exactly what he'd just said. Only, he didn't mean it. It *was* his business, because he was crazy about Emma Jean Frasier and had been for eleven years. Damned if he wanted her taking up with his brother again. Not when he was the one she really wanted.

And he knew he was.

Instead of saying any of that, however, he simply crossed his arms and leaned against the counter to watch her.

"Because, you know, it's not as if we're involved or anything," she said as she grabbed a knife and thrust it into the middle of a pecan pie. "I mean, just because we have sex when we feel the need to get off, that doesn't mean we mean anything to each other."

Christ, that hurt. Hurt badly. His jaw tightened and he bit out, "Yeah, right. Exactly."

She looked up, focusing her full attention on his face. Her eyes were stormy, her lips trembling, as if a world of turmoil was going on in her head and she didn't know what to say.

So she didn't say anything. She acted instead.

Before he realized what she was going to do, she'd scooped up a big handful of gooey pecan pie filling and lobbed it right at him. It hit him on the chin and jaw, a little of it landing on his lips.

Johnny stood there, shocked, feeling the oozy brown mess drip down his neck and onto his crisp white dress shirt.

"There, you have your pie," she snapped, her whole body shaking with emotion. "You can enjoy it after you get the hell out."

She'd doused him with pie. And she was absolutely furious. All because he'd said exactly what he thought she wanted to hear.

But maybe she *hadn't* wanted to hear it.

His heart sped up a bit as he acknowledged what she might be admitting. That there was something between them. Something more than sex, something emotional. On *both* sides.

Unsure how to react, Johnny started by flicking out his tongue to lick off some of the filling. "Good," he murmured, meaning it.

Then he slowly approached her. For every step he took forward, she took one back, watching him with wide eyes. She suddenly seemed to have realized what she had done, and how he might react to it. Nibbling on her bottom lip, she whispered, "It was an accident."

He stepped closer, until she was backed against the counter. "Bullshit."

Then, because words had never expressed things as well as actions when it came to Emma Jean, he lifted his hand to his chin and wiped off some of the filling. Reaching toward her, he smeared it on her neck, almost laughing at the look of shock on her face. Before she could react, he bent down to sample the sweet flavors of old Emmajean's famous pecan pie…and her granddaughter.

"Johnny," she said, moaning as he licked and sucked and tasted his way to the hollow of her throat, "what are you doing?"

"What do you think?" he whispered. "I'm eating my pie. You didn't really want me to take it to go, did you?"

She shook her head, and tilted her head back to give him better access. "No, I didn't."

Finally, when he'd licked her clean, he said, "All gone."

Emma didn't say a word. She simply opened her eyes

and looked at him. Then, still silent, she reached up to scrape more of the filling off his chin. He held his breath, dying to nip at her fingertips, to suck the sweetness from them, but wanting to see what she'd do.

With a seductive smile, she pressed her fingers—and the filling—to her throat, then slid it down in a straight line to below the neck of her shirt.

"I get seconds?"

"And thirds, if you want them," she whispered.

That answered a lot of unasked questions and Johnny's reservations melted completely away. He licked away the sweet goo from her collarbone and her throat. Then lower, pausing only to reach for the bottom of her shirt, and tug it up and off her.

She wore nothing underneath. His breath caught and he just looked at her, feeling hungry for so much more than dessert. Unable to resist, he cupped her, tweaking one tight nipple between his fingers until she gasped.

"Johnny…"

"Shh." Lifting her up by the waist, he set her down on the kitchen counter and stepped easily between her legs. Her eyes closed as her head fell back. She did nothing but moan as he devoured all of the filling she'd smeared on herself.

When it was gone, he reached for the pie, drew out more of the sweet gooiness and spread it lower. Across the top of one breast, then the other. Then down, smearing all that sticky stuff on her beautiful nipple.

She shivered and sighed, almost shaking as he played with her, toyed with her, not licking away the filling as she so obviously wanted.

"It's gonna get hard…"

"It already is," he growled.

She laughed, low in her throat, and he followed the sound, lowering his mouth to lick and taste and kiss her clean. When he reached her breast, he was very thorough, savoring every drop. Until finally he closed his lips over her nipple and sucked deeply, the sweetness of the pie not comparing to the sweetness of her skin.

She jerked and cried out in reaction, pressing harder against him as if begging for more. Then, when he pulled away, she met his stare and whispered, "Please…"

He knew what she wanted, and he wanted it too. Slowly, very slowly, he bent closer, watching her gold eyes grow molten and soft as she anticipated his kiss. Her lips parted, welcoming his and they both breathed a little, sighed a little, dreamed a little.

"Emma…"

"I know."

Then there were no more whispers, he couldn't wait and had to devour her, to sip from her tongue and taste the inside of her mouth. She was sweeter than any dessert and he savored every bit of her.

When they drew apart for a breath, he ran a tender hand through her curly hair. "You didn't mean what you said."

She shook her head. "You didn't mean it when you agreed."

"No, I didn't."

She hesitated for one moment, then added, "Nick just came over to apologize. He was only here for five minutes."

Relief flooded through him, though he'd suspected as much. He knew Emma Jean too well to believe she had any interest in Nick. Unfortunately, the green-eyed monster in his gut had been the one in charge of his emotions since he'd arrived.

"What does this mean, Johnny?"

He knew what she was asking, but he didn't know the answer. At least, he didn't know what kind of answer he could give her without scaring her off. Because the first one that came to his mind was one simple word: *everything*.

It…she…meant everything to him. She always had, she always would. He supposed some would call it both his blessing and his curse.

"Something," was the answer he finally settled on. "It means something."

She smiled, a sweet, lazy kind of smile, and replied, "I need you to kiss me now."

He paused, meeting her stare. Then he told her exactly what was in his heart. What had been in his heart for ten long years.

"I don't want you to *need* me, Emma." Wondering if she could hear the intensity of emotion coursing through him, he continued. "I want you to *want* me."

She lifted a hand and cupped his cheek, her skin cool and soft against his face. Then she really rocked his world. "Don't you know, Johnny? I've wanted you from the minute you stole my ankle bracelet."

He froze, taking her words in, letting them roll around in his mind as he wondered if he could believe them. If he could *allow* himself to believe them.

Emma didn't seem to care whether he did or not. She wasn't waiting. With a deep sigh, she drew him close again, tilting her head back for another kiss. But just before his lips met hers, she whispered, "Can we please do this in a bed for a change?"

Laughing, Johnny nodded. "On one condition…"

Emma's eyes sparkled and her expression was pure mischief. "That we bring the pie?"

"That we bring the pie."

CORA HAD FRETTED and stewed over the Jimbo Boyd situation all weekend. At church on Sunday she'd even asked for divine guidance. When she'd reached into her purse to find money for the collection plate—and found her wallet empty—she'd figured she'd gotten it.

Jimbo. He'd be the one she'd tell. Certainly she didn't believe in blackmail, heavens no, she was a God-fearing woman who hated sin. But she did believe in an eye for an eye. And if the man had to throw more work her way, and maybe raise her salary a bit, it was only just and right. Penance, one might call it.

Knowing she couldn't confront the man while his mistress was in the office, she waited in her car across the street Monday, watching for Daneen to leave on her lunch break. After she had, Cora went inside, past the reception desk.

Jimbo's office door was partially closed. From within the other room, she heard him speaking in what sounded like a one-sided conversation, and knew he was on the phone. "No, no, this isn't a problem. She can say that all she wants, it doesn't make it so," she heard him say. "If she goes out to the club one more time, we'll have a restraining order filed against her. I promise, nothing's going to interfere with your on-time opening this September."

The club. He was talking about Joyful Interludes. Talking to the mystery owner, who, everyone in town had heard over the weekend, was *not* Emmajean Frasier's granddaughter.

"It doesn't matter if she shouts to the world that she never sold the land, because she didn't." He laughed, the dirty kind of laugh little boys made when they'd done something nasty like breaking wind in church. Then he added, "Her grandmother did, before she died, you have my word on it."

Cora stiffened. Emmajean? Sell her family place? The place she'd crowed about every single time she won another blue ribbon at the fair for her pecan pies?

Never. Not in a million years would Cora believe it. Emmajean's family had farmed that land in the last century, and the old woman had held onto it with every bit of Southern stubbornness she'd possessed. Just as Cora would have done.

Something smelled stinky. As stinky as a pair of Bob's old work socks. She suddenly had to wonder if Mayor Jimbo Boyd hadn't been up to more nasty tricks than doing the desk mambo with his secretary. For some reason, the image of the jumble of papers she'd found in Emmajean Frasier's rolltop desk a couple of weeks back popped into her mind. Papers…deeds…things with signatures. All locked up in a house to which Jimbo held the key.

Seemed worth thinking about some more. Maybe even worth a trip to the county records building to do some nosing around in the land transfer files. It might even be worth mentioning to someone official.

Maybe even the *real* power in this town—first lady Hannah Boyd.

FOR THE REST of her life, Emma Jean Frasier would associate the smell of pecans with orgasms. It'd be instantaneous. Sixty years from now, she'd be an old lady, pushing her cart through whatever kind of high-tech grocery store they'd have in the future and would pass by the bakery where someone was handing out samples of pecan pie. Right then and there she'd start shaking and panting. She'd scare little children and her dentures would fall out and she just wouldn't care because the smell would *always* take her back to this place where, for the past half hour, Johnny Walker had been devouring pie—and her—until the climaxes were rolling over her in unrelenting waves.

Pecan pie was now officially the most heavenly food on earth. Ambrosia. The only bad thing about it was that the stuff turned into glue when it dried.

"Oh, God," she said with a moan as she buried her face in her pillow, only to smear a glob of dried sticky filling on her nose, "I'm going to have to throw these sheets away."

Johnny, who was busy nibbling the vulnerable skin on the back of her knee, mumbled, "Do you really care?"

"No."

She didn't. How could she when he kept doing these insanely wonderful things to her? Like now, smoothing that delicious stuff up the back of her thigh with one fingertip. He tortured her, his touch light and deliberate, laying the path of pie filling. He teased her to the point of begging, but wouldn't touch her where she most wanted to be touched until he was good and ready.

"Oh, *please....*"

She tried to roll over, but he wouldn't let her. "Ah, ah, I already ate my way across the entire top of your body," he whispered as he drew nearer and nearer to the apex of her thighs. "Now I want to finish the bottom."

He returned to his mission, nuzzling, licking, tasting his way up her legs, always taking delicious detours on the way. Like when he'd nipped at the tiny birthmark on her right thigh. Or now when he...oh, when he followed the curve where her thigh met her bottom with the tip of his hot, sweet tongue. Or, oh, heavens, when he slipped that tongue deeper, lifting her hips up to gain better access.

"Johnny," she wailed. Then she couldn't say anything

because her world exploded with color and intensity as his mouth went lower, deeper, to eat and drink his fill from her. Until he finally taunted her into another climax that had her practically screeching into the pillow.

"I'll get you for this," she whispered when she was somewhat sane again. "I will get even if I have to bake another pie."

Rolling her over, he gave her a lazy grin, then lay on his side next to her. "There's plenty left, sugar."

And Emma made very good use of every bit of it.

CHAPTER FIFTEEN

CLAIRE HAD FIGURED Tim would show up at her mother's house yesterday, for Sunday dinner, but he hadn't. Part of her was glad. Another part missed him like mad. She missed sitting with him at church, exchanging amused glances when the choir started to sing "Joyful, Joyful, We Adore Ye," considering how unholy this town was. She'd missed hearing he and Eve laugh together as he pushed her on the old tire swing in the backyard.

Her mother and father hadn't asked many questions. She had the feeling they knew what was going on. When she'd left, Mama had given her a big plate of food and told her to bring it home to Emma Jean, to thank her for getting Claire to dress in something that wasn't shaped like a sack.

She was still worrying over Tim's unexpected absence when she left the newspaper office Monday morning during her break.

"Hey, babe."

She immediately stiffened.

Tim looked tired. His hair was uncombed and he wore a pair of jeans, unthinkable on a weekday given the dress code at the engineering firm where he worked.

"Hi," she replied. "You look bad."

"I feel bad."

"I'm sorry about that," she admitted, meaning it. She was sorry, truly sorry her husband was going through this pain. His world had shifted, as had hers. But she'd been the one to cause the shift, and he hadn't quite caught up. At least not yet.

The sad look on his face, and the bunch of daffodils he held out to her, made her realize it might be time to bring him up to speed. On a lot of things. "Want to grab a cup of coffee?"

"I'd rather grab you and hug you and never let you go."

"Well, gee, imagine, you hugging me without being *ordered* by Eve to give us both a family hug. Don't hurt yourself."

His jaw dropped. Then he stared searchingly at her, his fine hazel eyes not hiding a thing. "You're not serious."

Breathing deeply, she replied, "Yeah, I am."

Tim didn't hesitate. He put his arms around her shoulders and pulled her close, holding her, rocking her a little, rubbing his hand up and down her back. "God, I love you so much, Claire, I'd never want you to think I don't love holding you."

She sniffled a little, sucking up his warmth, wondering how long it had been since her husband had taken her into his arms in broad daylight on a public street.

"Let's go talk," she murmured against his chest.

Claire didn't trust the open ears of the diner or the Denny's by the highway, so she suggested they grab some coffee and take a walk in the park. In spite of the stifling heat, it was a beautiful day, with a bright blue sky and a few puffy white clouds floating here and there. And yet she still felt like crying.

She didn't want to hurt her husband. She loved him. Loved him so much she never wanted to think about living without him.

You have to do this, she reminded herself. For their future, she had to get everything out in the open so they could work together to try to make things right.

"Your friend sure made a speech the other night."

She tensed, wondering if Tim was going to bash Emma Jean.

"Sounds like she had good reason, though. I heard those stories and never thought for a minute they weren't true."

"I told you they weren't."

Tim grinned. "As I recall, that was right after I came and bailed you out of jail. I wasn't much in the mood to be charitable after she got you arrested."

"I don't need anybody's help to get into trouble." Lowering her voice, she added, "At least, I didn't used to need any help."

Tim took her hand, lacing his fingers through hers. "I remember. You were hell on wheels."

"You used to like me that way."

"I like you *any* way." Then he clarified. "*Love* you any way. And I'm sorry I reacted so badly Friday. I know we agreed you'd go back to work sometime. I just hadn't figured you'd want to until Eve started school."

"I was going crazy," she admitted. "I love being with Eve, but sometimes I think if I don't have another adult to talk to, I'm going to lose my mind."

Tim led her to a park bench and sat down with her. "I guess I was mainly upset that you didn't even talk to me about it."

"I've tried to several times over the past year."

He shrugged in a typical "guy" way. "I didn't think you were serious. You always dropped it after bringing it up once."

"Because *you* seemed so against it."

"Because I thought you didn't really want it."

"Well, we were obviously both wrong."

He fell silent for a moment, probably thinking the same thing she was: *when did we stop being able to communicate?*

"Okay," he finally said, "so you're back at work part-time. And Eve seems to really like it at the day care."

Claire raised a brow. "She does?"

Tim nodded.

"She hasn't said anything to me, except that it's fine."

With a snicker, her husband said, "Because she knew you'd tease her. Turns out Courtney Foster goes there and she called Eve 'Angelica' the first day. Since then Eve has been working very hard to make Courtney her best friend."

Claire smiled, suddenly wanting to hug her baby.

"There's more to say isn't there?" Tim asked quietly.

"Well," she admitted, drawing on some inner strength she wasn't sure she'd find, "there is the fact that I feel invisible to the rest of the world…and ignored by you."

"What?"

Wow, she'd stepped into it. She might as well take the leap. "Sorry if it hurts to hear, but it's the truth. I can't remember the last time you walked in the door after work and laid a real kiss on me that wasn't just like the one you give Eve on the cheek or the forehead."

"What? I'm supposed to grab you and kiss the daylights out of you in front of Eve?" He sounded shocked.

"Why not? My parents always had a very loving relationship and I didn't grow up to be an ax-murderer or anything."

"Eew, can we please not talk about your parents' sex life?"

"Are we ready to talk about *our* sex life?"

"What sex life?" he muttered under his breath.

That made her gasp. "Oh, so you noticed?"

"Well of course I noticed, Claire. You think I'm a eunuch or something?" He leaned back on the bench, swiping a hand through his thick blond hair, then covering his eyes.

"So why haven't you done anything about it?"

Straightening, he admitted, "I kinda figured when you were ready for something normal again, you'd let me know. You're the one who made it very clear you were too tired or too unhappy with how you looked or too worried about the baby waking up in the middle for us to do anything."

"That was when she was a baby! Eve's four years old."

"Exactly," he shot back, his eyes dark and stormy. "So where's my Claire? Where's the woman I used to find naked and on top of me during the night? The one who'd climb into the shower with me in the morning or grab me under the table when we were in a public restaurant until I was tempted to toss you onto the table and dive on you right there in front of everyone?" He shook his head, looking weary and confused. "I thought she'd been replaced by someone who decided she was now a mother and that certain things weren't…proper. And weren't going to happen anymore. You sure didn't seem interested."

Claire stared at him, unable to believe what she was hearing. God, all the things she'd been feeling and thinking and believing and crying over—he'd been feeling, too.

His words almost angered her at first. He was the one who'd rolled over night after night. But then she thought about it, and had to admit the truth…the times they did have sex he usually initiated it. Unfortunately, she often had such difficulty letting go of her resentment for all the times they *weren't,* that she seldom enjoyed it.

Her feelings had obviously showed.

They sat there for several long moments, thinking things

over, their hands still touching. Finally Claire said what was deepest in her heart, knowing it was what she had to say. "I love you so much, Tim. And I want you." She squeezed his hand. "I want the man who can make love to me for two hours straight because he focuses on *our* pleasure, not just his."

He chuckled. "Oh, God, not that *Cosmo* thing again."

She rushed on. "I adore our daughter. I'd die to keep her safe, and I know you would, too."

His smile faded and he looked very serious as he nodded.

"But there will come a time when Eve grows up and leaves, and it's just Tim and Claire." She lifted a hand to his cheek, and he immediately turned his head to press a kiss in her palm. "Before that happens, we have to make sure there's a Tim and Claire who *want* to finish out their lives together."

She stood, ready to go back to work, knowing they'd said enough for now. Enough to get them both thinking.

"Eve's not the only one," Tim murmured as he rose to stand beside her.

She raised a brow.

Running his fingers through her hair, Tim drew her close and whispered, "I'd die to keep you safe and happy too, Claire." Then he kissed her, deeply and passionately, right there in the park in front of the mothers pushing strollers and the old guys playing checkers.

When he drew away to look down at her, Claire said, "I'll come home tonight."

He shocked her by shaking his head. "Stay at your friend's."

Her stomach clenched as she wondered if she'd hurt him too deeply, if it was too late for them to make things right.

"Ask her if she'll baby-sit Eve tonight, okay?" Tim said. "Because I want to take my wife on a date. If she'll have me."

Claire's lips widened into a smile as she began to feel, for the first time in ages, that they were going to be okay. "She'll have you all right," she said. "She can't wait to have you."

WITH ONE PIE GONE, devoured during the most delicious sex of her life, and another one cut into by Eve and Emma Monday night during their baby-sitting adventure—which had left her more exhausted than any four hours she'd spent on the floor of the New York Stock Exchange—Emma was left with only one pecan pie.

That one was spoken for. By the hair salon owner.

Seemed like a rather "flaky" thing to base her short-term future on, but, she figured, it was worth a shot. So she carried it into the Let Your Hair Down salon first thing Tuesday morning. Inside, she immediately looked for the owner, who'd introduced herself as Doris the other day. Doris, a middle-aged woman with blond hair and black roots two weeks past needing a color job, wasn't hard to spot.

Why, she wondered, did hairstylists always let their own hair get so bad? Kinda like the cobbler's kids being shoeless.

"Morning," Emma said brightly as she inhaled the familiar scents of hair products and shampoo and chemicals. She loved that smell. Salons were one of her favorite places—especially after last year. When her hair had started growing back, she'd experimented with different looks at varying lengths and had become addicted to her local salon.

Doris looked up from her station, where she was putting something blue and gunky onto the iron-gray hair of an old lady. Another stylist—young and snapping gum like she was trying to chew a wild animal into submission—was snipping away on a large woman. A third busily rolled fat rollers into the thick brassy hair of a buxom, middle-aged redhead. The waiting area was empty but for one customer, who sat there nosing through an old, tattered issue of the *Ladies' Home Journal.*

"Lord a'mighty, you found Emmajean's pecan pie recipe!" Doris cried out when she recognized Emma.

"I did."

"You're hired."

"You were serious?"

"Darn right I was." Doris had stripped off her gloves, leaving the elderly woman's head half-striped with blue colorant. "I didn't think you were seriously interested the other day. Now that I know you're not some rich, bored, porn movie queen, I figure I can give you a shot."

"Glad to see the rumor mill works both ways," Emma murmured.

"It sure does," Doris admitted. Then she snickered. "I wish I'da been there when you went after Melanie Forsythe. She's a pickle. Always claims her hair's not right and wants a discount."

"Yeah, she does," the young gum-snapping stylist said. "We all race for the bathroom when she comes in. Last one in hiding gets stuck with her."

The old lady with half a color job, who now resembled a blue-striped zebra, said, "Doris, my hair!"

"Don't matter, honey," the owner told the old lady. "You have barely enough left to fall out, anyway."

The woman, instead of being insulted, laughed. "Good time for a break, anyway, because I want a piece of that pie. Last September was the first time in forty years I didn't get to have a piece of Emmajean Frasier's pecan pie at the county fair."

Pie, it appeared, was as effective as cash when it came to bribery. Who knew?

Emma had thought to bring not only the pie, but also a knife, server, paper plates and plastic forks. Within three minutes of her entry, every woman in the place was eating a disgustingly fattening breakfast. Everyone except Emma, who didn't think she'd ever be able to eat pecan pie again after yesterday's sex adventures with Johnny.

My, oh, my, what adventures.

Claire's arrival with Eve late in the day had interrupted them. Otherwise they might still be in bed, though she didn't know if she'd be conscious by that point. She didn't know if a woman could die from having too many orgasms. For a day like yesterday, however, it would have been worth it.

"It's almost as good as your grandma's. I don't suppose you'd want to tell us her secret ingredient?" Doris asked.

Emma shook her head. "Sorry, I can't." She *literally* couldn't. Emma couldn't tell them what the secret ingredient was, since she'd never made a pecan pie before and had no idea whether Grandma Emmajean's ingredients were normal or secret or what.

"Aren't you gonna have some of your own pie, honey?" asked the red-haired woman, who'd introduced herself as Mona Harding.

"I devoured almost an entire one myself yesterday."

Well, not entirely by herself. She'd had more than a little help. Johnny had been very hungry. Insatiable. He'd made love to her so many times, in so many ways, that Emma felt she was dreaming. Only in her dreams had sex ever been as powerful, as perfect. And then, only in her dreams of Johnny.

A smile crossed her lips as she imagined telling these ladies one more tidbit about pecan pie. That it tasted ever so much yummier when it was being licked off a man's...

"Johnny didn't tell me you'd changed your hair. I like it."

That interrupted Emma's wicked memories. She looked closer at the woman who'd spoken—the one who'd been sitting in the waiting area. And suddenly she recognized her. "Mrs. Walker," she stammered, feeling heat rise in her cheeks. Good lord, to be thinking about doing *that* with a man when his mother sat right across from you!

"Welcome back to Joyful, Emma Jean," Mrs. Walker said with a sweet smile. "I meant to come and see you last week, but I had one of those awful summer colds."

Emma believed her. Johnny and Nick's mother didn't have a mean, gossiping bone in her body. She likely hadn't believed the stories for one second. Too bad there hadn't been more like her in town. "Thanks. I appreciate it."

"It's okay, Aunt Jane, the Walkers have been well represented in welcoming Emma Jean back." This came from the heavy woman who'd been getting inches cut off her long brown hair. The smile on the woman's face was genuine and teasing.

Emma liked her on sight. "You're right. But do I know you?"

"I'm Minnie Walker. Virgil's wife."

Emma remembered Virgil, though he'd been a year younger than she and Nick. A nice Walker. Not as bad or troublesome as a lot of the other family members. He was just a laid-back Southern boy who never had an unkind word for anyone.

"Yes," Mrs. Walker said, a sparkle in her brown eyes, so like Nick's, "I heard *both* my boys were at your house yesterday."

Oh, God.

"Nick waited for Johnny to show up out at my place, and he never did. Couldn't reach him at work all afternoon, either."

The woman's slightly arched brow, and amused smile, told every woman in the place exactly where Johnny had spent the previous afternoon. And hinted at what he'd been doing.

As Emma's face flushed redder, all the other women in the place began to laugh uproariously.

"Girl, if I'da known you had Johnny Walker on your tail, I woulda hired you last week," Doris said with a frank wink. "'Cause if that boy comes by my shop to visit you every woman in town's gonna decide she needs a make-over."

"He's not…" *On my tail…?* "We aren't…"

"Leave her be," Johnny's mother said. "First time my son's shown any interest in a girl from Joyful, and I'd just as soon you all not scare her off."

A girl from Joyful. She wasn't exactly that, was she? Nor would she ever be.

"I hear tell Nick's drop-dead gorgeous, like his brother," Doris said. "Whoo-ee, if I were only twenty years younger. I'd let that son of yours rescue me anytime." Then she turned to Emma. "Did you know your high school honey turned into a big hero? Got his picture on the cover of *Time* magazine and everything."

"I had no idea." She gave Mrs. Walker a curious look.

"When he was in the service, he rescued some children in Bosnia and the picture ended up in all the papers," she explained.

Emma vaguely recalled the incident, from several years back. She hadn't recognized her high school boyfriend in the Marine hero.

For the next several minutes, Emma sat back and watched the women devour the pie, with the help of the next customer who came in and pulled up a fork. Though she chatted lightly, her mind remained focused on Mrs. Walker's comment—about Johnny and a girl from Joyful.

She and Johnny hadn't talked about anything but how much they wanted each other. Not about emotions. Not about the future—which, for her, didn't include a longtime stay in Joyful. And for him, didn't include leaving. Desire and heat and air conditioners and pecan pie had taken the place of rational decision making when it came to her and Johnny. They hadn't thought one minute beyond every sexual encounter they'd shared.

She only hoped she didn't live to regret it.

"Yum, nothing like homemade pie," Minnie said, licking her lips when she was done. "I swear, I could probably make nothing but pies at the tavern, serve them with beer, and keep the place packed day and night."

Mrs. Walker frowned. "You shouldn't have to be serving up your food in that place."

"Noplace else is gonna hire someone who's only ever cooked in her own kitchen," Minnie replied with a philosophical shrug. "Not even if I were as good a cook as you, Aunt Jane." Then she turned to Emma. "Speaking of pie, are you going to be seeing Johnny today, Emma?"

"Actually, yes, I told him I'd come by the county courthouse to see where he works. Why?"

Minnie pointed to a brown sack sitting on a chair in the waiting room. "Could you bring that to him? He called last night in a tizzy saying he simply *had* to have one of my peach pies."

Emma sucked her lips into her mouth to hold back a laugh, knowing darn well why Johnny wanted the pie. After they'd o.d.'d on pecans the day before, Johnny had said something interesting.

That it was time to move on to the fruit food group.

"Is it true you work with money, stocks and things?" Doris said as she walked to the trash to throw away her paper plate.

Emma nodded. "I did. I'm…between jobs right now. But I can provide proof of employment, if you need it."

"Nah," Doris said, looking thoughtful. "Think you could give me some advice about retirement stuff while you're washing heads tomorrow? The only accountant around here is too busy and too lazy to do more'n file tax return extensions."

Tomorrow. She started her new job tomorrow. Grinning, Emma replied, "You bet." Then she looked around at the other women and said, "and the same goes for you all. If you have any questions, I'd be glad to help you out."

Thirty minutes later, she almost wished she hadn't offered. Because the women of Let Your Hair Down were *very* interested in talking money. And soon Emma wondered if she'd stumbled into a second part-time job…a completely unexpected one: financial advisor to the women of Joyful.

"SO ARE YOU feeling okay after all the unhealthy, addictive stuff you gobbled up yesterday?"

Johnny looked up from the case file lying open on his desk and saw Emma standing in the open doorway to his office. He instantly rose to his feet, a smile curling his lips. "I don't think you're unhealthy."

"But I might be dangerously addictive."

Oh, yeah, he knew that already. Hadn't he been addicted to her from the time he was a kid? To the point that he'd compared her to every other woman he'd ever met or dated, every one of them falling short of the magic that was Emma Jean?

The thoughts whizzed through his brain, but he didn't put voice to them. Their relationship—if he could call it that—was too new to handle such an admission. They'd crossed a bridge yesterday—a big one—but they weren't ready for rings or promises or anything. At least, he didn't think *she* was.

As for Johnny, well, he had to wonder if she wasn't exactly what he'd been waiting for all along. Ever since that hot summer night ten years ago when he'd finally taken her into his arms, knowing he'd never be able to find anyone else who fit there so well.

"Mornin'," he finally said, knowing she heard all the other things he didn't say. *I want you. You're beautiful. Thanks for yesterday and let's do it again. Now.*

"Good morning to you, too."

She sauntered into the room, glancing out into the reception area. "There's no one working your secretary's desk so I just let myself in. Hope that's okay."

Johnny shrugged. "I share a secretary with the county animal control officer. Lotta puppies born this spring here in Joyful."

She laughed, sounding carefree and joyous, while looking fresh and luscious. Emma wore the same raspberry-sherbet colored miniskirt she'd been wearing the day she hit town, which looked cool and appetizing, as it was likely meant to. Thankfully, though, on her feet were a pair of low-heeled sandals, instead of those high-heeled monstrosities she'd wobbled around in that day.

His groin tightened up at the sight of her. God, she was beautiful, her short platinum hair springy and shiny, her smile bright and warm. Her eyes luminous and her expression sassy. Her body…good lord, her body had given him a long night of heavenly dreams. After a long day of heavenly pleasures.

"What are you wearing under your skirt?" he asked, his voice nearly a growl. "I was dying to know the day you hit town."

She took one step into the office and kicked the door shut behind her. "Thong. Jungle pattern. Black and tan. Leopard spots."

"Who told you that one?"

"Your mother."

Her admission surprised a bark of laughter out of him. "Now, were you *really* wearing a pair of black and tan leopard-spotted underwear, Ms. Frasier?" he asked, sounding like a prosecutor.

Her expression remained coy. "Maybe not then…"

"Now?"

"Wouldn't you like to know."

"Yeah, I would. Get over here."

Watching her cross the room, his heart rate kicked into high gear. He recognized the expression on her face—both tender and a little naughty. When she held out the brown paper bag and he caught a whiff of Minnie's peach pie, he understood why. "Oh, my, why do I suddenly have a hankerin' for dessert?"

"It's time to eat healthy for a change. Peaches are such a nice, wholesome fruit. They're very good for you…much better than fattening nuts."

He tugged her into his arms and caught her laughing mouth in a deep, wet kiss that picked up where they'd left off the previous afternoon. "You're good for me," he whispered when their kiss finally ended and they drew apart enough to share a breath.

"She sure looks to be."

They instantly sprang apart as a male voice intruded. Somehow, Johnny couldn't muster any surprise when he saw his brother Nick standing there watching him.

Nick wasn't smiling, but he didn't look angry, either. Damn good thing, considering he had no claim on Emma whatsoever. Which Johnny emphasized by keeping her firmly in his embrace as he stared his brother down.

Finally Nick grinned. "Jeez, Johnny, you're gonna give the public officials of this town a bad name if you get caught going at it on your desk."

Emma lifted her nose and sniffed. "I closed the door."

"Not all the way," Nick replied. "Something's wrong with your door, it doesn't look like it stays closed."

"It's warped from the last time the roof sprung a leak," Johnny admitted. "But you still could have knocked."

"Don't worry. Considering who the public officials in this town are," Emma said, "I think we'd have to be swinging naked from the light fixture in the courtroom to surprise anyone."

"Ouch. Who you mad at?" Nick asked as he sauntered in.

"Jimbo?" Johnny asked.

Emma nodded. "Yep. I'm going over there to hash this out one way or another later today."

Johnny frowned. "No, you're not. We're working on it together, and you're staying away from him. I left some copies of the sale documents at your place the other day, and that's enough of a start. They're under your coffee table."

Nick raised a brow, but didn't ask.

"I don't want you arrested for assaulting the mayor," Johnny added. "You've made it eight whole days without getting thrown into the Joyful jail again. I want to keep a good thing going."

Nick whistled. "Why, Emma Jean Frasier, you've done turned into a woman suitable for a wicked Walker man."

The exaggerated Southern drawl and look of amusement in Nick's eyes made Johnny relax for the first time since his brother had entered the room. Nick obviously wasn't holding any kind of grudge over Em. So that was one less thing the two of them were going to be fighting over in a few minutes.

Sitting down in a chair across from Johnny's desk, Nick leaned back and stretched out his legs in front of him. Looked like his brother was here to stay. Which was fine since they did need to talk. Johnny'd had every intention of doing so yesterday, at least until Emma had, uh, sidetracked him. Last night, when he'd called his mother's house, he'd learned Nick had gone out.

"Emma, maybe I could show you around the courthouse tomorrow," he said, never taking his gaze off his brother.

She nodded, obviously sensing he and Nick had some talking to do. "All right. I need to go to the land development office, anyway."

He raised a questioning brow.

"I won't go see Jimbo. But I'm not going to sit back and do nothing while you investigate." Then she added, "As a matter of fact, some of the women at the hair salon told me there's an antinudity rally planned for this weekend. You'll never believe who's helping arrange it."

"Who?"

"Hannah Boyd, aided by Cora Dillon."

That startled him. "You're kidding! Even though Hannah's own husband handled the deal for the owners?"

Emma nodded. "Yep. Rumor has it the mayor's wife was very unhappy with him when she found out what the site was being used for. I guess her family has been in this town forever."

"You know what they say about those rumors…."

She laughed, but tossed her head in disinterest. "I know. But this seems reliable. She's coming here to get a permit for the protest and everything. I hope her husband finds out and chokes."

She sounded bloodthirsty. That kinda turned him on.

"Now, I have to go," Emma continued. "And don't you even try to stop me from looking into the records."

Knowing she didn't need his permission, and would do whatever she wanted anyway, Johnny nodded. "Okay, but *just* look through the paperwork. Promise."

She lifted her right hand into the air. "Scout's honor."

"*Were* you a Girl Scout?" he asked.

Emma shrugged. "Details, details."

Before she left, she stood up on tiptoe to kiss his cheek. He turned his face and caught her mouth, instead, needing a real kiss in spite of their audience.

Wrapping her arms around his neck, she curled into him, kissing him back. She sighed a little, then, when they pulled apart, blushed a little, before walking out on wobbly legs.

He and Nick both watched her leave. Only after she was gone did his brother admit, "She grew into one beautiful woman."

"Yes, she did." Johnny heard the edge in his own voice.

Nick appeared amused. "Back off, big man, I know I blew things with her years ago. I don't hold a grudge."

"I do," Johnny shot back.

"For?"

"Let's start with your son."

Nick's body tensed, almost imperceptibly, but Johnny recognized the reaction. A muscle in his brother's cheek began to tick, and some of the sparkle left his eyes.

Johnny pushed harder. "And your ex-wife."

Nick nodded. "You're right. It's about time this all gets out in the open. I already told Mama the truth on Saturday afternoon, so you oughta hear it, too."

Johnny leaned against his desk, almost subconsciously going into prosecutor mode by crossing his arms and looking down from above, as if about to question a witness.

"I'm a cop, Johnny. That shit doesn't work on me. And besides, I came here to clear the air. Not to hide anything."

"Came here to the office, you mean? Or here to Joyful?"

Nick rose from his chair and walked across the room, glancing out the window overlooking the downtown street below. "Here to town. To the reunion." Then he turned and faced Johnny. "I came here because I got sick and tired of Mama living a lie."

"What lie?"

Nick didn't flinch as he delivered a completely unexpected answer. "Daneen's boy is not my son, Johnny."

He wasn't sure he'd heard right at first. "What the hell are you talking about?"

Nick didn't flinch at his angry tone. "I figured it out pretty fast after we got married. I confronted her when she was about eight months pregnant. She admitted it." He rubbed a weary hand through his hair. "There was no way she could deny it unless she was gonna have the biggest preemie baby ever born."

Johnny put a hand on the back of his chair, his fingers

curling reflexively as his head began to pound. "Mama and I have been treating Jack like our own since the day Daneen brought him back to town. You let us…let *her*…fall in love with him…."

"I didn't know Daneen had continued her lie after I split," Nick admitted. "I was too humiliated, too *furious* over what she'd done—over what I'd lost—to want to talk to anyone after I found out. In case you've forgotten, I pretty much dropped off the face of the earth for the next year."

He hadn't forgotten a moment of that long, worry-filled time.

"How'd Daneen convince you to marry her, anyway?"

Nick ran a weary hand through his hair. "She told me she was pregnant and that her dad was looking for me, out for blood. I thought we'd had sex, but I wasn't totally sure. I just woke up with her on top of me after a senior party that year."

Johnny kept quiet, not about to interrupt Nick, though he wanted to shake him for being so careless.

"I had no idea there could have been anyone else. When I found out the truth, I left and we filed for divorce," Nick continued. "I joined the Marines and went away to basic for a couple of months. Then straight overseas."

By which point Daneen had been back in Joyful, playing the poor, dumped divorcée with the needy, fatherless baby.

"Honest to God, Johnny, I figured Daneen would have come back to Joyful and confronted one of the other suckers she thought could be the father. I *never* thought she'd go introducing her son to Mama as her one and only grandbaby."

Johnny began to see. It infuriated him, but he began to

understand what had happened. "I wrote to you, once we heard where you were."

Nick frowned. "Yeah, and I had every intention of coming back and making you eat every word of that letter."

Johnny suddenly remembered the circumstances of Nick's one previous return to Joyful. "But the time you came back…"

"It was for the funeral." Nick's flat, unemotional tone said he hadn't ever completely gotten past their childhood, either. "Mama seemed crushed." He looked away and muttered, "Though for the life of me I'll never understand why."

Johnny didn't understand any better than Nick. He could only imagine their mother had found something to love in their father back when he'd been young and sober, and that was the person she mourned after he died.

Nick had continued speaking. "The only thing that seemed to make her happy in her life was Daneen's little boy."

Johnny shook his head. "So you let it go on. For *years.*"

"You think I didn't hate it? But I didn't want to be responsible for breaking her heart."

"It wouldn't have made any difference to how we felt about him, you know," Johnny admitted. "It still doesn't."

Nick gave one brief nod. "I know."

"Maybe you could have, too, if you'd—"

"Don't." Nick threw a hand into the air, palm out, and his mouth pulled tight. "Don't even say it. I was nowhere near reasonable or mature enough to think that way when I made the choices I made. Maybe a better man would have stayed with Daneen and raised Jack, but not me. Not then."

Johnny slowly felt the anger recede from his brain as he acknowledged the kind of sacrifice his brother had made, and the kind of man he'd become if he could admit his mistakes. "You let all of us think you were a scumbag."

Nick shrugged. "Maybe I was."

"You were eighteen." Then Johnny added something he knew to be true. "You never loved Daneen. And you must have downright hated her for costing you the girl you did love."

Nick's jaw tightened more, but he said nothing. He turned to again look outside, finally murmuring, "I was a kid. That boat has long since sailed. I've moved on and life's okay."

Yeah, apparently it was. From what his mother had told him, Nick had done all right for himself in the Savannah police department. His kid brother—first a Marine hero, now a cop. Well, he supposed it wasn't any more bizarre than Johnny being a prosecutor. He got a perverse sense of amusement, wondering what the old man would have had to say about such a turn of events.

He'd probably be horrified.

"So," he asked, suddenly feeling weary, "what now?"

"One more person to hash this out with."

"Daneen."

"Uh-huh."

"You really think she'll admit the truth to the world?"

Nick shrugged. "I don't know. Maybe it's best she doesn't, until her son's older. It won't be easy on a boy to find out his mama's lied to him all his life, when he might well have a daddy living here in Joyful who would've been proud to claim him."

"Really?"

Nick nodded. "If Daneen wasn't so scared of what her father'd say or do, she might've been honest from the get-go."

Johnny, who'd only ever seen Dan Brady dote on his

"little girl," questioned that. But Nick seemed pretty sure. "Why?"

A look of disgust crossed his brother's face. "Well, because of Dan Brady's renowned temper…and because of who a couple of the possible fathers are."

"Do I even want to know?"

"Probably not."

But Nick told him anyway, first naming one guy Johnny remembered from high school.

"He's still in town," he said, wondering how it would feel to have a woman knock on your door and introduce you to your ten-year-old son.

"That's not the only one," Nick said. Then he added two names, both of which made Johnny's jaw drop.

"You're not serious."

"Oh, yeah, I am. So you can see why Daneen would be a little concerned about our gun-happy sheriff finding out."

Yeah, he could see that. Bad enough for the sheriff to find out his grandson's father could be one of his own deputies, but the other option was even worse.

His very best friend. The *mayor.*

Johnny absorbed the shock for a moment, thinking of the implications. Jimbo Boyd was Chief Brady's age and had been married to Hannah for over two decades. Daneen had gotten pregnant with Jack when she was a seventeen-year-old girl.

He felt sick. "You're sure about Daneen and Jimbo?"

Nick nodded. "I wouldn't be at all surprised if that's why she's working for him now. The way she told it, he had her pretty well wrapped around his finger from the time she was a kid. Sick son of a bitch."

Before he could express his dismay to his brother, they both heard the sound of something falling out in the reception area. The door, which Emma had closed on the way out, had swung open again, as it often did. Curious as to whether Emma had come back, he walked over and looked at the secretary's desk. Nobody was there. But a pile of files that had been on the edge of the desk was now scattered on the floor. He suddenly had a bad feeling.

"This isn't good," Nick murmured from behind him.

"No, it's not."

"Please tell me there's no way Sheriff Brady was standing here listening to us talking about his little angel."

Johnny shook his head. "Can't be. He's speaking at the state police headquarters today. He's been bragging about it for days."

Nick breathed a visible sigh of relief.

"It still doesn't matter," Johnny said with a frown. "Because, here in Joyful, any overheard information can very quickly become public knowledge."

As he knew only too well.

CHAPTER SIXTEEN

"I HATE TO TELL YOU this honeybun, but I'm gonna have to let you go."

Daneen had barely been paying attention when she answered the phone Wednesday evening, since she'd been yelling to Jack to wash up for supper. She immediately assumed the person calling had dialed the wrong number.

"Did you hear me? I have to let you go. I've got no choice."

Yes, the words the man spoke meant it had to be the wrong number, no matter how familiar the voice sounded. Because it couldn't be…he wouldn't…

"Daneen? You there?"

Her heart leaped into her throat. "Jimbo?"

"Yeah, it's me. I'm sorrier'n hell about this, sugarbaby, but I gotta do it."

Let her go. As in… "You're *firing* me?" Her voice rose in disbelief. She quickly lowered it since Jack was right in the kitchen. "You can't be serious."

Jimbo's long, drawn out sigh told her he was. "I'm sorry, I have no choice. Something's going on with Hannah."

Hannah? What did she have to do with the business? She never bothered coming down to the office and had no idea how much work Daneen did to keep things running smoothly. Then she realized… "Oh, my God, she found out about us, didn't she?"

Another sigh. "Yeah. I'm pretty sure she did."

Part of her reacted with dismay to the news that her lover's wife had finally learned the truth about them. The part of her who'd worshipped her own good and proper mother was struck hard with a deep sense of shame. Another part, the harder part that had taken over when she'd been forced to grow up all too soon because of her mother's death, was glad. "So you *think* she knows. Maybe it's time to make sure it's all out in the open." She took a deep breath, assessing everything. "We could finally stop hiding."

"Well…"

Hearing hesitation in Jimbo's voice, she instantly stiffened. "Well what? You've always said you couldn't leave her because it would hurt her too much to find out. Now, if she already has, there's no point waiting." Feeling her pulse pound wildly, and knowing her voice was getting loud again, Daneen walked out the back door, tugging the phone cord after her. "You know what this means. We can be a family. You, me…and Jack."

She didn't press any harder. Knowing Jimbo the way she did, she wondered if she'd already said too much. Jimbo didn't like kids, didn't want them, though he always treated Jack well enough. But surely, if his marriage was over, he could see how perfect things could be.

Particularly now. Because after a very heated conversation with her ex-husband the night before, Daneen had realized that Nick's family knew the truth of Jack's parentage. Meaning others would soon find out, too. She just had to figure out what to tell her son, who was completely innocent in all of this.

Thankfully, Nick had agreed to let her do it on her own timetable. He might have turned into a hard man, but he wasn't an unkind one. He wouldn't force her to tell Jack the truth until she was ready. And until she thought her son was, too.

Lucky for her, Jack had always been a breezy, carefree kid who'd taken his one-parent upbringing in stride, since so many of his friends were the products of divorced homes. He'd never really asked about his absent father, seeming content to know he had a grandmother, and his Uncle Johnny, to care for him.

God, please, let them still. Knowing them the way she did, she suspected her son would still have that feeling of extended family, for the rest of his life.

And maybe now, with Jimbo there to step into their lives permanently, he could have more.

"I'm sorry, Daneen," he said, sounding like he meant it. "I love you darlin', but Hannah doesn't want you working for me anymore. So I'm gonna have to let you go." Then, in a magnanimous voice, he added, "I won't fight your unemployment claim."

Her jaw dropped open in shock. The man who'd seduced her during a multifamily camping trip when she was sixteen years old was telling her to hit the unemployment line. With his own son.

"You're *not* serious."

Then he hammered home the spike that felt like it was splitting her skull in two. "I can't lose Hannah. I'm afraid you and I are finished, Daneen. I can't see you anymore at all."

"SO HOW WAS your first day at work?"

Emma looked up from where she stood chopping vegetables for a salad in the kitchen of Johnny's house on

Wednesday evening. He'd invited her to his place for the first time, and she'd enjoyed getting a snapshot of his life as an eligible bachelor.

He lived in a small house in an older neighborhood a few blocks from downtown. His quiet street was the kind that probably housed retired couples or else young families just starting out. Though his fenced yard was neatly cut, it didn't have so much as a single flower bed, so she assumed he didn't get to work outside much.

The inside was just as sparse. It had the comforts, at least in terms of furniture and big-boy toys like the huge TV in the living room. But not much else. She'd bet a lot of women in Joyful would probably have liked to help him hang curtains over the blind-covered windows, or pick out some pictures for the empty walls.

Or test out the springs on that massive king-size bed of his. *Yum.*

The fact that the house was so decidedly male and undecorated gave her an inordinate amount of pleasure. As if she was the first woman he'd ever invited over.

"Em?"

"Oh, my day. Uh, good," she admitted, surprised to realize it was true. "Though, not for the reasons you might suspect."

He stopped beating the life out of a couple of sirloins and looked up at her. "How so?"

"Well, I spent less time washing hair than I did explaining the differences between an IRA and an SEP to Doris. And helping one woman decide between a Roth and a conventional, and another determine what to do with her husband's rollover."

He grinned as he went to the sink to wash his hands. "And you thought nobody would trust you with their money."

"They're probably better off trusting me with their money than with their hair. Speaking of money, do you know Mrs. Harding?"

"Sixtyish redhead? Kinda flamboyant?"

She nodded. "She must have some big bucks squirreled away. She cornered me leaving the salon and bought me a cup of coffee while we talked about some cap stocks. She knows her stuff."

"I think her late husband had a lot of money," he replied. "She moved to town a couple of years ago and bought one of those old estates out on Tanner Mill Road."

"She's sharp. I liked her. She told me I should open up a pie shop," Emma said. Then, remembering the other reason her first day on the job had been a big hit, she added, "Word got out about the pies, you see. Several people came in and asked me if they could place orders."

"Sounds like you've got a regular little business going."

Yeah, it did sound like that. Six months ago she would probably have laughed at the picture of her dispensing financial advice and pecan pie while bent over the wash sink of a Joyful beauty parlor. Today, though, she'd actually enjoyed herself. It beat sitting at a desk all day.

She didn't tell him who one of her financial "clients" had been today: his mother, who apparently had a small sum of money tucked away—proceeds from a life insurance policy.

"So you brought the papers I left at your house Friday?"

"Yes. I haven't had a chance to look at them. Maybe we could go over them after dinner?"

He stepped close, crowding her against the counter. "I'd rather go over you. Before dinner. After dinner."

"Before dessert? After dessert?"

"*During* dessert," he said with a wolfish chuckle, the

husky sound sending shivers up and down her body. As did his closeness. He put his hands on either side of her, flat on the countertop. Johnny pressed against her, his breath hot on her neck, his chest touching her back, his groin tucked against her bottom.

Emma couldn't contain a small moan as she leaned into him. "You hungry man, what is it with you and kitchens?"

"Just don't go lobbing that cucumber at me," he said, looking over her shoulder at the cutting board. "I don't think it'd have the same effect as pie."

"Speaking of which…"

He grinned. "Lemon meringue."

"Mmm. I've become a pie addict. You won't ever tell anyone why I'm becoming as big as a house, will you?"

"Darlin', you've got nothin to worry about," he said, nuzzling her neck. "You work off every bit of pie the minute after you…lick it all up…."

"Suck it all down," she whispered, just as suggestively.

Dropping the cucumber she'd been slicing, she turned around in his arms and leaned up to catch his mouth in a hot and hungry kiss. When their lips finally parted, she had to gasp in a few deep breaths to try to calm her raging pulse.

"Think I'll go outside and cook the steaks," he said, sounding as out of breath as she felt. "Unless you want to start with dessert."

"Then we'll never get to dinner." She patted his chest. "You need the protein."

"Planning on working me hard, huh?"

She nodded and almost purred, "Very, very hard." Then she pushed him away, patting his awesome butt as he walked away. "Now, go cook us dinner."

JOHNNY HATED for Emma to leave late that night, but knew she should. She'd just gotten herself out of the limelight of Joyful's gossipmongerers. Her red convertible parked in his driveway early tomorrow morning would thrust them both right back into it. That was the way it went in small towns.

Pulling on a pair of gym shorts, he watched her dress. "I'm sorry you can't stay. Next time I'll pick you up."

"Better yet, stay at my place," she whispered as she leaned up to kiss his lips. "I have a garage."

Chuckling, he slid his arm around her waist and walked her to the front door.

"Wait. We didn't go over the papers." She glanced toward the manila envelope she'd deposited on his dining room table as soon as she'd arrived. "Maybe I should take them with me?"

She could have, but he wanted the excuse to keep her around a little longer. It was only ten. Surely whatever biddies had their binoculars trained on his driveway would stay up another hour to watch Emma drive away.

"Let's look at them together before you go."

A few minutes later, he was glad he'd made the suggestion. Because as he and Emma sat at the table, sorting through the tax records, deed and transfer paperwork he'd been able to dig up at the courthouse, she began to mutter under her breath.

"What?"

"I said something's wrong," she replied, sounding distracted. "This is *wrong*."

"I know you're unhappy about it, Em, but the paperwork is all here."

"No, it's something else," she said, scrunching her brow as she studied one of the documents. She ran a frustrated hand through her hair, sending those crazy wavy curls, that he could practically still feel against his fingertips, in all directions. "I swear I wonder if the surgeon took out some of my brain cells because sometimes I have the hardest time grabbing thoughts as they whiz by."

His stiffened, the reaction completely instinctive. God, he hated the thought of Emma banged up, lying in a hospital bed. What if she'd died? What if he'd lost her before he'd ever had the chance to have her again? The stab in his gut at the very thought of it was physically painful. "Emma…"

"Oh, my God," she snapped, her mouth dropping open. With her index finger, she jabbed at one of the legal documents spread out in front of her. "That's it, that's *it*."

"What?"

Her eyes practically sparked with fire. "Look at this, Johnny, just look."

He looked at the paper, a copy of the contract signed by her grandmother. "What am I looking at? This is a pretty standard contract. I mean, it's a little strange to go to closing so soon after the purchase contract had been signed, but since the buyer, this MLH Enterprises, paid cash, it's not entirely out of the question."

"That's not what I meant."

"Are you trying to say it's not her signature? I compared it to the one registered with the DMV and the elections office. I'm no handwriting expert, but it looked identical to me."

"It's not," she said, her voice shaking with anger, indignation or excitement. Maybe all three. "And I am absolutely certain of it." She lifted the paper and thrust it into his hands. "My grandmother did not sign the contract for the sale of the lot, Johnny. Meaning she also didn't sign the closing documents, so conveniently dated for the day before she died." Crossing her arms in front of her, she leaned back in her chair and flatly added, "They're forgeries."

She sounded absolutely convinced. "How can you be sure? You admitted your grandmother told you she was thinking of selling."

"Look at the date."

He did. "April sixth."

"Know when I had my accident? April fifth."

He began to understand. "Okay, but Em, it's *possible* she signed this before she left to go to New York."

She shook her head. "No, it's *not* possible. I got hit on my way home from work at 6:00 p.m. Grandma Emmajean found out right after my parents did, that very night, Johnny. Not the next day."

As with any interesting legal puzzle, he began to get caught up in the details. "When did she arrive in New York?"

"Late night on the sixth. Because she couldn't get a flight out any earlier."

Thinking aloud, he said, "Meaning, technically, she *could* have had time to sign some papers."

Emma merely shook her head. "Think about it."

He did. Legally, he knew the timetable didn't prove anything. Old Emmajean could have done just about anything during the day of the sixth before making the two hour drive to the closest major airport in Atlanta. Including accepting an offer on her land.

Only, she wouldn't have. Absolutely no way on God's green earth would Emmajean Frasier have spared two seconds to think about anything except the life-or-death situation facing her beloved only grandchild. Certainly not something as important as deciding to give up her family's legacy, a place she knew that injured granddaughter loved.

Emma Jean was right. He couldn't prove it, at least not yet. But there was no doubt in his mind...someone *had* stolen her birthright. And judging by the signature that appeared on all these documents, he had a good idea who to start looking at.

Jimbo Boyd.

EMMA SHOULD HAVE driven straight home after she left Johnny's. She was tired and had another full day of "hair-washing-slash-financial-advising-slash-pie-dispensing" on the schedule for tomorrow.

So why, she wondered, was she sitting in her parked car in front of the residence of Mayor Jimbo Boyd?

"Stupid, Emma Jean," she whispered, knowing Johnny would kill her if he found out she'd come here after leaving his place.

She hadn't even realized she was taking the long way home until she pulled onto Sycamore Way, where Hannah Boyd's family had lived for decades. Everyone in town knew where the mayor lived, because the house was the biggest one in town. The society set of Joyful all angled for invitations to the Boyd Christmas party, which had once been covered by *Vanity Fair* magazine.

If the house had been dark and quiet late on this week-night, she probably would have just sat outside, staring at it, doing nothing. She'd have planned all the things she would say to the man the next day when she confronted him with her suspicions. Then she would have driven home and slept off some of her fury.

But it wasn't dark. The bottom floor of the graceful, col-umned, two-story mansion was alight. A few cars were parked in the driveway. Through the quiet night air, she could hear the hum of music. Shadows moved across the front windows.

The Boyds were entertaining.

She wondered how they'd feel about one more guest.

Her feet were on the ground before her mind even completely decided to get out of the car. And once there, they kept on walking, right up the driveway, onto the front porch.

The door was answered by a uniformed maid, who didn't look the least bit surprised to have someone show up at eleven o'clock at night. "They're in the front room," she said with a nod, turning to lead the way for Emma, who she must have assumed was a guest arriving late for the party.

Emma's steps clicked on the polished tile floor, sounding like tiny little starter pistols. She was definitely about to start something. If it took tackling the lion late at night in his own den, she'd do it. Jimbo sure wasn't making it easy for her to speak to him during business hours.

Entering the tastefully decorated drawing room, she immediately assessed the situation. The gathering was a small one. Just Hannah Boyd, perched elegantly on the edge of an antique settee, speaking with a red-haired woman Emma recognized as Mona Harding, from the hair salon. In another corner of the room, Jimbo stood face-to-face with Sheriff Dan Brady.

Oh, great. Lord a'mighty, if she got arrested again tonight, Johnny was just gonna kill her.

Keep calm.

"Well, what a surprise," Mona Harding said as she spied Emma in the doorway. Standing, she offered her a big smile. "I was telling Hannah here what sharp advice you gave me today. Girlfriend, you belong up with the sharks on Wall Street, not down here with the laid-back Joyful folks."

Ha. The sharks in this town had made her feel more like chum than anyone she'd ever known in New York.

"Why, thank you," she managed to say.

Jimbo, who'd looked over immediately, walked across the room, wearing a big, phony politician's smile. "Well, hello there, Ms. Frasier. I've been looking forward to seeing you since you got back to town."

Emma managed to avoid snorting at that one. Instead, keeping her voice neutral, she said, "How interesting. Especially since I've been unable to reach you at all." Glancing at Hannah Boyd, who watched them with a detached, aloof expression, she added, "I apologize for interrupting your party. But since I can't reach Mr. Boyd during the day, I took a chance and stopped by on my way home."

Hannah acknowledged the apology with a slight incline of her head. A cool creature, that one. Quiet and alert and always watching. Emma suspected the brains in Joyful's royal family belonged to the queen, not the florid court jester standing in front of her.

"I'm sorry 'bout that," Jimbo said. "I have been busy this week. You call me in the morning and we'll have us a sit-down."

Sheriff Brady, out of uniform and dressed in a suit and tie, walked over and stood behind Mrs. Harding. His hand on her shoulder said the two of them were a couple. Very interesting. She wondered if Daneen knew her long-widowed daddy was seeing the brassy, wealthy woman.

"That won't be necessary," Emma replied, amazing herself with her own calm tone. "I've just come to inform you that, whether I stay in Joyful or not, I am removing you as manager of my property."

Jimbo didn't look disturbed. In fact, she almost noted a flash of relief on his face, as if he'd expected her to say something else. Not surprising. He *had* to suspect she might catch on sometime and had probably anticipated an attack.

"I sure do understand, and no hard feelings," he replied with a nod that made his thick, black hair—which Emma suspected was fake—flop a little over his forehead.

Emma looked at the others in the room, all of them watching curiously, as if feeling the undercurrents between she and Jimbo. How could they not, when she was fighting an inner battle not to punch the man in his smiling face? She somehow managed to remain cool as she nodded at everyone and murmured goodbye, letting Jimbo have one more second of peace.

But before she left the room, she met Jimbo's stare with a piercing one of her own. "Oh, and by the way, I am hiring an attorney to look into the supposed sale of my grandmother's property." She paused for a heartbeat, watching his cheeks grow red. Then she continued. "I know she didn't sell it. Certain things have come to light, and now I'm completely certain I've been defrauded." She mentally crossed her fingers, knowing she was too broke to do any such thing, and added, "I'm sure the lawyer's private investigator and handwriting analyst can help to shed new light on the situation."

Hannah's face grew pale while Mona Harding's eyes widened in shock. Dan Brady shook his head, appearing distressed. But Jimbo managed to keep his smarmy smile in place, in spite of his red and shiny cheeks.

"Well, now, I'm sorry you don't like what your grandma

did with her land, Ms. Frasier, but what's done is done. I'm afraid you're wasting your time and your money. You might as well go on back up north and forget all about Joyful."

"Oh, no," she snapped. "I won't be forgetting about anything. And believe me, Mr. Boyd, I will not allow you to just forget about me, either." Satisfied, she sailed out of the room, ignoring the quick rumbling of conversation breaking out in the room behind her.

A big part of her prayed Boyd would follow. He wouldn't speak in front of Hannah, or the others, that was sure. But she really thought he'd come after her, to try to make excuses or come up with a story...*anything*. And hopefully he'd trip up, giving her some tidbit to use as evidence against him.

He didn't follow, to her deep disappointment. She even stood on the porch for a long expectant moment, but the front door remained firmly closed.

So be it. He wanted to call her bluff. She'd have to do this the hard way, meaning she'd be in his office bright and early tomorrow morning to start hitting him hard with dates and signatures.

But not until after she'd made a phone call to her parents. It was time to stop acting like a kid in trouble and bring them up to speed on what was happening. She might not have the means to hire an attorney or private investigator, but they sure did. That land had been part of her father's childhood, too. He'd be as horrified as she about what had happened.

Feeling better about things, Emma got into her convertible. Before she even started the car, however, she heard the roar of another engine. In her rearview mirror, she watched as a small sedan pulled out from the curb a few car lengths behind her. Its engine revving, it sped up toward her, burning rubber, and careening dangerously close to her rear bumper. Then it sped past, probably going four times the legal speed limit.

"Crazy driver," she muttered, deciding to stay a few lengths back, in case the person in the other car had been drinking.

For once, karma seemed to be smiling. Because for all the times on the road when she'd seen a reckless driver tailgating, speeding or passing on the shoulder, and had wished for a cop to appear out of nowhere, one finally did. A blue light flashed ahead as a police cruiser turned onto Sycamore from a side street where it'd obviously been waiting.

"Speed trap. Serves you right. I hope they do a Breathalyzer," she muttered as she drove by. She felt so good about it, she even gave a little wave of her fingers to Deputy Fred, who'd just stepped out of his car. She barely spared a glance for the sedan's driver, whose silhouette she could make out through the windows. "Have a fun night," she whispered to the woman, hoping she'd learn a lesson.

Arriving home, she locked her front door, wondering how Claire and Eve were doing back home with Tim. Claire had seemed very confident that things would work, and she was happy for them. But the house did feel awfully empty.

Though she figured she'd be too hyped up to sleep that night, Emma actually crashed hard and long. Maybe washing hair—which was already shaping up to be the most interesting job she'd ever had, given the side duties—was more tiring than she thought. Or maybe confronting loathsome thieving creeps was.

Or being involved in the most passionate affair of her life.

Johnny. He was the last thing she thought of before she fell asleep, and the first image that filled her mind Thursday morning. She was falling in love with him all over again. Just like she had when she was seventeen and he'd been dangerous and unattainable and more exciting than any girl could hope for.

Only, no, it wasn't like that. This was different, she realized as she showered and got ready for work. This wasn't merely an infatuation. If it were simply that—if it had *ever* been anything that simple—would the raw feelings have remained during a decade of separation?

She didn't think so. The reason she'd held on to the hurt for so long was because her feelings for Johnny hadn't been just a girlish infatuation, even when she'd been a high school kid. She may not have understood exactly what love was back in those days, but she'd experienced it nonetheless.

Which made it easier to believe she was experiencing it again.

Unfortunately, knowing the truth about their past didn't help her figure out what, exactly, she could do about their present. For all the passion, all the wild *storms* they shared, they were still moving in two different directions. Not just geographically, either.

Emma might have realized she loved him, but did Johnny love her back? She didn't know if he'd even allow himself to. He'd flat out said he'd never marry. She couldn't blame him, given his history.

Which left her holding a bag of unrequited emotion.

Forcing thoughts of him away, Emma packed up the paperwork she was convinced was fake, and headed out of the house. Because of the time difference and her parents' work schedule, she hadn't been able to reach them yet, but planned to call again later today.

In the meantime, she was going to the Boyd Realty office.

When she arrived, she saw two cars parked in the lot outside, and assumed Daneen was already at work. Too bad. She'd hoped to beat the woman in, which was why she'd shown up before eight. Steeling herself to see derision, annoyance or dislike in Daneen Walker's eyes, she entered the office.

But Daneen's desk was unattended, the reception area empty. Or, at least, she thought it was, until a small noise drew her attention to a person standing in the interior doorway.

"You probably should go back outside."

Looking up, she saw Cora Dillon, the old cleaning lady who'd given her the key to the house her first day in town. "Good morning, Mrs. Dillon." Then, seeing the pinched look around the woman's mouth, and the paleness of her face, she stepped closer. "Are you all right?"

The woman nodded, raising a hand to her face. That was when Emma noticed how much it was shaking.

And what it held.

"Good, God, what is that?" she asked, noticing the clump of black furry stuff clutched in the woman's death grip.

Cora glanced at her own hand, appearing almost dazed, then snapped her fingers apart, as if she hadn't realized she was holding anything until then. The black clumpy thing fell to the floor.

Emma studied it with distaste. "Was that a dead rat you were holding?"

Cora merely shook her head. "Nope."

Hearing something that sounded like dread in the woman's voice, Emma raised a questioning brow.

Cora pursed her lips and blew out a long, slow breath, eyes wide with disbelief. Then, pointing toward the inner office, she explained, "It's the head of hair offa the dead snake in the other room."

CHAPTER SEVENTEEN

IF THERE WAS one sight in the world Johnny never wanted to see again, it was Emma Jean Frasier standing inside a jail cell, looking angry and forlorn, frightened and shell-shocked all at the same time.

Goddamn it, Dan Brady had locked her up for the third time in two weeks. He wanted to grab her and hold her, to carry her out of here and never let anyone put her in this filthy place again. Hell, never let her leave his side again.

He didn't pause to analyze that thought. Whatever happened between him and Emma Jean in the future needed to remain there…in the future. At least until he took care of this unsettling present.

He stood in the open doorway between the office and the holding cells of the Joyful jail. Taking a moment before she was aware of his presence, he hoped the sight of her—safe and sound—would wash over him like a cool breeze, calming him down.

Huh-uh. He only grew more angry.

Having blown past the sheriff, who stood at the desk talking to Fred, he felt a sense of déjà vu sweep over him. But this time, Johnny wasn't laughing or resigned about seeing Emma in a cell. He was boiling mad. Somehow, however, he managed to hide it. "Hey, darlin', we've really gotta stop meetin' like this."

"Johnny!" She darted over to the front of the cell, extending her hand through the bars. "Thank God you're here. This is insane."

He gave her a tender smile. "Hold on, honey, you'll be out in a second." Then he barked over his shoulder, "Let her out. Right now."

"Now, *you* just hold on a minute there, *honey*," Chief Brady said from behind him as he approached. "I'm not ready to let her go anywhere."

Johnny stepped out of the way so the barrel-chested chief could get through the narrow doorway with the keys to open Emma's cell. Which he was going to do, even if Johnny had to grab him by the scruff of the neck and drag him.

"Let her out now, Dan," he bit out.

The older man instantly stiffened. "I'm questionin' her."

"No, you're not." He shook his head in disgust, tired of the old argument which was suddenly so much more serious than it ever had been in the past. "You can't ignore the law whenever you feel like it. You've got no right to just throw somebody into a cell at your whim. Now let her out, or I'll be the first one testifying against you when she files charges against you and the town."

Brady frowned, but he did approach the front of the cell with the huge key ring that usually hung on the hook by the front desk. "She's the prime suspect in a murder."

Murder. Right. It'd almost make him laugh…if only it weren't true. Little old Joyful had seen its first murder in the past eight years. Now, under his watch.

Unbelievable. The whole thing was like a bad dream.

First, that anyone would walk into the Boyd Realty office and stab Jimbo Boyd in the heart with the wooden stake from one of his own damn campaign signs. Like a freakin' vampire.

But worse, the sheriff had turned a suspicious eye toward Emma. The woman who'd shared his bed last evening.

This wasn't nightmare stuff, it'd gone straight to horror movie status.

"I want to talk to you, young lady," Dan said, towering over Emma. "You said you'd talk when the D.A. got here, and he's here."

She opened her mouth, but Johnny threw his hand up, palm out, to stop her. "Don't say anything." Boy did that go against every prosecutorial instinct he possessed.

"It's all right," Emma replied, looking much less panicked than when she'd stood on the other side of the steel bars. She stepped closer, not touching him, but seeming to need the solid warmth of his body as near as possible. Then she turned to Sheriff Brady. "I do have something to say." Her jaw stiff, she snapped, "I didn't do it. The end."

Brady turned red. "You were there…"

"So was Mrs. Dillon, even before me! Good lord, she was holding the man's *hair* in her hand when I walked in the place."

Johnny winced. He hadn't heard that part.

Probably seeing his surprise, Emma explained. "She said it came right off when she tried to lift his head up off the floor to see if he was breathing. I guess she was too shocked to drop it." Then she turned her attention back toward the sheriff. "She can tell you I showed up *after* the man was dead."

"Doesn't mean anything," the sheriff said with a scoffing frown. "You coulda followed him from the house. You mighta waited all night outside and followed him into the office to do your dirty work, then came back later to try to throw us off the scent." His eyes widened. "Or 'cause you realized you dropped your earring and had to come back to find it."

Emma's hands immediately rose to touch her ears. Pretty gold hoops dangled from each one.

Oh, such colossal intellect. Johnny imagined Perry Mason would be right proud of this moment. Actually, he thought he'd seen that particular case on an old *Matlock* rerun. "You're reaching, Dan. You've got absolutely nothing. No evidence, no motive, no nothing."

"She threatened him last night."

Last night. The words pierced through the red haze of anger in his brain. Twice now Brady had said something about last night. "She was at my house last night," Johnny admitted through clenched teeth.

He heard a soft, nearly imperceptible sigh. Casting a quick glance at Emma, he immediately noted her pinkening cheeks. *Hell.*

"Not at eleven o'clock she wasn't," Brady said. "I was standing right there in the room when she threatened the man."

"I did no such thing."

"You said you'd make him wish he'd never heard of you."

Oh, no. No, no, no. Emma had *not* left his house and gone over to Jimbo's to confront the man, full of righteous anger and fire. And threats.

The way she nibbled her bottom lip told him she had.

A keeper. That's what she needed. Either that or a pair of handcuffs to prevent her from leaving home and getting into trouble.

Emma continued to defend herself to the frowning sheriff. "I said I wasn't going to let him forget me, which wasn't a threat. And I most *certainly* did not sit outside his house on Sycamore Avenue stalking him all night."

A sharp crack caught the attention of all three of them. Glancing over, Johnny saw Deputy Fred, picking up a notebook he'd dropped near the doorway. He'd probably kicked it, wanting to get nice and close for the best eaves-dropping angle.

Beside him, Emma snapped to attention. "Wait, if you don't believe me, ask your own deputy. I drove right by him when I left the neighborhood. He had somebody pulled over."

His analytical mind kicked in. Whether Fred had seen her leave or not, it really didn't matter. Emma wouldn't have had to follow Jimbo to know he'd show up at work today.

What was he thinking? He shook his head, hard, forcing himself to think like a lover. Not a prosecutor.

"Well?" Emma asked, looking at Fred, who opened and closed his mouth a few times.

Finally, the red-faced man merely shook his head. "I don't know what she's talking about."

Emma gaped. Sheriff Brady immediately got back to questions about Jimbo. And Fred stood there, frowning, looking very confused. Not to mention secretive…though about what, Johnny had no idea.

How strange that Fred would lie—as he so obviously was—when the truth wouldn't matter a bit, anyway. He couldn't imagine why the normally straight-laced deputy would do such a thing.

But it suddenly seemed very important to find out.

EMMA HAD NEVER seen Johnny so furious. As they drove away from the jail, his hands grew white from his death grip on the steering wheel. His pulse pounded in his temple and his jaw looked stiff enough to crack. Though she knew his anger wasn't directed at her, it was still some-what intimidating to see.

"The mentality in this town is going to make me lose my mind someday," he muttered through clenched teeth.

Dropping her hand onto his leg, she rubbed up and down as much to distract as to console him. "You're the one who wanted to move back here."

"So I could batter my head against an idiot sheriff and small-minded people for the rest of my life. What was I thinking?"

She thought about it. "About your mother. And your nephew," she finally murmured. Then, speculating about some of Johnny's choices, she continued. "About living in a place where you don't have to lock your door at night. Where you can open a window on a summer day and hear kids playing ball in the park."

A slight shrug was his only response. But she didn't give up. "About having neighbors who are always ready to come over to help you fix your lawnmower or offer you a beer."

He gave her a disbelieving look. "Yeah, right."

"You're telling me it's not like that, *now?*" she asked, knowing he'd started remembering his childhood as a white-trash Walker, instead of the life he lived today.

"I suppose," he admitted, his tone grudging.

She nodded, glad he could admit it. "Besides all that, I suspect you came back here because you know there are people in this town who deserve to have at least one public official who knows how to do his job."

The tightness returned to his lips. She almost regretted mentioning town officials, which immediately brought to mind the dead, hairless mayor and the blustery sheriff.

Moving her hand up to his cheek, she scraped the back of her fingers along his jawline. "I'm okay, Johnny. I'm really okay."

He glanced over, emotion, stark and raw, evident in his eyes. That emotion told her she'd reached the right conclusion. He was afraid for her. More, *enraged* for her.

Johnny had never been the fighter of the Walkers. His temper had always been slow to rise to a boil, unlike Nick who'd punched his way out of a lot of situations. Johnny had never needed to. He'd been the sexy rebel with the wicked smile and the irresistible charm. On the rare occasions when he did get mad, he yelled, got it out of his system and moved on. It would take a lot to bring the man to violence.

Right now he looked ready to rip someone to shreds.

"Don't take me home yet," she murmured, knowing they both needed a distraction. "I can't stand the thought of every set of eyes on the block watching us walk into my house together. And we probably shouldn't go to your place, either."

He immediately turned the car in another direction, without telling her where they were going. During their silent drive, Emma tried to think of anything except how that black toupee had looked in Cora Dillon's hand. Her tummy felt queasy thinking about it. Thank God she hadn't gone into Jimbo's private office. Otherwise she'd be picturing his dead body on the floor instead of just his saggy hair.

She'd distrusted the man, but she'd certainly never wanted him dead. And she couldn't imagine who would.

Emma would have liked to talk about it, but kept quiet. Johnny finally seemed to have calmed down a bit. The last thing she wanted to do was stoke his anger again.

They'd get to it, eventually. He'd certainly have something to say about her going over to the Boyd house last night. But not now. Now, she just wanted to be alone with him, to crawl into his arms and kiss him and forget the ugliness of the morning.

Seeing the top of the grange building, Emma suddenly realized where he was taking her. "The gazebo."

He didn't say anything, didn't ask for permission or offer to go someplace else. There was no place else for them, no place as right, anyway.

The gazebo stood near a small playground on the edge of a tiny lake, where Emma remembered feeding the ducks with her grandparents as a child. And hanging out with her friends late at night during high school.

It'd been a pretty spot, off the main road. With not a house in sight—the old grange building was the only structure within a half mile—the place had been secluded, almost separate from the rest of the world.

That hadn't changed...it was still secluded. But the park itself was a surprise.

"It looks abandoned," she murmured.

Weeds had sprung up through the gravel of the parking lot, until it resembled a mere clearing. The trees and shrubs circling the playground had become overgrown and tangled. Orange rust covered the chains of one swing, while the other was gone altogether. And only a very foolish parent would allow a child to slide down the mangled remains of the sliding board.

"Doesn't anybody come here anymore?" she asked.

"The city built a big new park downtown. This one's been pretty much forgotten."

"Sad," she murmured.

"Private."

Ah, yes, it would be that.

Getting out of the SUV, she walked around to the front and held her hand out. When he took it, lacing his fingers with hers, she immediately began to feel safe, calm and relaxed. For the first time all day.

Judging by the condition of the park equipment, she half feared the gazebo would have fallen into disrepair as well. Almost holding her breath, she glanced past two ancient oak trees dripping with Spanish moss, and breathed an audible sigh of relief to see it standing just where it had a decade ago.

Near the lake, surrounded by a tangle of jasmine, the once white structure was now a milky gray, with brownish water stains on its roof. Some of the vines had curled up over the railing, providing a thick wall of privacy that had been absent years ago. If it'd been there on prom night, she might not have been so, umm, *exposed* to her classmates.

By unspoken agreement, they stepped up inside, Emma inhaling deeply to savor the scent of the jasmine.

"Johnny?"

He didn't reply, didn't need to. Because he obviously heard the need in her voice. His arms opened to her and she launched into them. Stroking her back, he whispered sweet things into her hair, absorbing the confusion and fear that had consumed her since she'd stumbled into a murder scene this morning.

And soon he did even more. Because the hard strength of his form, the feel of his breath on her neck and the soft rumble of his voice brought all her senses into full alert. Their bodies touched from top to bottom, and Emma became aware of a different kind of tension building inside her. The hungry, wicked kind this man had always inspired.

Tilting her head back, she looked up at him and moistened her parted lips. Johnny responded with a groan, then gave her what she'd silently been begging for. His mouth opened on hers as he kissed her deeply. She circled her arms around his neck, sinking her fingers into his thick hair.

A lot was said in the kiss…a lot of tender things that spoken words might have diminished. She thanked him and he told her he was glad she was safe. They shared emotion and kindness and a sweet, languorous kind of want so appropriate for this place on this hot summer day.

Finally, after their long, intimate kiss, he pulled away. Emma drew in a few deep breaths to calm her raging pulse, wondering how he'd managed to make every other thought completely evaporate from her mind. Except one: how much she wanted him. Here and now. In a place that had once been so important to them both.

"How do you always have this effect on me?" she asked, not meaning to voice the question aloud.

"What effect?" He kissed the corner of her mouth. Then traced his tongue across her lips. "Making you want to rip off your clothes, not caring where we are or who's nearby?"

Tilting her head back, she nearly purred when he kissed his way down her throat. "Exactly. Like the last time we were here."

He hesitated for the briefest moment and she almost bit her own tongue for mentioning their last time here. *Prom night.*

His hands were at her waist, his fingertips sliding under the edge of her top, caressing her hips with featherlight touches. Closing her eyes, she gave herself over to the sensation, wanting more. Wanting it all. Especially the delightful kisses he was placing on her neck.

"We ever gonna talk about it, Em?" he whispered against her sensitized skin.

Talk about it? About what? Were they talking? How could she possibly know when he continued to press hot, wet kisses onto the hollow of her throat, and then lower.

He whispered something against her collarbone.

"Hmm?"

"I said I'm sorry."

Sorry? For this? Goodness, no man should ever apologize for being able to reduce a woman to a five-foot-six pile of jelly with just his lips and oh-so-sweet tongue.

"I'm sorry I took off that night."

She stiffened, suddenly realizing they were still talking about prom night.

Lifting his head, he whispered, "I'm sorry I left you standing here alone, Emma Jean."

She couldn't help it. Moisture gathered in the corners of her eyes, and she blinked rapidly, mentally willing the tears to disappear. It was hard. His words brought back what had been the most awful moment of her life, up until that night.

Now, as an adult, being caught naked in the headlights of a bunch of cars would be darned embarrassing, but she might be able to laugh at it. Eventually.

Then, however, at age eighteen, having just lost her virginity to a guy she was crazy about—who'd morphed into an angry stranger for some unknown reason—it was absolutely devastating.

"You were a prick."

And a prince.

"I wanted to kill you."

I wanted to lose myself in you.

"I hated you."

I loved you.

Johnny didn't flinch from her hard words. "I hated myself once I had a chance to calm down."

He stepped away, giving them both some distance to continue with what she sensed was going to be an important conversation. The kind they had to have if they wanted this…*thing*…between them to have any chance of going further.

"Why did you do it?" she asked softly. "Why did you turn into a stranger?"

Crossing his arms, he leaned his hip against the railing and countered with a question of his own. "Why did *you* do it? Why did you let me make love to you?"

Because I loved you.

The words leaped to her lips, but she quickly adjusted them. "Because I wanted you." Remembering something he'd said the other night, she wondered if he'd doubted that over the years. She approached him, lifting one hand and placing it flat on his chest, over his strongly beating heart. "I *wanted* you. I didn't *need* you."

Seeing a quick flash of relief on his face, she was glad she'd admitted it. "Now, why did you get so angry? It wasn't because I was a virgin, because you were so…" Her face grew hot and she realized she was blushing like a kid. She pressed on, her voice a little shaky. "You were so wonderful when you realized."

"It was the locket," he admitted, his words thick and tight. "When you started crying about the locket and I realized you'd practically been engaged to my brother, well…"

Her jaw dropped. "Engaged? *What?*"

"Nick asked you to wear the locket on your honeymoon, remember? And you cried like someone whose heart had been completely trampled on when it broke."

Yes. She had. But not for the reasons he thought. Not because of Nick, or a necklace or any engagement that didn't exist and never would have existed.

"I suddenly realized you'd been planning on losing your virginity to your fiancé on prom night," Johnny added. "And I was a convenient substitute."

Oh, God, of course he would have thought that. Because he'd never known…she'd never told him the truth about which brother she'd really wanted. "Johnny, to start with, I never intended to marry Nick. Never. You know how I was back then…you certainly knew me better than *he* did. I couldn't wait to turn eighteen and get out on my own."

He remained silent.

"I don't know if you can understand what I'm about to say, since you're not a girl."

"Thanks. I think."

"I mean, this might not make sense to you, because you're not used to having mood swings that make you cry at a Hallmark commercial on TV one minute, when what you're really sad about is the fight you had with your best friend three years ago."

He rolled his eyes. "Okay, that logic totally escapes me."

"Of course it does. You're a man. But go along with me."

Sighing, he replied, "I'm trying."

She grabbed his hand and stepped closer, until their bodies were separated by an inch of summer air and a decade of memory. Taking a deep breath, she continued. "Think about it. I was a teenager who'd just lost her virginity to a fantasy guy every girl I knew had been whispering about since the day I hit town."

His eyes widened. She lifted her fingers to his mouth to keep him quiet, knowing if he interrupted, she'd lose her courage. "I'd gone from being a good girl having a nice, simple girlfriend-boyfriend relationship with a guy who never did more than kiss me, to a woman—a *real* woman—who'd had the most perfect lover anyone could dream about."

He remained silent, just watching, his face revealing nothing of his thoughts.

"I cried. Yes. Because I'd gone from girl to woman. From childhood to adulthood. It was all wrapped up together for me, the break between the past and the future as vivid as the snap of the chain on the locket. And suddenly, it was just…emotional…like the tears during a Hallmark commercial."

His eyes widened a tiny bit, then his jaw tightened. She wished Johnny was an easier man to read, because right now she had absolutely no idea what he was thinking. Rushing on, she said, "I wasn't crying out of regret. I didn't…*don't*…regret what happened between us on prom night. It was perfect." Then, to make absolutely sure he got the point, she added, "You were not a substitute for *anyone,* Johnny Walker. I can guarantee you, if Nick and I had ended up here that night, I would still have been a virgin the next morning."

Staring searchingly into her eyes, he remained silent, as if looking for more, knowing there was something yet unsaid.

There was more. There was a *lot* more she could have said. She could have told him she'd been crazy for him since the day she'd given him a ride. That she'd fantasized for weeks about that teasing kiss he'd given her. That she'd dreamed of him for ages and had felt guilty for wanting him during every minute she'd spent with his brother.

But those words would push her too close, far too close, to an admission she wasn't ready to make. One *he* wasn't ready to hear.

If she admitted she loved him, Johnny would have to respond. She suspected he had feelings for her, but also knew it wouldn't be easy for a man like him to admit them. The few times they'd talked about his childhood, and his feelings about love, it'd been pretty clear he still had scars—deep ones. It wouldn't be easy for him to admit he'd fallen in love.

Not even to himself.

Which explained why he'd resisted the women of Joyful, who'd tried so hard to get his attention. She knew it. Johnny was too nice a man to let any woman fall in love with him, when he didn't think he'd ever be able to love her in return. Including Emma.

Finally, as if realizing she wasn't going to say anything else, he let out a long, slow breath. When she tried to pull her hand away from his face—still not knowing what he was thinking—he wouldn't let her. Instead, he kissed her palm, curling his rough cheek against it. "I didn't know, Em."

"No, you couldn't have."

"Why didn't you tell me?"

"I thought I had," she whispered, hearing her voice break a bit. "Every time I kissed you and touched you that night, I was telling you you were the one I wanted."

"And I didn't get the message."

"Obviously not." She stepped back, out of his arms, her eyes never breaking their stare. "See if you can get this one."

Without another word, she reached for the bottom of her shirt and pulled it up and off.

His eyes narrowed even as a slight smile played about his lips. "Hmm…"

She didn't pause. Her bra came next, joining her shirt on the dusty floor of the gazebo. Johnny's jaw visibly tightened, his eyes narrowing as he stared at her bare breasts.

"You getting the picture?" she asked with a saucy smile.

"Some picture."

"I mean, are you following me?"

"Anywhere you want to lead."

"Johnny!"

"Pardon me, ma'am," he said in his wicked Walker drawl, never taking his eyes off her nipples, getting hard and ripe in anticipation of his touch, "I'm just a slow Southern boy. I might need a little more to go on."

"Uh-huh." She reached for the elastic waist of her skirt. "Maybe this'll help." Then she easily pushed the filmy thing down over her hips and off her body.

His eyes dropped. Straight down. Widening when he saw what she'd been wearing underneath. "Why, ma'am, I do believe that'd have to qualify as a leopard-spotted pair of drawers you got on."

"Not for long," she retorted.

With one quick move, the panties dropped, too. She kicked them—and her strapless sandals—off, standing completely naked, highlighted by the sun, shadowed by the vines, enveloped in the security of Johnny's never-ending desire for her.

Fisting one hand, she put it on her hip and lifted her chin, nearly purring, "Am I making myself clear enough, Mr. Prosecuting Attorney?"

"Right clear, ma'am." His words sounded thick as if he'd had to force them out of a very tight throat.

Umm, how she savored that hungry tone. That needy look. That anticipatory smile.

"So there's no misunderstanding?" Taunting him, loving the way his eyes glazed over with hunger and his breaths came in audible gasps, Emma lifted one hand and cupped her own breast, stroking her nipple with her fingertips. "You are aware there is no one in this gazebo but you and me?"

"Be damned embarrassing for you if there was."

She ignored him and continued her seduction. "There's *nobody* else I want touching me."

"You're doing pretty good on your own," he replied, sounding like he hoped she'd continue.

Smiling wickedly, she did exactly that. She smoothed her hand down her body, over her stomach, her pelvis, lower, knowing he was dying to touch her the way she touched herself.

Johnny's eyes remained glued to her and finally the teasing look faded away, replaced by one of raw hunger. His control was about to break. Just before it did, Emma said, "I want you, Johnny. I choose *you*. Right here, right now, exactly like I did that night."

Those were the last words she could manage, because before she could think of another one, he was on her. With one hand thrust in her hair to tug her mouth to his, the other curling against her backside, he dragged her to him, kissing every thought out of her head. His kiss was wet and hungry and carnal, his tongue tasting so sweet, so hot, she whimpered and pressed harder against him. She gasped with pleasure when she felt the hard ridge of his erection.

Not letting their mouths break apart, he began to jerkily open the buttons of his shirt. Impatient, she reached for his belt, wanting to hurry things along. Then, finally, he was as gloriously naked as she, slick skin sliding together as they exchanged kiss after hungry kiss. The sweet fragrant perfume of the jasmine was soon mingling with the heady, musky odor of delicious sexual need.

"Come here," he growled against her mouth, backing up to the built-in wooden bench and tugging her with him.

She didn't hesitate as he pulled her down to straddle him on the bench, until she was taking him—all of him—inside herself in one slow, deep, wet thrust.

Closing her eyes, Emma tilted her head back and savored his deep penetration. Not moving, barely breathing, she focused only on the delicious sensation of Johnny buried to the hilt inside her body. So good, so hot, so full she nearly lost her mind.

He thrust up, slowly, deliberately, grinding into her until she whimpered. Then tilting away.

"You getting the point now, Emma Jean?" he asked as he held her hips and delivered another slow, maddening stroke that removed all thought and all reason, replacing them with pure physical pleasure.

She nodded, managing to whisper, "I'm definitely getting it." Then she sighed. "And I want to keep getting it."

"Good," he growled against her throat as he picked up the pace, rocking into her hard enough to take her breath away.

"Because I intend to keep giving it to you."

CHAPTER EIGHTEEN

THOUGH CLAIRE had gone home yesterday, feeling confident that she and her husband were on the right path to working things out in their marriage, she still had a key to Emma's house.

So she used it.

She'd heard about Jimbo Boyd's murder early this morning from a neighbor, but it wasn't until Tim had come home from work at around eleven that she heard the rest of the rumors.

Emma Jean was a suspect. She'd been taken into custody, but her lover, Johnny Walker, had spirited her out of the jail.

Well, she doubted the spirited part, considering Sheriff Brady had been present at the time, but she could easily imagine Johnny getting Emma the heck out of there.

"You're sure she won't mind us just coming on in?" Tim asked as they sat in Emma's living room.

"No, she won't." Then she squeezed her husband's hand. "Thanks for coming with me. You didn't have to."

He squeezed back. "I was a jerk and listened to stories about her once. I'm not stupid enough to do it again." He shook his head in disgust. "I don't know her well, but I can sure see she's no killer."

Tim had definitely changed his tune about Emma, not

only because he'd felt badly about the porn star rumors, but also because of Eve. Claire had overheard their daughter telling Tim that Auntie Emma had told her she was the luckiest girl in the world to have a mommy and daddy who loved each other—and *her*—so very much.

Emma had earned Tim's lifelong loyalty when she hadn't even been in the same building.

"Eve sure is starting to like day care," Tim said as he dropped his arm across Claire's shoulders and pulled her closer on the couch. "She wanted to go there instead of to your mom's this morning."

"Courtney Foster," Claire replied absently. "Eve found out she has a My Size Barbie and she's dying to get invited over to play with it."

Tim snickered. "She's a little hellion, our kid."

"Uh-huh. You have a problem with that?"

He shook his head. "Nope. I happen to like hellions."

"Glad you finally remembered."

"I never forgot," he countered. Then he pulled her closer for a sweet, gentle kiss. "You the kind of bad girl who lets guys take advantage on the sofa in somebody else's house?"

Giggling, Claire nodded, then drew her husband close for another kiss. The past couple of days had been magical—they'd reminded her why she'd fallen so madly in love with the man to begin with. Once they'd gotten past their misunderstandings about their marriage—and their sex life—they'd both been doing whatever it took to make things right. Out of the bedroom…and in it.

Ohhh, yeah, *in* it.

Before they could do much more than exchange a few deep kisses, she heard a car pull up outside. They sprang apart, like two guilty teenagers. Meeting her husband's eye, Claire giggled. Then she suddenly felt bad for being happy when so many people here in Joyful were feeling anything but. Like Emma.

Hearing footsteps outside, Claire rose, fully expecting Emma to walk through the front door. Instead, the doorbell rang. When she answered it, she got another surprise. "Nick? I didn't know you were still in town."

A scowling Nick Walker strode into the house without waiting for an invitation. Not that Claire had any right to issue one, since this wasn't her house.

"I'd left early this morning. Got halfway home when Mama called me and told me what happened. I drove back right away. Where's Emma and Johnny?"

"I dunno. We're waiting for them," Claire replied.

After introducing her husband to Nick, Claire returned to her seat. Nick took the chair near the front door, and got right down to business. "Tell me as much as you know about the murder."

Claire raised her hands in resignation. "I don't know much of the *facts*. Mayor Boyd was found dead in his office this morning by Cora Dillon. Murdered, though I haven't heard how. And Emma showed up a few minutes later."

"What about Daneen?"

Claire shrugged. "Haven't heard a word about her."

"She wasn't at work this morning?"

"No idea. Have you tried to reach her?"

He nodded. "Yeah, I went to her place first, but she wasn't around." He muttered something under his breath. She wasn't quite sure she'd caught it, but it sounded like he was almost worried about Daneen being devastated.

Well, she imagined any woman would be upset at losing her employer so violently. But at least she hadn't been the one to accidentally rip the man's hair right off his head.

Or so said the rumor mill. Not that she was listening.

"You gonna wait here?" Nick asked, rising to his feet as if he couldn't stand the inactivity.

Tim nodded. "Yes. And I'm staying with her."

"Good. When Emma and Johnny get here, have my brother call me on my cell phone." He pulled out his wallet and opened it to retrieve a business card, which he dropped onto the table.

While his wallet was open, Claire caught a quick glimpse of a badge inside. So, the stories about the younger bad-ass Walker boy were true. Nick, the guy who'd once gotten into a brawl with half the football team from Bradenton High—and *won*—was a cop. Would wonders never cease.

Nick strode toward the door, tall, lean, full of simmering anger and energy. Where his brother had a cocky grin and sexy charm that could make a woman's clothes fall right off her body, Nick put off enough pure dangerous heat to make them melt off.

Made Claire scoot closer to Tim on the couch. She preferred her men romantic and tender, able to make love to her for hours until she wanted to cry at the beauty of it.

Leave the bad boys and the wicked ones to women like Emma, who seemed to like them.

"Where are you going?" she asked.

Nick glanced over his shoulder as he opened the door. His eyes dark and intense, he admitted, "To find Cora Dillon." Then, his jaw growing stiff, he bit out, "And my ex-wife."

THOUGH HE WOULD have loved nothing more than to spend the entire day making love to Emma in the shadows of the gazebo, Johnny knew he couldn't. Not only because it would be downright uncomfortable after a while, but because there was work to be done.

Still, it was tempting. Particularly after their talk.

Emma had wanted him all along. He hadn't been alone in what he'd been feeling on prom night, nor had he stolen something his brother ever would have had.

After ten years of wondering, he could finally relax, secure in the knowledge that he hadn't imagined a thing about what they'd shared that night.

Which made him wonder if he also hadn't imagined how he'd felt about it. His emotions had been in a tangle over Emma Jean Frasier for as long as he'd known her. That had made it easy to convince himself he'd felt nothing but the hots for her. Even when, deep down, he'd known better.

He hadn't believed himself capable of it, but even way back then, when he'd just been a dumbass kid, he'd been in love with her.

And still was now.

This wasn't, however, the time to talk about that. They'd rounded a bend in their relationship, certainly, but there were still a lot of forks in the road. Not the least of which was the possibility of Emma facing murder charges.

Driving her home, he updated her on his plans. "I have to call the state police in on this one, because it's too big for Brady. Plus, of course, there's his personal bias."

"Oh?"

Johnny's jaw stiffened as he bit out a few of the less sordid details Nick had shared with him the other day.

"Oh, God, you mean Daneen had an affair with Jimbo?"

He nodded, not even broaching the possibility of Jimbo having been Jack's real father. He hoped, for the boy's sake, that it wasn't so.

"Does the sheriff know?"

"I don't think so." But if he did, Johnny damn sure wanted to find out about it. Soon.

"So, what about *your* personal bias," she murmured, sounding worried.

He'd expected the question. "If the sheriff convinces the state guys to look at you as a serious suspect, I'm going to have to step aside, allowing the state to provide a special prosecutor."

"Will it come to that?"

"Hell, no," he replied, taking her hand in his as he pulled onto her street. "Something like this…well, Joyful hasn't seen a murder in a good long time. I have to think it was a crime of passion, which usually means a quick confession or a sloppy killer. Once the state guys get here, they can do a professional investigation and will probably have a real suspect in custody right away."

At least, he hoped so.

Part of him wished his brother hadn't left this morning. He wouldn't mind having Nick do some investigating. It almost seemed worth giving him a call later, just to bounce some ideas around.

Their conversation in his office the other morning wouldn't leave his head. Because of what Nick had revealed about Jimbo. Christ, the man had been a slime. He'd swindled Emma, seduced Daneen, who knew what else he was capable of? Not that he'd deserved the Dracula treatment. Still, he couldn't say the world was gonna be a worse place without Jimbo Boyd in it.

A hint of concern about who had overheard him and Nick during their conversation flashed through his mind. He made a mental note to make sure Dan Brady had shown up at his luncheon Tuesday.

"You expecting company?" he asked when he saw the strange car parked in Emma's driveway.

"It's Claire. She's probably checking to see if I'm okay."

Johnny walked her inside, surprised to see Claire's husband waiting with her. The two of them sat mighty close together on the couch. The sight brought an unexpected smile.

Claire got up to hug Emma, and Tim rose, watching, his hands thrust in his pockets.

When the women's hug ended, Claire reached up and pulled a dry leaf from Emma's hair. "Geez, if you two are going to go to the gazebo, you oughta at least bring a blanket."

Johnny coughed into his fist as Emma turned red.

"That's what Claire insists we do," Tim interjected, giving his wife a quelling look.

This time, she was the one who flushed.

"So the gazebo's not our little secret?" Emma asked.

"Hate to break it to you, guys," Claire replied, "but you started your own lover's lane on prom night."

Johnny was suddenly very thankful he hadn't known that before they'd gone to the gazebo. Otherwise he might not have been as comfortable getting bare-ass naked in broad daylight.

"Johnny," Tim said, handing him a business card, "your brother was here. He wants you to call him on his cell."

"He stayed in Joyful?"

Claire shook her head. "Your mom called him and he turned around and came right back."

"Good," he murmured as he thought of the ground work his brother, as a detective, could do. "He'll be a big help."

Then Claire looked at Emma, nibbling her lip and looking a bit sheepish. "You had a call, too. We didn't mean to pry, but I turned up the answering machine, just in case it was…important." Then she sighed. "I guess it was."

"Oh? Who was it?"

Claire didn't so much as glance toward Johnny as she

answered. "Somebody from a company called Pierce Watson. They got your résumé and want to set up a meeting."

Unable to help it, Johnny immediately stiffened.

"They're one of the major brokerage houses in Manhattan," Emma murmured, sounding subdued.

A brokerage house. A résumé. Christ, she was going back to New York. Not thinking about it, he snapped, "You can't leave."

She jerked her attention toward him. He didn't know if she was surprised more by his words or his angry tone. Actually, he didn't know which surprised *him* more, either.

All he knew was the response had come from a place deep inside that had panicked at the thought of Emma Jean flying out of his life again.

"I can't, huh?"

Feeling like a controlling jerk, he backpedaled, lying to them both about what had prompted his instinctive response. "I mean," he explained in an even tone which revealed nothing of his raging emotions, "if Brady or the state police are considering you a suspect in this murder, you can't just leave town, Em. It wouldn't look good."

She nodded slowly, her eyes wide and searching as she held his stare. As if she expected him to say more.

Only he didn't. He couldn't. Because he had no idea what to say.

He was saved by the ringing of the phone. The sharp peal sounded three times before Emma finally pulled her attention off him—while he stood there trying to appear calm and noncommittal. Then she finally answered.

Please don't be calling to offer her a job.

Not until he figured out how to keep her in his life.

"Hi, Doris," Emma said, looking surprised when she realized who was on the other end of the line.

Johnny, Claire and Tim all listened to her side of the conversation, just waiting for a hint of concern in Emma's expression. He'd personally go down to Let Your Hair Down and tell the gossiping hair salon crowd to ride their wave of rumors straight to hell if they hurt her again.

"You mean, you really want me to come to work today?" Emma said into the receiver. "I figured…no, no, I'm sorry, I thought you wouldn't be willing…yes, sure, I'll be there. Give me a half hour."

When she hung up, a pleased smile was evident on her lips. She seemed, for the time being, to have forgotten that heavy, question-filled moment they'd shared before the phone call.

"It was Doris. She said the sheriff is a moron, and for me to get myself to work." Then she grinned. "She also ordered me to bring my calculator…and a pie."

Johnny liked seeing the frown disappear from Emma's brow, and damn sure wanted to keep a smile on her face. So, after chatting with Claire and Tim, he insisted on taking her to get her car, then following her to the beauty salon. He walked her inside, his arm draped over her shoulders, to make sure everybody in the place got the message, loud and clear.

That she was his. And that he supported her.

Doris waved him off. "Get on outta here, boy, we got some questions for your girlie."

He tensed, wondering if Doris and the handful of women in the place were going to ask for lurid details on Jimbo's murder.

"Emma, Mary-Anne here says she saw something on MS-NBC today about second quarter earnings being low for the big three automakers. What's that gonna do to the market? Should I get out of the mutual funds?" Doris asked, not pausing for a second as she continued to clip away at Mary-Anne Tucker's hair.

Johnny almost laughed as Emma launched into a detailed answer. She paused only long enough to give him a quick kiss before striding to the wash sink. Grabbing an apron, she began to explain things like quarterly earnings, faulty predictions and market hedging to the attentive women.

Feeling sure she was among friends, he left, wishing his next stop could be as pleasant. He somehow suspected it wouldn't.

Because he was on his way to find Daneen.

EMMA WOULD NEVER have believed anything could take her mind off the horror of her morning, or the sultry perfection of her early afternoon. But over the next hour, the ladies of Let Your Hair Down somehow managed to do exactly that.

"Mrs. Walker, you just got a cut on Tuesday. You can't tell me you really need another trim," Emma said as she and Johnny's mother stood in the back of the salon, near the wash basins.

Jane Walker, a pretty, petite woman who looked younger now than she had a decade ago when her husband had been alive managed an earnest look. "I do. I'm not so sure about this length."

Emma raised a brow, looking at Mrs. Walker's barely more than an inch long hair. The pixie cut suited her. Baldness wouldn't. If anyone knew, it was Emma. "You don't have to get your hair done to come in and ask me for financial advice."

"Oh, honey," said Susie, one of the stylists Emma had met Tuesday—the gum-chewer with the black and blue hair. "They're not coming in for advice."

Doris chimed in. "They're coming in for support."

Emma's mouth dropped open and she looked around to see two women getting cuts and two more waiting up front. All of them wore looks ranging from fondness to amusement.

"You're…"

"This town did enough damage when you showed up. Not one person here believes you killed anybody," Jane Walker said.

"Even," a new voice added, "if he might have deserved it."

Mona Harding. The redhead who'd been at Jimbo's house the other night entered the salon, letting the door swing shut behind her as she strode toward Emma. "I didn't hear you *threaten* him. Even though if I suspected what *you* suspected, I woulda gone over there armed and ready to go medieval on that man's ass."

All the other women in the room were now paying careful attention to Mrs. Harding. The woman had that kind of presence—large, flamboyant and ballsy.

"Thank you. Maybe you could tell the chief that."

Mona nodded once. "I already did." Lowering her voice a bit, and inhaling a shaky breath, she added, "He confessed some things to me." At Emma's surprised look, she clarified. "No, he wasn't in on anything he thought was really wrong. Jimbo convinced him your grandma had signed the contract and agreed to everything, but she up'n died before the deal could go to closing."

Emma knew better, but wasn't about to argue.

"He figured you were gone forever. So he helped Jimbo set up an illegitimate closing with a buddy of his who does title work."

The room remained so silent, the sound of one of Doris's bobby pins dropping would likely have sent them all leap-

ing out of their seats as they realized the importance of
what Mona had revealed.

"The sheriff has confessed to doing something illegal,"
Emma said.

The woman nodded. "He'll have to resign and face the
music." Then she put her hand on her hip and tilted her chin
up in challenge. "I'll stand by him. Because he's seeing
things differently today. Definitely about his former buddy,
the mayor. Do you know that bastard fired Daneen last
night? The slime."

Emma's brow shot up, particularly because of what
Johnny had told her earlier, regarding Daneen and Jimbo's
personal relationship. "Slime indeed."

"Yeah. Dan was pretty upset."

She could imagine. And a trickle of suspicion coursed
through her. *How upset?*

"He's with Daneen now. Poor girl was sitting in her car
in the parking lot of the jail bawling her eyes out when I
left."

The image brought an unexpected hint of empathy.
Emma didn't like Daneen. She never had. But she ached
a little for the woman, who'd apparently also been used,
though in a different way, just as Emma had. The image
of her unable to get out of her car as she sobbed over a man
who wasn't worth *anyone's* tears got to Emma more than
she'd ever have expected.

"Well," she said to Mona, "thank you very much for
backing me up, and for coming here to tell me what you
found out. You didn't have to involve yourself, and I do appreciate it."

Even as she spoke, part of her wondered why Mona had
done it. Not only standing up to her boyfriend, but also
confessing the truth of the matter to Emma, especially so
publicly.

"It was the least I could do." Then Mona quirked a brow, fully aware she was in the spotlight. "After all, I feel partly responsible for what happened to your grandma's land."

"Why? It wasn't you, it was Jimbo and this MLH Enterprises."

Oh, my God. An unbelievable possibility flickered through her mind.

A half smile lifted the woman's bright red lips "Have we ever been fully introduced?" She extended one heavily ringed, perfectly manicured hand. "My name's Mona Lisa Harding."

A few of the women tittered at the flamboyant name, probably thinking that it suited the woman. Emma was the only one who fully absorbed the implications.

Mona Lisa Harding. MLH Enterprises. In the flesh.

"I understand," Emma murmured.

"I don't think anybody else does," Mona said with an exaggerated sigh. "What's it take to get a public confession across around here, self-flagellation and a hair shirt? What I'm saying is, I'm the one building the club, Joyful Interludes."

Every other woman in the room shot straight up. With dropped jaws, they stared at Mona, who'd been one of them a moment ago, and who was now admitting to…all kinds of things.

"I like this place," the woman said with an unrepentant shrug. "I have money squirreled away from my, um, *career.* I wanted to open a business, get some of those highway drivers to get off the exit and maybe give Joyful a try."

Naked dancers. That'd get 'em off the highway all right. Emma didn't argue the woman's motives, since she obviously believed them legitimate. "How'd the pecan grove come into this?"

"I got together with Jimbo, who suggested some property that might be suitable for the kind of establishment I had in mind."

"What establishment?" someone said from the front of the room.

"She's talking about the hootchie-cootchie girl place," a woman in the waiting area explained—loudly—to another. Then she looked up at Mona. "Sorry, she's hard of hearing. Go on."

Eyes twinkling with amusement, Mona did. "I looked at the site and loved the idea of building my club in the middle of a beautiful place, classy-like, leaving a lot of the trees intact."

Not a *lot*. But Emma wasn't going to interrupt.

"Jimbo handled everything. He told me the offer was accepted and took the deal from contract to closing, so I could stay out of it." Mona shook her head, looking regretful. "It was right here in this room where I first heard Emmajean had owned the land I'd bought. I wondered if I had all the facts, because, though I didn't know her well, I knew your grandma a little. I couldn't believe she'd really wanted to part with the land. But it was too late to ask her, obviously. And Jimbo swore it was true."

"Bastard," Emma muttered, unable to help it.

The entire shop remained quiet as all the women in the place digested Mona's words. Emma focused primarily on Jimbo and the grove. She imagined the other women in the salon had quickly moved past those issues and were now wondering how to tactfully ask Mrs. Harding whether or not she'd really made porn movies. Whether she'd liked it. And if the bountiful breasts gracing the billboard were hers.

Judging by the woman's more than generous bustline, Emma suspected they might be…or might have *been*, back in her heyday.

"So," Doris finally said as she slowly lifted her shears and again started clipping at her customer's dark brown hair, "what's all this mean? Is Joyful Interludes gonna open or not?"

Mona and Emma stared at each other. The legal implications were obvious. With the information Mona had just handed her, Emma could prove she was the rightful owner of the land on which Mona's club had been built. She was no lawyer, but as far as she knew, improvements belonged to the owner of the land.

Not to the person who'd paid for them.

Mona's suspiciously bright eyes told her she'd reached the same conclusion. Realizing how much the woman stood to lose, Emma wanted to reach out and take her hand, but wasn't sure the gesture would be appreciated. The redhead appeared to be hanging on to her bawdy bravado by a loose thread.

"I hope Jimbo's professional liability insurance was paid up," the other woman finally said with a toss of her head. "I invested my life savings in that place. If there's anybody to sue, I'll sure do it."

Emma wanted to cry for the woman, who'd been duped, as Emma had, by Jimbo Boyd. "Mrs. Harding..."

The other woman held up a hand. "You don't have to say anything. We were both used." Then she turned to look at the others. "I didn't realize how much everybody around here would hate the idea of, uh, *that* kind of business. So I'm thinking if I get my money back, maybe Bradenton might be a better place for it." With a sigh, she added, "But I gotta admit, *Bradenton* Interludes doesn't work the way Joyful did." Her voice lowering the tiniest bit, she added, "I didn't mean to hurt anyone."

Doris immediately murmured assurances and Susie

stepped close to give Mona a hug. "I woulda liked your place. I was thinking about trying to get a job there."

Mona looked her over. "You coulda, kid. You got the body."

"But she dances like Elmer Fudd on Prozac," Doris cracked, immediately lightening the tension. Then she added, "You know, maybe you could answer a question for me. Is it true the, uh, *biggest* ones pass out if they get a real woody because all their blood rushes to their little head insteada their big one?"

Mona didn't bat a lash. "Quite true."

A few shocked titters greeted the response, then Doris sighed. "I know I'll never have that worry. The only way my Donald'd pass out during sex is if he had to last longer'n ninety seconds. Or if I made him turn off the TV."

This time the laughter was loud and cleansing.

As a more comfortable silence descended, the normal clicks of shears and hiss of hairspray gradually resumed. Mona, deciding she wanted a change of look to go with her change of status from respectable widow to former porn queen, took a seat up front, secure in the knowledge that the women in this room, at least, weren't turning their backs on her. Kinda gave Emma a renewed sense of faith in Joyful.

Though she intended to get right to work, Emma had a hard time getting refocused. Something was tickling the back of her mind. Mona had given her a lot to think about, and at first she figured the thought whizzing around, un-catchable, in her brain, was somehow related. But she didn't think so. There was something else, something that had put her on edge as soon as she'd started thinking about Daneen. Even more so than thoughts of Daneen usually put her on edge. For the life of her, though, she couldn't figure out what it was.

Finally, knowing she'd never grab the thought if she continued to hunt it down inside her head, she forced herself to focus on her work. "Mrs. Walker? Ready for your completely unnecessary wash and cut? Want a perm to go with it?"

But the woman wasn't listening. She was staring into the air, her lips moving, though she didn't speak aloud. Then, finally, she smiled. An "aha" look which usually accompanied a good idea got Emma curious. "Mrs. Walker?"

"I think," Jane Walker slowly replied, "I have a possible solution." She patted Emma on the shoulder. "Of course, nothing can put those trees back, honey. Your grandma's place is never gonna be able to be the way it was. But you know, when life hands you pecans…sometimes, you just gotta make some pie."

Emma didn't think the pecans-for-lemons thing worked, but she was too interested in hearing the woman's idea to say so.

"What are you getting at?" Doris asked.

"Yes, please explain," Emma added.

And Jane did.

CHAPTER NINETEEN

JOHNNY HAD FIGURED there were only three places Daneen could be. The first was a bust—she wasn't home. He'd even checked her garage to make sure her little blue car wasn't parked inside.

Next he cruised past Dan Brady's house. It was possible Daneen would have gone to her father for support. Dan might not know about Daneen and Jimbo's personal relationship—*might* not—but he'd certainly lend a shoulder to a daughter whose boss had been murdered in her place of employment.

Nobody was there, either. Which left the jail.

Pulling up outside, he saw a number of familiar cars in the lot. A couple of cruisers—including Dan's and Fred's—plus Daneen's car. And, to his surprise...

"Hey, you didn't return my call," his brother Nick said as he stepped out of his car.

"I tried a bunch of times. It's been busy," Johnny replied as he joined his younger brother on the sidewalk.

"Sorry. I've been checking up on some things." With a shrug he admitted, "Dan Brady *did* give his speech Tuesday."

"We're on the same wavelength, I guess," Johnny said, pleased his brother was already at work.

"That doesn't mean whoever heard our conversation in the office Tuesday didn't tell him about it afterward."

Johnny nodded. "Speaking of our conversation…"

"Yeah?"

Johnny voiced another possibility, one he'd been mulling over all day. "Remember what Emma said? Hannah was supposed to come to the courthouse to get some protest permits on Tuesday."

Nick raised a brow. "The victim's *wife?*"

"He was a slug. And maybe, if she heard for herself just how much of a slug, she went over the edge." He knew it was implausible, given Hannah Boyd's cool, demeanor and reputation. Still, stranger things had happened.

"Possible." Then Nick, sounding more resigned than concerned, asked, "You think Sheriff Dan's gonna go for his gun the minute I walk in the station?"

"I'll go first to block the way."

"You always did," Nick murmured.

Johnny paused.

"I mean," Nick said evenly, "with Pop."

Their eyes met and held, saying a wealth of things they'd never said before. Then, with a brief nod of understanding that came from surviving the same hardships—and coming out stronger for them—they walked into the jail.

Inside the building, Johnny immediately spied Dan Brady, sitting in his private office with his daughter. Fred stood at the front desk, talking quietly with another deputy.

"Have you heard from the state police yet?" Johnny asked.

Fred nodded, though his eyes flashed with resentment. Not unexpected. Any cop disliked the interference of outsiders on his turf. "They'll be here by six." Then Fred turned to eye Nick. "Didn't get a chance to welcome you home the other night."

Nick managed a smile. "Hey, Fred, good seeing you. I didn't expect you to come back here after college."

Johnny suddenly remembered that Nick and Fred had once been friends, though they'd been complete opposites. Quiet, studious Fred, volatile troublemaker Nick.

They'd both played on the Joyful High football squad—with Johnny during his senior year, then again together during their own. Fred, for all his quiet demeanor and unprepossessing features, had once been a hell of a fullback, strong as a bull and fast on his feet. He wondered when the man had started looking so old and worn-down by life.

"I dropped out after freshman year," Fred told Nick. "Missed Joyful too much. Like your brother, I guess. And other folks."

Ha. When he'd been off at college, Johnny had missed Joyful about as much as a sailor would miss a case of the clap.

Before Nick could comment—and he could only imagine the kind of disdain his brother would show at the idea of moving back here—another voice interrupted.

"What do you want?"

Johnny stiffened at Dan Brady's words. The man stood in the doorway, shielding his daughter from their view.

"We were looking for Daneen," Johnny said.

"She doesn't want to talk to you." Then he cast a hard glare at Nick. "Either of you."

Nick, completely unperturbed, leaned his hip against the front desk and crossed his arms, leaving things in Johnny's hands. Johnny stepped smoothly between the two men. "We thought she might be able to help with the investigation."

Dan pointed an index finger at Nick. "He's not investigating this. My people are."

"Actually, the state police are," Johnny replied, his voice low and even, and deadly serious. "There's no reason we can't get some background information for them to go on."

"I don't want him here."

From inside the office, Johnny heard Daneen's voice. "Let them in, Daddy. Please."

Retaining his surly expression, Dan stepped aside, though he continued to scowl as they entered his office.

Daneen sat in a chair opposite her father's desk, clutching a big, white handkerchief to her makeup-smeared face.

"Where's Jack?" Johnny asked, concerned for the boy who was *still* his nephew, as far as he was concerned.

"He went home from school with a friend," Daneen replied. Then she focused on Nick. "You can sit down. Daddy's not going to…do anything. I've told him the truth about us."

His brother and the sheriff exchanged a long, disdainful look which said more than words ever could have. Dan obviously didn't care about the circumstances of his daughter's marriage—just that Nick had left her. And Nick still smoldered with resentment at the man whose temper and reputation had forced him into one of the biggest mistakes of his life.

"You okay?" Nick finally asked his ex, managing to sound concerned, though Johnny knew he could hardly stand her.

Daneen nodded. "I can't believe he's dead. I mean, I wanted to kill the son of a bitch myself last night, but knowing someone actually did it is too horrible to believe."

"What?" Johnny asked, stunned at her words.

Dan answered for his daughter, disgust ringing in his

voice. "Jimbo fired her last night. After all the years she worked so hard for him in his two-bit office, he let her go."

Daneen shot a quelling look toward Nick, which Johnny intercepted. So, she hadn't been completely honest with Daddy about her uh, more *personal* relationship with Jimbo. Hence Dan's relative calm. Either that, or the man was one hell of an actor, and he'd known the truth for a while. At least long enough to pay an early morning visit to Jimbo's office.

But before Johnny could think too hard on which of the two Bradys knew more about Jimbo's death, the ring of his cell phone interfered. He almost ignored it. Then he saw the name on the caller ID: Let Your Hair Down. "Excuse me," he said to the others before answering. "Hello?"

"Johnny, it's me," Emma said. "I need to talk to you."

"Uh, I'm in the middle of something right now, can it wait?"

"No," she said, sounding out of breath and near panic. "I think I know who killed Jimbo."

Trying to maintain a calm expression, he asked, "Who?"

"Daneen. I remembered something just now when I was washing the permanent solution out of your mother's hair. By the way, Johnny, she looks adorable with curls."

Like he wanted to hear about his mother's hair now, when Emma had just accused the woman sitting next to him of murder? "What were you saying?"

"Oh, yeah, I had to reach you because I want you to stay away from Daneen. Remember the driver I saw Deputy Fred pulling over by Jimbo's house? It was Daneen. I saw her car the night of the reunion, but didn't connect it with the one I saw last night until a few minutes ago."

He sensed there was a lot more to the story, and that

Emma was trying to cut to the chase. But the way her voice shook also told him she was very upset. He tried to calm her down. "It's okay, that might not mean anything."

"It means she was in a rage. She was driving like a bloody maniac, after being parked outside the victim's house, furious…because he'd fired her!"

"I heard."

Suddenly Emma sucked in an audible breath. "Oh, my God, you're with her right now."

"Correct again."

She muttered a hard curse word that sounded shocking coming from what he knew were two beautifully soft lips. "Get out of there before she does her Van Helsing act on you, too."

This time, he couldn't prevent the small chuckle. Lord have mercy, the woman could be warped. He liked that about her. "Look, Nick and I are here in the sheriff's office, but when I'm done I'll meet you at your place, okay?"

"You're not alone with her? There are witnesses?" She sounded only slightly relieved. "Okay. But show up by five-thirty or I'm coming out looking for you. And Daneen had better have more than a frickin' campaign sign to fight me off if she hurts you."

"Bloodthirsty, aren't you?" he couldn't help mumbling, even as he chuckled a little.

Saying goodbye, he hung up, only to see his brother, Nick, grinning like a man who sees another man acting like a total sucker over a woman.

Johnny managed to smother a sigh, knowing he was doomed. A man in love. With a woman who threatened violence to anyone who might hurt him, no less.

Getting back to business, he hit Daneen with the information he'd gotten from Emma. "Daneen, why were you parked outside Jimbo's house last night?"

His ex-sister-in-law sat up straighter, looking wary.

"She wasn't," her father said. Then he studied Daneen's face. "Were you, baby? Did you come out to Jimbo's last night?"

Daneen's slowly nodded. "I was upset. I had a neighbor pop in to stay with Jack after he went to bed, and I went for a long drive." She gave them all a pleading look. "But I didn't mean to do anything, or confront him about dumping…I mean, *firing* me. I just parked there. Then I took off. Fred can tell you I left while your car was still right there in Jimbo's driveway, Daddy."

Fred's lie earlier today suddenly made sense. He'd been protecting Daneen. The man hadn't cared that he'd been leaving Emma Jean out to dry, which enraged Johnny.

Dan stood and called to his deputy, who entered so fast, Johnny suspected he'd had his ear pressed to the closed door. After being confronted by his boss, Fred admitted that he had pulled Daneen over the night before.

Dan frowned. "No record of it in your nightly report."

Stiff-jawed, Fred replied, "I didn't think it was worth embarrassing anybody by making a record."

"And you didn't think it was worth coming clean when Emma Jean Frasier looked to you to help prove she hadn't been stalking the victim last night," Johnny bit out from between clenched teeth.

Fred flushed. But didn't say a word.

"So," Nick said from his chair, where he'd been sitting quietly for the past few minutes, observing them through partly lowered lashes, as if bored by the entire conversation, "Daneen, you were in quite a state last night. How about this morning?"

"You watch your mouth," Dan said.

"It's a reasonable question." Nick rose to his feet and towered over Brady. "One the state police are going to ask as soon as they start nosing into this."

Daneen's eyes were wide, her mouth working, but no sound was coming out. And Johnny began to wonder, for the first time, if maybe Emma hadn't been onto something. Because Daneen looked about as guilty as anyone he'd ever seen.

Fred cleared his throat. "She didn't go to Jimbo's office this morning. She didn't kill anyone." Shooting a half-tentative look toward his boss, he added, "Because, after I followed her home, I stayed. She was with me, right up until I got the call about the murder." He swallowed visibly. "We were together *all night long.*"

EMMA WATCHED the minute hand of her watch sweep down to the six and glared at the front door, ordering it to open. Just before she grabbed her keys, determined to go find Johnny, it did. "You're here," she said, launching herself into his arms before he'd even had a chance to cross the threshold.

He was warm and solid and fine. Just fine. Wrapping her hands in his hair, she tugged his mouth to hers and gave him a slow, lingering kiss, wanting to imprint his taste and his scent on her brain, to store up her reservoir of calm against future moments of panic.

When they parted, she gave him a wobbly smile, breathing normally for the first time in an hour. "Where is she? Has Daneen been arrested?"

"It's not that simple," Nick said.

Emma hadn't even noticed him entering the house behind his brother. Shooting him a grateful look for serving as Johnny's backup, she gestured toward a chair. "Sit down and tell me."

Johnny she kept firmly by her side, dragging him to sit with her on the sofa where they'd made such incredible love last weekend.

"I don't think she's strong enough to put a stake through a man's heart," Johnny said.

"Ever heard of adrenaline? Extraordinary strength produced by rage?" She glared at Nick. "You're a cop, back me up."

"I think that's just in comic books," Nick said with an apologetic shrug.

Emma nearly growled in annoyance.

Chuckling, Johnny tenderly brushed his fingers through her hair before tugging her closer. "Daneen's got an alibi."

Across the room, Nick watched them, an enigmatic smile on his face. "And while my ex-wife might be a lying, cheating little she-devil, I honestly don't think she's a murderer."

"Neither do I," Johnny said.

Men. Pfft. "If Jimbo fired her and dumped her, all on the same day…"

"There are other people who might have done it, Em," Johnny said, obviously trying to calm her down.

"The victim's wife," Nick pointed out.

Johnny nodded. "Daneen's father. Or Jimbo's mysterious business partner."

"No, it's not her." Seeing Johnny's surprise, she quickly explained everything she'd learned today at Let Your Hair Down.

"You mean Mona Harding made sex movies? She's gotta be in her sixties." Then he chuckled. "Wait'll I tell Virg."

Nick snorted. "Bet he'll be looking at his video collection differently from now on."

They were laughing, grinning like fools while they sat here discussing murder. "I think you're crazy. Daneen had to be out of her mind angry with Jimbo."

"She has an alibi, darlin'. Believe it or not, she spent the night—and the morning—with Fred Willis."

Emma let that sink in. Daneen and Fred. Wow. "You're sure?"

Johnny nodded. "He confessed it right in front of her father, who looked ready to tear him a new one. We got outta there quick."

"Fred Willis," she whispered again, having a hard time picturing brassy, sexy Daneen with someone so…so ordinary. "He's so quiet. And nice. He seemed really embarrassed about having to lock me up last week. He could barely meet my eye when I ran into him at the reunion and at the courthouse Tuesday."

"Fred had a crush on Daneen in high school," Nick admitted. "Followed her around like a puppy dog through freshman year. 'Course, she hardly gave him the time of day."

"Well," Johnny said, drawing out the word in a slow drawl, "she obviously gave it to him at least *once* in high school." He and Nick met each other's stares and Nick slowly nodded.

"What?"

"As it turns out, Fred might very well be Jack's real father."

Emma couldn't help it. Her jaw dropped completely. Then she looked back and forth between the two impossibly handsome men sitting in her living room.

"Somebody start explaining. Right now."

DANEEN *ALMOST* DID IT. She almost allowed Fred to cover for her. But in the end, full of grief and guilt and shock and dismay, she just couldn't.

She had to admit the truth, though not to her father. She'd barely gotten out of the jailhouse without breaking down under his disappointed frown.

God love Fred, he'd put himself right into the line of fire of a much-too-overprotective father with his lie. He'd lied to help *her*. Heaven forgive her for every unkind thought she'd ever had about the man.

Knowing there was one person she had to confess to— before the state police showed up—she headed straight toward a house she'd never imagined visiting. Emma Jean Frasier's.

When she arrived and saw all the cars in the driveway, she realized this wouldn't be as easy as she'd hoped. She wouldn't only be confessing in front of Johnny and Emma, but also her ex-husband. Who happened to answer the door after she halfheartedly knocked.

"Nick."

"Hello, Daneen."

He somehow managed to look unsurprised, as unflappable and unreachable as ever. God, how different might her life have been if she'd been able to hold on to this man?

"She's here?" she heard from inside. Emma Jean strode to the front door, shouldering Nick out of the way and blocking Daneen out. "What do you want?"

Ms. Ladylike Emma looked all riled up and angry. Protective, even. It almost made Daneen smile, the thought of Emma needing to protect the wicked Walker brothers from her.

"Is Johnny here?"

"He is."

"I need to talk to him." Daneen swallowed her pride. "Please, may I come in?" Then, softly, so softly she almost didn't hear her own voice, she added, "I have a confession to make."

JOHNNY WASN'T entirely sure what to expect. He damn sure didn't think his ex-sister-in-law was going to confess to murder. Because he didn't think she'd done it, whether she had an alibi or not.

As he watched Daneen lower herself to the edge of the chair Nick had vacated, a number of scenarios ran through his head. Anything was possible—because Daneen looked...broken. That was the only way to describe the slump of her shoulders, the pinched, weary look on her face and the emptiness in her eyes.

Emma, it seemed, noticed as well. "Can I get you something cold to drink?" she murmured softly. "Some iced tea?"

Offering sweet tea to a woman she thought was a murderer. Heaven help anyone who claimed Emmajean Frasier's granddaughter hadn't inherited her good Southern manners.

Daneen shook her head. "No. I just want to get this over with."

Steeling himself, Johnny said, "I'm not the police, Daneen. You don't have to talk to me, or to anybody else, without a lawyer."

Daneen turned her full attention on him. "I'm not coming to you as a prosecutor. I'm coming to you as a friend, because you deserve the truth." Swallowing, she admitted, "Fred lied. I didn't spend last night with him. He pulled me over outside Jimbo's, then followed me home to make sure I was okay. Then he left."

"He was protecting you," Nick murmured.

Daneen looked up at her ex and nodded. "God knows why." Leaning forward, she put her elbows on her knees and rubbed a weary hand over her eyes. "But I swear on my life, I didn't kill Jimbo. I might have *wanted* him dead for a while last night after he threw me over, but I'd never have killed a man I loved. A man who might be my boy's father."

Beside him, Emma sucked in a shocked breath. For a woman who'd publicly admitted to having had only three lovers in her life, he supposed today's revelations about Daneen *were* pretty shocking. He squeezed her hand, though he continued to focus on Nick's ex-wife.

"I didn't know anything about Jimbo's death until I went to the office after Jack left for school this morning. I planned to have it out with him." She laughed bitterly. "Only, I had it out with his wife, instead."

Ouch. "Hannah was there?"

Daneen nodded. "She was with Cora Dillon, and the police."

"Mrs. Boyd was arriving as our estimable sheriff was hauling me off to jail," Emma said.

Daneen shot her an apologetic look. "Anyway, Hannah said some things…things I guess I deserved. Cora watched every bit of the spectacle." Daneen shook her head. "You know, I think Cora was the one who told Hannah about me and Jimbo. She was almost clapping the whole time I was being called a slut and a whore and a home-wrecker."

Emma's hand tightened reflexively in his. The dead look in Daneen's eyes, and the resigned tone of her voice revealed more than anger ever would have. She was crushed. Completely crushed.

Some would say she deserved it, that she *was* all the things Hannah had called her.

Johnny preferred to remember the young girl who'd

been seduced by her father's best friend not long after the death of her mother.

Finally, as if she'd come to the end of her rope, Daneen rose wearily to her feet. "That's all I've got to say. I'd best go get Jack now." She crossed her arms, hugging herself. "I want to see my baby."

Emma rose and walked the other woman to the door. Johnny swore he saw her give Daneen's shoulder a little squeeze, though she'd probably never have admitted it.

"You need a ride?" Nick asked his ex.

She shook her head. "I'm okay." Then she looked back at Johnny. "Don't go too hard on Fred, okay? He was just trying to protect me. He's always been...well, he's always liked me, I guess." And without another word, she left.

"My God, how sad," Emma murmured once she was gone. She gently pushed the front door closed, then moved to the window air conditioner to crank it up a notch.

It was damn hot in here. Not as hot as it had been last Friday—but pretty bad. Made more so by the thick layer of unhappiness Daneen had worn like a cloak.

"I still don't like her, but I feel very sorry for her." Emma admitted. "And I think you're right. She didn't kill Jimbo."

"No, she didn't." Johnny remained still, sitting on the couch as he analyzed all the bits and pieces of information floating around in his brain.

"My," Emma said, shaking her head, "Fred must really care about her to lie like that to protect her."

That made him pause.

Fred. Good old Fred.

Noble Fred who'd loved Daneen for years.

Fred, who'd come back to Joyful after one year in college—right around the same time Daneen had come back.

The man who'd been unable to look Emma in the eye…
on, oh, God, Emma had said…*Tuesday.* At the *courthouse.*

And suddenly everything came together.

Daneen hadn't killed Jimbo. Johnny knew it, just as sure
as he knew who had.

Not two seconds later, his brother's jaw dropped. "That
lying sack of shit."

"Yeah," Johnny said as he rose from the couch.

"What?" Emma asked, obviously reading their sudden
mood change. She looked confused.

Of course, she would be. Because she didn't know everything. Didn't know Fred had loved Daneen for *years.*
Didn't know about the conversation Johnny and Nick had
had in his office the other day…Tuesday…the day Emma
had seen Fred in the courthouse. She couldn't have realized how violently a deceptively strong former football
player would react to the truth about what Jimbo had done
to Daneen when she'd been practically a kid.

Johnny pressed a quick kiss on Emma's lips. A kiss of
reassurance that everything was going to be okay. Because
it was.

She practically stamped her foot in annoyance. "Is
somebody going to tell me what's going on?"

"Fred wasn't protecting *Daneen* with a phony alibi,"
Nick said.

"No," Johnny agreed. "He was protecting himself."

CHAPTER TWENTY

FOR THE FIRST couple of days after Deputy Fred Willis was charged with Jimbo's murder, everybody in Joyful talked about nothing else.

If he'd done it—yes. He'd confessed almost immediately after being confronted by Johnny Walker and the state investigators.

When he'd done it—sometime around 7:30 a.m., immediately after Jimbo had shown up for work on Thursday.

Why he'd done it—for Daneen, who'd been having an affair with the mayor. And who Fred had loved most of his life.

How he'd done it—with a wooden stake. Snicker, snicker.

And what would happen—anyone's guess.

Emma was glad when the gossip finally died down, at least at the beauty parlor. After all, they had other things to talk about. Other plans to make.

Speaking of those plans…it was about time to fill Johnny in on them, she decided Tuesday afternoon. Ever since Friday, he'd been tied up with the investigation. He'd been the key liaison to the state police working on the case, since Sheriff Brady had resigned.

That resignation had added more fire to the scandal. The women of Let Your Hair Down were the only ones who really knew why the chief had quit. So far.

Johnny had called at lunchtime, saying he was finally going to leave the office at a reasonable hour, after working ungodly long days straight through the weekend. And Emma was going to be ready for him. Pies at hand, a confession in her heart, she would be ready.

She planned to tell him the truth. Those tense moments Thursday when she'd been near to panic at the thought of him being alone with a possible murderer had made her realize something. Whether he wanted to hear it or not—whether she was a fool to tell him or not—she was going to let Johnny know how she felt.

She loved him. Madly. Passionately. Always had, always would, forever and ever, amen.

A hint of self-doubt whispered in her brain, reminding her of his views on love, relationships, commitment.

As in, never.

As for marriage? Not in a million years.

"Tough," she told her reflection in the misty bathroom mirror. "You're telling him."

"Telling who what?"

She whirled around, shocked to see Johnny standing in the doorway of her bathroom, wearing a salacious grin. No wonder, considering she was dressed in nothing but a loose towel, which she'd tucked around her breasts.

"You scared me. You're early."

"Want me to leave?"

She grabbed his arm. "Don't you dare." Then she stood up on tiptoe, holding her towel with one hand while, with the other, she cupped his head and pulled him close for a kiss. She kissed him deeply, holding nothing back, letting him feel the emotions that had so far gone unvoiced between them.

When they finally drew apart, he stared searchingly into her eyes. "Emma? You okay?"

She nodded. "Yeah. Let me get dressed, okay?"

"You don't have to on my account."

Nibbling her lip, she looked away. "Yes, I do. We need to talk."

WE NEED TO TALK.

God, were there four worse words in the English language for a man to hear, when spoken by a woman he loved? Usually they preceded some horrible news, quite often followed by, "It's not you, it's me." Or, "I just need my space."

At least, so he'd heard. He wasn't entirely sure since he'd never been involved long enough with any one woman to actually be dumped by one.

"Wanna tell me what about?" he finally asked, keeping his voice slow and even. She shook her head, then ducked past him out of the bathroom.

He followed her to her room, watching as she disappeared into her closet and came back out wearing her short pink robe.

Her hair was twisted up in a towel, her face bare of makeup, her whole body moist, sweet and fragrant from her shower. And she was mouthwateringly beautiful.

If she told him they were finished before he ever got the chance to tell her he loved her, he was gonna die. "Emma Jean…"

"So what's the latest?" she asked, looking nervous, as if she didn't want to proceed to their real conversation any more than he did.

He suddenly began to suspect why. New York had come calling again. He'd bet his last dollar on it. She was leaving.

"Johnny? Is anything new?"

He shook his head absently. "Not really. Just what I told you on the phone earlier. Daneen is taking Jack and moving down to Atlanta to live with her cousin for a while."

"She needs a new start," Emma said, a slight frown pulling at her brow. "And she certainly doesn't need her son hearing all the gossip flying around this place."

Emma walked by him, heading toward her dresser, probably to get some clothes. But Johnny couldn't wait any longer. He caught her arm, holding her still. "Tell me."

She looked down, staring at her pretty pink toenails, at the wall. At the bed. Then her face turned pinker than her nail polish and she looked away from the bed.

That was definitely one place where the two of them had no trouble communicating.

"What is it?"

She shrugged, resigned. "This is hard for me."

He could have let it remain hard, made her come up with the words to tell him she was going away, but he didn't want to see her hurting any longer than she had to. "I know what you're going to say."

"You do?"

He nodded. "I expected it, Emma. I've been waiting for you to give me this kind of news almost since the day you arrived."

She rolled her eyes. "Well, gee, if I'd known it myself as soon as I'd arrived, it might have saved us both a lot of trouble."

Trouble. The weeks they'd spent together had been trouble? His heart took a hit. "So I guess that means you're not going to change your mind."

"Who can change their mind when their mind's not calling the shots?"

"I guess your wallet is," he admitted, knowing she had to look out for herself.

"Huh?"

Shaking his head, he drew in a deep breath, about to

tread into very deep water. Where he'd never attempted to swim before.

She was worth it. What they had was worth it. What they *could* have was worth it most of all.

He wasn't about to ask her to stay. But he sure as hell wasn't going to sit back and watch her go. "I'm not a bad lawyer, you know."

She looked surprised by the change of topic.

"I mean, I've been sitting here with my thumb up my ass for eighteen months. Then, all of a sudden a real murder happens and wham, I remember I used to be pretty good at my job back in Atlanta."

"But did you like it?"

He shrugged, looking away. "I can like any job under the right circumstances."

"Those being?"

This time he didn't hesitate in meeting her stare and holding it. "That *you're* in the vicinity."

Her eyes widened in shock as she finally understood what he was getting at. "Johnny, you…"

"Shh," he said, holding his fingers up to her lips. "You don't have to decide anything now. But there's something between us, Em, there always has been. And if I have to follow you to some big northern city to make sure we give it a shot, then so be it."

"Oh, my God," she whispered, looking stunned. "Are you saying what I *think* you're saying?"

"You want me," he said, not letting her obvious dismay change his mind about being honest. "You admitted you've always wanted me. I want you, too."

This time, she was the one who put her hand to his mouth. "You're wrong," she said softly.

No. God, please no.

A part of him died. Just shriveled up and died inside.

"I didn't always *want* you, Johnny Walker."

He almost called her a liar, but before he could, she cut his legs right out from under him.

"I always loved you."

Loved. *Loved?*

She must have seen his disbelief. "I loved you. I was infatuated with you from that hot summer day when your truck broke down and I gave you a ride. I fell a little harder for you every time you were home from college, when I'd see you standing up for Nick or Virg, or working your butt off to help your mom."

That word, love, was still bouncing around inside his brain, making it hard to focus on the rest of her words.

Emma loved him? Had *always* loved him?

"And I lost my heart to you forever the minute I opened my front door and saw you standing there in that tux, holding those wildflowers you'd picked from Nelson's field."

Her beautiful amber eyes glittered with emotion. Her soft voice held no hint of doubt. And the way she cupped his cheek in her hand—as if reaching up to touch him for the first time—nearly brought him to his knees.

"I know you don't believe in it, don't believe yourself capable of truly loving anyone, or of making a real relationship work. But I love you enough to order you to try."

"Order?" he finally croaked out through a mouth as dry as dust.

"Yeah. I *order* you to give yourself a chance to love me, Johnny Walker. If you don't, I'll…I'll never give you another piece of pie again as long as you live." Though her voice held a note of teasing, her eyes narrowed as she threatened, "And I'll make sure you aren't capable of sharing pie with any *other* woman for the rest of your life, either."

Unable to help it, he let out a bark of laughter. Grabbing her, he hoisted her up until they were nose to nose. Then he kissed her, tasted, for the first time in his life, the sweetness of a mouth that had just said, "I love you."

This time the words they communicated in their kiss were deeper. More meaningful. He told her with his lips what he hadn't yet put into words. *I love you, Emma Jean.*

When they pulled apart, he let Emma slide down his body to stand on her own. Her eyes were wide, her breaths coming in short, shallow gasps as she waited. Waited for a response

There was only one he could give her.

He took a step back, seeing her sudden frown, but needing room to reach into his back pocket. Withdrawing his wallet, he opened it and reached inside for something very familiar. Very precious.

In a small plastic sleeve, which was made to hold a wallet-sized photograph, was a tiny, delicate, thin strip of gold. He heard her gasp as he drew it out, letting the cool metal slide over his fingertips. Then he lifted it higher.

So she could see the butterfly.

"Oh, my God, that's my anklet."

"It hung on my bedpost in my dorm for a long time," he admitted hoarsely. "But ever since prom night, it's been in my wallet. I've carried it with me every day for the past ten years."

She knew, then. Of course she did, judging by the shaking of her lips and the brightness of her eyes. But Johnny gave her the gift of the words, anyway. Just as she'd done for him. "I love you, Emma Jean Frasier. I've loved you, and *only* you, for as long as I can remember."

The moisture in her eyes turned into full-fledged tears, though her beautiful face was practically alight from the huge smile on her lips.

"Hallmark, huh?" he asked with a gentle laugh as he touched one teardrop with the tip of his finger.

"Yeah," she whispered.

Then there was nothing left to say. She twined her fingers in his, the ankle bracelet winding between both their hands, creating a large ring of gold. Then she kissed him again, like she needed him to breathe.

Which was just what he needed from her.

Her kiss to breathe. Her laughter to melt. Her smile to exist. Her love to survive.

Their long, sweet embrace eventually moved to her bed, where they continued to kiss, slowly, languorously, as the late-afternoon sun slid through the half-open blinds over her bedroom window. That sunlight cast lines of shadow and light across her body as he drew her silky robe off, kissing her, all over, as if for the first time.

But before he removed his own clothes to make love to her, truly, in every sense of the word this time, she frowned.

"What is it?"

"Did you really have your heart set on going with me to New York?"

"I'm not letting you get away again, Em."

She nodded, thinking about it. "Can I reserve the right to take you up on that in the future?"

Not sure what she was getting at, and wanting very much to get back to the much more interesting task of getting naked with her, he nodded absently. "Sure."

"Good."

Getting naked was definitely more interesting. But he'd only gotten as far as his shirt, which he tossed to the floor, when he had to ask, "Why do you need to reserve judgment?"

She shrugged, moving her cool hands all over his chest, as if testing the curves and contours of his body. He nearly shuddered under the power of her soft, delicate touch, completely forgetting what he'd just asked her.

"Well, your mother would kill me if I up and moved to New York with you right now," she finally whispered, her words riding her tiny little pants of arousal.

"My mother can visit me anywhere I go," he mumbled, not wanting to think of anyone else, *especially* not his mother, when Emma was doing such remarkable things with her hands. Her lips.

Oh, God, he silently moaned, *her amazingly sweet mouth.*

Emma chuckled, then moved down his body, using that mouth to unfasten his pants, then reaching to tug them down and out of her way.

She climbed on top of him, looking down with heavy-lidded, desire-filled eyes. Her wet hair tangled around her face, and he put his hands in it, delicately caressing her scalp, thinking, as he always did when he tangled his fingers in her soft, bright hair, how much he wanted to get down on his knees and thank God that she'd survived her accident.

"I didn't mean she'd kill me for taking *you* away," she admitted as she stretched and curved like a cat, sliding her body over his, tempting him with her heat and her softness. "I meant, she'd be upset if her business partner bailed on her."

"Business…"

"Later," she whispered, leaning down and nibbling on the corner of his mouth. Then tilting her hips, doing crazy, *insane* things to him until he forgot who and where he was.

"I'll tell you all about it later," she said, licking at his lips. "Right now, I want you to tell me you love me, over and over again, while you're making love to me."

And Johnny was only too happy to oblige.

EPILOGUE

EMMAJEAN'S PECAN GROVE opened the following September.

The very first customers—members of Sylvie Stottlemyer's bridge club—decided after sampling some amazing homemade desserts to hold their annual Christmas party in one of the diner's private party rooms. They booked it, stuffed a bit more pie between their cheeks, then left to spread the word that Emmajean's was divine.

When not ordering Emmajean's Famous Pecan Pie, or Minnie's Perfect Peach, the diner's patrons happily consumed the delicious home-cooked meals whipped up by the two cooks: Minnie and Jane Walker. The guys from the machine parts factory north of town took a particular liking to the mighty fine meat loaf.

Which they told to whoever would listen.

The rumors circulated and floated through the autumn air, fast and varied, like leaves caught in a strong wind. They landed here, were passed along there, then took off again, carried on until they'd covered most every square foot of Joyful.

Yessir, before long, every soul in the county knew Emmajean's Pecan Grove was a bona fide hit.

As an investor, Jane had a lot at stake in making sure the regular folks kept coming back, and that strangers getting off the highway remembered to stop on their return trip. So she worked hard to make every meal as good as many a home-cooked one, and *better* than some.

With even more at stake—as a full-fledged partner—Mona Harding kept the business side of things running smoothly. She also, the male populace was pleased to note, did the hiring.

Meaning the waitresses at Emmajean's Pecan Grove were all young, perky and buxom.

As for the co-owner, well, the granddaughter of the diner's namesake didn't have much to do with the day-to-day operations of the diner. No, she was much too busy running her thriving financial consulting business out of one of the upstairs offices.

Not to mention planning her wedding to the *formerly* most eligible bachelor of Joyful, Georgia.

* * * * *

Don't miss bad boy Nick Walker's story in
She's Got the Look,
available September 2005 from HQN.

HQN™

We *are* romance™

Special Agent Cece Blackwell is smart, savvy and knows her way around race cars…and Blain Sanders.

Award-winning author

pamela britton

NASCAR star Blain Sanders can't believe that sexy lead investigator Cece Blackwell is the same drag-racing tomboy who used to dog his steps! But Cece has grown up, and while catching a killer is her main objective, she's not entirely above making the man who used to ignore her squirm just a little….

Dangerous Curves

Two people on a surefire collision course…in love.
Available in March.

NORA ROBERTS

THE CALHOUNS:
Suzanna and Megan

Atop the rocky coast of Maine sits the Towers, a magnificent family mansion—home to a legend of long-lost love, hidden treasures and a family determined to save their home against all odds. Don't miss the concluding stories in the spellbinding Calhoun family saga!

Suzanna's Surrender—Ex-cop Holt Bradford just wanted to relax, but he couldn't say no to Suzanna Calhoun's plea for help. And she wouldn't risk her well-ordered life for a man who made her mouth go dry...

Megan's Mate—Calhoun sister-in-law Megan O'Riley and her young son traveled far to become the Towers' newest residents, but she never expected that Captain Nate Fury would find a home in her heart.

Available at your favorite bookstore March 2005.

Silhouette®

Where love comes alive™

If you enjoyed what you just read,
then we've got an offer you can't resist!

Take 2 bestselling novels FREE!
Plus get a FREE surprise gift!

Clip this page and mail it to MIRA®

IN U.S.A.
3010 Walden Ave.
P.O. Box 1867
Buffalo, N.Y. 14240-1867

IN CANADA
P.O. Box 609
Fort Erie, Ontario
L2A 5X3

YES! Please send me 2 free MIRA® novels and my free _____ at the receiving them, if I don't wish to receive anymore ____ book and applicable statement marked cancel. If I don't cancel, bargain price of $5.49 plus 25¢ every month, before they're available ____ That's the complete bargain price of $4.99 plus 25¢ and applicable taxes**. what a great deal! I sales tax, if any*. In Ca____ over 20% off the cover prices____what a great deal! I shipping and handl____ the 2 free books and gift places me under no price and a sa____ accepting the 2 free books and gift places me under no unders____ ever to buy any books. I can always return a shipment and cancel at obli____ Even if I never buy another The Best of the Best™ book, the 2 free any time. Even if I never buy another The Best of the Best™ book, the 2 free books and gift are mine to keep forever.

185 MDN DZ7J
385 MDN DZ7K

(PLEASE PRINT)

Name _____

Apt.# _____

Address _____

State/Prov. _____   Zip/Postal Code _____

City _____

Not valid to current The Best of the Best™, Mira®,
suspense and romance subscribers.

Want to try two free books from another series?
Call 1-800-873-8635 or visit www.morefreebooks.com.

* Terms and prices subject to change without notice. Sales tax applicable in N.Y.
** Canadian residents will be charged applicable provincial taxes and GST.
- All orders subject to approval. Offer limited to one per household.
® and ™are registered trademarks owned and used by the trademark owner and or its licensee.

©2004 Harlequin Enterprises Limited

BOB04R